ANN M. MARTIN

THE BABY-SITTERS CLUB

KRISTY AND THE SNOBS

A GRAPHIC NOVEL BY

CHAN CHAU

WITH COLOR BY BRADEN LAMB

graphix

An Imprint of

SCHOLASTIC

In memory of Neena and Grandpa
A. M. M.

For Erik Munson, Danya Adair, Alice Woods,
Bleb, and Maddi Gonzalez for being there
when I needed someone the most.

And to my incredible friends and family.
C. C.

Text copyright © 2021 by Ann M. Martin
Art copyright © 2021 by Chan Chau

Library of Congress Control Number: 2020946441

ISBN 978-1-338-30461-9 (hardcover)
ISBN 978-1-338-30460-2 (paperback)

10 9 8 7 6 5 4 3 2 1   21 22 23 24 25

Printed in China   62
First edition, September 2021

Edited by Cassandra Pelham Fulton and David Levithan
Book design by Phil Falco
Publisher: David Saylor

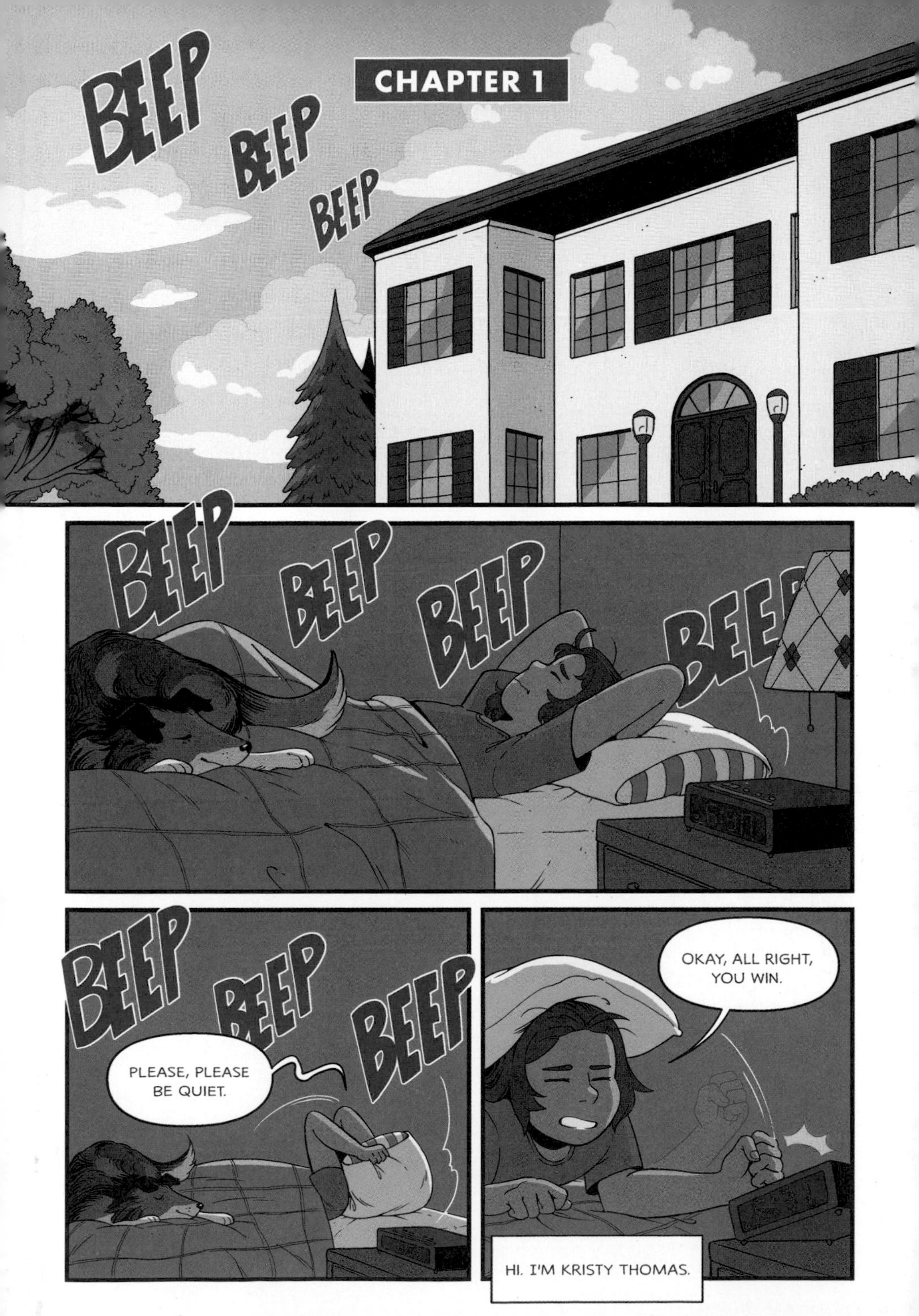
CHAPTER 1
BEEP
BEEP
BEEP
BEEP
BEEP
BEEP
BEEP
BEEP
BEEP
BEEP
PLEASE, PLEASE BE QUIET.
OKAY, ALL RIGHT, YOU WIN.
HI. I'M KRISTY THOMAS.

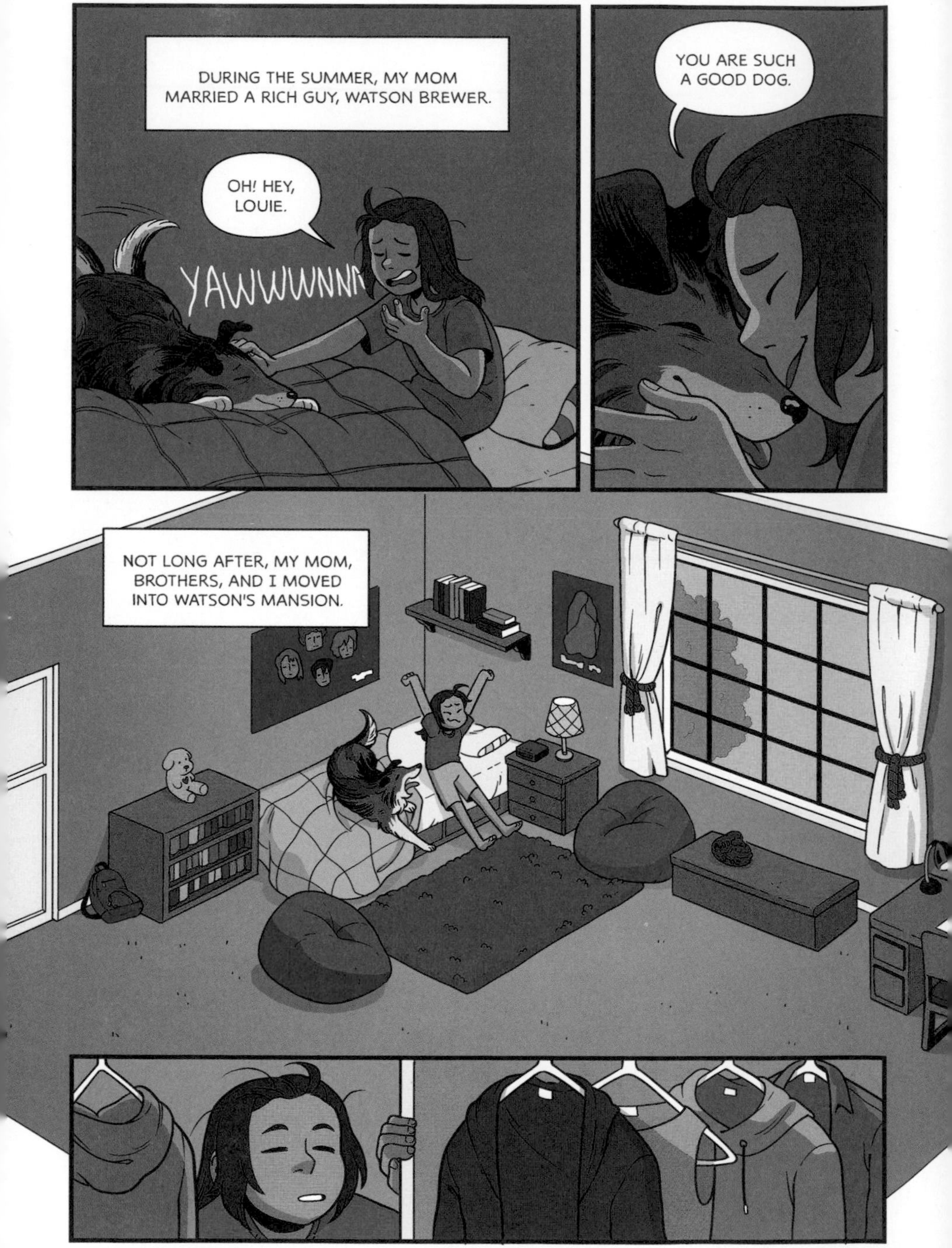

DURING THE SUMMER, MY MOM MARRIED A RICH GUY, WATSON BREWER.
OH! HEY, LOUIE.
YAWWWNNN
YOU ARE SUCH A GOOD DOG.
NOT LONG AFTER, MY MOM, BROTHERS, AND I MOVED INTO WATSON'S MANSION.

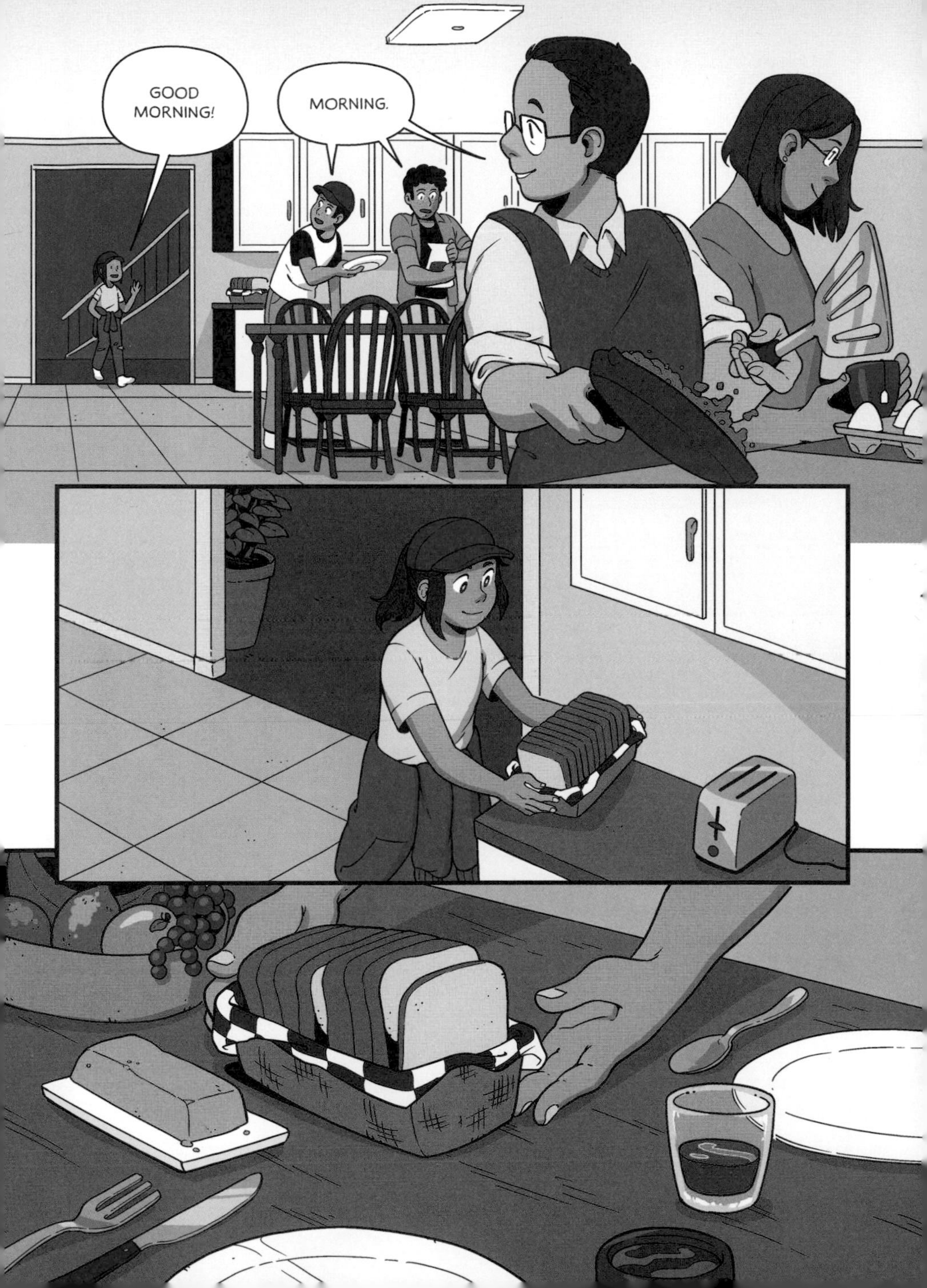
GOOD MORNING!
MORNING.

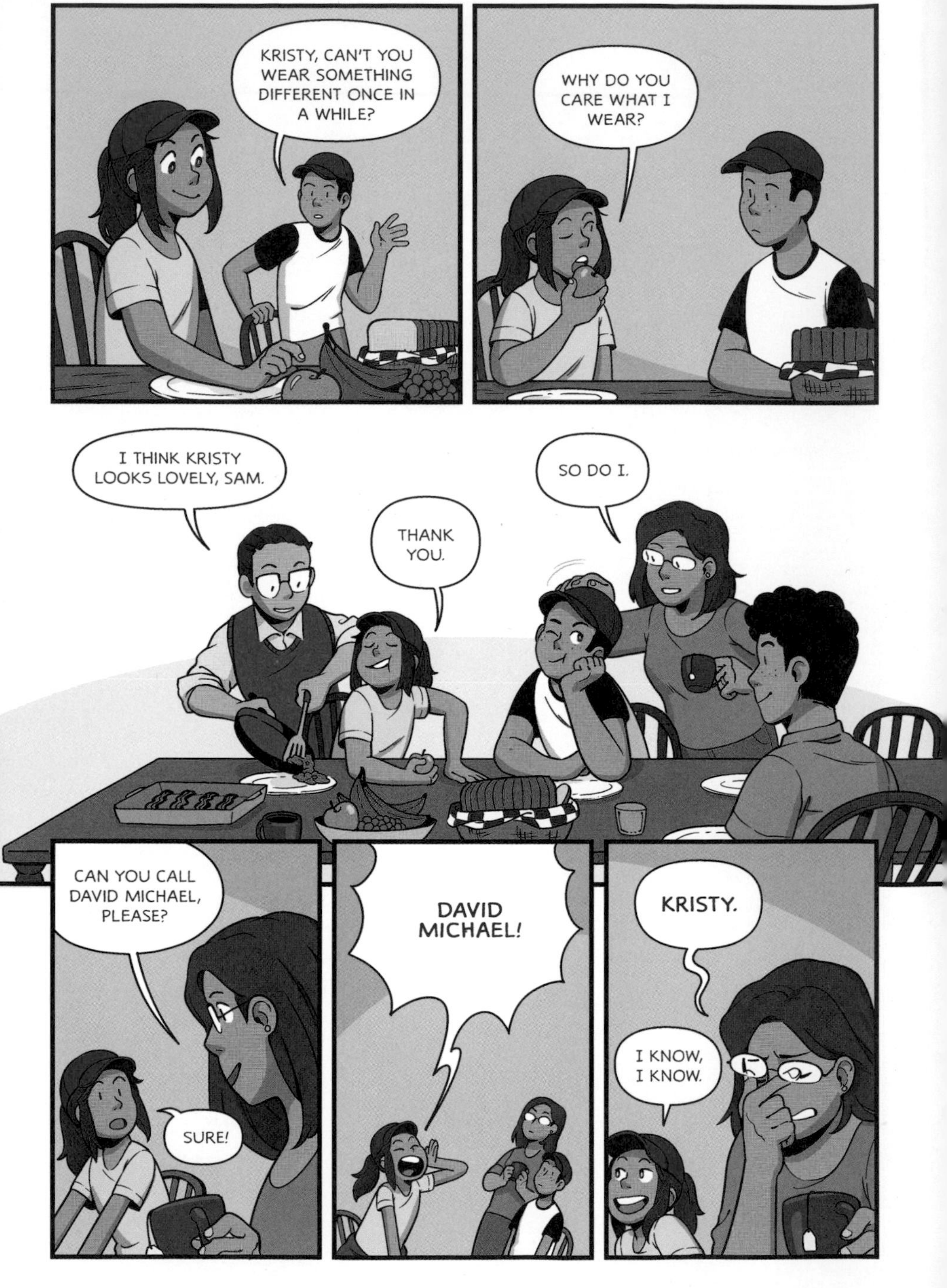
KRISTY, CAN'T YOU WEAR SOMETHING DIFFERENT ONCE IN A WHILE?
WHY DO YOU CARE WHAT I WEAR?
I THINK KRISTY LOOKS LOVELY, SAM.
THANK YOU.
SO DO I.
CAN YOU CALL DAVID MICHAEL, PLEASE?
SURE!
DAVID MICHAEL!
KRISTY.
I KNOW, I KNOW.

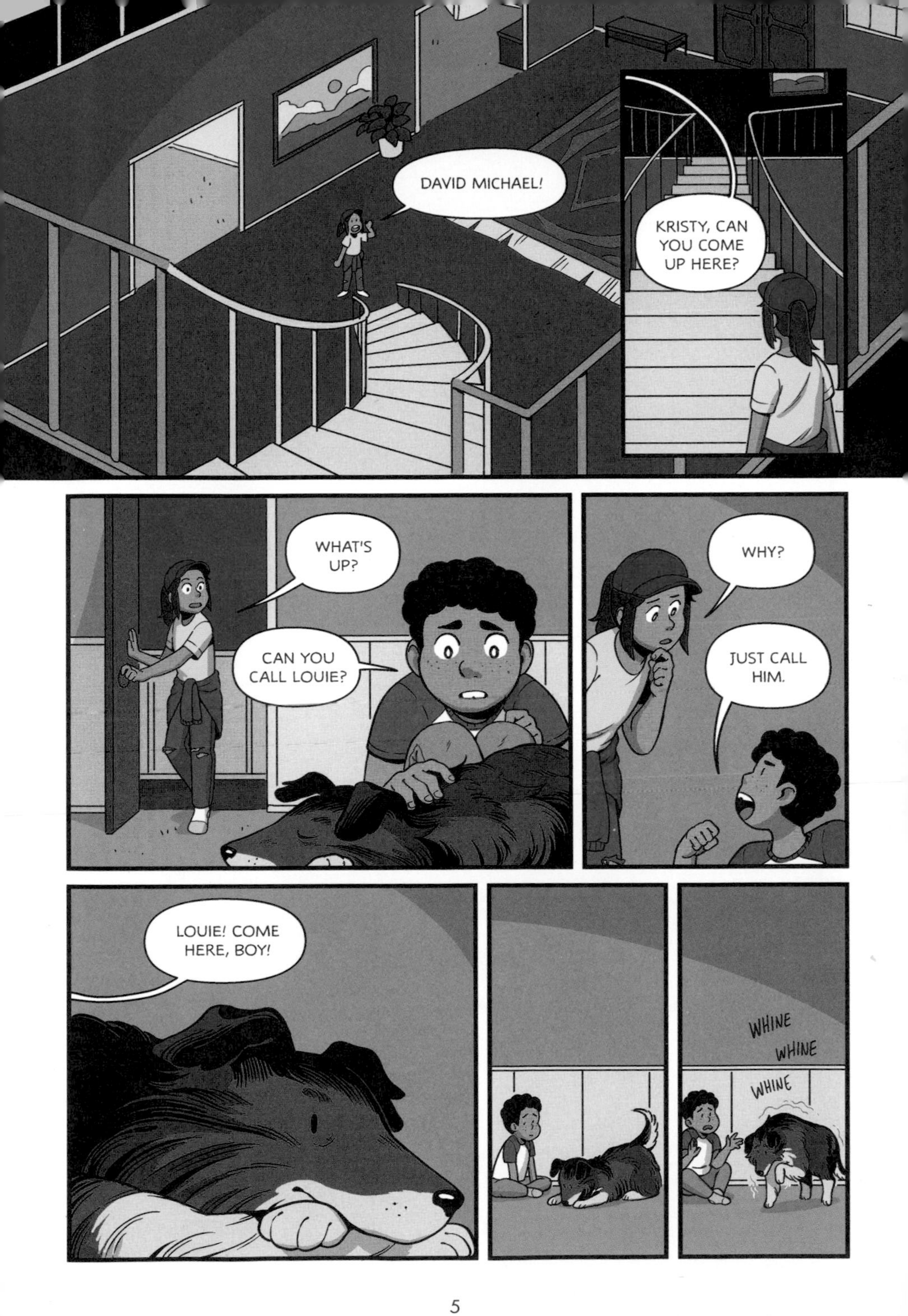
DAVID MICHAEL!
KRISTY, CAN YOU COME UP HERE?
WHAT'S UP?
CAN YOU CALL LOUIE?
WHY?
JUST CALL HIM.
LOUIE! COME HERE, BOY!
WHINE
WHINE
WHINE

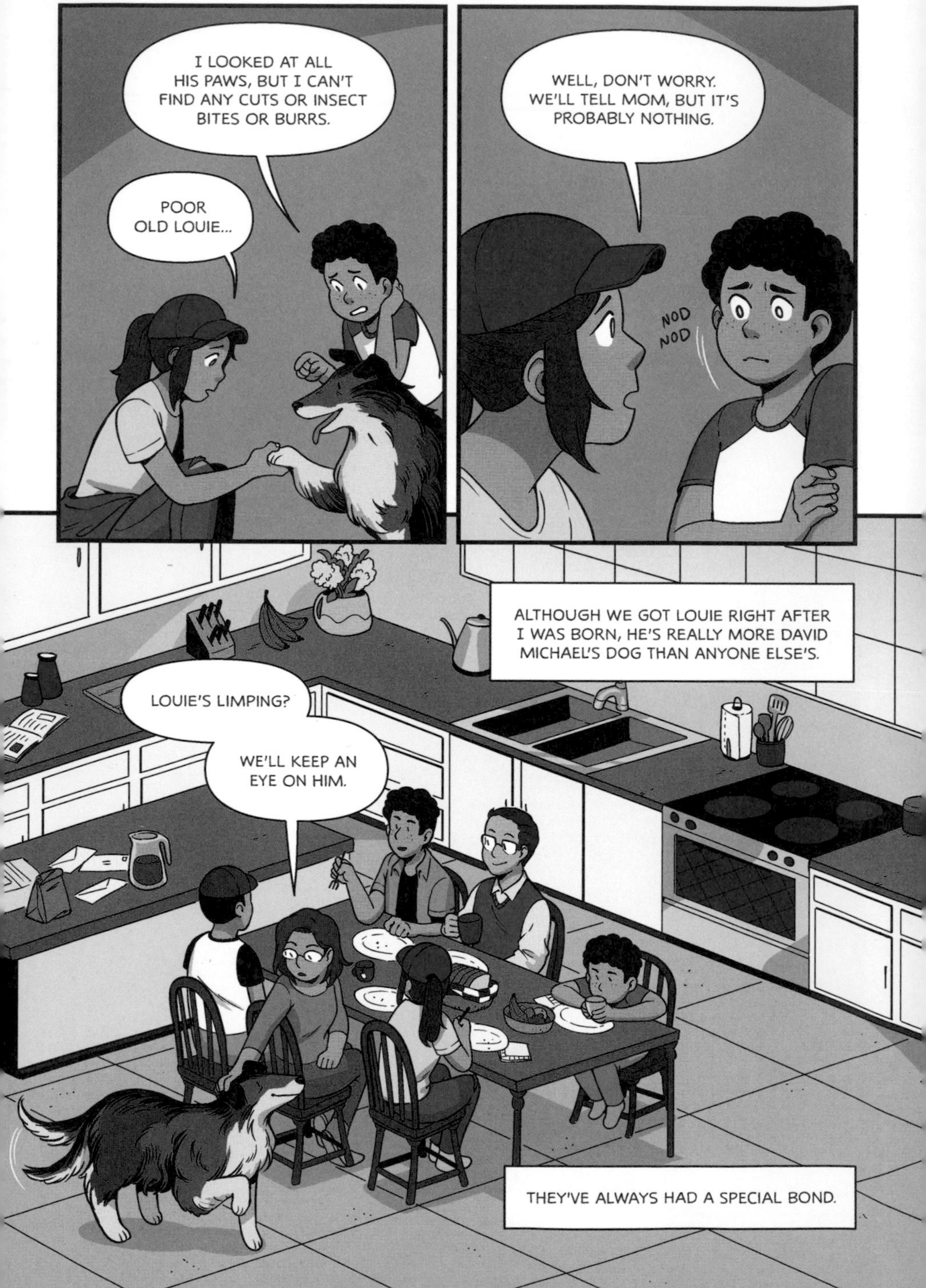
I LOOKED AT ALL HIS PAWS, BUT I CAN'T FIND ANY CUTS OR INSECT BITES OR BURRS.
POOR OLD LOUIE...
WELL, DON'T WORRY. WE'LL TELL MOM, BUT IT'S PROBABLY NOTHING.
NOD NOD
ALTHOUGH WE GOT LOUIE RIGHT AFTER I WAS BORN, HE'S REALLY MORE DAVID MICHAEL'S DOG THAN ANYONE ELSE'S.
LOUIE'S LIMPING?
WE'LL KEEP AN EYE ON HIM.
THEY'VE ALWAYS HAD A SPECIAL BOND.

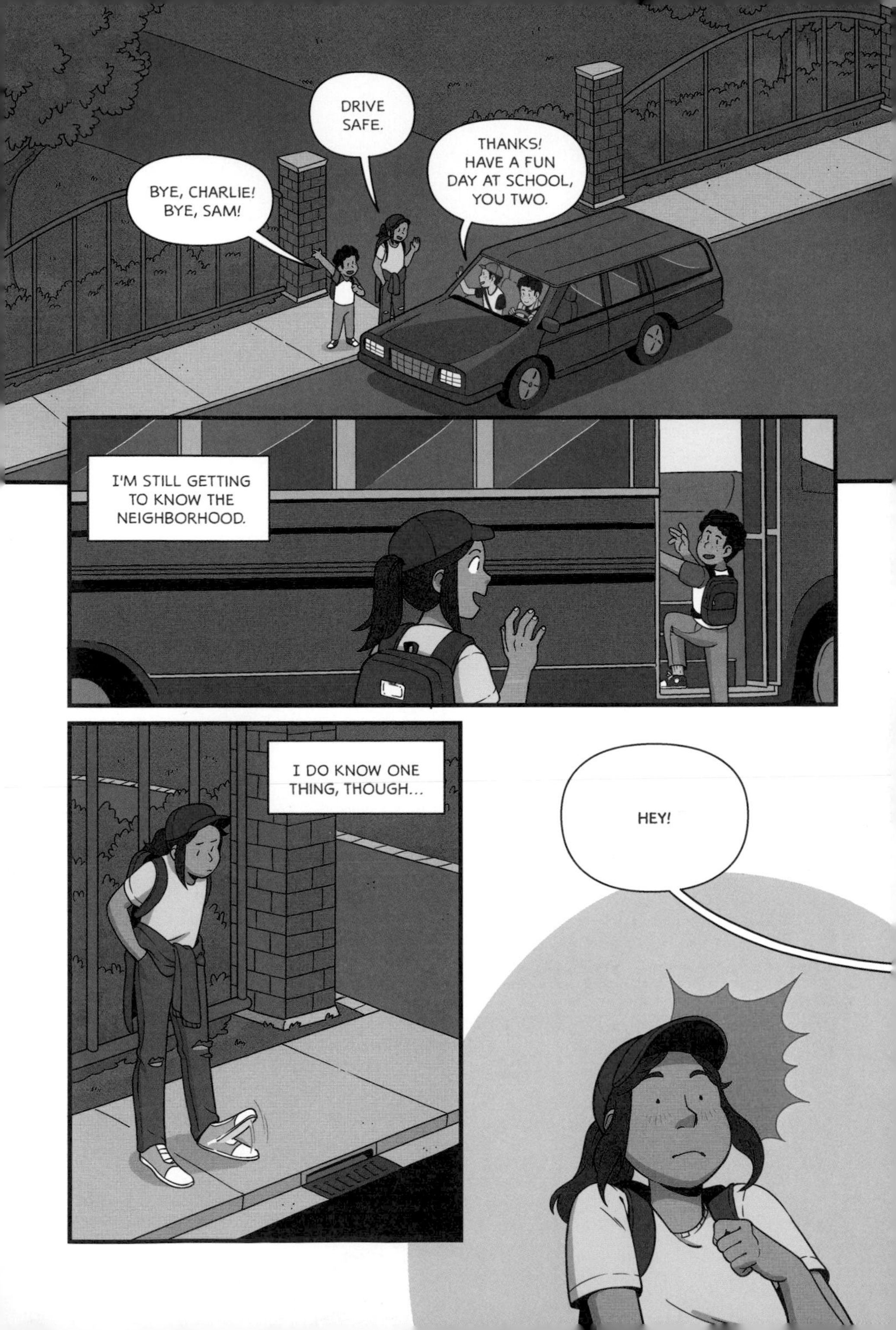
BYE, CHARLIE!
BYE, SAM!
DRIVE SAFE.
THANKS! HAVE A FUN DAY AT SCHOOL, YOU TWO.
I'M STILL GETTING TO KNOW THE NEIGHBORHOOD.
I DO KNOW ONE THING, THOUGH...
HEY!

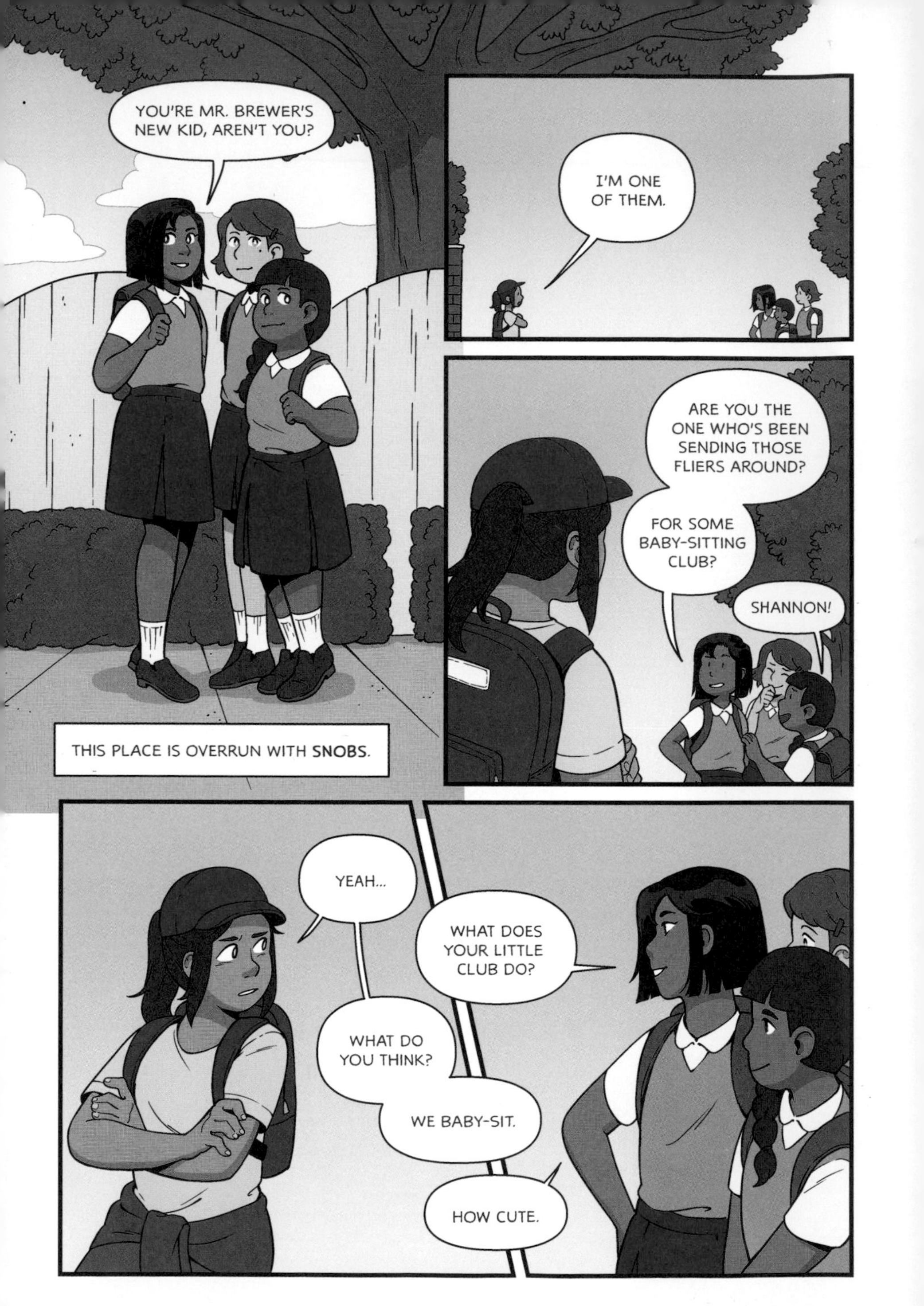
YOU'RE MR. BREWER'S NEW KID, AREN'T YOU?
THIS PLACE IS OVERRUN WITH SNOBS.
I'M ONE OF THEM.
ARE YOU THE ONE WHO'S BEEN SENDING THOSE FLIERS AROUND?
FOR SOME BABY-SITTING CLUB?
SHANNON!
YEAH...
WHAT DOES YOUR LITTLE CLUB DO?
WHAT DO YOU THINK?
WE BABY-SIT.
HOW CUTE.

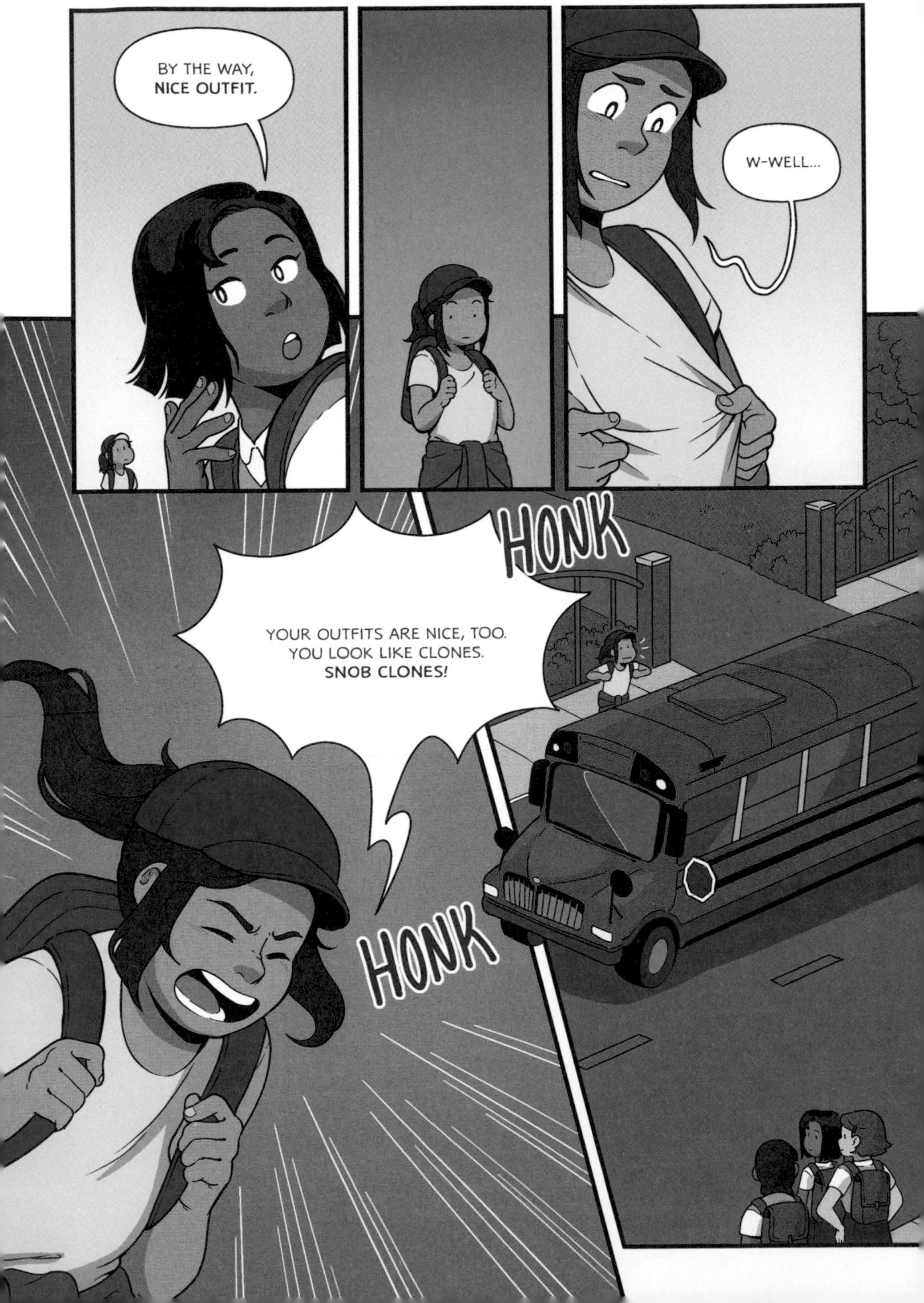
BY THE WAY, NICE OUTFIT.
W-WELL...
HONK
YOUR OUTFITS ARE NICE, TOO. YOU LOOK LIKE CLONES. SNOB CLONES!
HONK

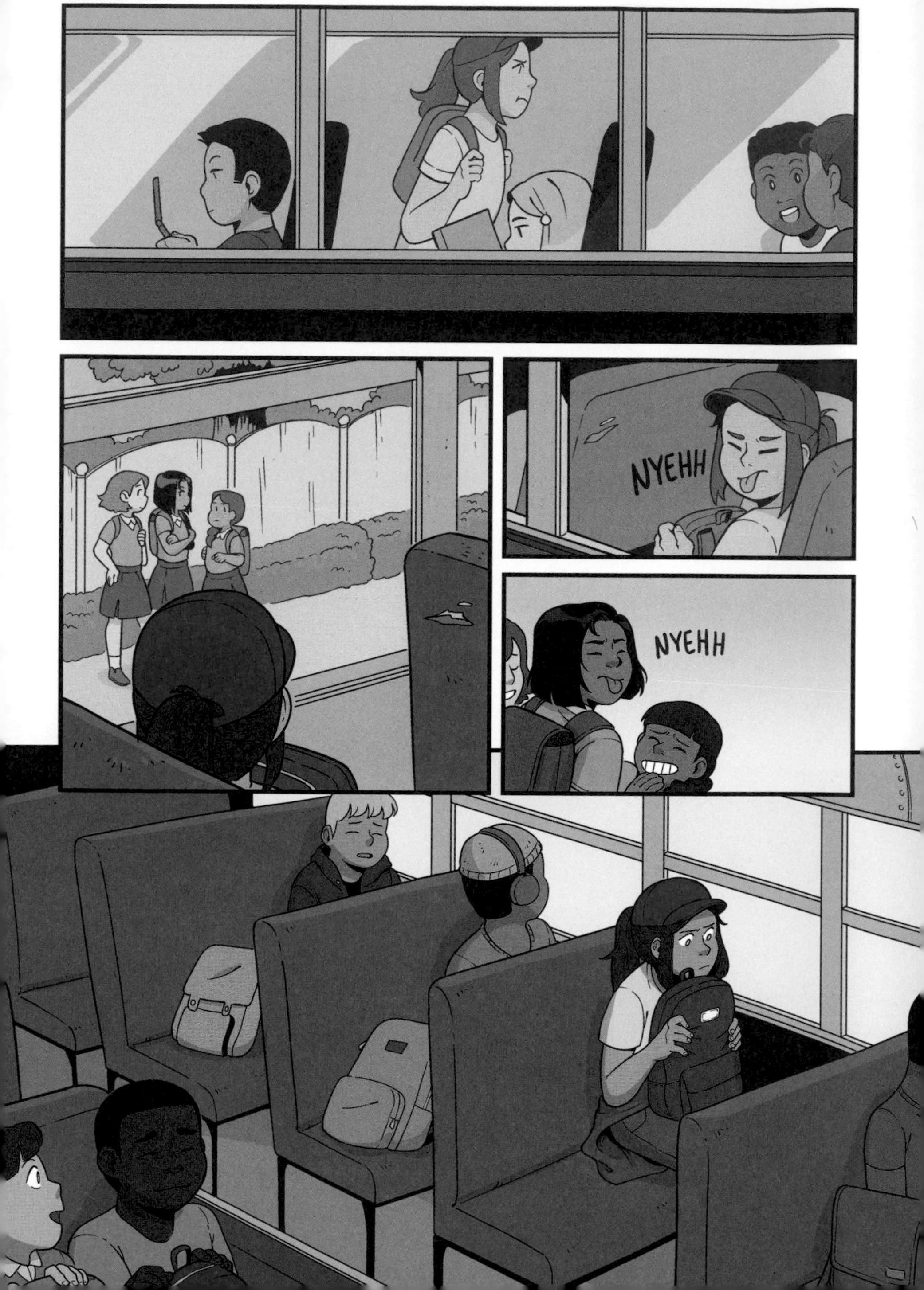
NYEHH
NYEHH

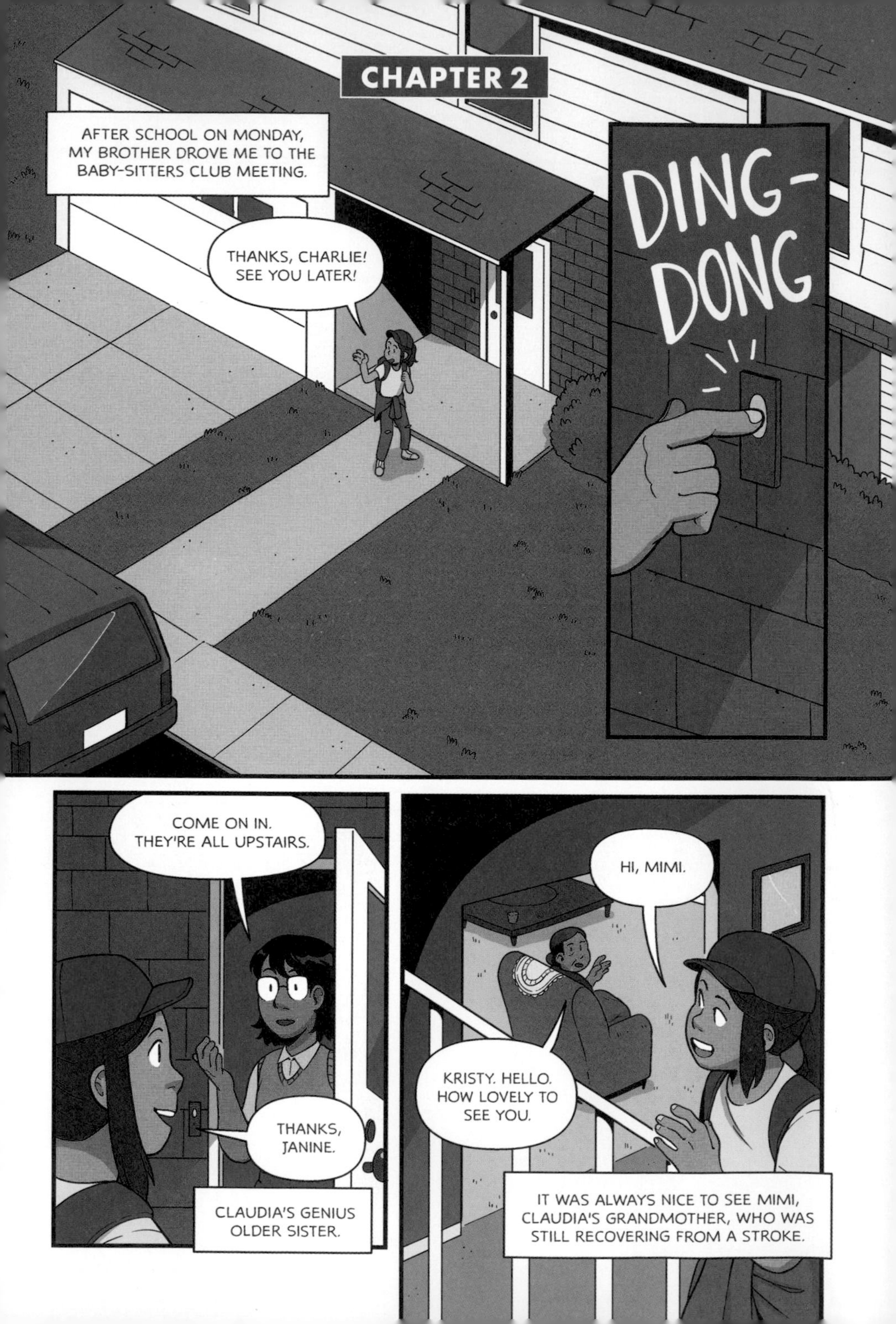
CHAPTER 2
AFTER SCHOOL ON MONDAY, MY BROTHER DROVE ME TO THE BABY-SITTERS CLUB MEETING.
THANKS, CHARLIE! SEE YOU LATER!
DING-DONG
COME ON IN. THEY'RE ALL UPSTAIRS.
THANKS, JANINE.
CLAUDIA'S GENIUS OLDER SISTER.
HI, MIMI.
KRISTY. HELLO. HOW LOVELY TO SEE YOU.
IT WAS ALWAYS NICE TO SEE MIMI, CLAUDIA'S GRANDMOTHER, WHO WAS STILL RECOVERING FROM A STROKE.

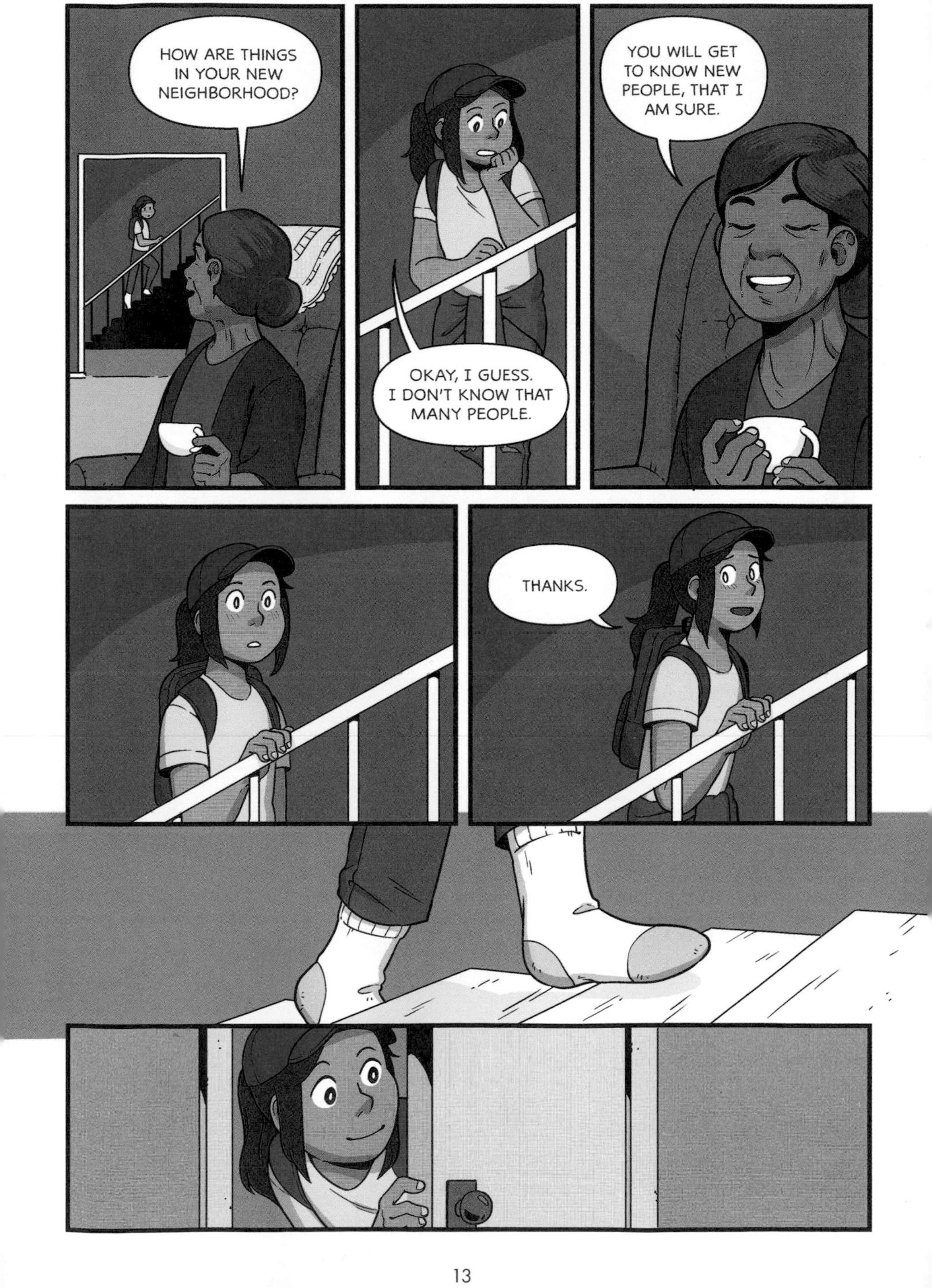
HOW ARE THINGS IN YOUR NEW NEIGHBORHOOD?
OKAY, I GUESS. I DON'T KNOW THAT MANY PEOPLE.
YOU WILL GET TO KNOW NEW PEOPLE, THAT I AM SURE.
THANKS.

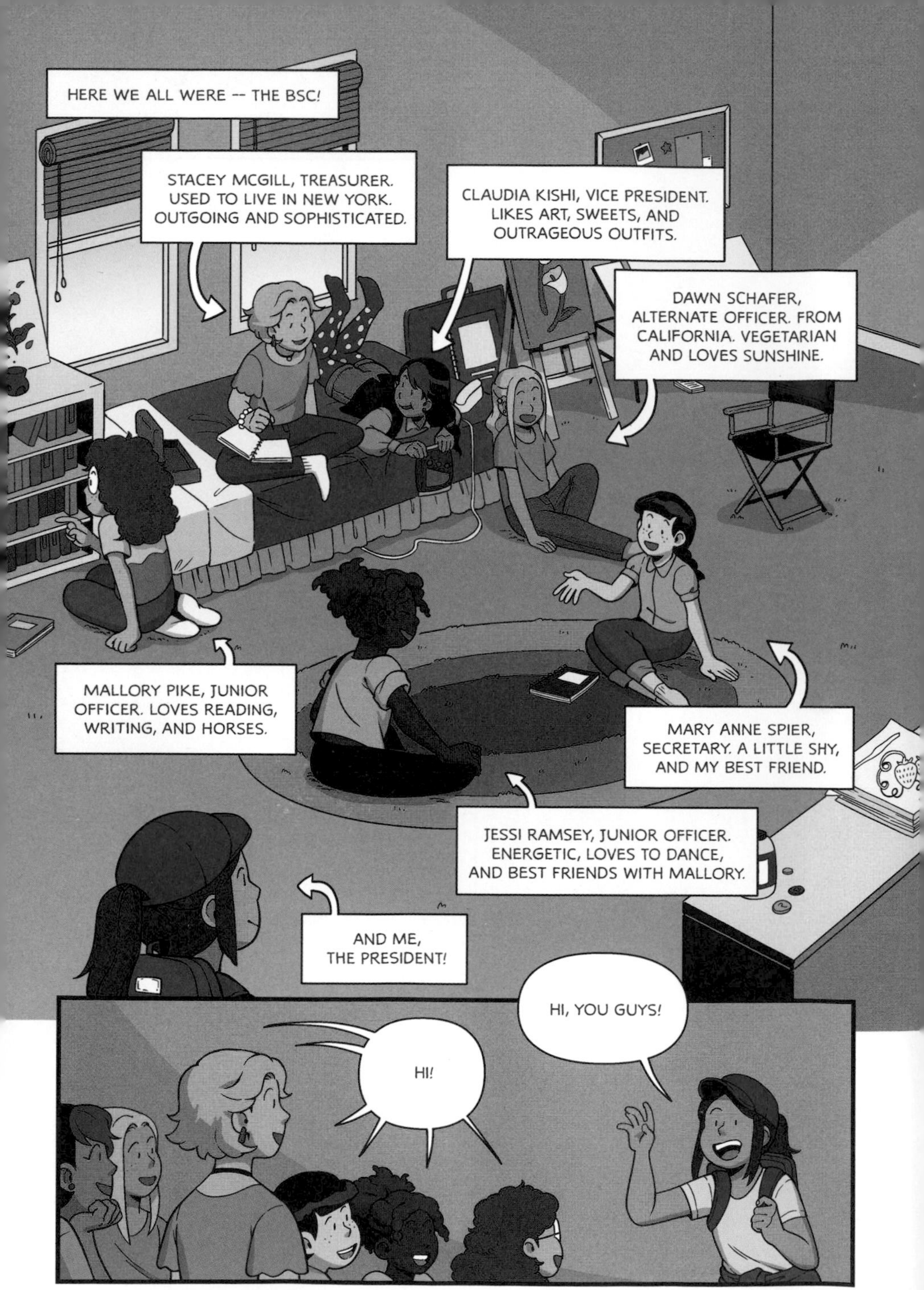
HERE WE ALL WERE -- THE BSC!
STACEY MCGILL, TREASURER. USED TO LIVE IN NEW YORK. OUTGOING AND SOPHISTICATED.
CLAUDIA KISHI, VICE PRESIDENT. LIKES ART, SWEETS, AND OUTRAGEOUS OUTFITS.
DAWN SCHAFER, ALTERNATE OFFICER. FROM CALIFORNIA. VEGETARIAN AND LOVES SUNSHINE.
MALLORY PIKE, JUNIOR OFFICER. LOVES READING, WRITING, AND HORSES.
MARY ANNE SPIER, SECRETARY. A LITTLE SHY, AND MY BEST FRIEND.
JESSI RAMSEY, JUNIOR OFFICER. ENERGETIC, LOVES TO DANCE, AND BEST FRIENDS WITH MALLORY.
AND ME, THE PRESIDENT!
HI, YOU GUYS!
HI!

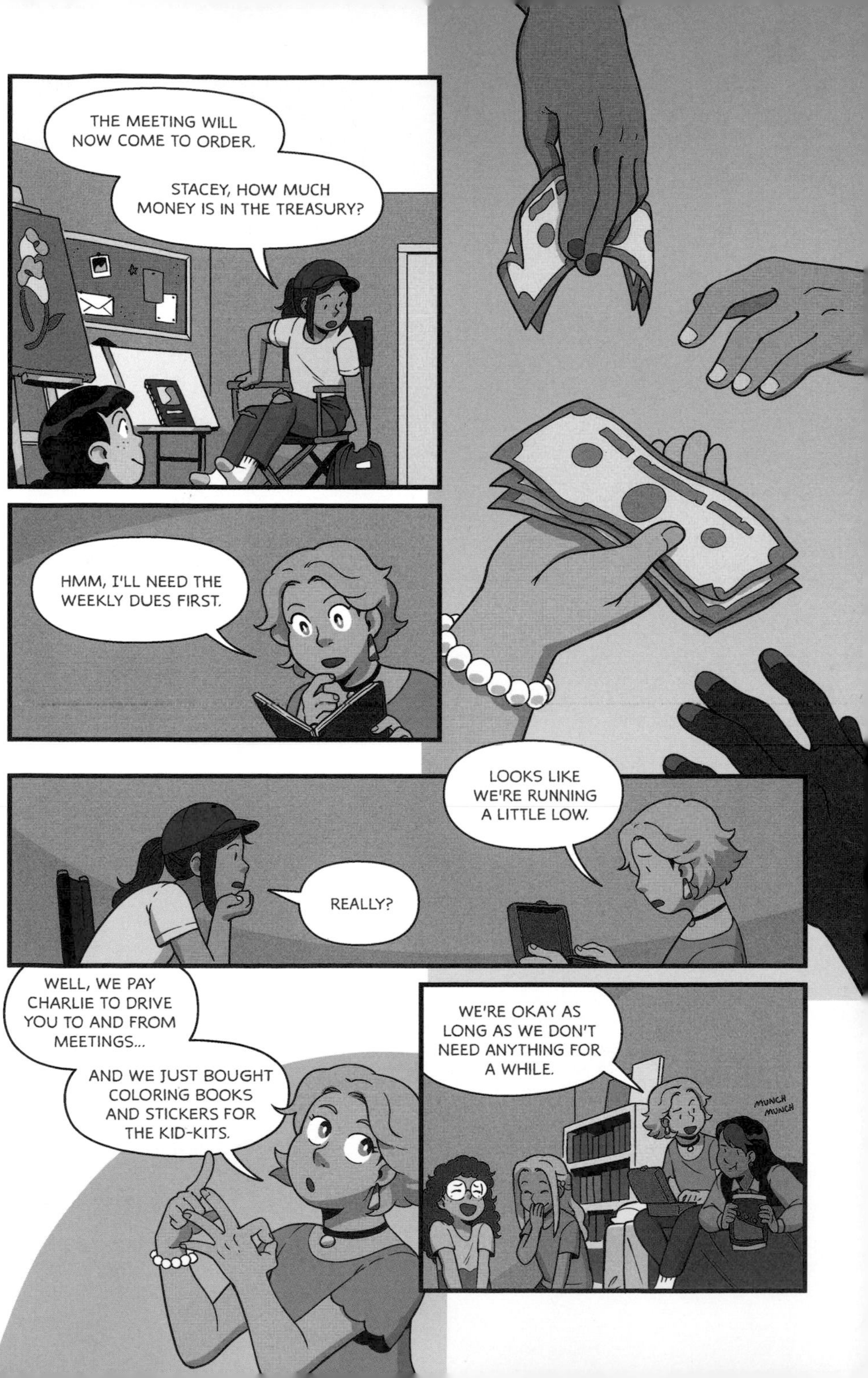
THE MEETING WILL NOW COME TO ORDER.
STACEY, HOW MUCH MONEY IS IN THE TREASURY?
HMM, I'LL NEED THE WEEKLY DUES FIRST.
LOOKS LIKE WE'RE RUNNING A LITTLE LOW.
REALLY?
WELL, WE PAY CHARLIE TO DRIVE YOU TO AND FROM MEETINGS...
AND WE JUST BOUGHT COLORING BOOKS AND STICKERS FOR THE KID-KITS.
WE'RE OKAY AS LONG AS WE DON'T NEED ANYTHING FOR A WHILE.
MUNCH MUNCH

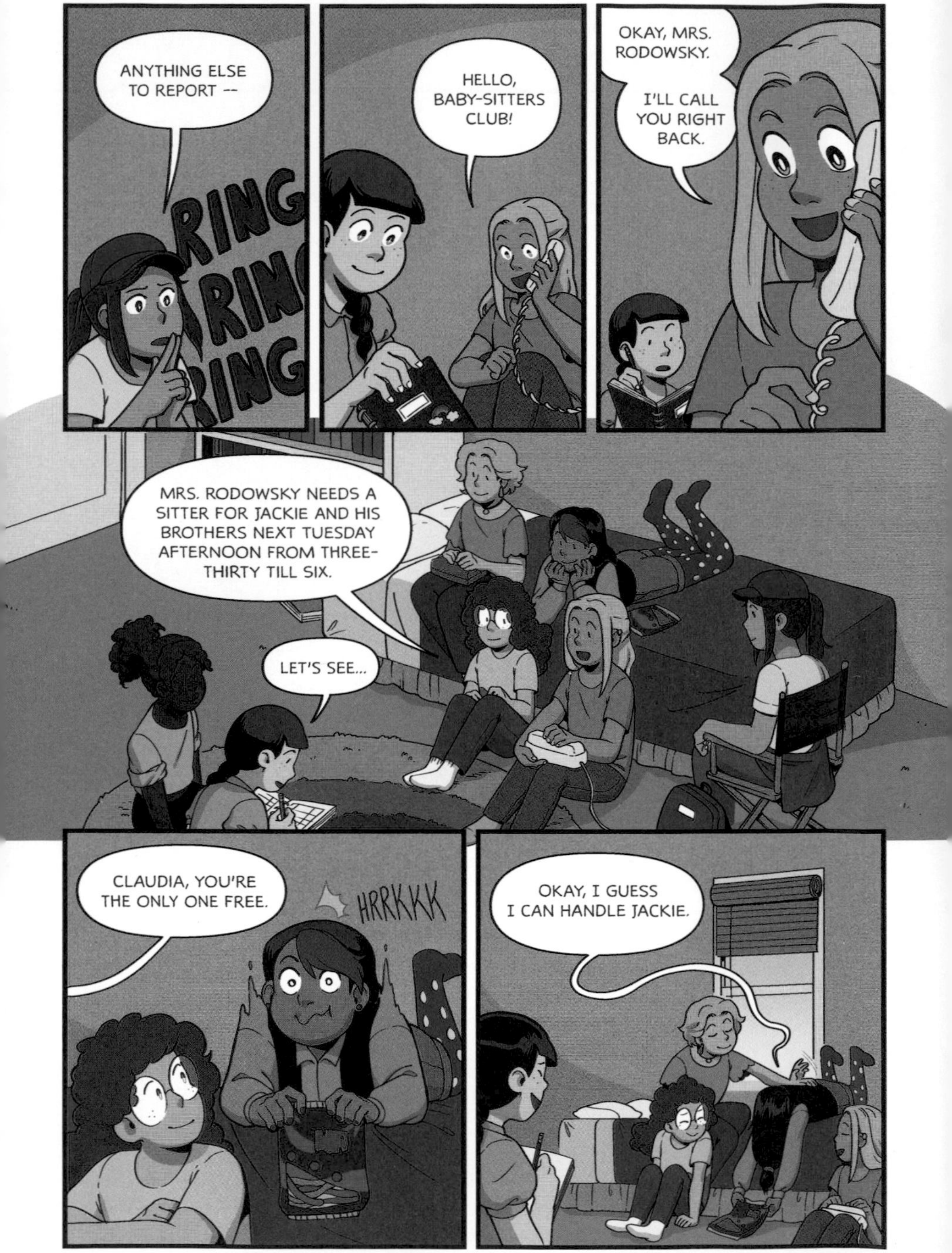
ANYTHING ELSE TO REPORT --
RING RING RING
HELLO, BABY-SITTERS CLUB!
OKAY, MRS. RODOWSKY.
I'LL CALL YOU RIGHT BACK.
MRS. RODOWSKY NEEDS A SITTER FOR JACKIE AND HIS BROTHERS NEXT TUESDAY AFTERNOON FROM THREE-THIRTY TILL SIX.
LET'S SEE...
CLAUDIA, YOU'RE THE ONLY ONE FREE.
HRRKKK
OKAY, I GUESS I CAN HANDLE JACKIE.

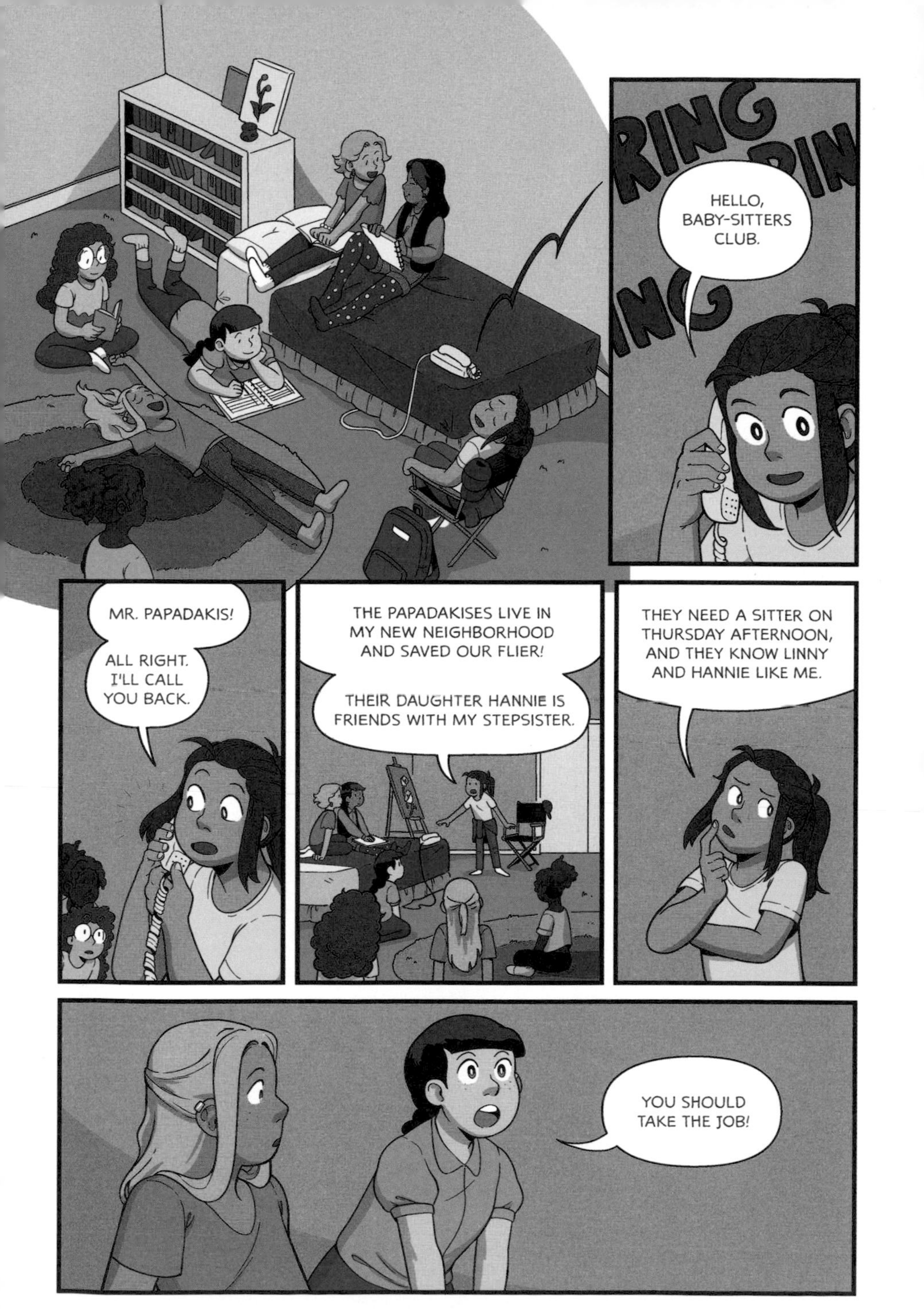
RING RIN
ING
HELLO, BABY-SITTERS CLUB.
MR. PAPADAKIS!
ALL RIGHT. I'LL CALL YOU BACK.
THE PAPADAKISES LIVE IN MY NEW NEIGHBORHOOD AND SAVED OUR FLIER!
THEIR DAUGHTER HANNIE IS FRIENDS WITH MY STEPSISTER.
THEY NEED A SITTER ON THURSDAY AFTERNOON, AND THEY KNOW LINNY AND HANNIE LIKE ME.
YOU SHOULD TAKE THE JOB!

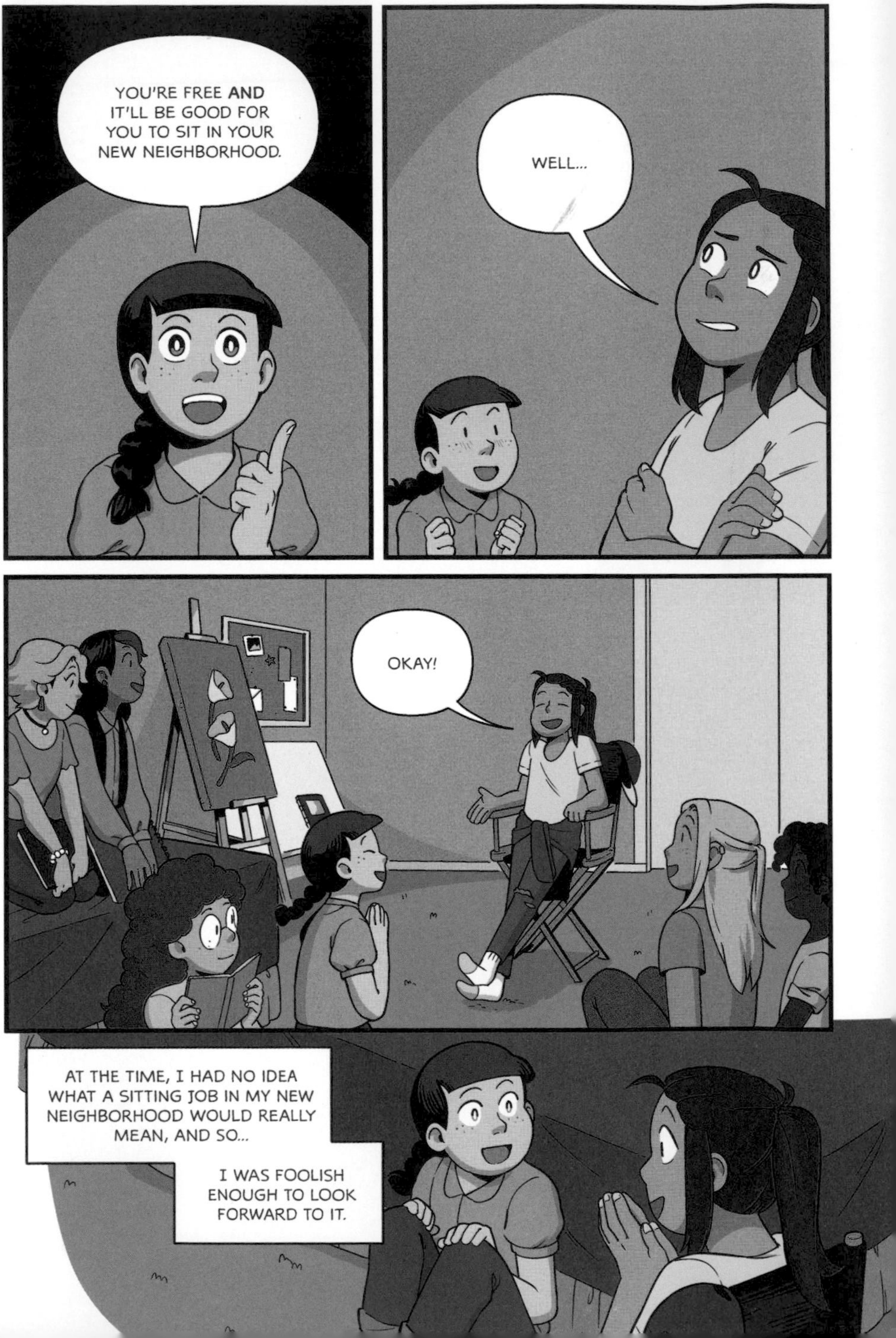
YOU'RE FREE **AND** IT'LL BE GOOD FOR YOU TO SIT IN YOUR NEW NEIGHBORHOOD.
WELL...
OKAY!
AT THE TIME, I HAD NO IDEA WHAT A SITTING JOB IN MY NEW NEIGHBORHOOD WOULD REALLY MEAN, AND SO...
I WAS FOOLISH ENOUGH TO LOOK FORWARD TO IT.

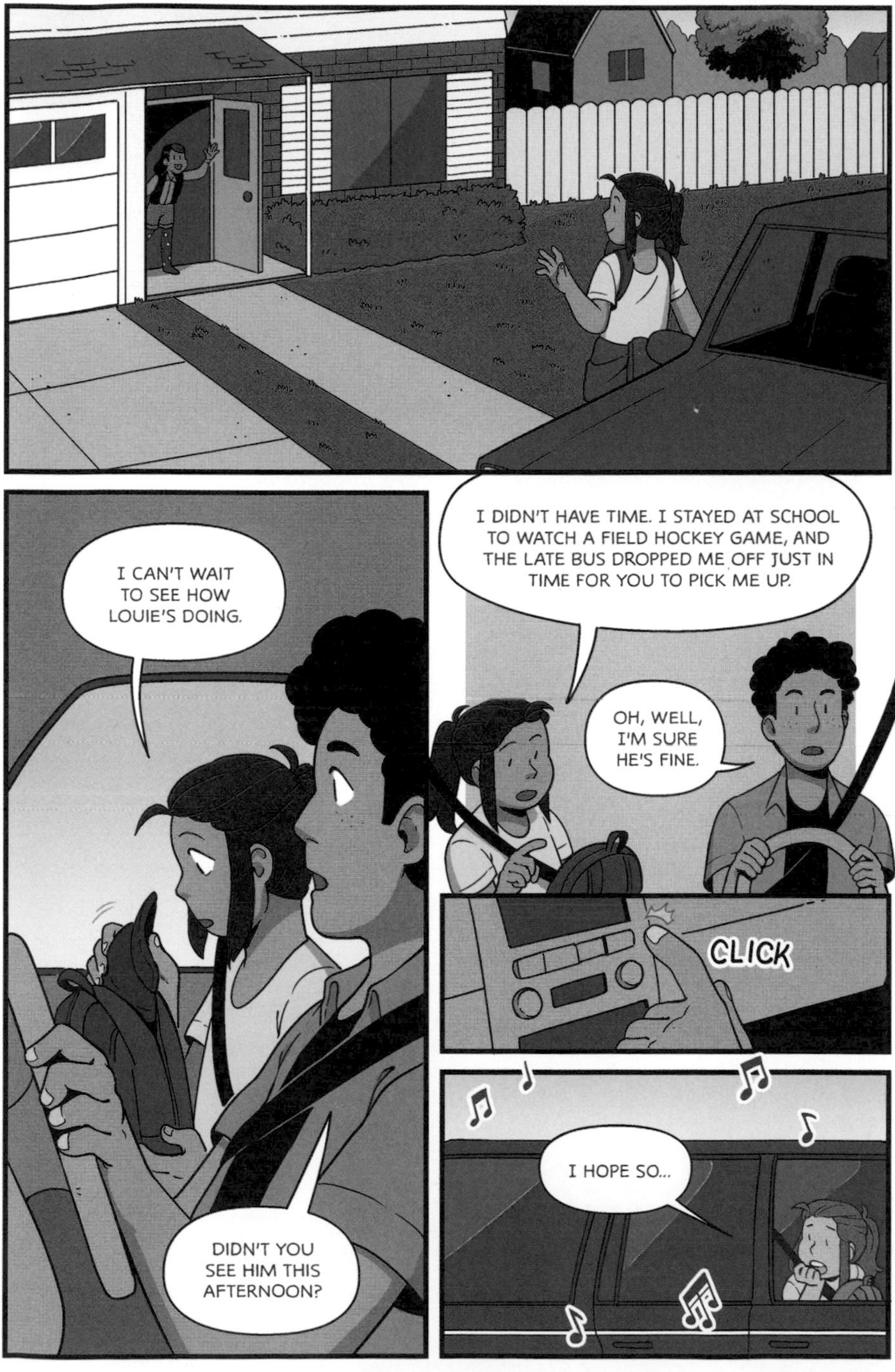
I CAN'T WAIT TO SEE HOW LOUIE'S DOING.
DIDN'T YOU SEE HIM THIS AFTERNOON?
I DIDN'T HAVE TIME. I STAYED AT SCHOOL TO WATCH A FIELD HOCKEY GAME, AND THE LATE BUS DROPPED ME OFF JUST IN TIME FOR YOU TO PICK ME UP.
OH, WELL, I'M SURE HE'S FINE.
CLICK
I HOPE SO...

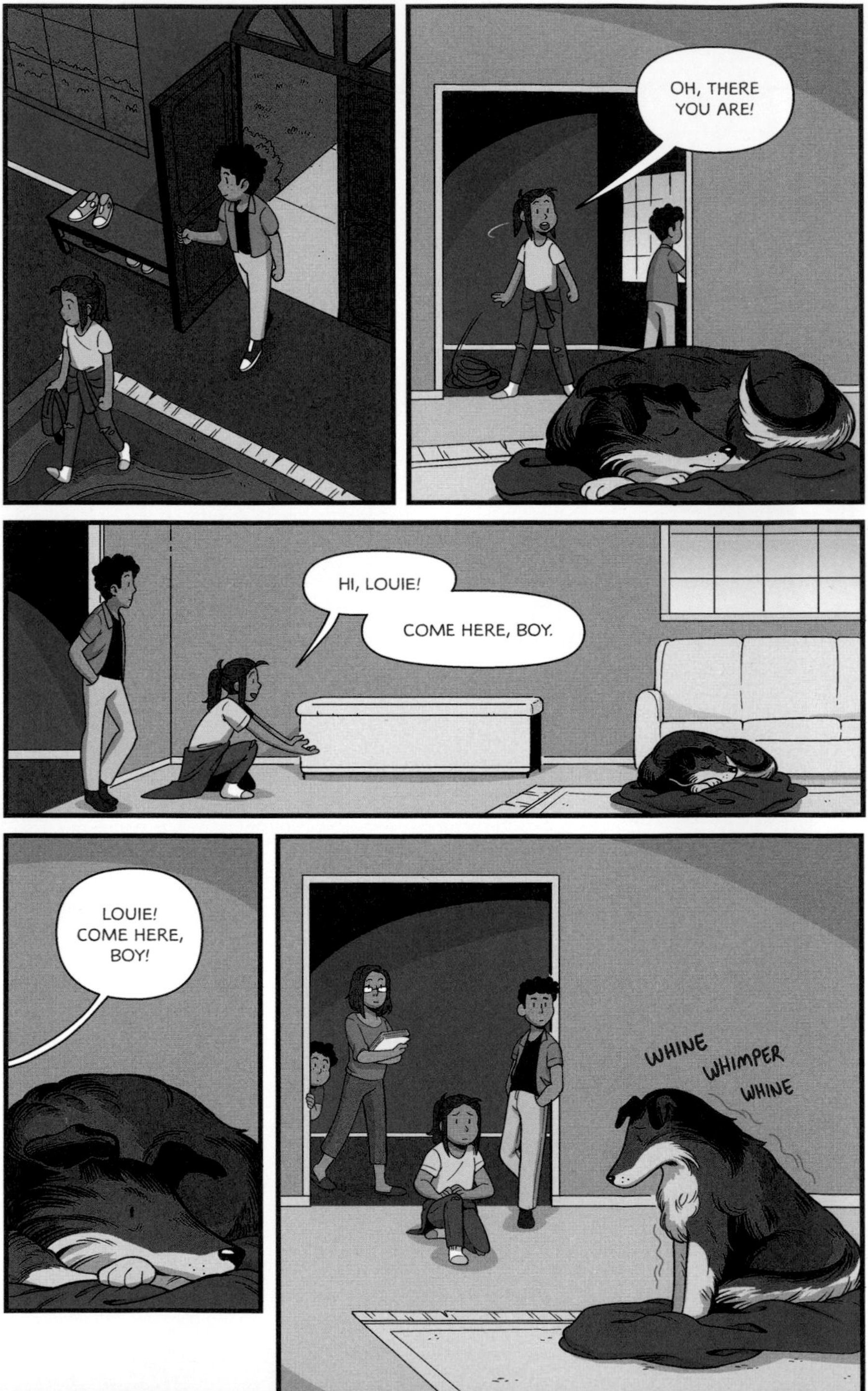
OH, THERE YOU ARE!
HI, LOUIE!
COME HERE, BOY.
LOUIE! COME HERE, BOY!
WHINE
WHIMPER
WHINE

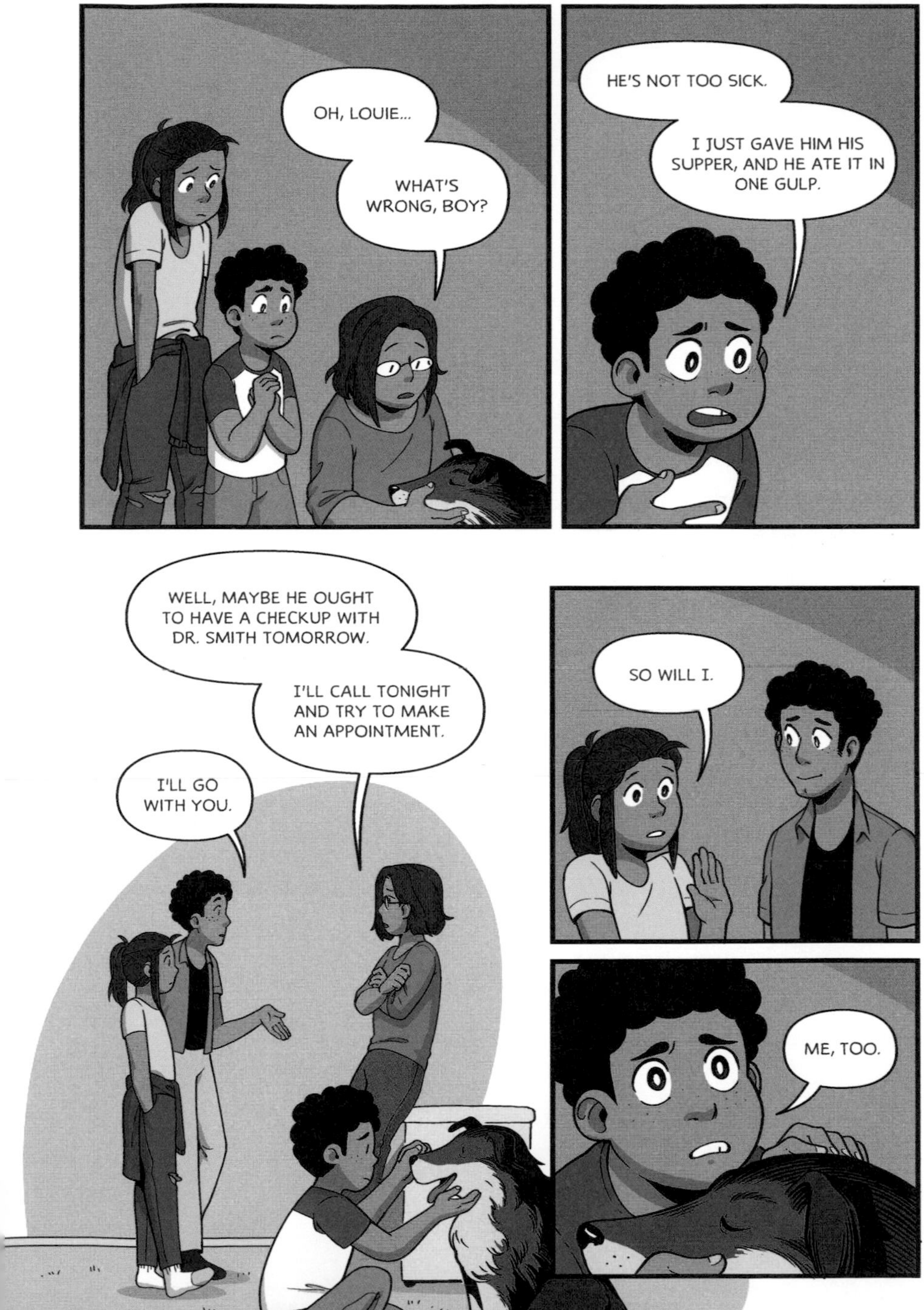
OH, LOUIE...
WHAT'S WRONG, BOY?
HE'S NOT TOO SICK.
I JUST GAVE HIM HIS SUPPER, AND HE ATE IT IN ONE GULP.
WELL, MAYBE HE OUGHT TO HAVE A CHECKUP WITH DR. SMITH TOMORROW.
I'LL CALL TONIGHT AND TRY TO MAKE AN APPOINTMENT.
I'LL GO WITH YOU.
SO WILL I.
ME, TOO.

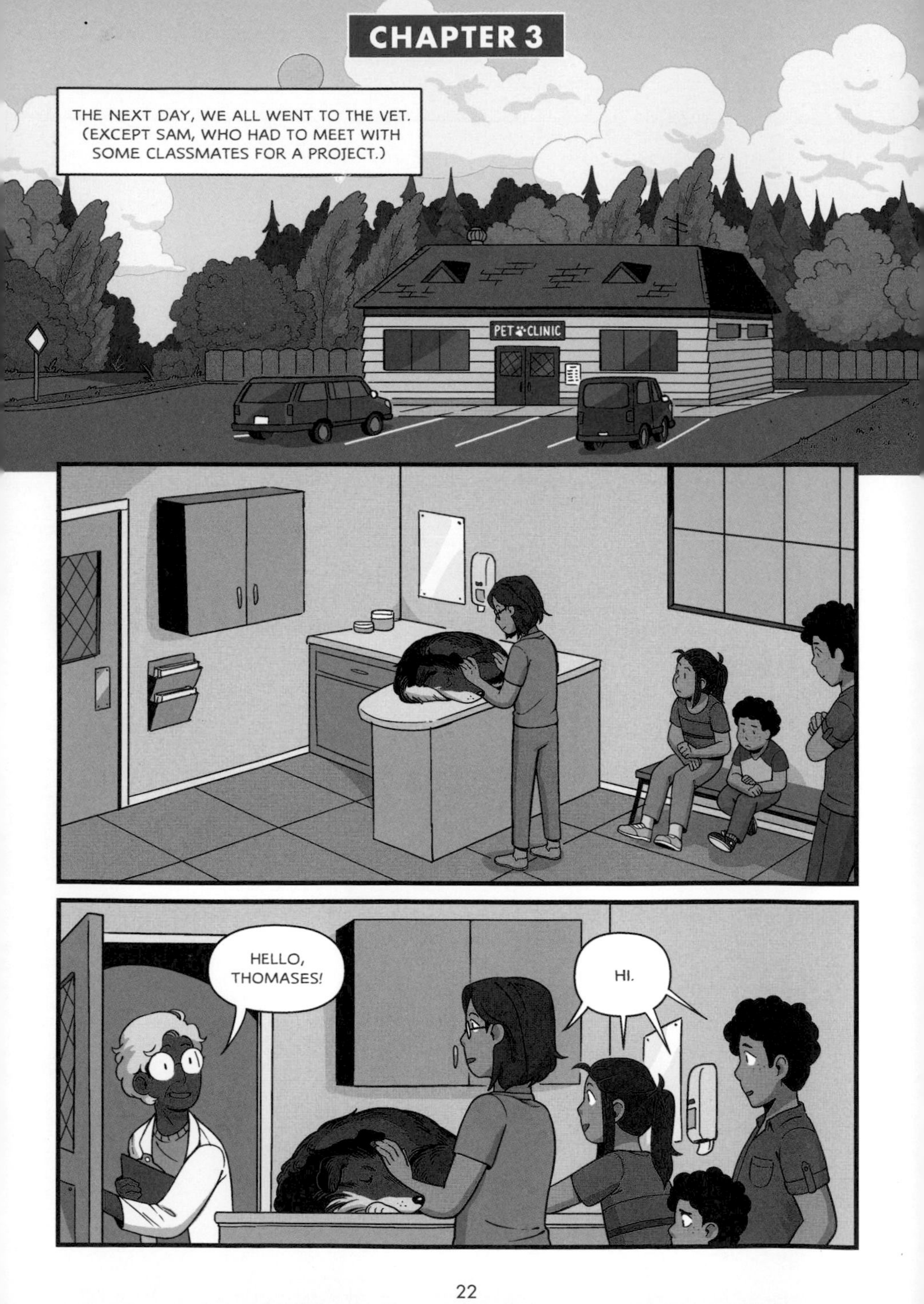
CHAPTER 3
THE NEXT DAY, WE ALL WENT TO THE VET. (EXCEPT SAM, WHO HAD TO MEET WITH SOME CLASSMATES FOR A PROJECT.)
PET CLINIC
HELLO, THOMASES!
HI.

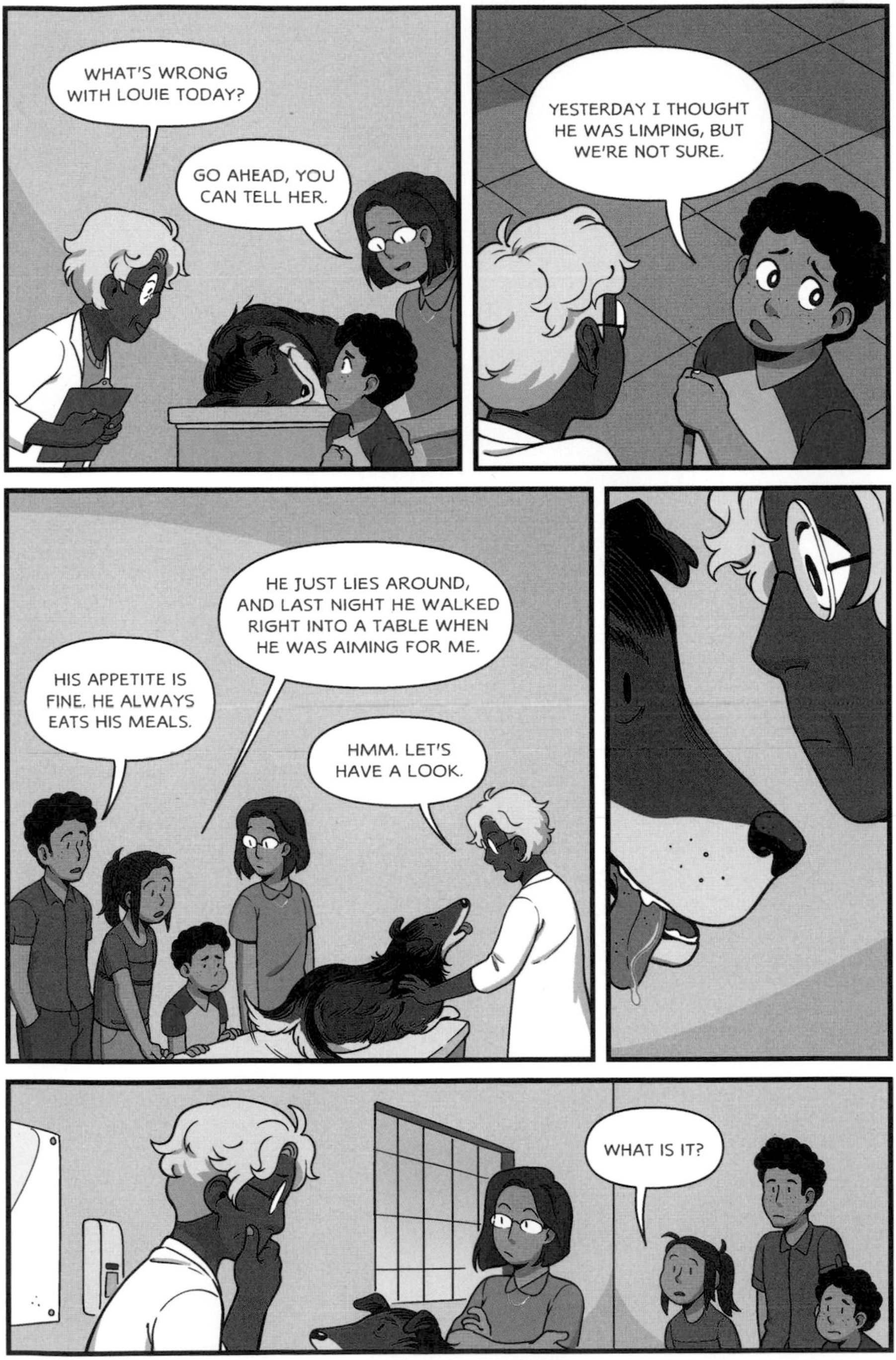
WHAT'S WRONG WITH LOUIE TODAY?
GO AHEAD, YOU CAN TELL HER.
YESTERDAY I THOUGHT HE WAS LIMPING, BUT WE'RE NOT SURE.
HIS APPETITE IS FINE. HE ALWAYS EATS HIS MEALS.
HE JUST LIES AROUND, AND LAST NIGHT HE WALKED RIGHT INTO A TABLE WHEN HE WAS AIMING FOR ME.
HMM. LET'S HAVE A LOOK.
WHAT IS IT?

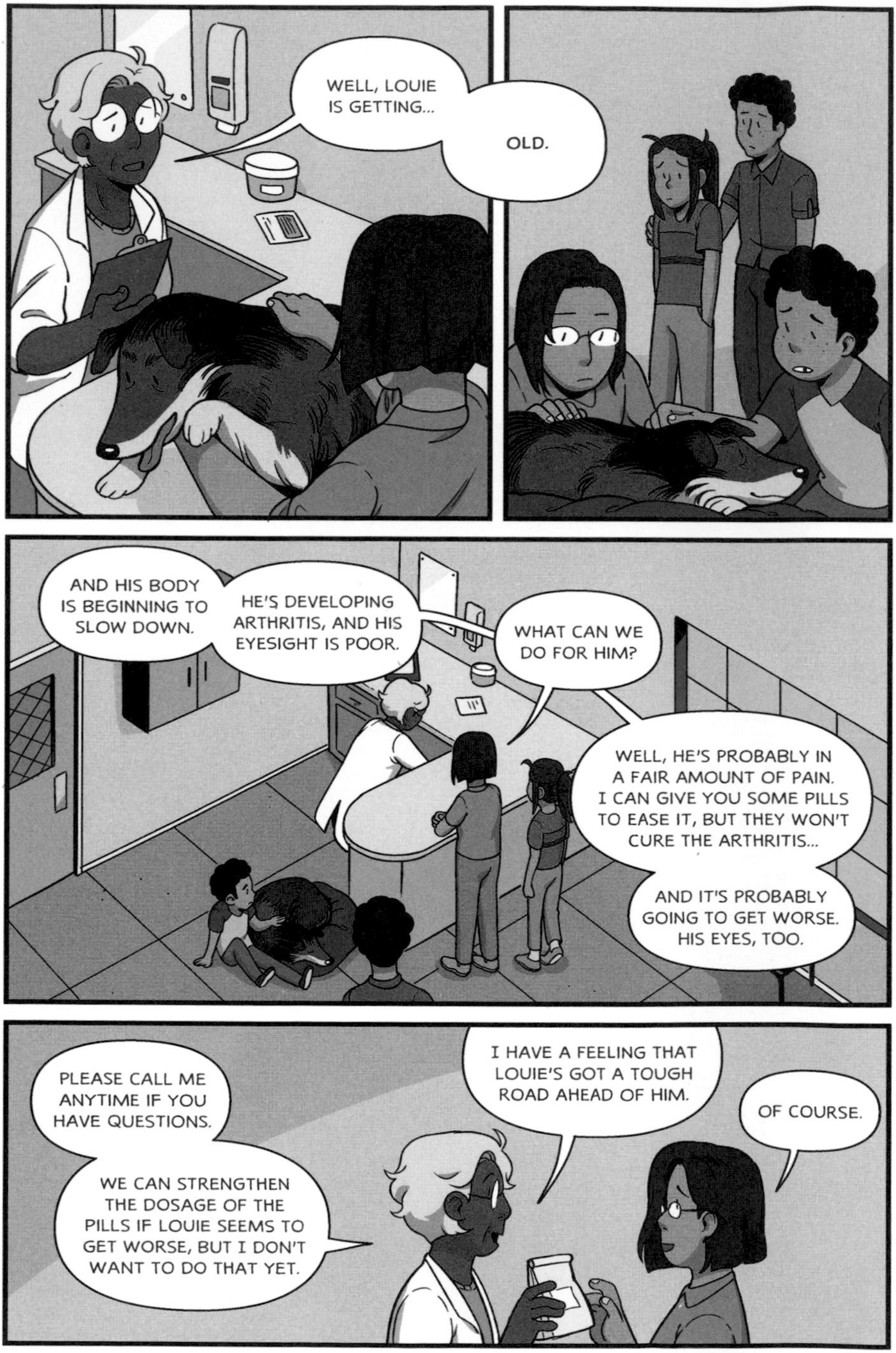
WELL, LOUIE IS GETTING...
OLD.
AND HIS BODY IS BEGINNING TO SLOW DOWN.
HE'S DEVELOPING ARTHRITIS, AND HIS EYESIGHT IS POOR.
WHAT CAN WE DO FOR HIM?
WELL, HE'S PROBABLY IN A FAIR AMOUNT OF PAIN. I CAN GIVE YOU SOME PILLS TO EASE IT, BUT THEY WON'T CURE THE ARTHRITIS...
AND IT'S PROBABLY GOING TO GET WORSE. HIS EYES, TOO.
PLEASE CALL ME ANYTIME IF YOU HAVE QUESTIONS.
WE CAN STRENGTHEN THE DOSAGE OF THE PILLS IF LOUIE SEEMS TO GET WORSE, BUT I DON'T WANT TO DO THAT YET.
I HAVE A FEELING THAT LOUIE'S GOT A TOUGH ROAD AHEAD OF HIM.
OF COURSE.

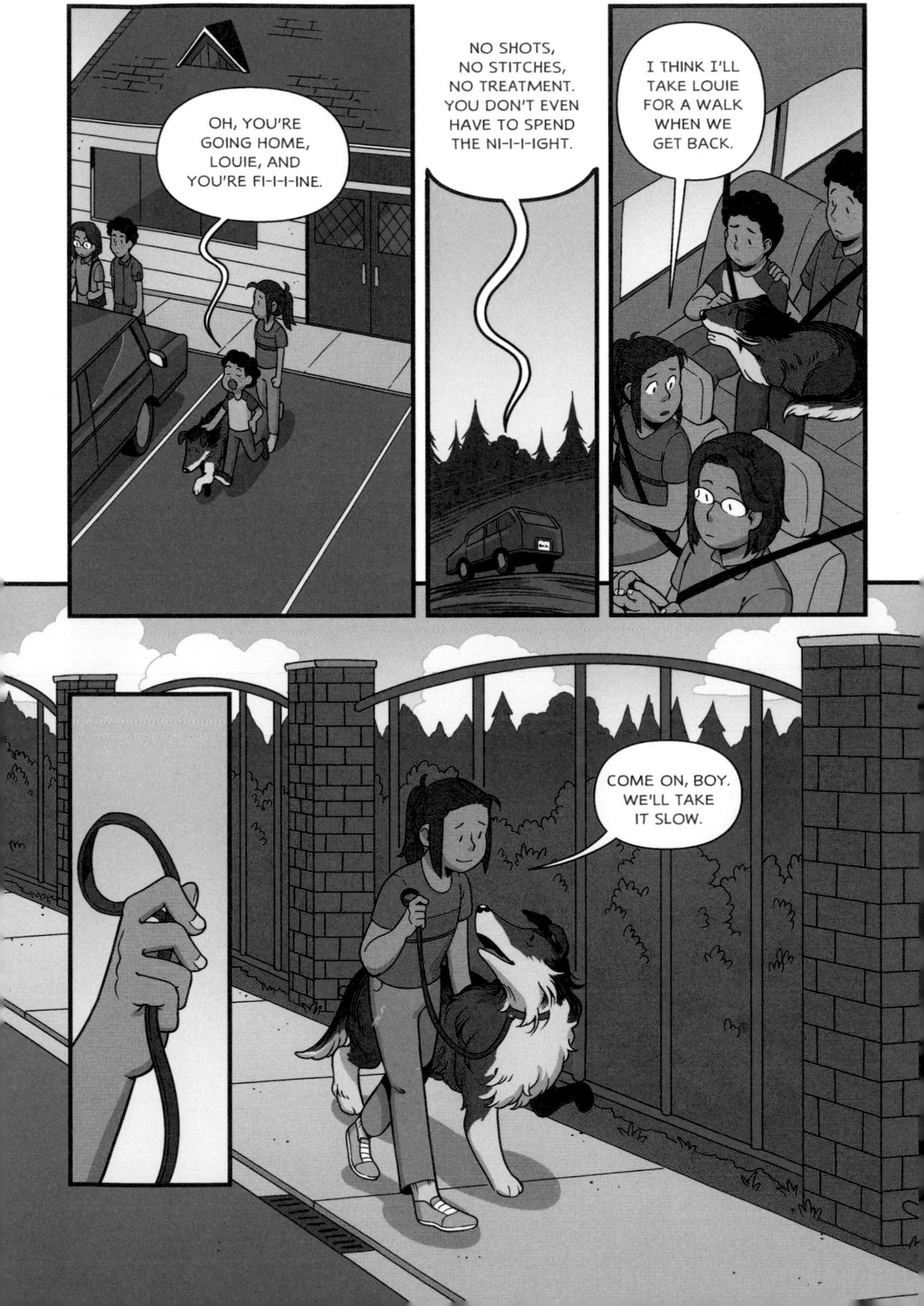
OH, YOU'RE GOING HOME, LOUIE, AND YOU'RE FI-I-I-INE.
NO SHOTS, NO STITCHES, NO TREATMENT. YOU DON'T EVEN HAVE TO SPEND THE NI-I-I-IGHT.
I THINK I'LL TAKE LOUIE FOR A WALK WHEN WE GET BACK.
COME ON, BOY. WE'LL TAKE IT SLOW.

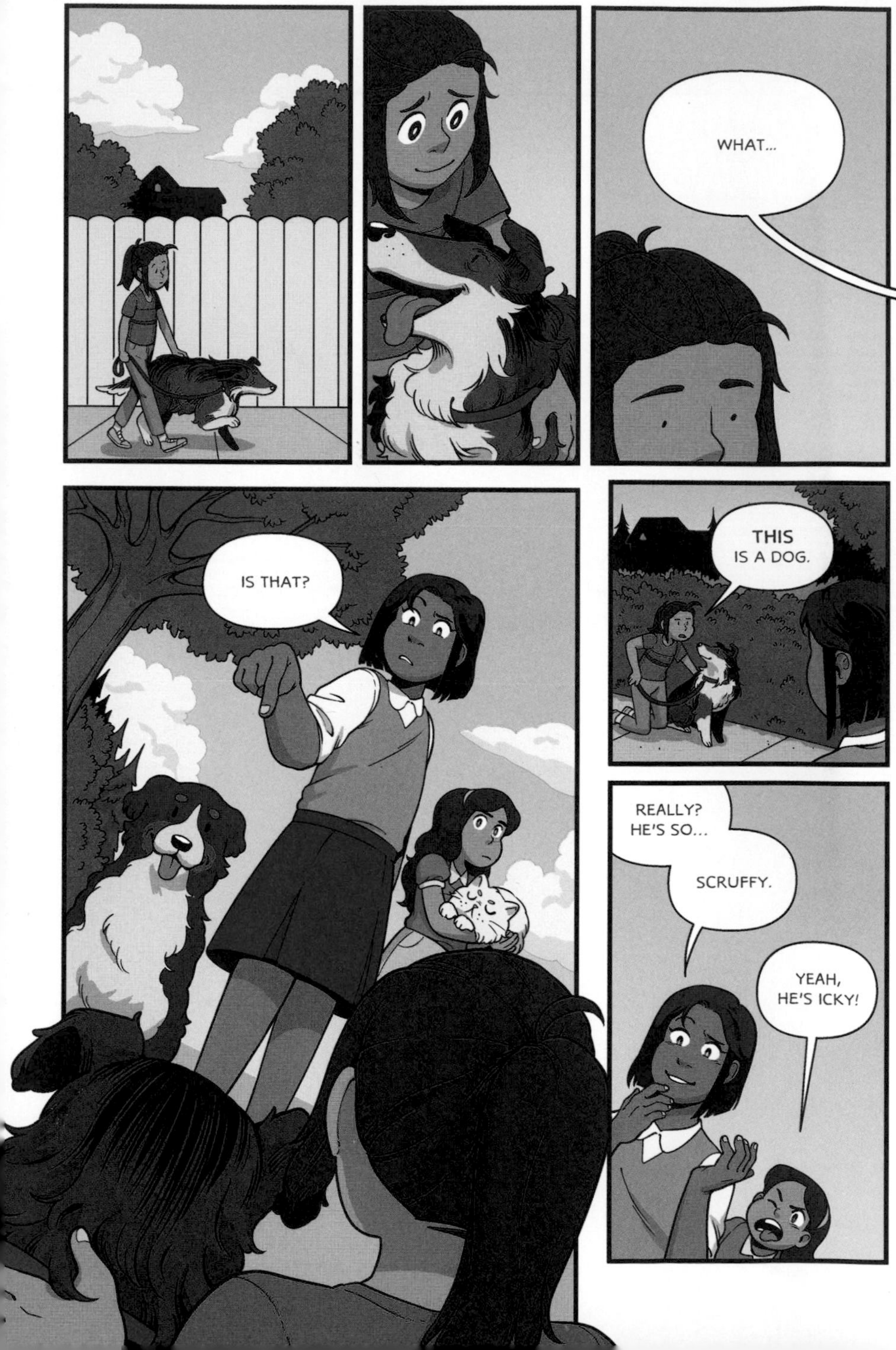

WHAT...
IS THAT?
THIS IS A DOG.
REALLY? HE'S SO...
SCRUFFY.
YEAH, HE'S ICKY!

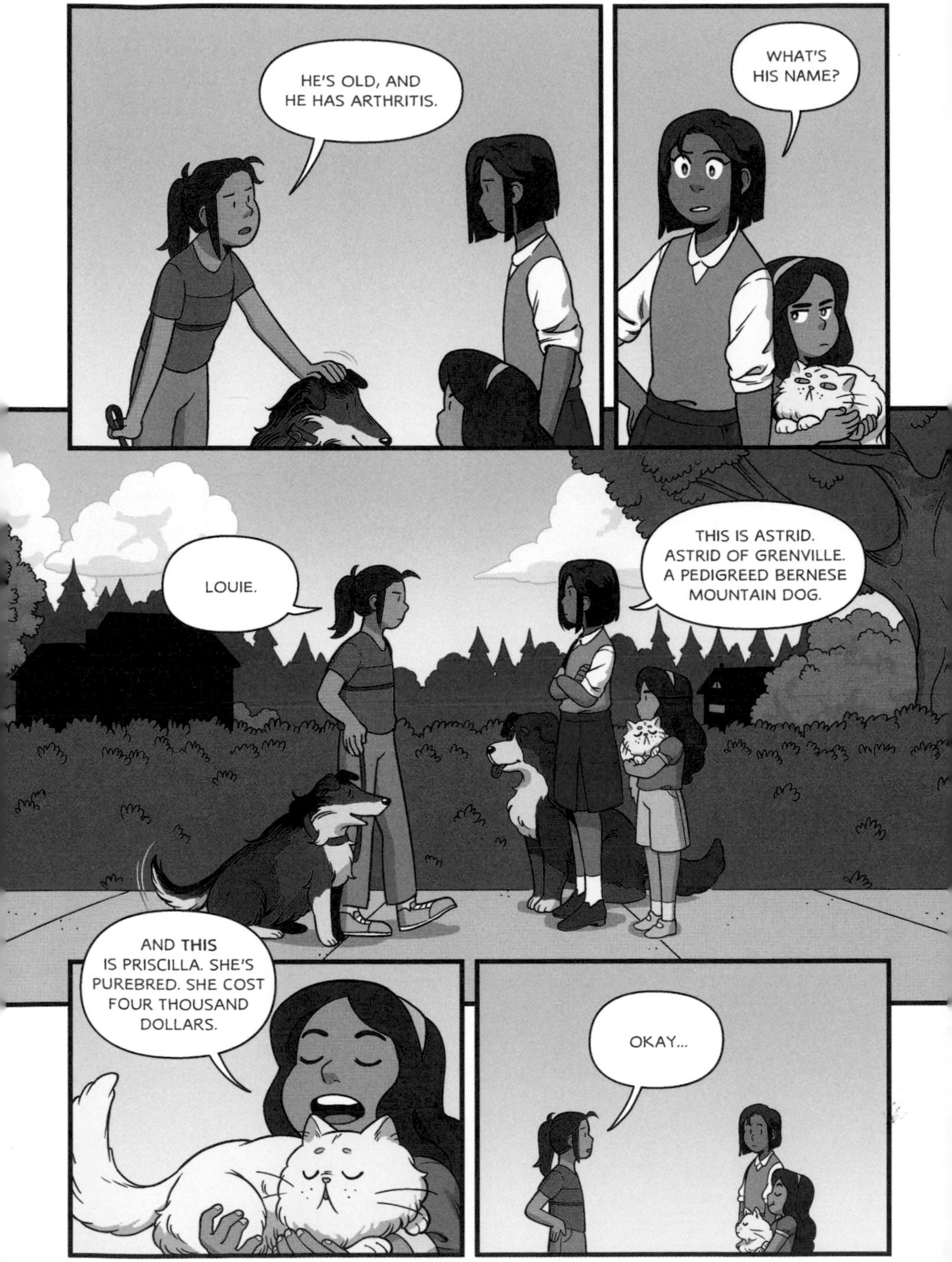
HE'S OLD, AND HE HAS ARTHRITIS.
WHAT'S HIS NAME?
LOUIE.
THIS IS ASTRID. ASTRID OF GRENVILLE. A PEDIGREED BERNESE MOUNTAIN DOG.
AND THIS IS PRISCILLA. SHE'S PUREBRED. SHE COST FOUR THOUSAND DOLLARS.
OKAY...

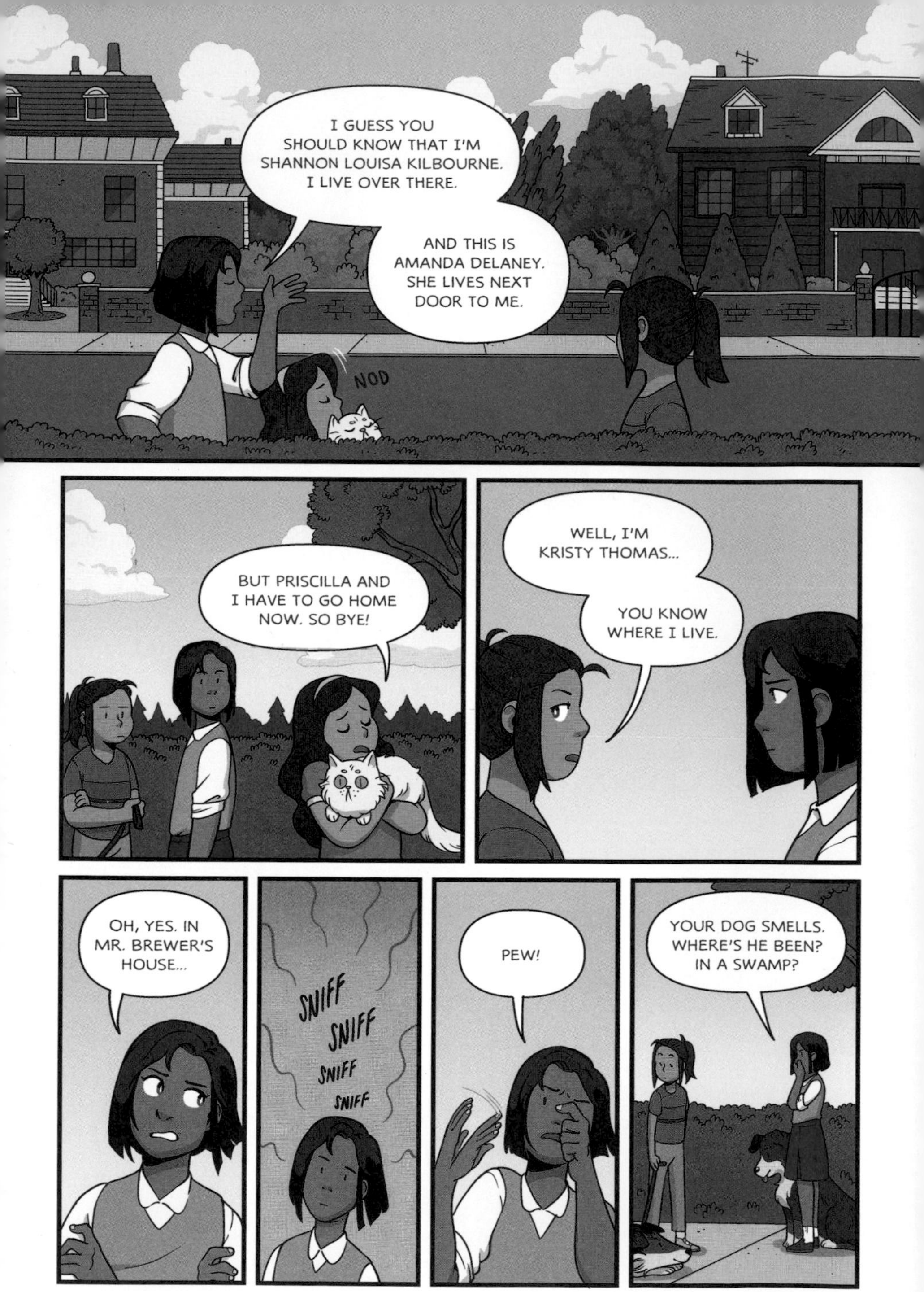
I GUESS YOU SHOULD KNOW THAT I'M SHANNON LOUISA KILBOURNE. I LIVE OVER THERE.
AND THIS IS AMANDA DELANEY. SHE LIVES NEXT DOOR TO ME.
NOD
BUT PRISCILLA AND I HAVE TO GO HOME NOW. SO BYE!
WELL, I'M KRISTY THOMAS...
YOU KNOW WHERE I LIVE.
OH, YES. IN MR. BREWER'S HOUSE...
SNIFF
SNIFF
SNIFF
SNIFF
PEW!
YOUR DOG SMELLS. WHERE'S HE BEEN? IN A SWAMP?

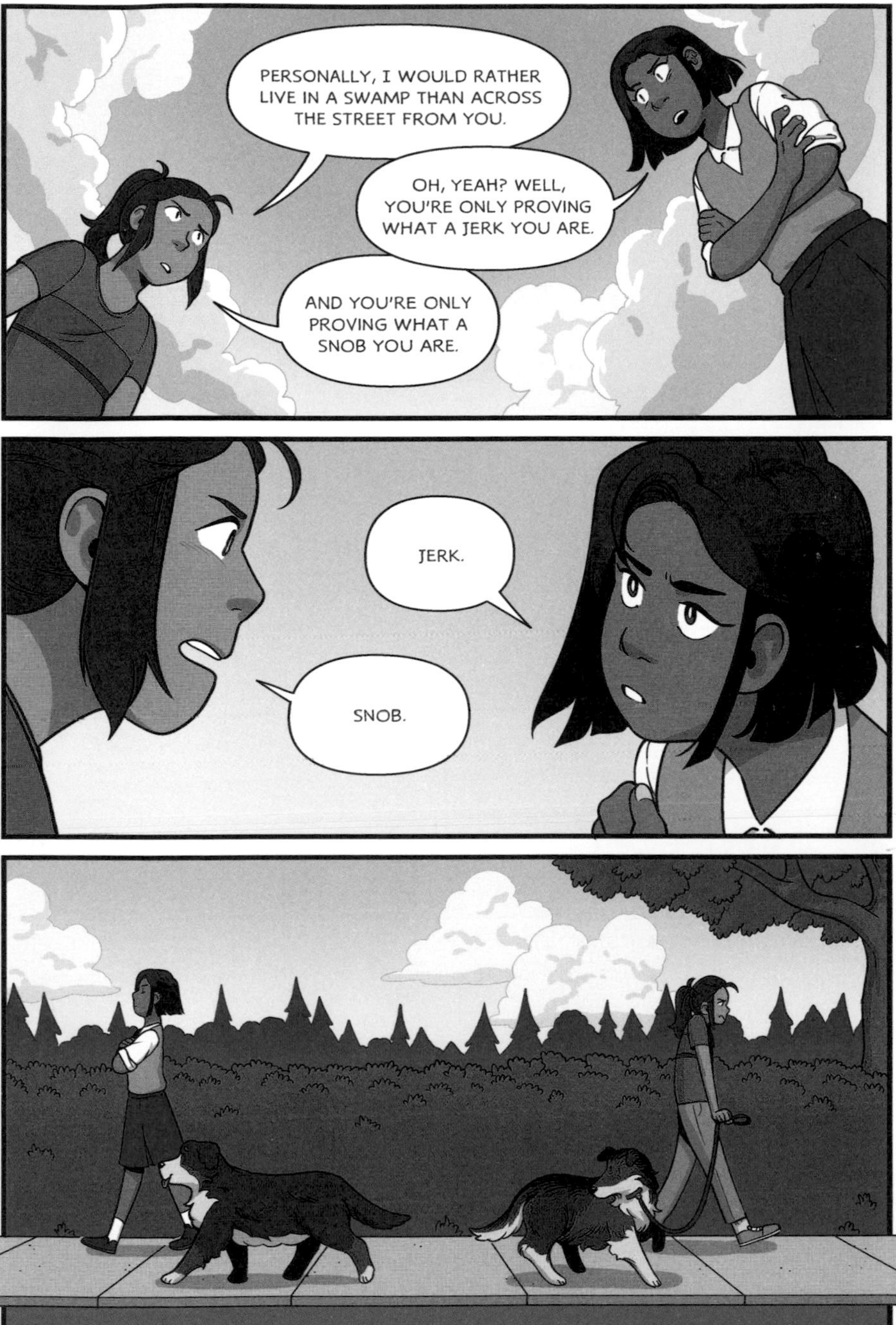
PERSONALLY, I WOULD RATHER LIVE IN A SWAMP THAN ACROSS THE STREET FROM YOU.
OH, YEAH? WELL, YOU'RE ONLY PROVING WHAT A JERK YOU ARE.
AND YOU'RE ONLY PROVING WHAT A SNOB YOU ARE.
JERK.
SNOB.

CHAPTER 4

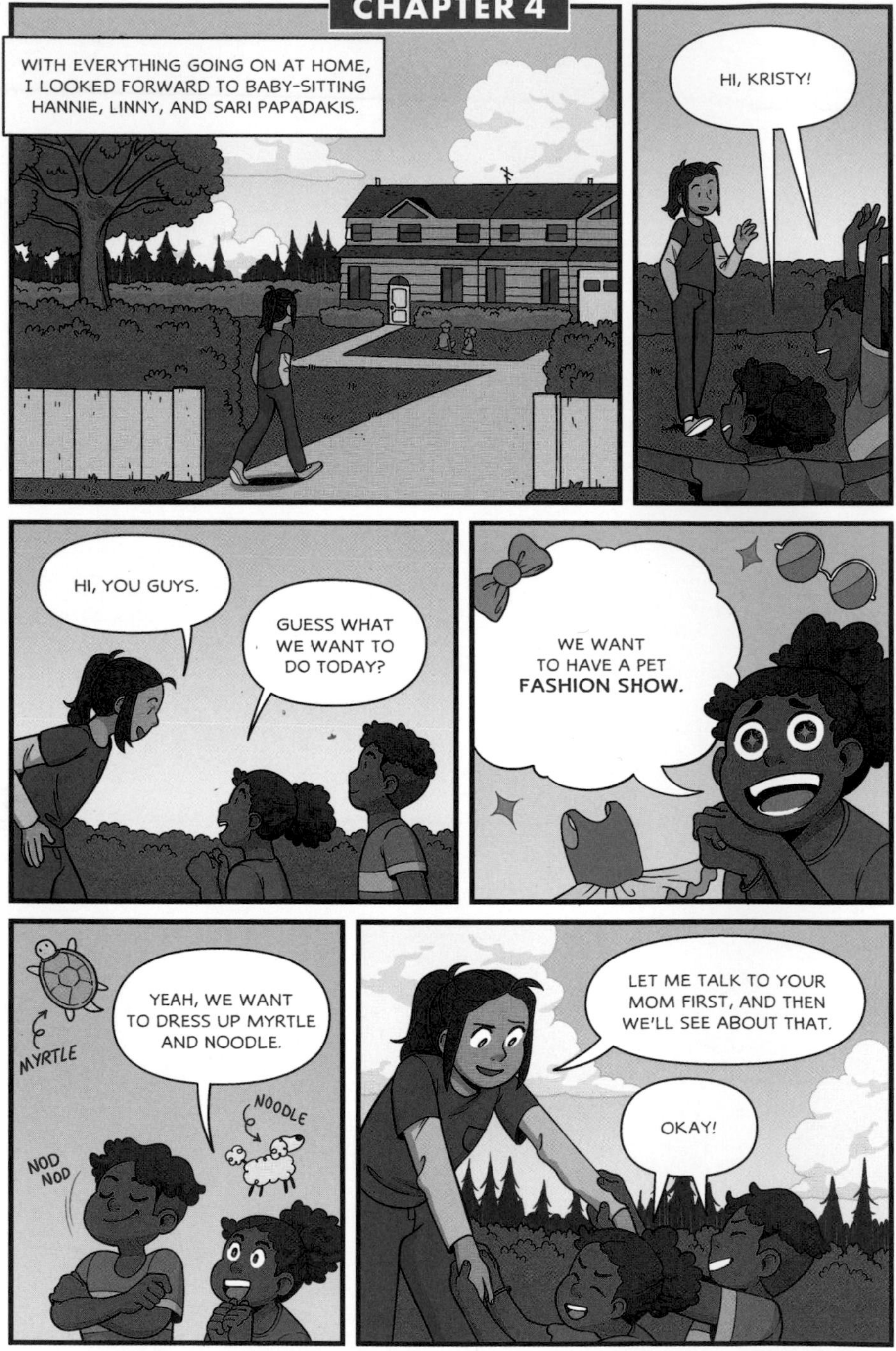
WITH EVERYTHING GOING ON AT HOME, I LOOKED FORWARD TO BABY-SITTING HANNIE, LINNY, AND SARI PAPADAKIS.
HI, KRISTY!
HI, YOU GUYS.
GUESS WHAT WE WANT TO DO TODAY?
WE WANT TO HAVE A PET FASHION SHOW.
MYRTLE
YEAH, WE WANT TO DRESS UP MYRTLE AND NOODLE.
NOODLE
NOD NOD
LET ME TALK TO YOUR MOM FIRST, AND THEN WE'LL SEE ABOUT THAT.
OKAY!

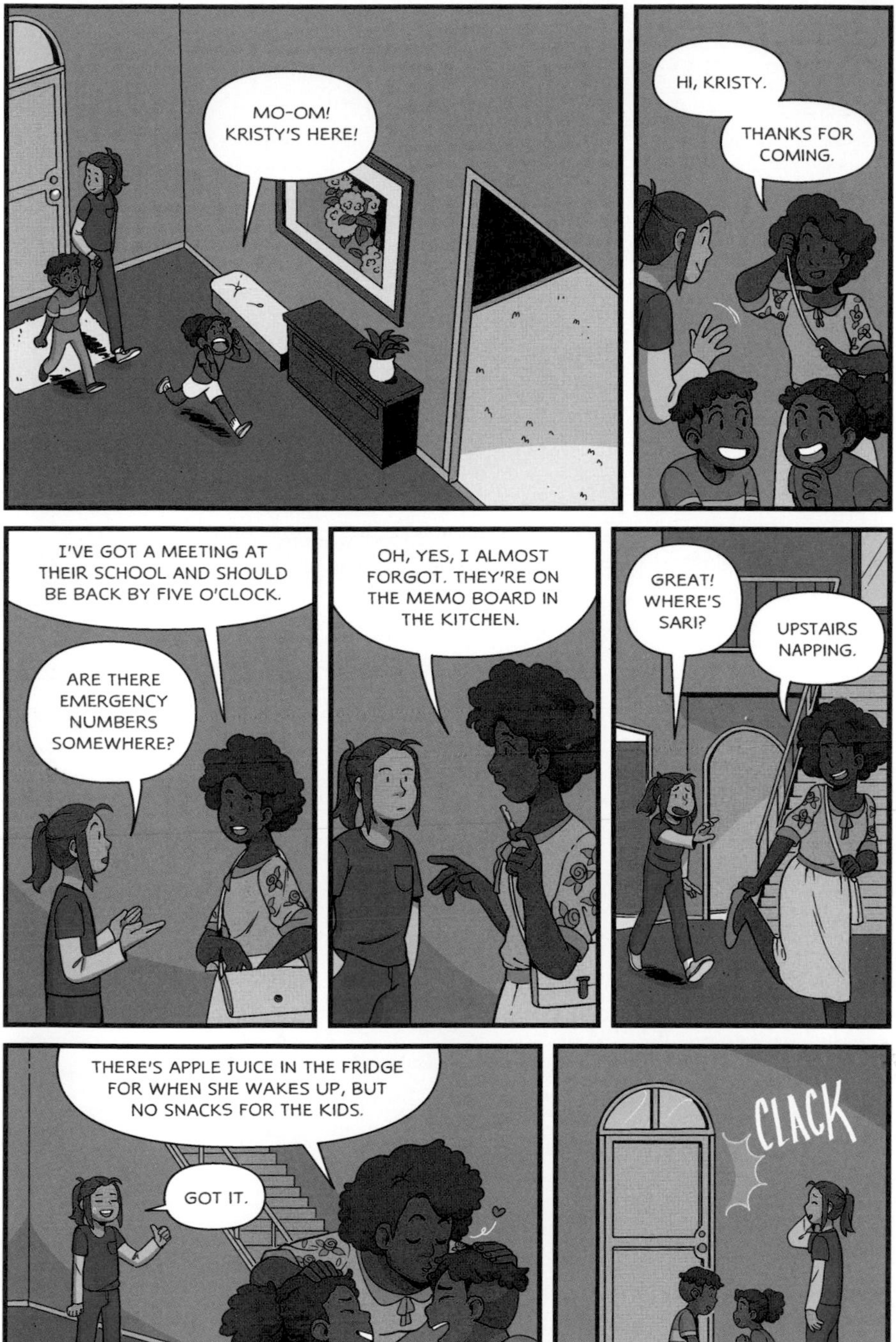
MO-OM! KRISTY'S HERE!
HI, KRISTY.
THANKS FOR COMING.
I'VE GOT A MEETING AT THEIR SCHOOL AND SHOULD BE BACK BY FIVE O'CLOCK.
ARE THERE EMERGENCY NUMBERS SOMEWHERE?
OH, YES, I ALMOST FORGOT. THEY'RE ON THE MEMO BOARD IN THE KITCHEN.
GREAT! WHERE'S SARI?
UPSTAIRS NAPPING.
THERE'S APPLE JUICE IN THE FRIDGE FOR WHEN SHE WAKES UP, BUT NO SNACKS FOR THE KIDS.
GOT IT.
CLACK

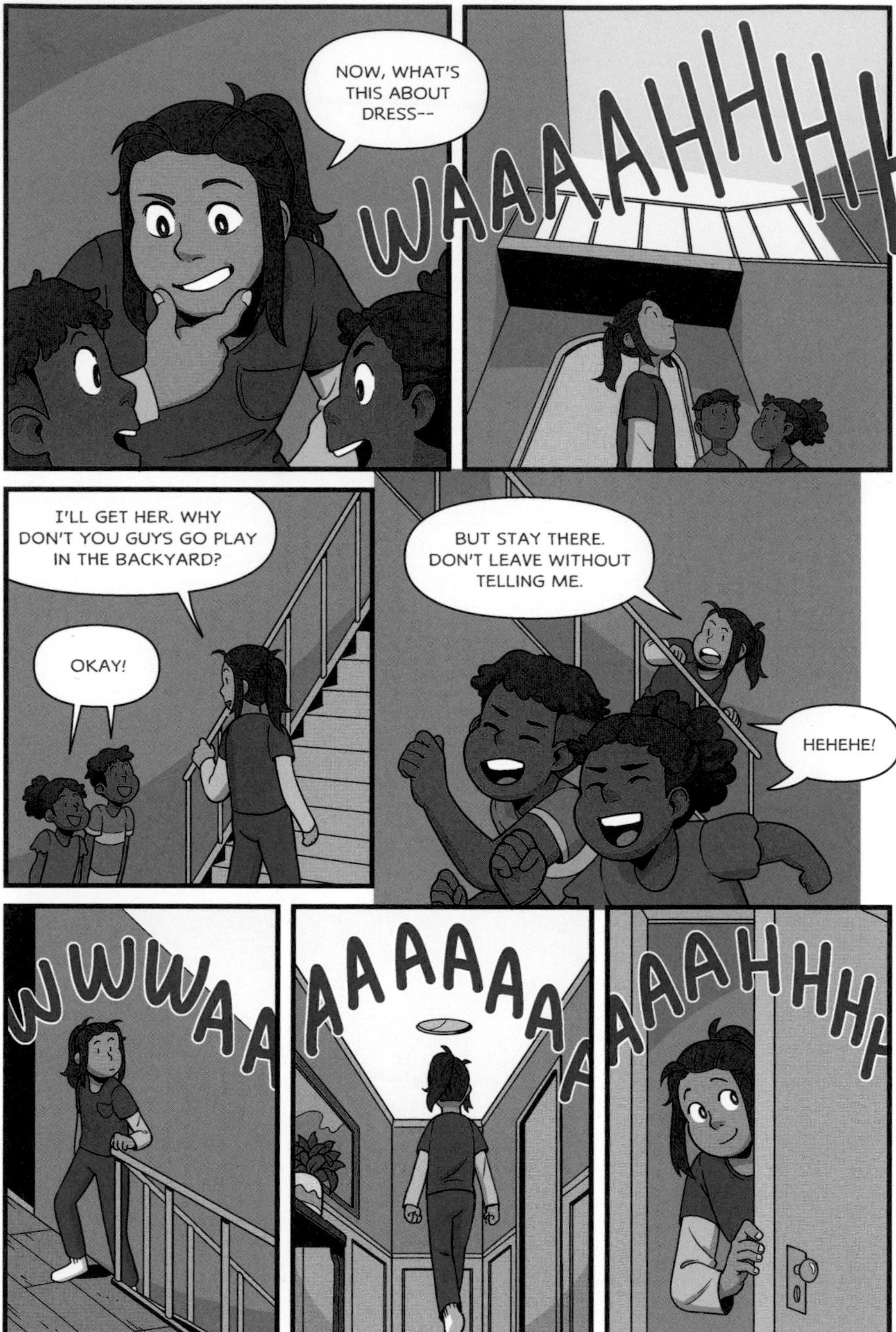
NOW, WHAT'S THIS ABOUT DRESS--
WAAAAHHHHH
I'LL GET HER. WHY DON'T YOU GUYS GO PLAY IN THE BACKYARD?
OKAY!
BUT STAY THERE. DON'T LEAVE WITHOUT TELLING ME.
HEHEHE!
WWWAAAAAAAAAAAAHHHH

HI, SARI!

WAAHH

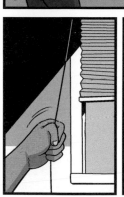

WE'RE GOING TO HAVE FUN PLAYING THIS AFTERNOON.

NO NO NO NO NO NO

HELLO, MR. BEAR, CAN I HELP SARI GET CHANGED?

THANK YOU.

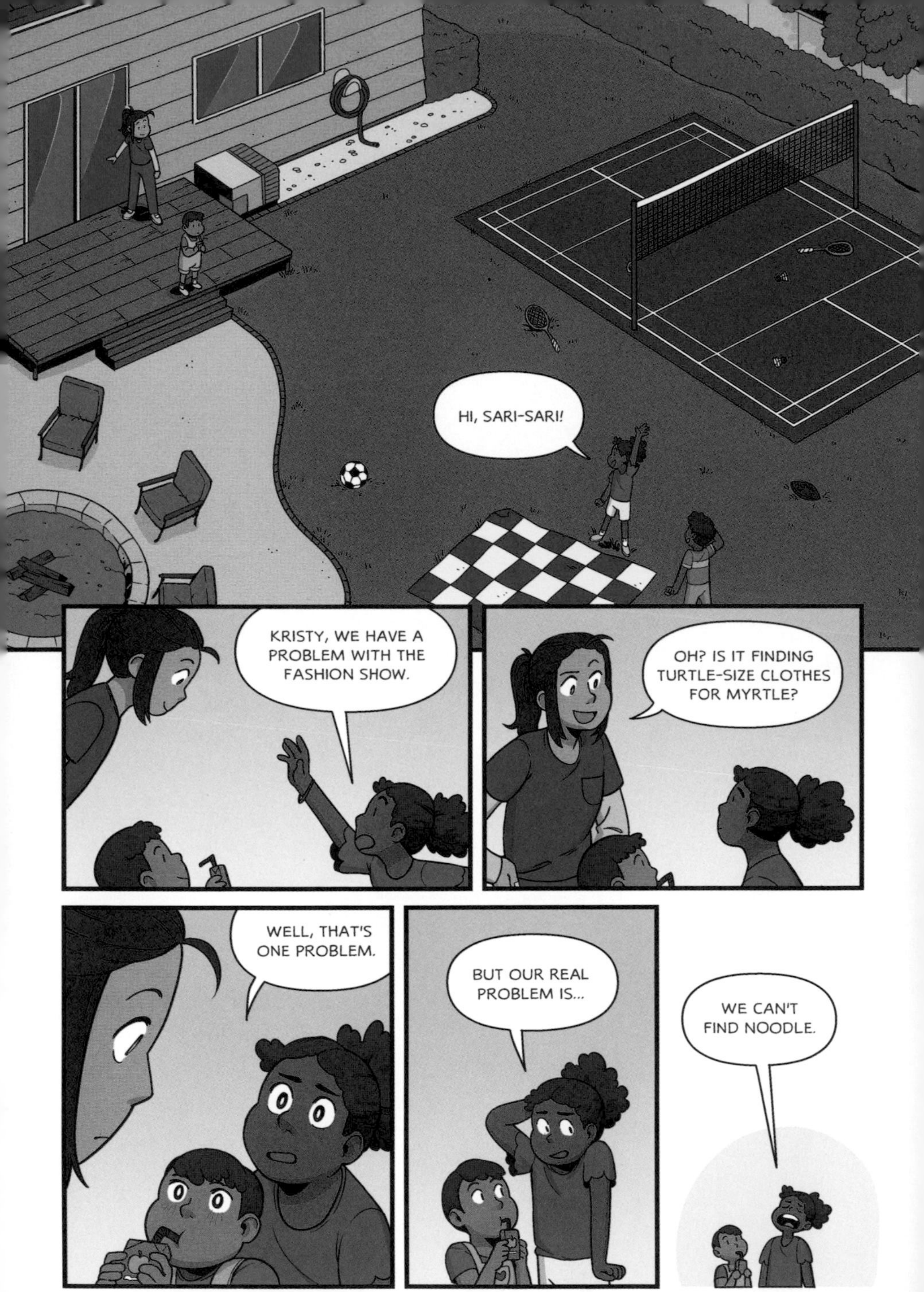
HI, SARI-SARI!
KRISTY, WE HAVE A PROBLEM WITH THE FASHION SHOW.
OH? IS IT FINDING TURTLE-SIZE CLOTHES FOR MYRTLE?
WELL, THAT'S ONE PROBLEM.
BUT OUR REAL PROBLEM IS...
WE CAN'T FIND NOODLE.

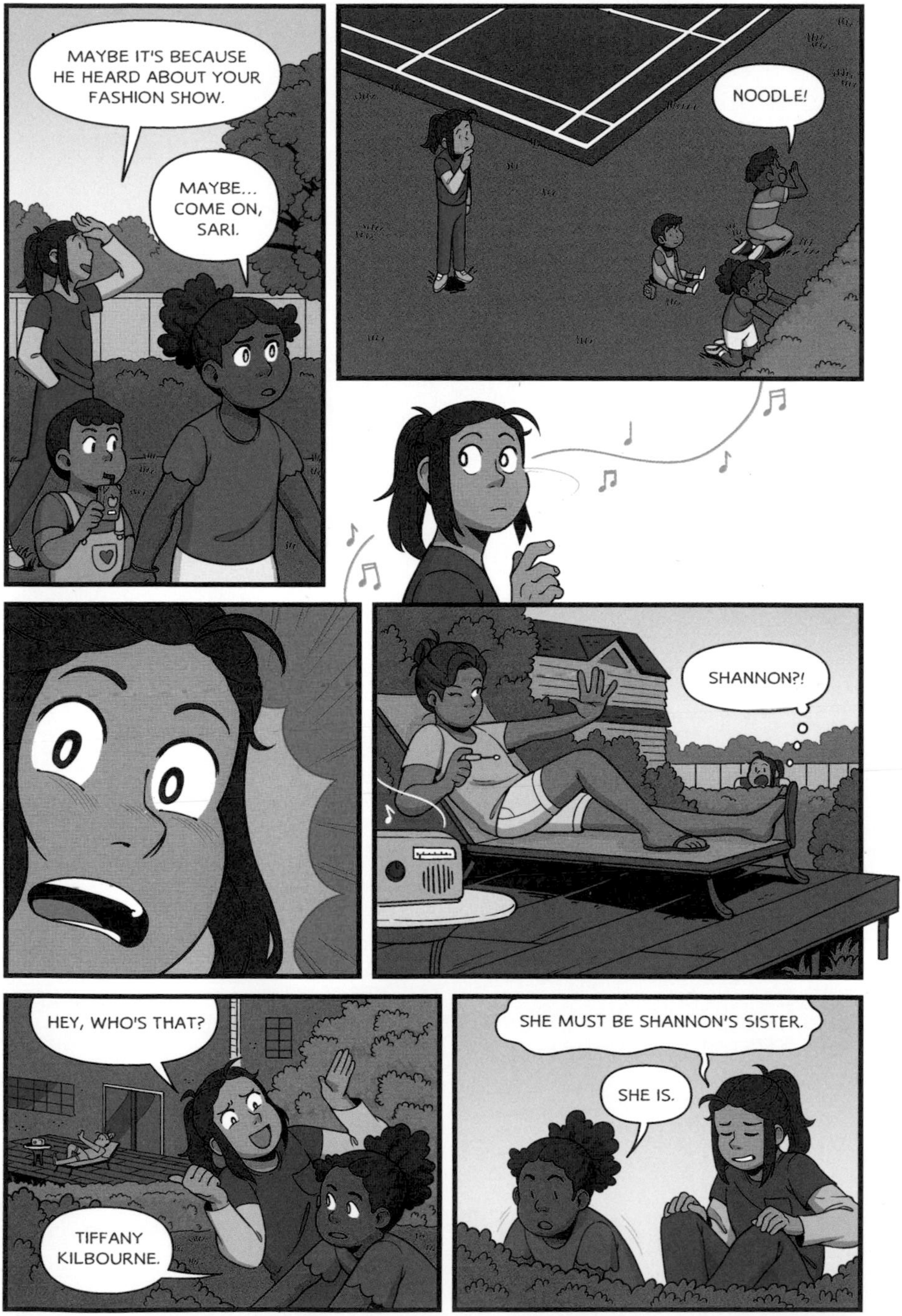
MAYBE IT'S BECAUSE HE HEARD ABOUT YOUR FASHION SHOW.
MAYBE... COME ON, SARI.
NOODLE!
SHANNON?!
HEY, WHO'S THAT?
TIFFANY KILBOURNE.
SHE MUST BE SHANNON'S SISTER.
SHE IS.

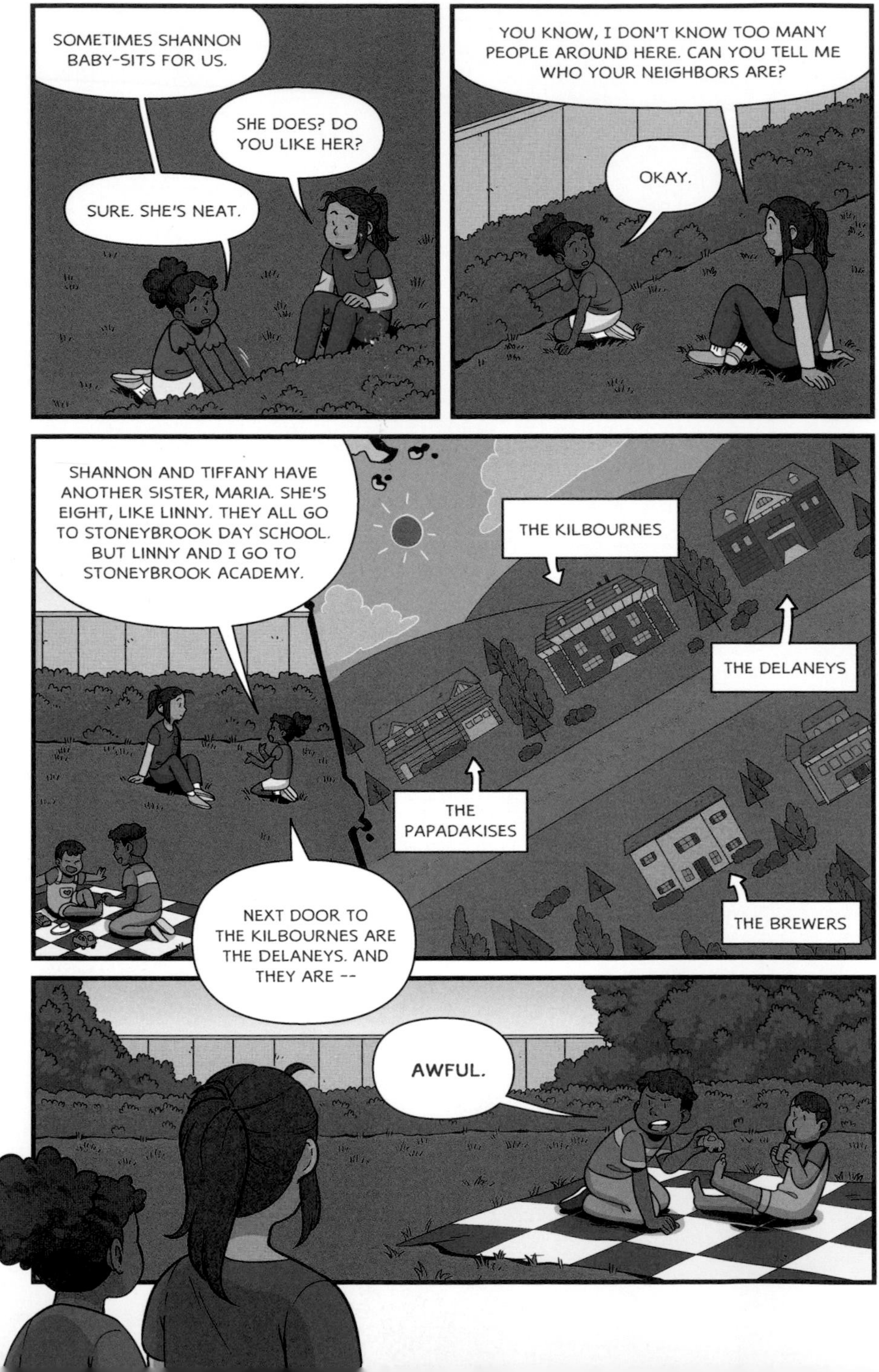
SOMETIMES SHANNON BABY-SITS FOR US.
SHE DOES? DO YOU LIKE HER?
SURE. SHE'S NEAT.
YOU KNOW, I DON'T KNOW TOO MANY PEOPLE AROUND HERE. CAN YOU TELL ME WHO YOUR NEIGHBORS ARE?
OKAY.
SHANNON AND TIFFANY HAVE ANOTHER SISTER, MARIA. SHE'S EIGHT, LIKE LINNY. THEY ALL GO TO STONEYBROOK DAY SCHOOL. BUT LINNY AND I GO TO STONEYBROOK ACADEMY.
THE KILBOURNES
THE DELANEYS
THE PAPADAKISES
THE BREWERS
NEXT DOOR TO THE KILBOURNES ARE THE DELANEYS. AND THEY ARE --
AWFUL.

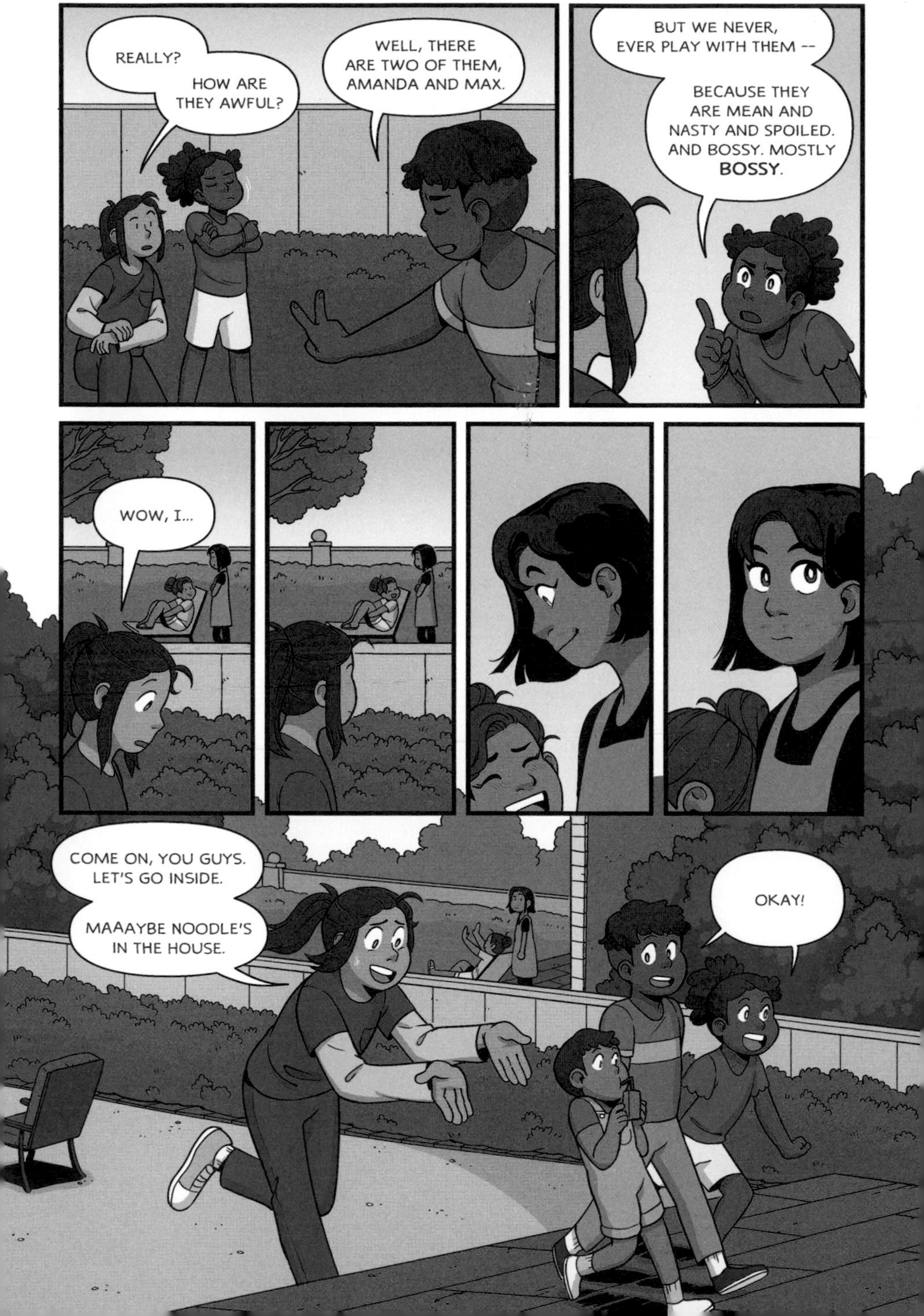
REALLY?
HOW ARE THEY AWFUL?
WELL, THERE ARE TWO OF THEM, AMANDA AND MAX.
BUT WE NEVER, EVER PLAY WITH THEM --
BECAUSE THEY ARE MEAN AND NASTY AND SPOILED. AND BOSSY. MOSTLY **BOSSY**.
WOW, I...
COME ON, YOU GUYS. LET'S GO INSIDE.
MAAAYBE NOODLE'S IN THE HOUSE.
OKAY!

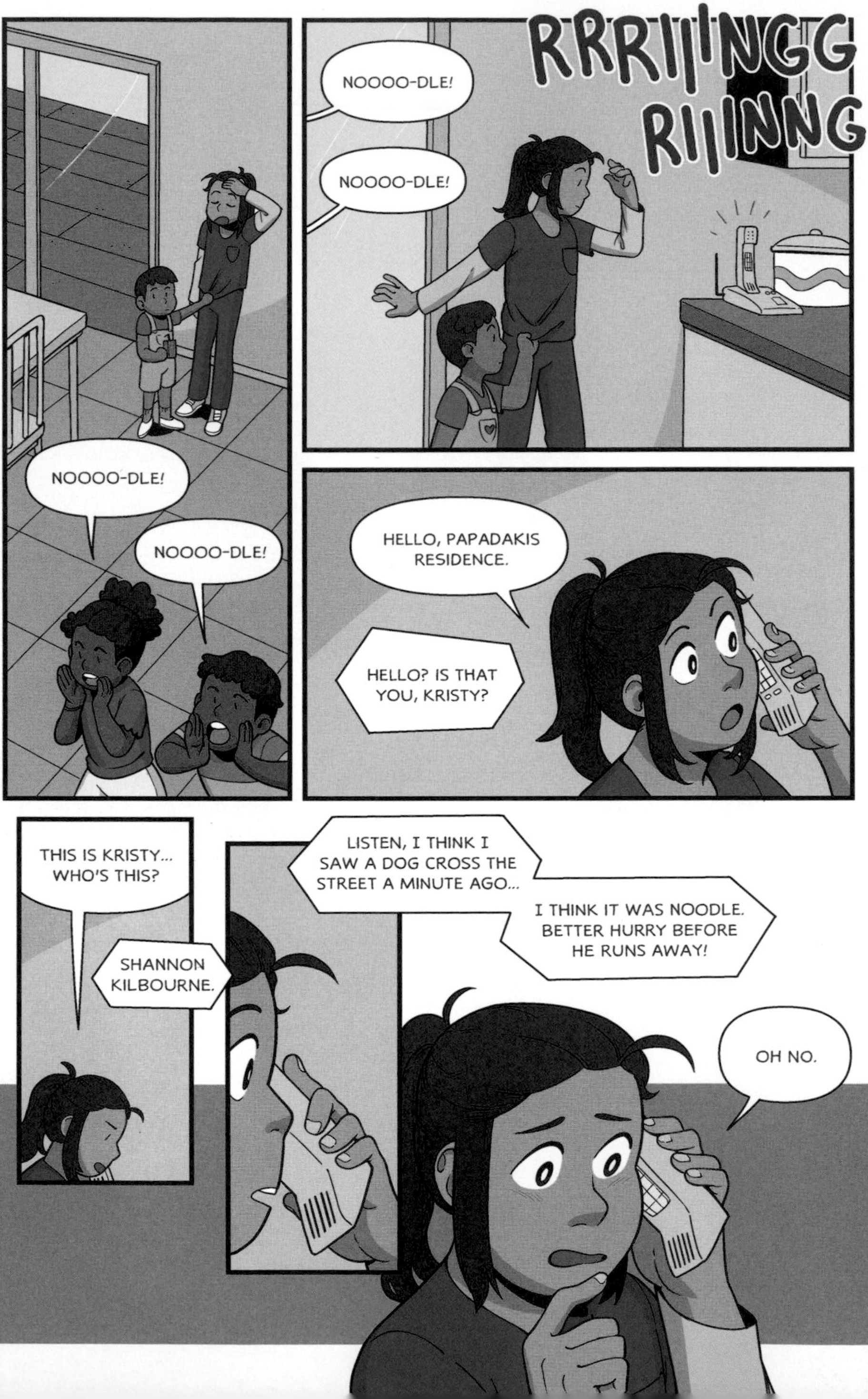
NOOOO-DLE!
NOOOO-DLE!
RRRIIINGG
RIIINNG
NOOOO-DLE!
NOOOO-DLE!
HELLO, PAPADAKIS RESIDENCE.
HELLO? IS THAT YOU, KRISTY?
THIS IS KRISTY... WHO'S THIS?
SHANNON KILBOURNE.
LISTEN, I THINK I SAW A DOG CROSS THE STREET A MINUTE AGO...
I THINK IT WAS NOODLE. BETTER HURRY BEFORE HE RUNS AWAY!
OH NO.

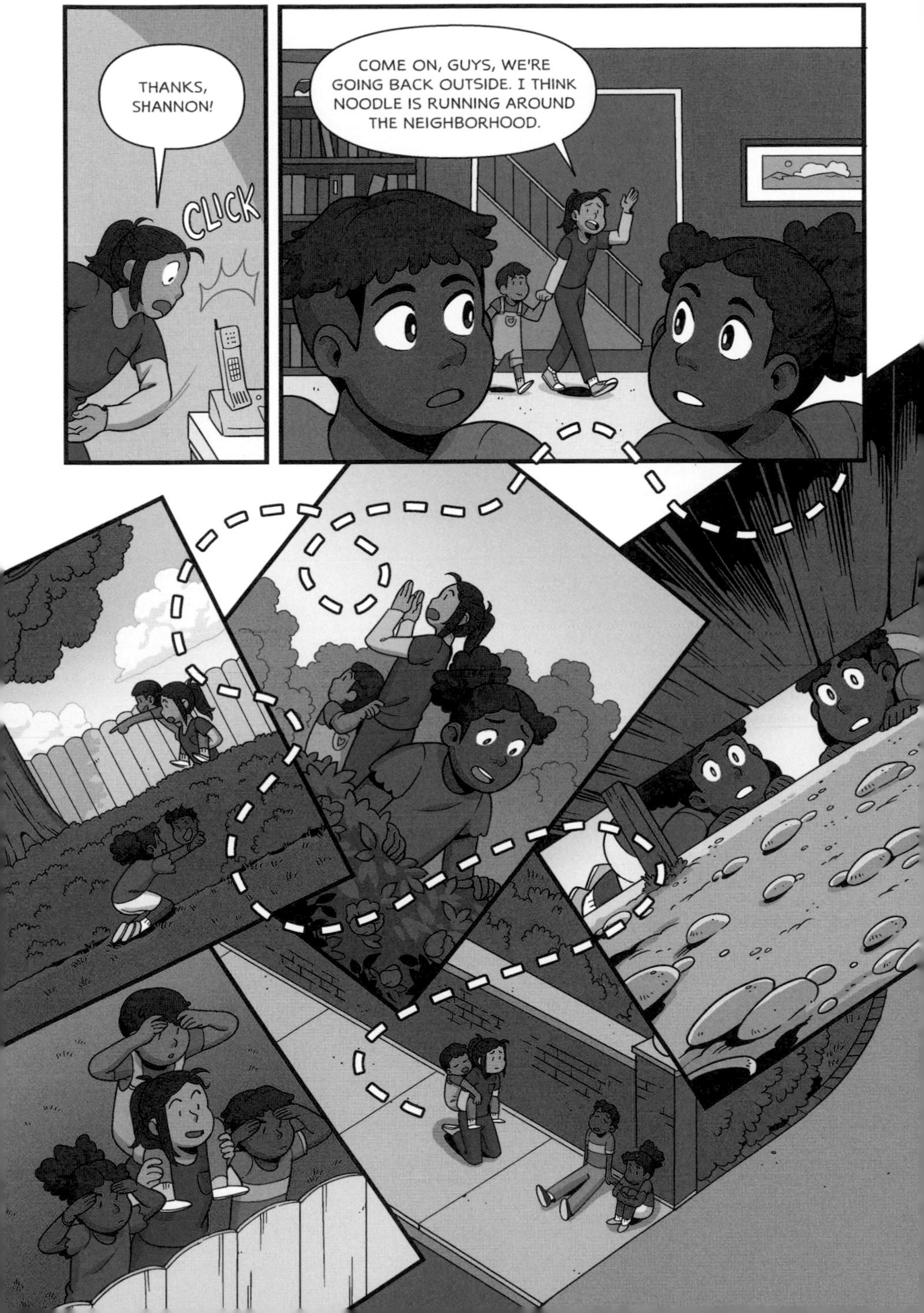
THANKS, SHANNON!
CLICK
COME ON, GUYS, WE'RE GOING BACK OUTSIDE. I THINK NOODLE IS RUNNING AROUND THE NEIGHBORHOOD.

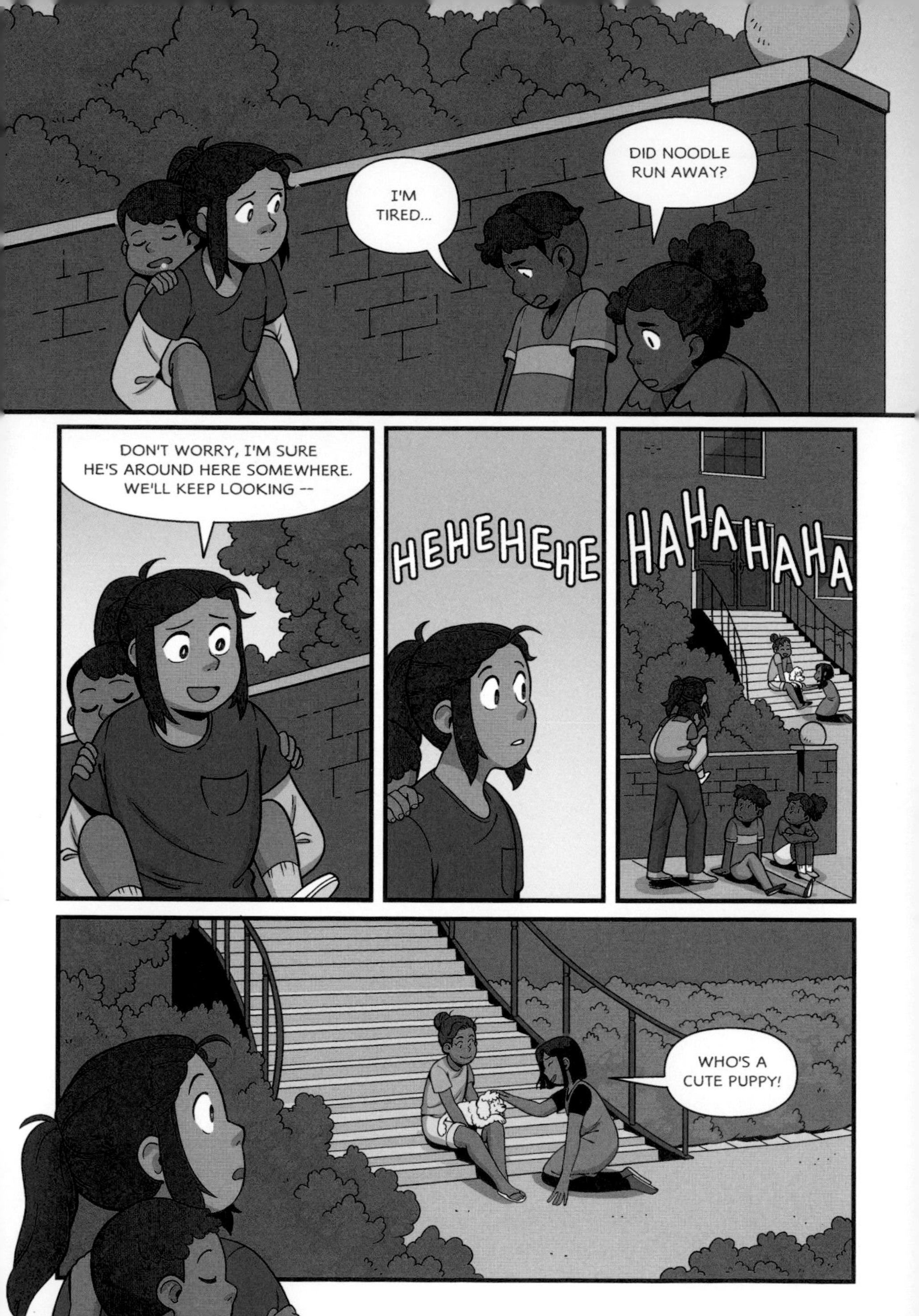
I'M TIRED...
DID NOODLE RUN AWAY?
DON'T WORRY, I'M SURE HE'S AROUND HERE SOMEWHERE. WE'LL KEEP LOOKING --
HEHEHEHEHE
HAHAHAHAHA
WHO'S A CUTE PUPPY!

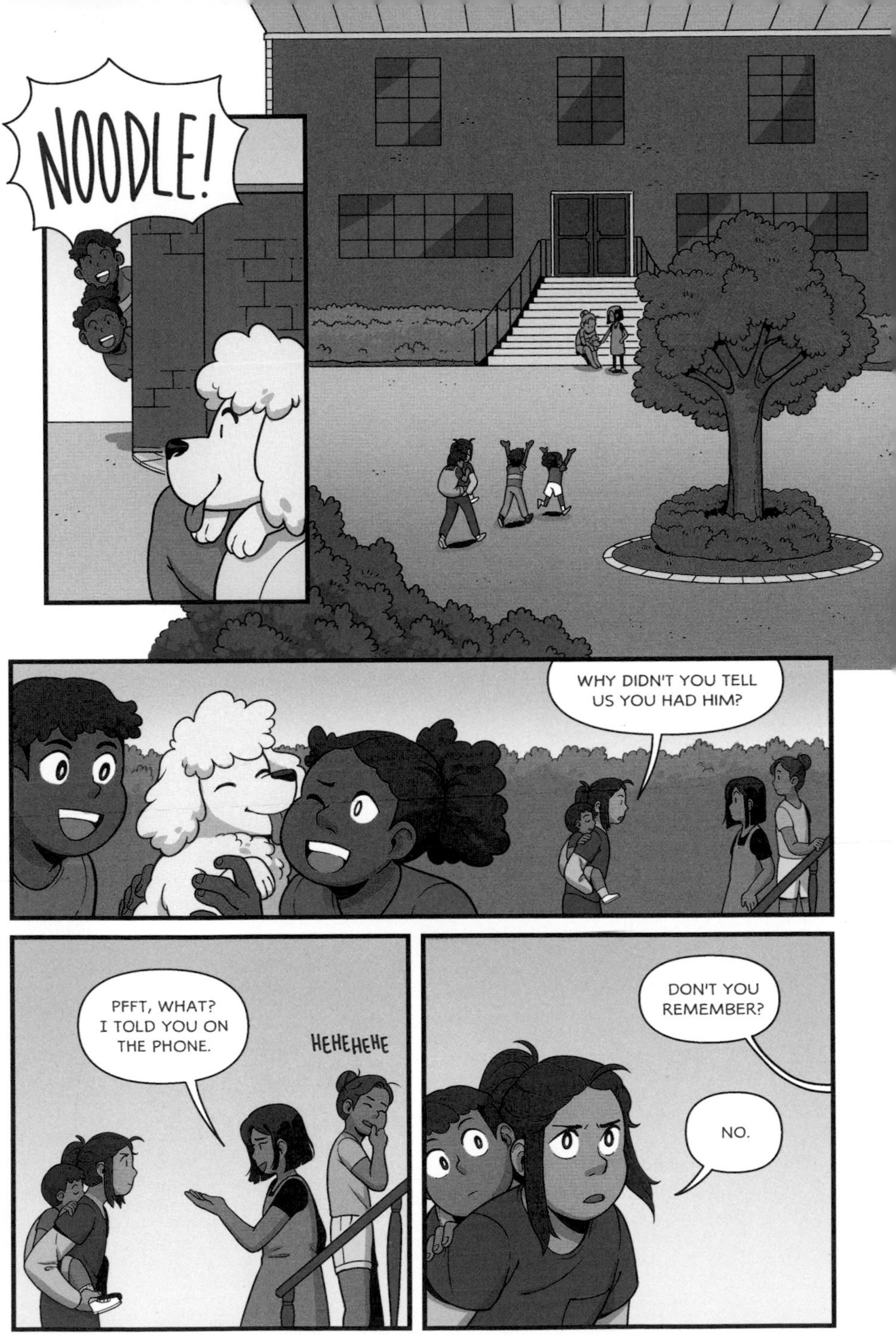
NOODLE!
WHY DIDN'T YOU TELL US YOU HAD HIM?
PFFT, WHAT? I TOLD YOU ON THE PHONE.
HEHEHEHE
DON'T YOU REMEMBER?
NO.

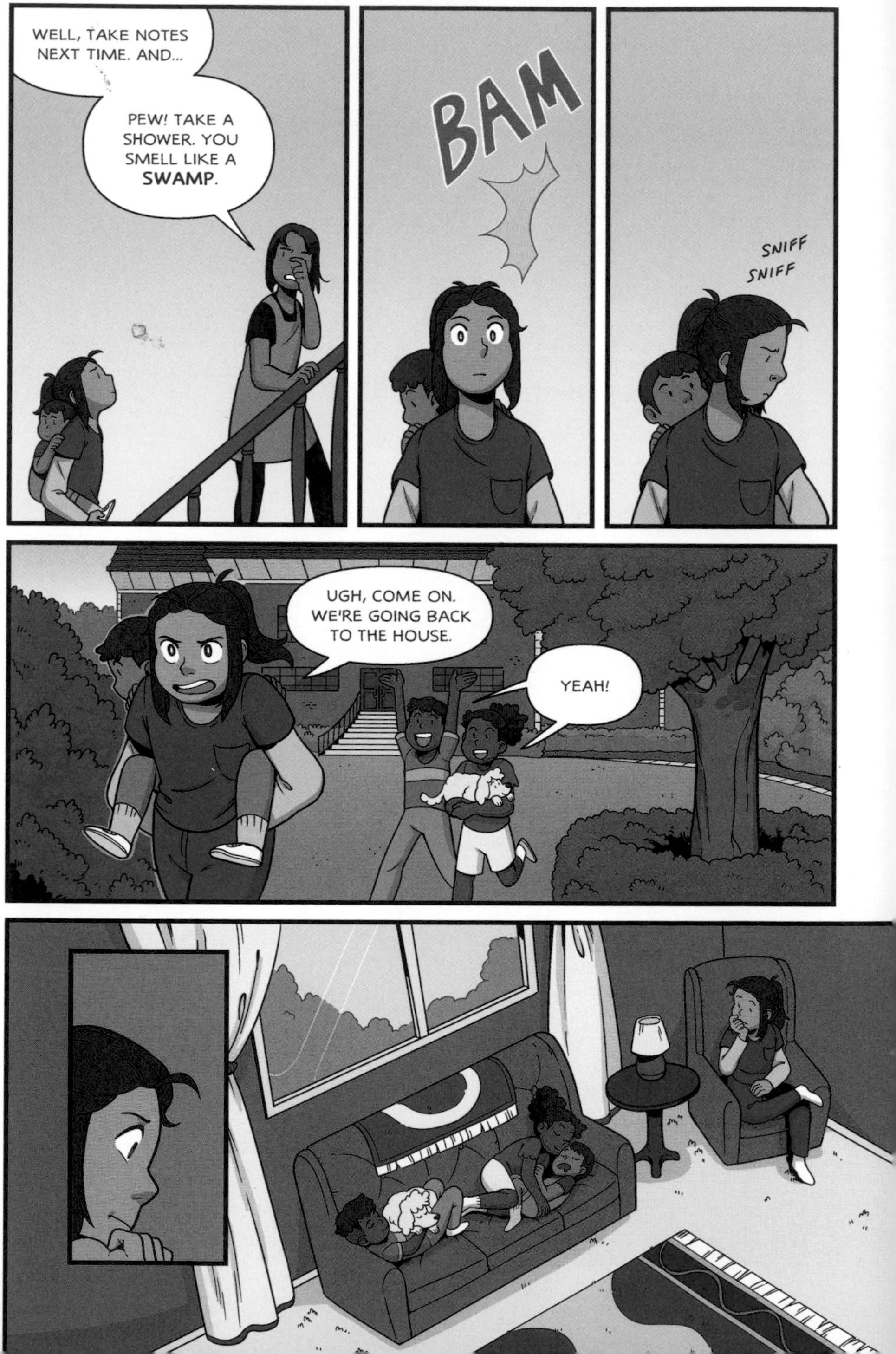
WELL, TAKE NOTES NEXT TIME. AND...
PEW! TAKE A SHOWER. YOU SMELL LIKE A **SWAMP**.
BAM
SNIFF SNIFF
UGH, COME ON. WE'RE GOING BACK TO THE HOUSE.
YEAH!

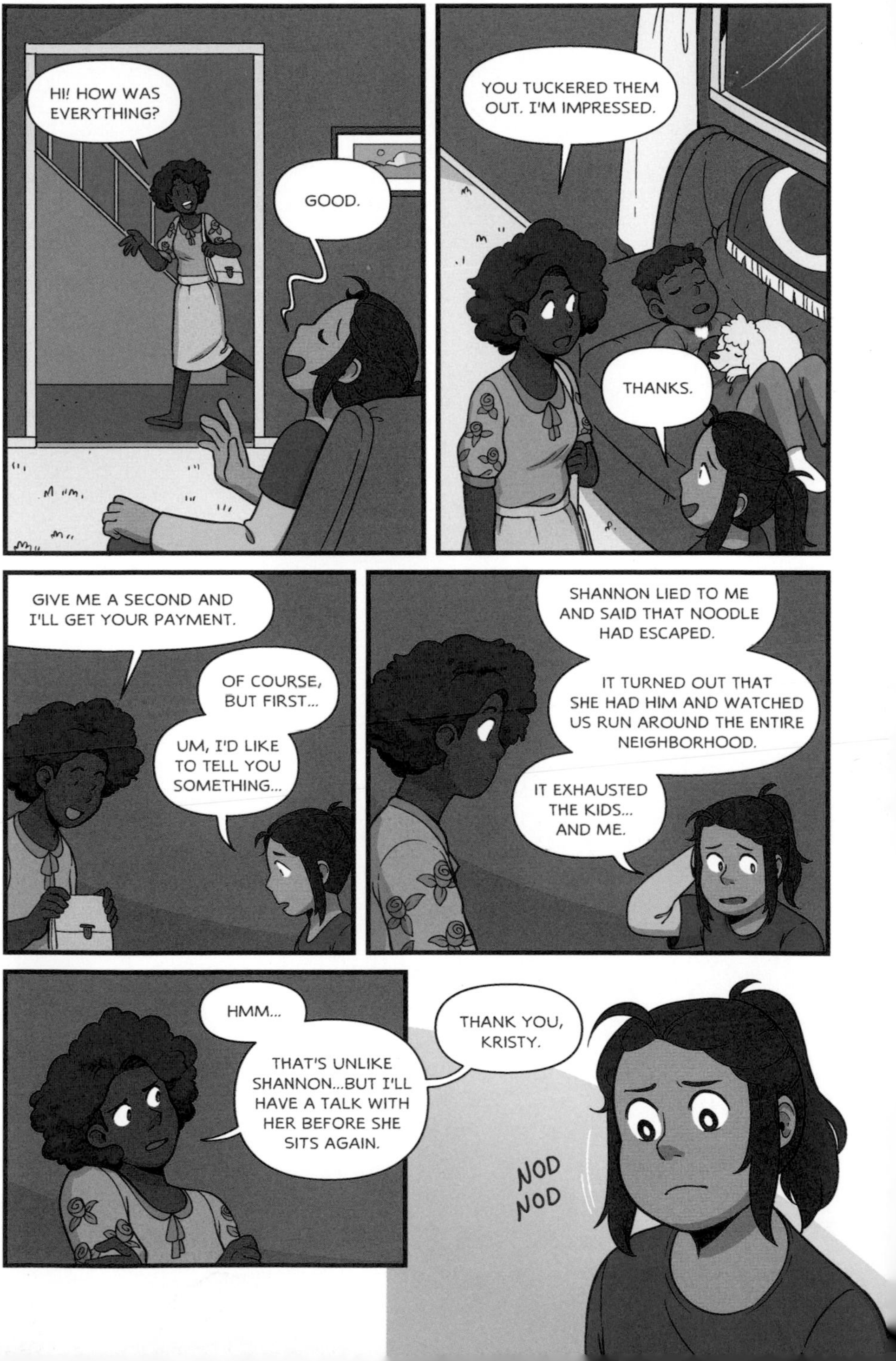
HI! HOW WAS EVERYTHING?
GOOD.
YOU TUCKERED THEM OUT. I'M IMPRESSED.
THANKS.
GIVE ME A SECOND AND I'LL GET YOUR PAYMENT.
OF COURSE, BUT FIRST...
UM, I'D LIKE TO TELL YOU SOMETHING...
SHANNON LIED TO ME AND SAID THAT NOODLE HAD ESCAPED.
IT TURNED OUT THAT SHE HAD HIM AND WATCHED US RUN AROUND THE ENTIRE NEIGHBORHOOD.
IT EXHAUSTED THE KIDS... AND ME.
HMM...
THAT'S UNLIKE SHANNON...BUT I'LL HAVE A TALK WITH HER BEFORE SHE SITS AGAIN.
THANK YOU, KRISTY.
NOD NOD

UP

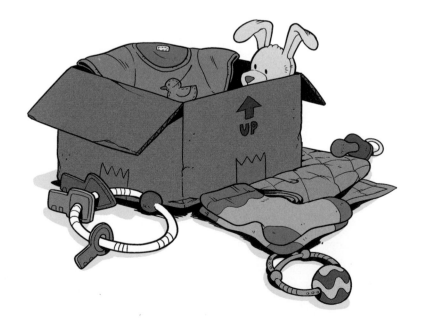

Thursday

I baby-sat for Myriah and Gabbie this afternoon, and we had a little trouble. Mrs. Perkins is getting ready for the new baby. She's fixing up the room that used to be David Michael's. (You guys should see it. There are bunnies and alphabet letters everywhere!) Mrs. Perkins is also sorting through Myriah and Gabbie's baby toys and clothes. The kids have been helping out, but Gabbie is _so_ excited that she doesn't understand why anyone wouldn't be. So when Jamie Newton came over to play, he started to tell Gabbie how he felt about his sister. Poor Gabbie didn't understand at all...

Mary Anne

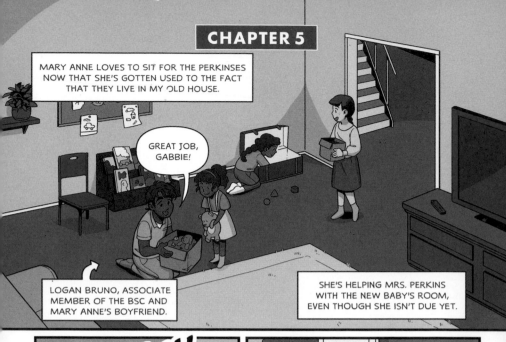

MARY ANNE LOVES TO SIT FOR THE PERKINSES NOW THAT SHE'S GOTTEN USED TO THE FACT THAT THEY LIVE IN MY OLD HOUSE.

GREAT JOB, GABBIE!

LOGAN BRUNO, ASSOCIATE MEMBER OF THE BSC AND MARY ANNE'S BOYFRIEND.

SHE'S HELPING MRS. PERKINS WITH THE NEW BABY'S ROOM, EVEN THOUGH SHE ISN'T DUE YET.

KNOCK KNOCK

I'LL GET IT! I'LL GET IT!

HI, JAMIE!

HEY, MYRIAH.

COME LOOK AT THE BABY'S ROOM. IT IS SO, SO BEAUTIFUL.

THANKS FOR HELPING, LOGAN.

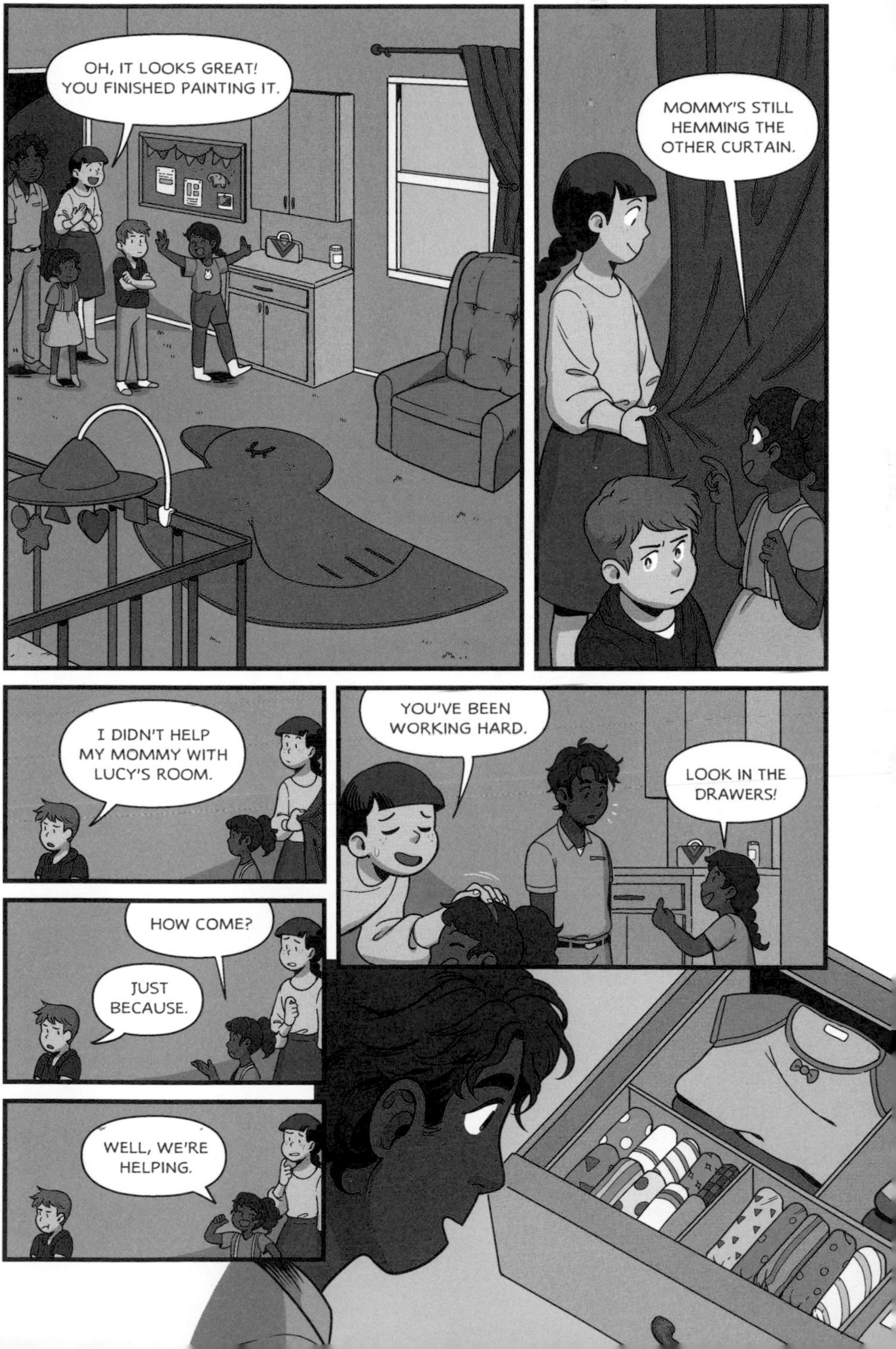
OH, IT LOOKS GREAT! YOU FINISHED PAINTING IT.
MOMMY'S STILL HEMMING THE OTHER CURTAIN.
I DIDN'T HELP MY MOMMY WITH LUCY'S ROOM.
YOU'VE BEEN WORKING HARD.
LOOK IN THE DRAWERS!
HOW COME?
JUST BECAUSE.
WELL, WE'RE HELPING.

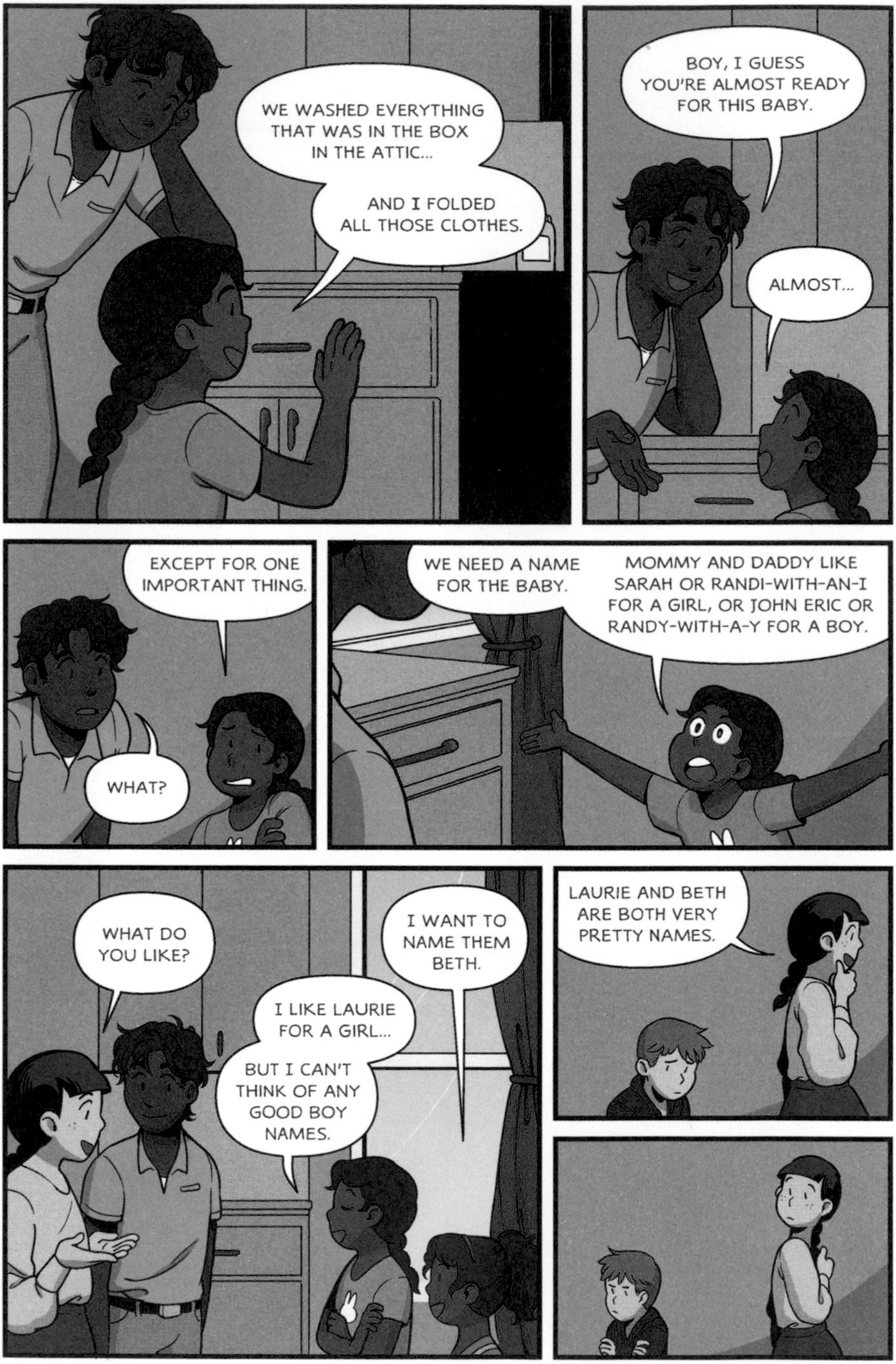
WE WASHED EVERYTHING THAT WAS IN THE BOX IN THE ATTIC...
AND I FOLDED ALL THOSE CLOTHES.
BOY, I GUESS YOU'RE ALMOST READY FOR THIS BABY.
ALMOST...
EXCEPT FOR ONE IMPORTANT THING.
WHAT?
WE NEED A NAME FOR THE BABY.
MOMMY AND DADDY LIKE SARAH OR RANDI-WITH-AN-I FOR A GIRL, OR JOHN ERIC OR RANDY-WITH-A-Y FOR A BOY.
WHAT DO YOU LIKE?
I LIKE LAURIE FOR A GIRL...
BUT I CAN'T THINK OF ANY GOOD BOY NAMES.
I WANT TO NAME THEM BETH.
LAURIE AND BETH ARE BOTH VERY PRETTY NAMES.

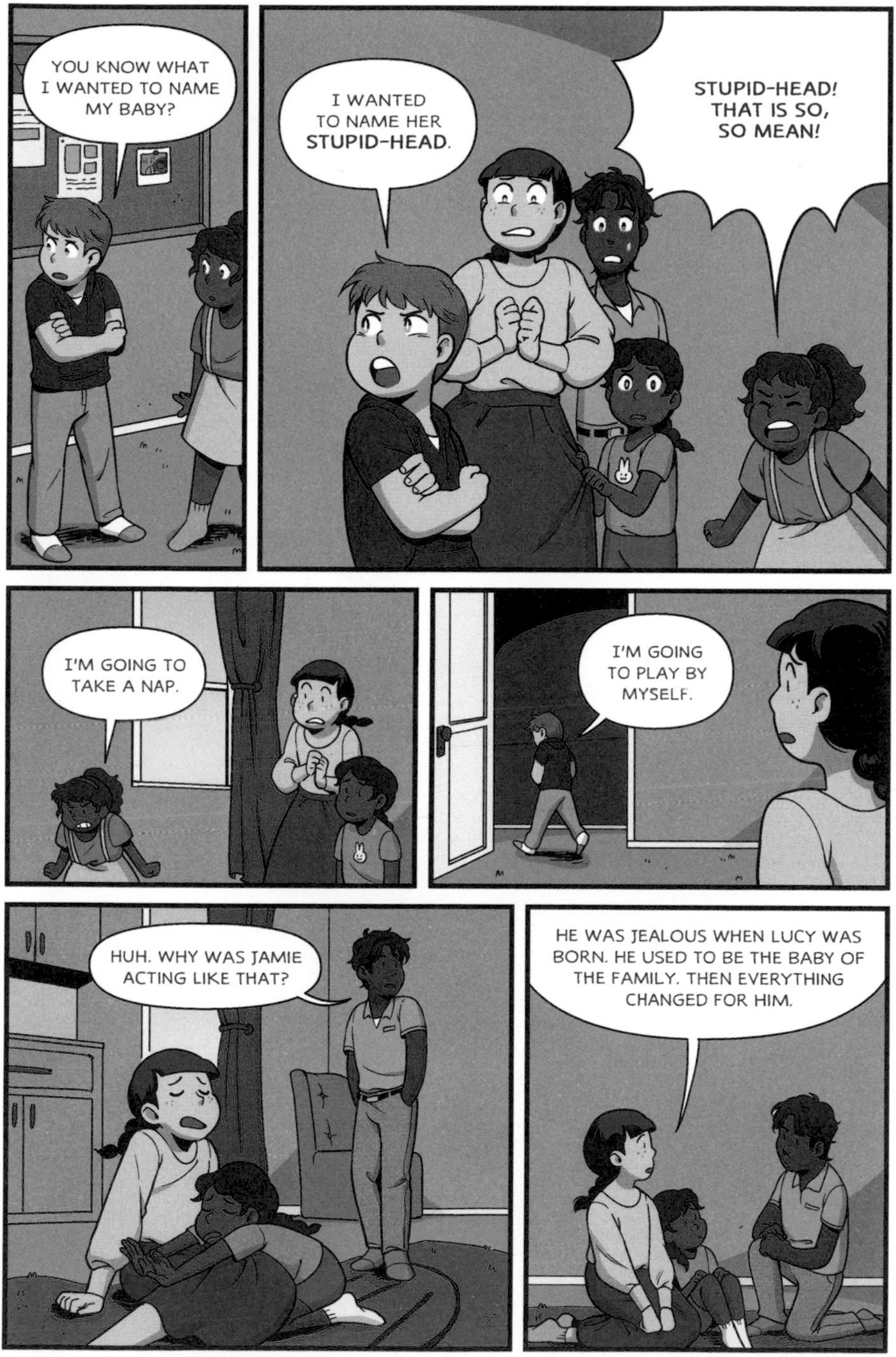
YOU KNOW WHAT I WANTED TO NAME MY BABY?
I WANTED TO NAME HER STUPID-HEAD.
STUPID-HEAD! THAT IS SO, SO MEAN!
I'M GOING TO TAKE A NAP.
I'M GOING TO PLAY BY MYSELF.
HUH. WHY WAS JAMIE ACTING LIKE THAT?
HE WAS JEALOUS WHEN LUCY WAS BORN. HE USED TO BE THE BABY OF THE FAMILY. THEN EVERYTHING CHANGED FOR HIM.

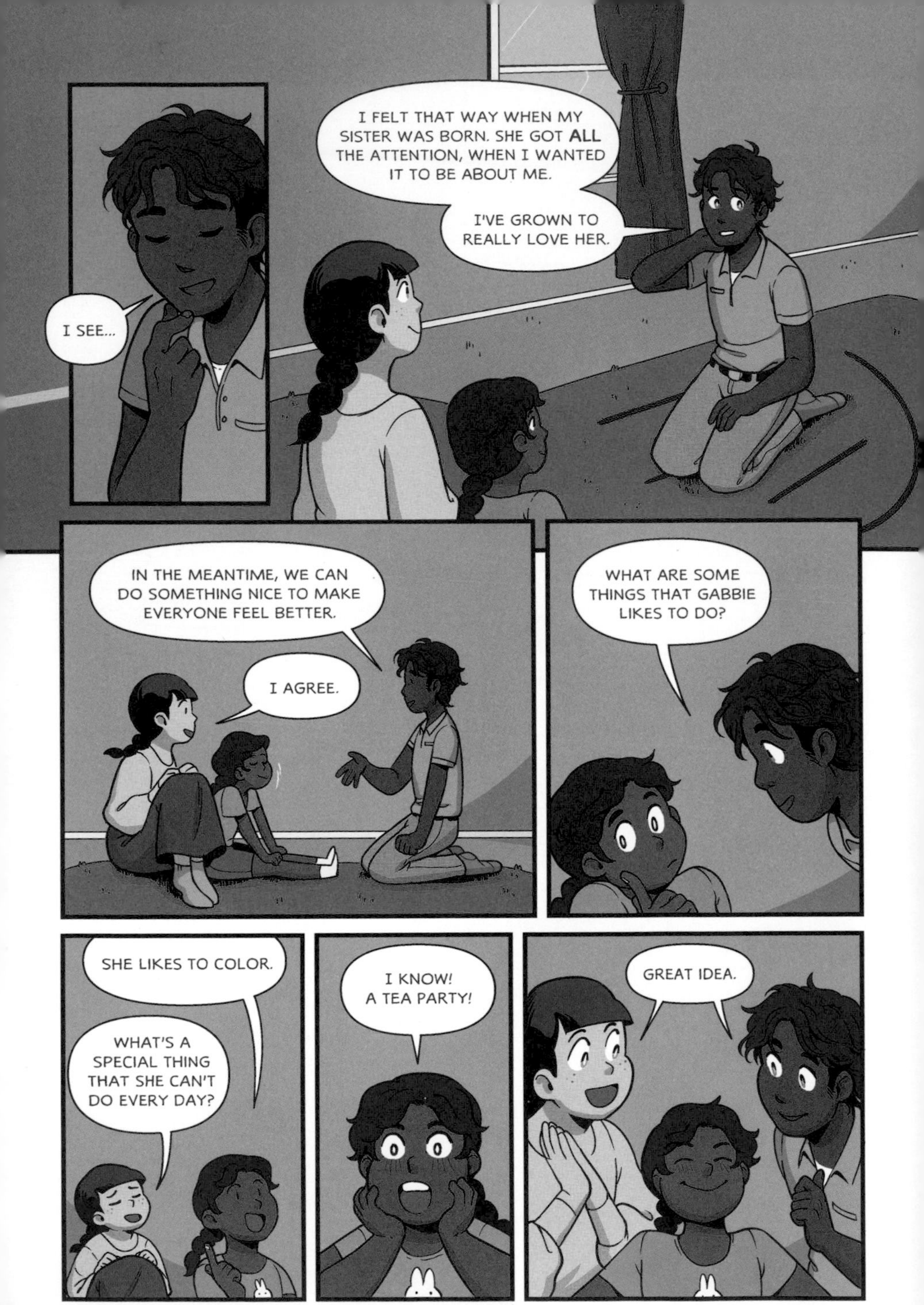
I FELT THAT WAY WHEN MY SISTER WAS BORN. SHE GOT **ALL** THE ATTENTION, WHEN I WANTED IT TO BE ABOUT ME.
I'VE GROWN TO REALLY LOVE HER.
I SEE...
IN THE MEANTIME, WE CAN DO SOMETHING NICE TO MAKE EVERYONE FEEL BETTER.
I AGREE.
WHAT ARE SOME THINGS THAT GABBIE LIKES TO DO?
SHE LIKES TO COLOR.
WHAT'S A SPECIAL THING THAT SHE CAN'T DO EVERY DAY?
I KNOW! A TEA PARTY!
GREAT IDEA.

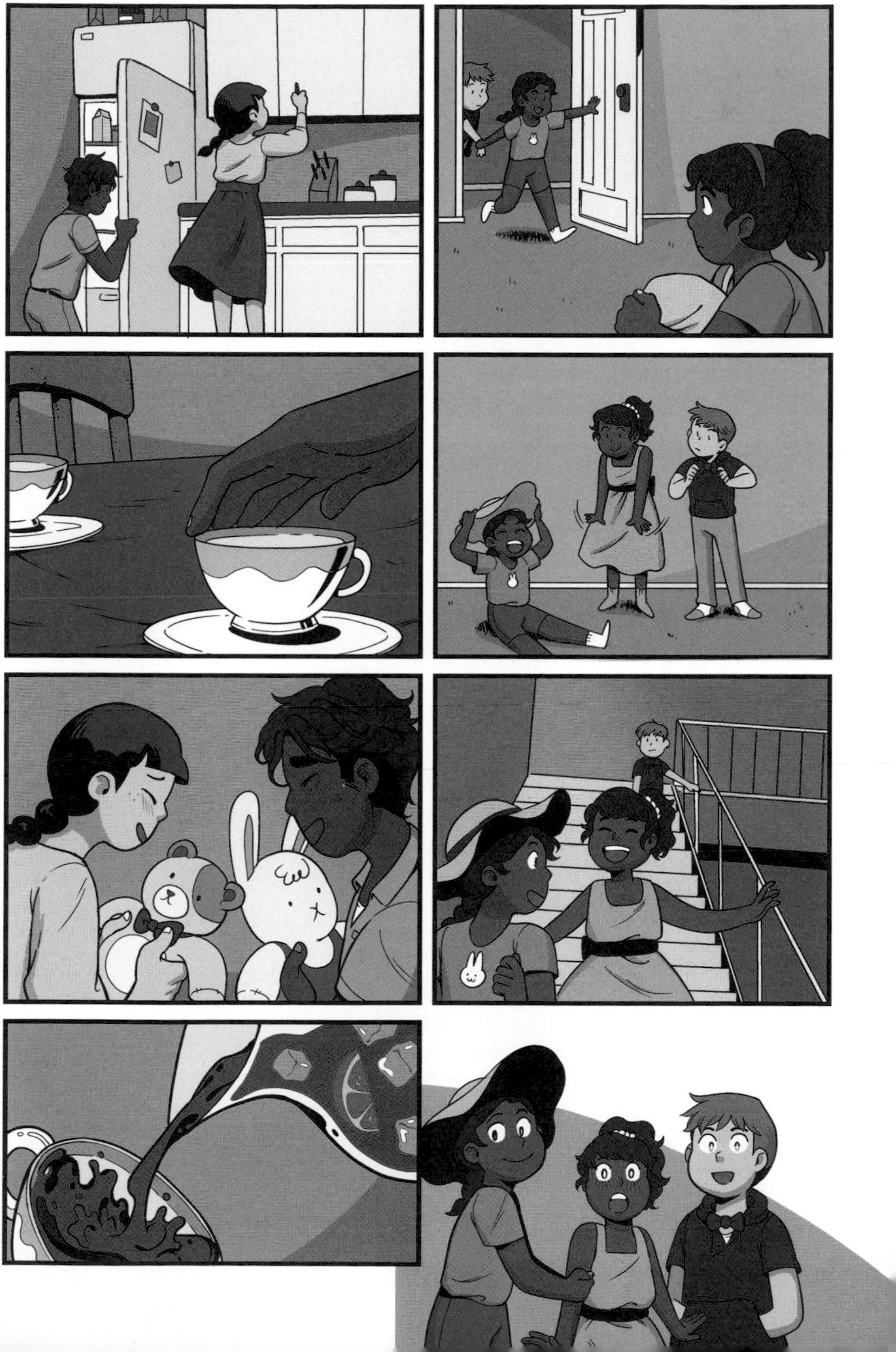

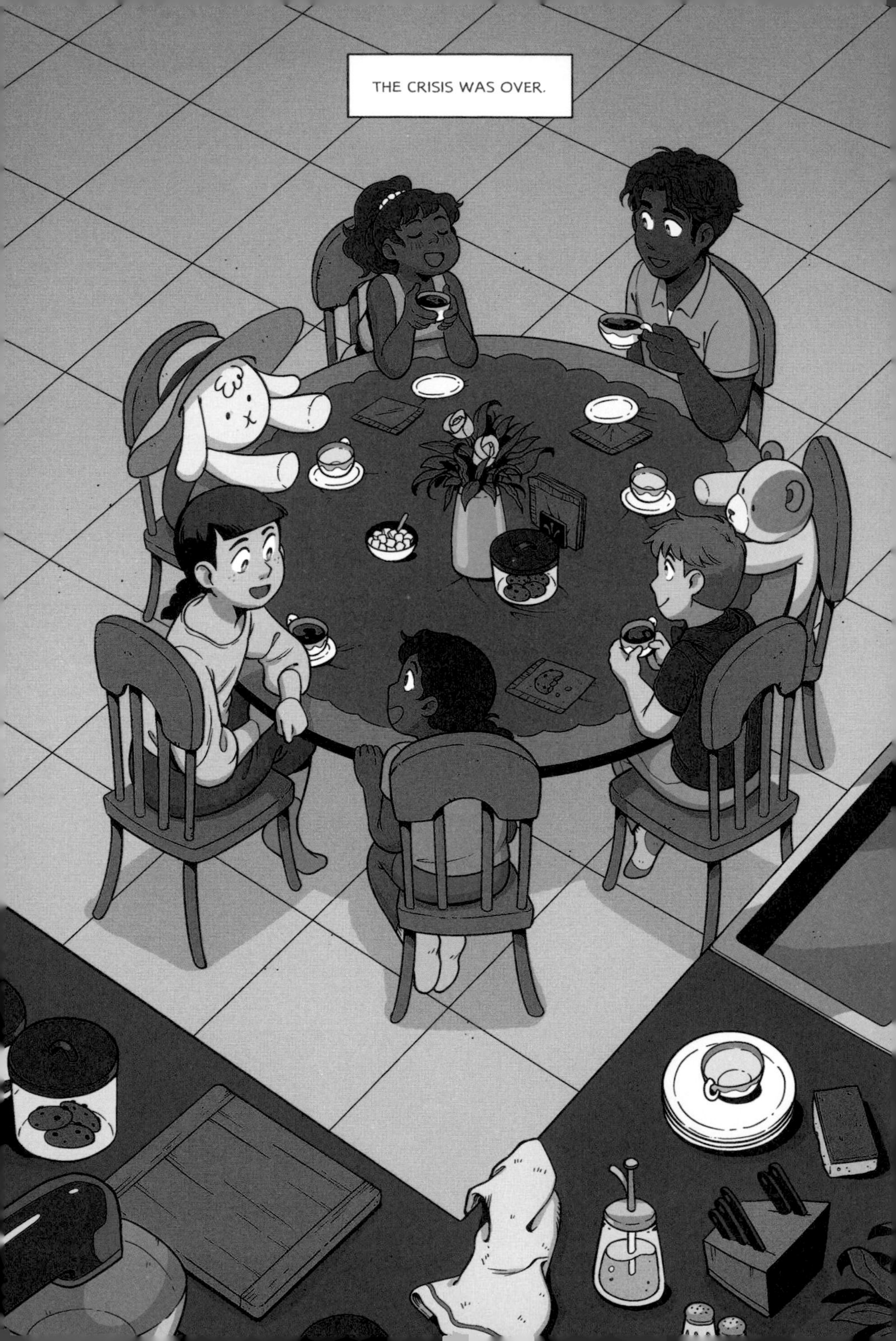
THE CRISIS WAS OVER.

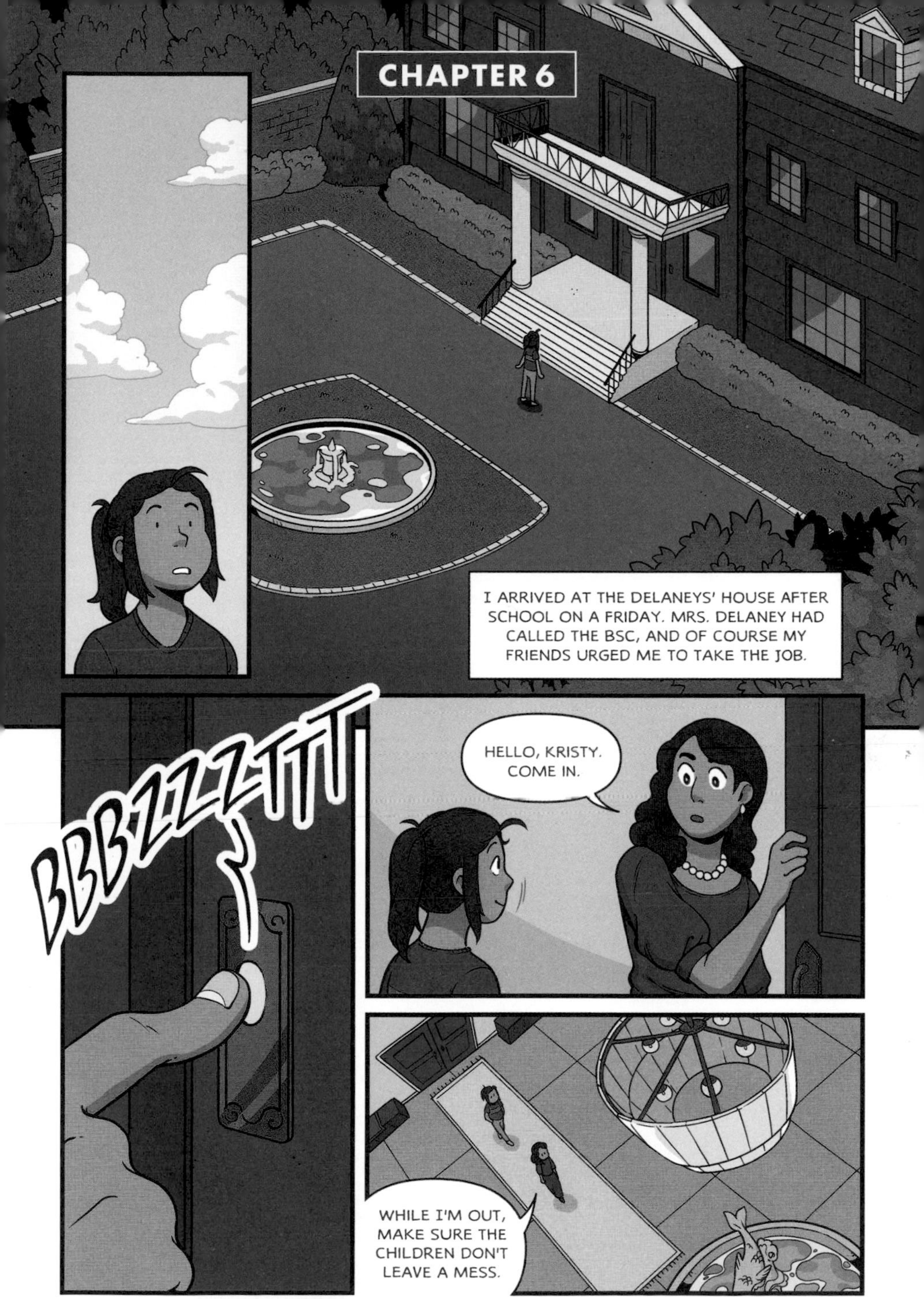
CHAPTER 6
I ARRIVED AT THE DELANEYS' HOUSE AFTER SCHOOL ON A FRIDAY. MRS. DELANEY HAD CALLED THE BSC, AND OF COURSE MY FRIENDS URGED ME TO TAKE THE JOB.
BBBZZZZTTT
HELLO, KRISTY. COME IN.
WHILE I'M OUT, MAKE SURE THE CHILDREN DON'T LEAVE A MESS.

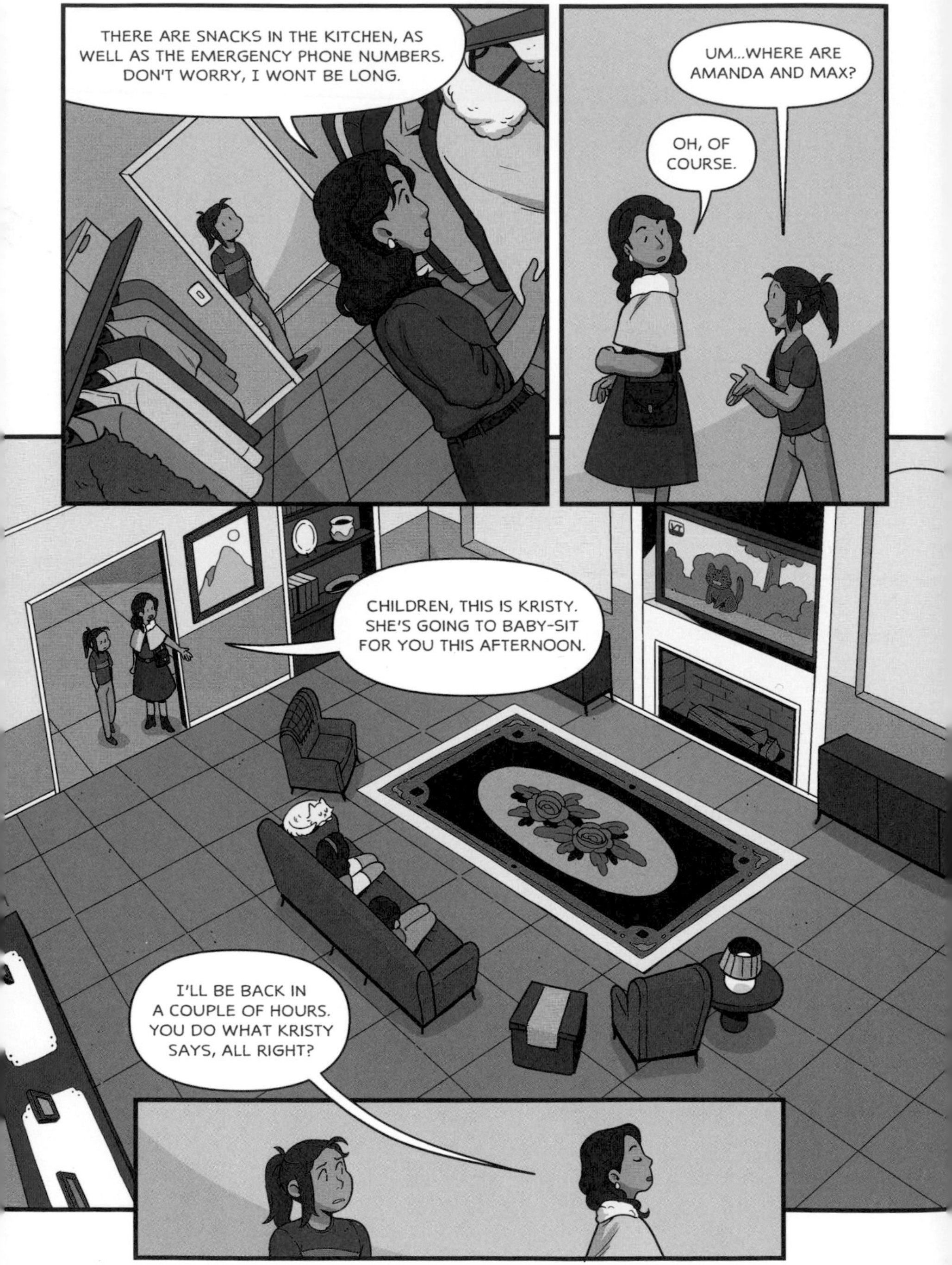
THERE ARE SNACKS IN THE KITCHEN, AS WELL AS THE EMERGENCY PHONE NUMBERS. DON'T WORRY, I WONT BE LONG.
UM...WHERE ARE AMANDA AND MAX?
OH, OF COURSE.
CHILDREN, THIS IS KRISTY. SHE'S GOING TO BABY-SIT FOR YOU THIS AFTERNOON.
I'LL BE BACK IN A COUPLE OF HOURS. YOU DO WHAT KRISTY SAYS, ALL RIGHT?

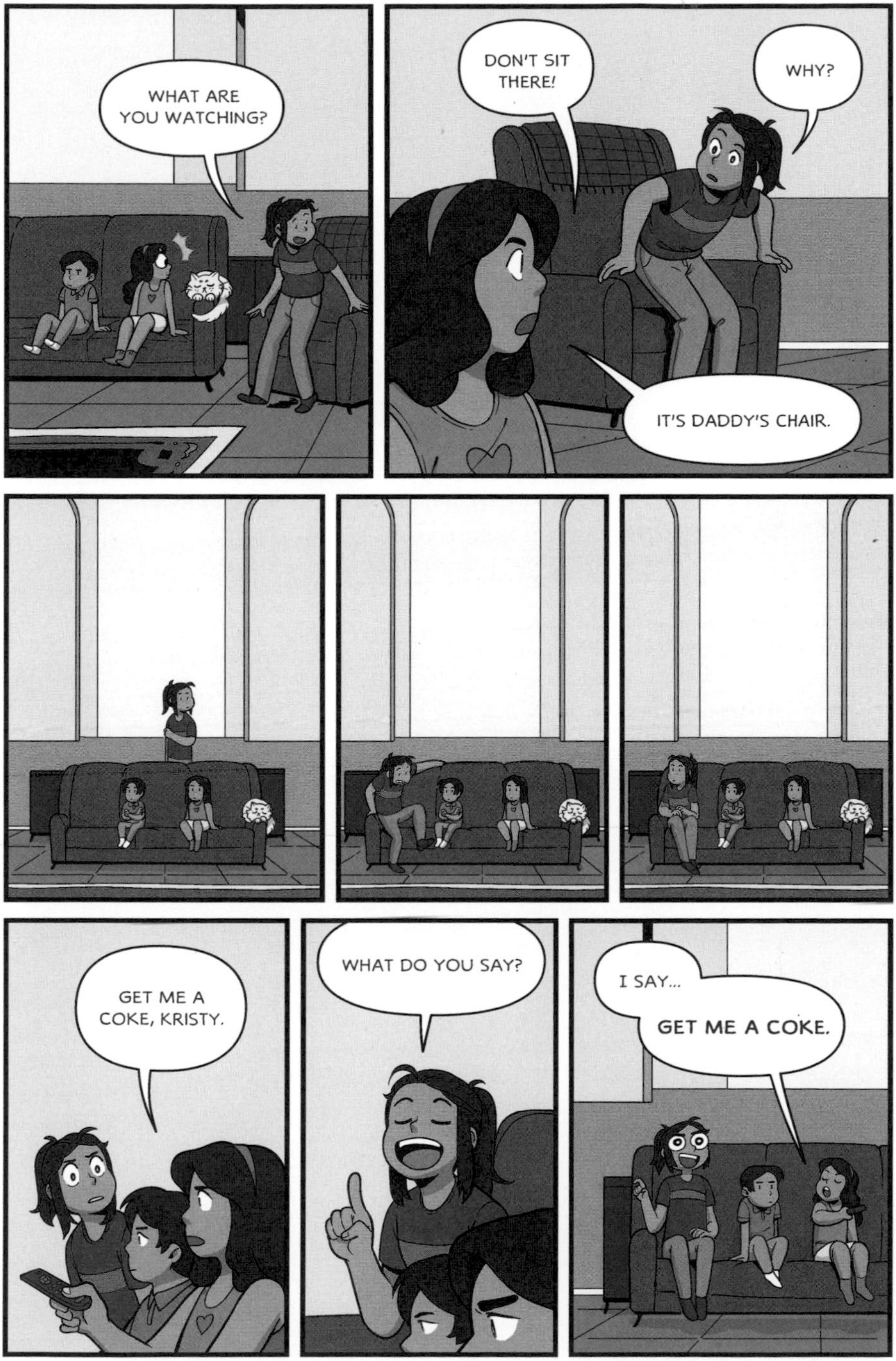
WHAT ARE YOU WATCHING?
DON'T SIT THERE!
WHY?
IT'S DADDY'S CHAIR.
GET ME A COKE, KRISTY.
WHAT DO YOU SAY?
I SAY...
GET ME A COKE.

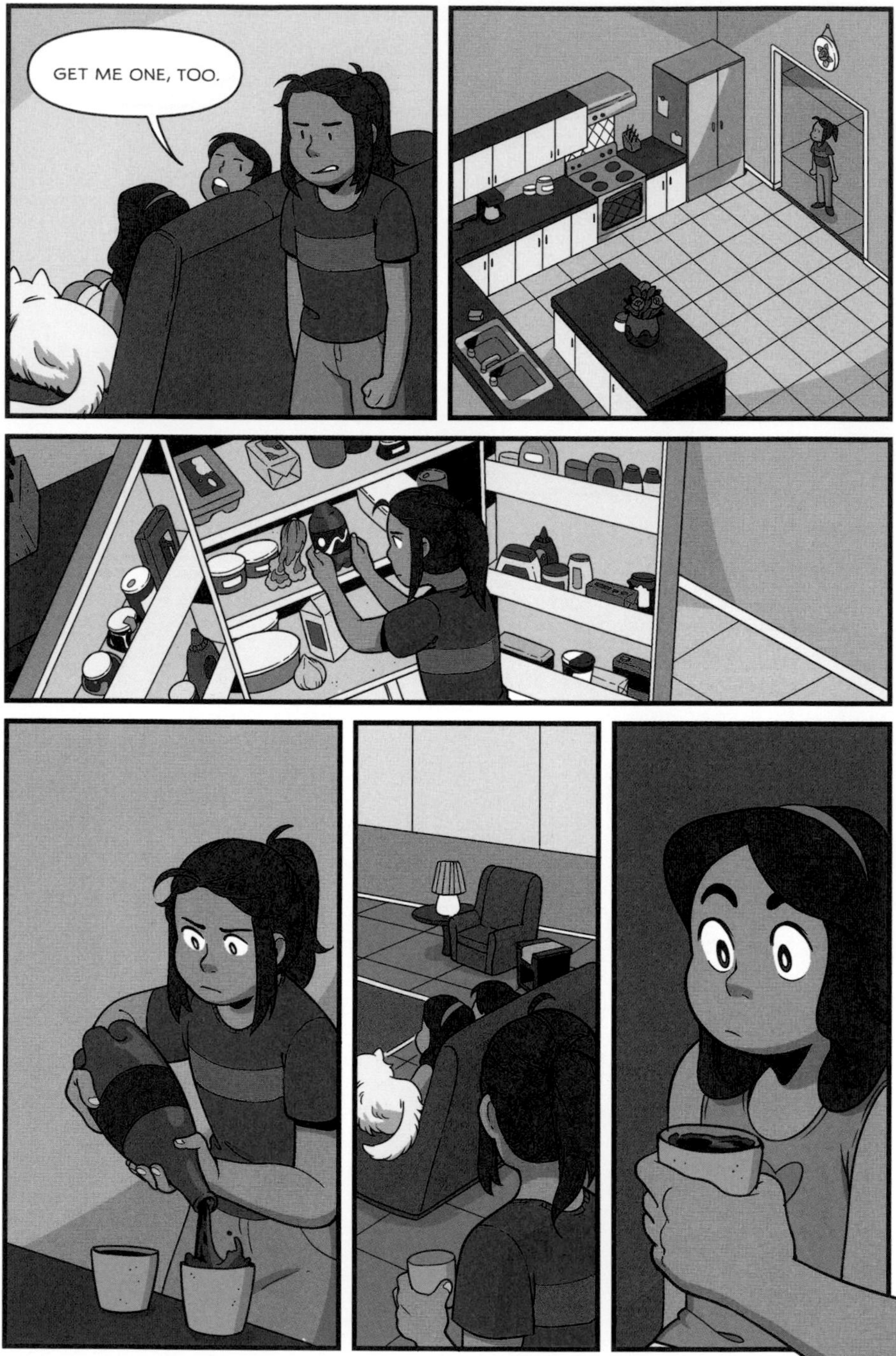
GET ME ONE, TOO.

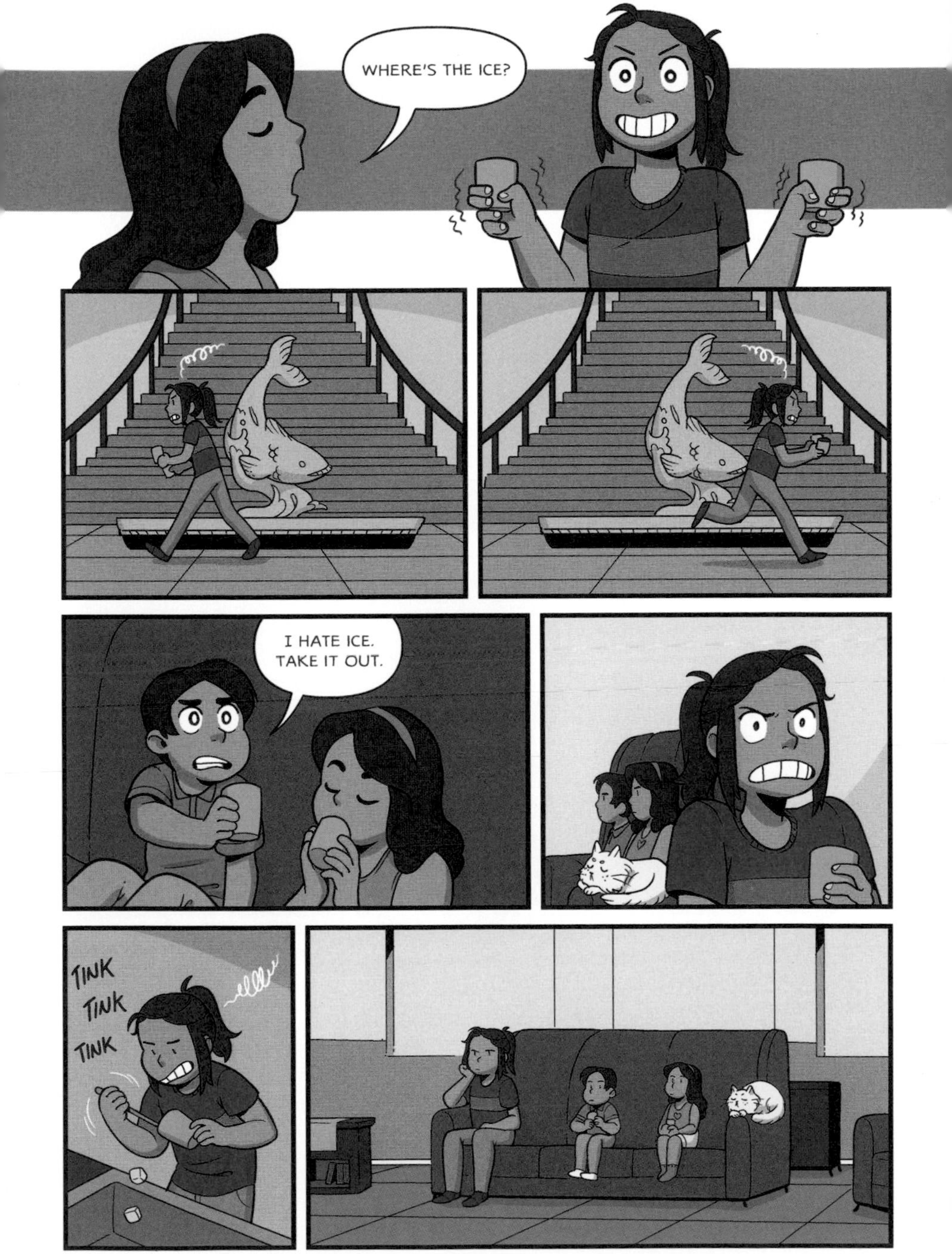
WHERE'S THE ICE?
I HATE ICE. TAKE IT OUT.
TINK
TINK
TINK

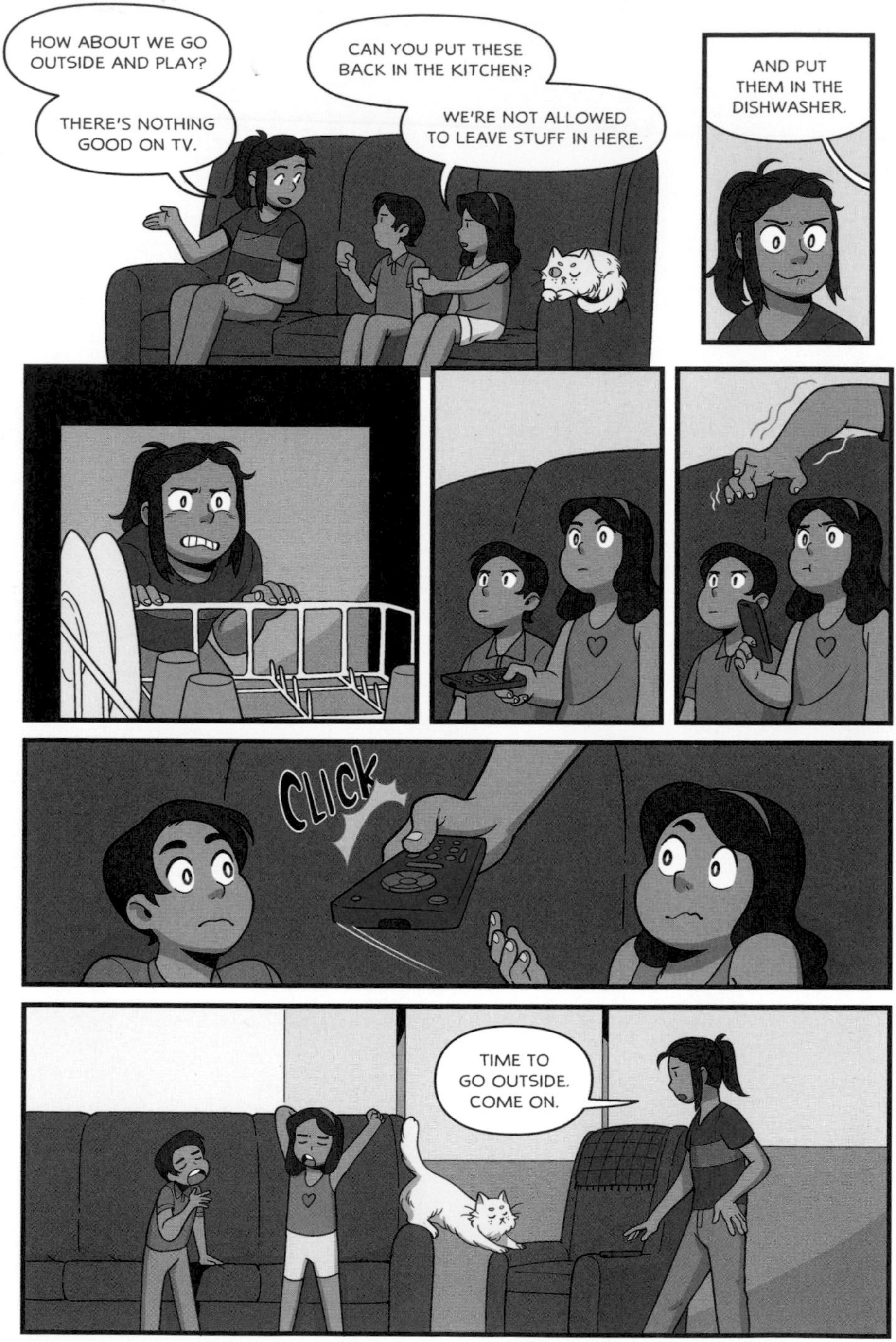
HOW ABOUT WE GO OUTSIDE AND PLAY?
THERE'S NOTHING GOOD ON TV.
CAN YOU PUT THESE BACK IN THE KITCHEN?
WE'RE NOT ALLOWED TO LEAVE STUFF IN HERE.
AND PUT THEM IN THE DISHWASHER.
CLICK
TIME TO GO OUTSIDE. COME ON.

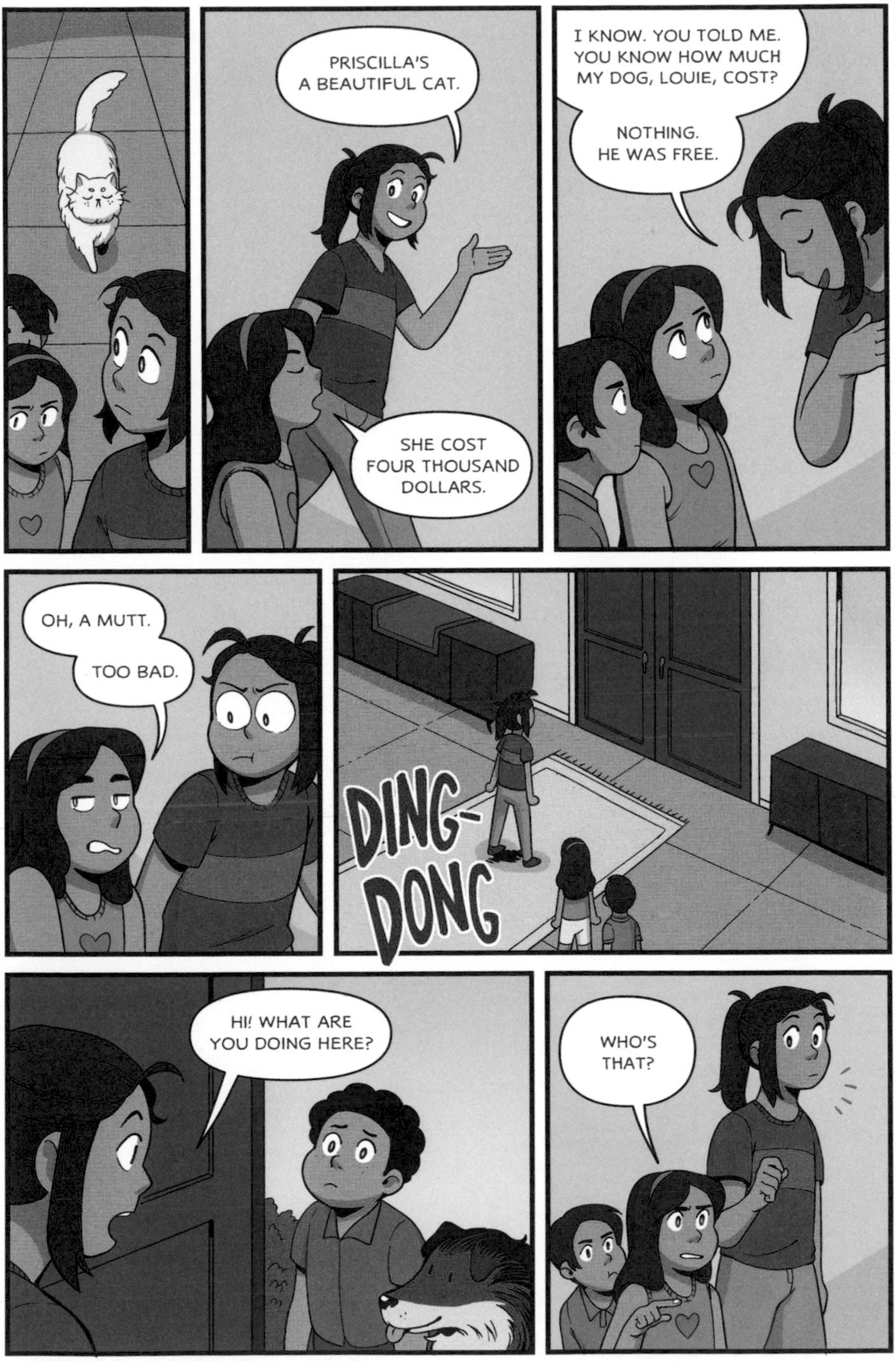
PRISCILLA'S A BEAUTIFUL CAT.
SHE COST FOUR THOUSAND DOLLARS.
I KNOW. YOU TOLD ME. YOU KNOW HOW MUCH MY DOG, LOUIE, COST?
NOTHING. HE WAS FREE.
OH, A MUTT.
TOO BAD.
DING-DONG
HI! WHAT ARE YOU DOING HERE?
WHO'S THAT?

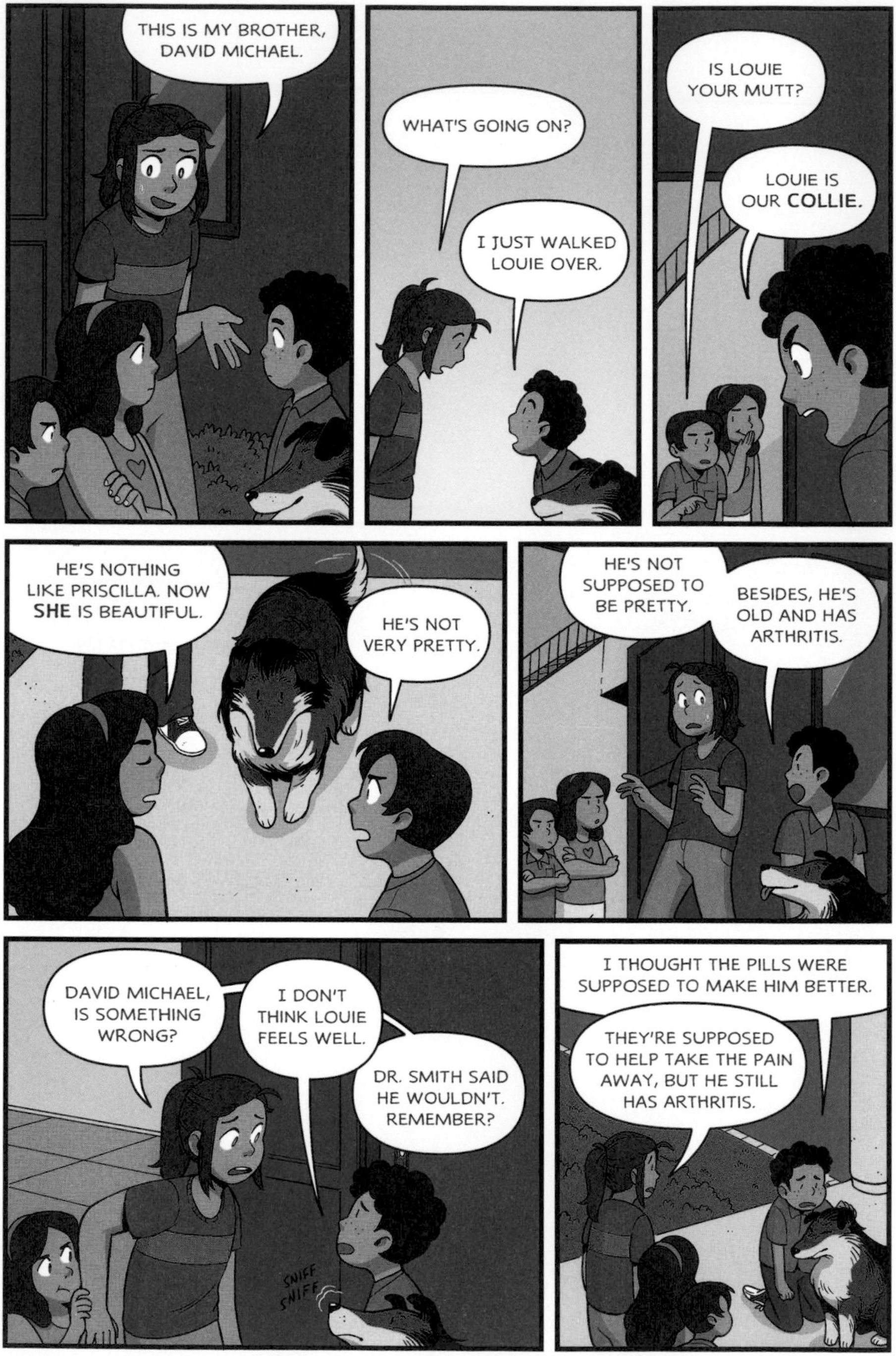
THIS IS MY BROTHER, DAVID MICHAEL.
WHAT'S GOING ON?
I JUST WALKED LOUIE OVER.
IS LOUIE YOUR MUTT?
LOUIE IS OUR **COLLIE.**
HE'S NOTHING LIKE PRISCILLA. NOW **SHE** IS BEAUTIFUL.
HE'S NOT VERY PRETTY.
HE'S NOT SUPPOSED TO BE PRETTY.
BESIDES, HE'S OLD AND HAS ARTHRITIS.
DAVID MICHAEL, IS SOMETHING WRONG?
I DON'T THINK LOUIE FEELS WELL.
DR. SMITH SAID HE WOULDN'T. REMEMBER?
SNIFF SNIFF
I THOUGHT THE PILLS WERE SUPPOSED TO MAKE HIM BETTER.
THEY'RE SUPPOSED TO HELP TAKE THE PAIN AWAY, BUT HE STILL HAS ARTHRITIS.

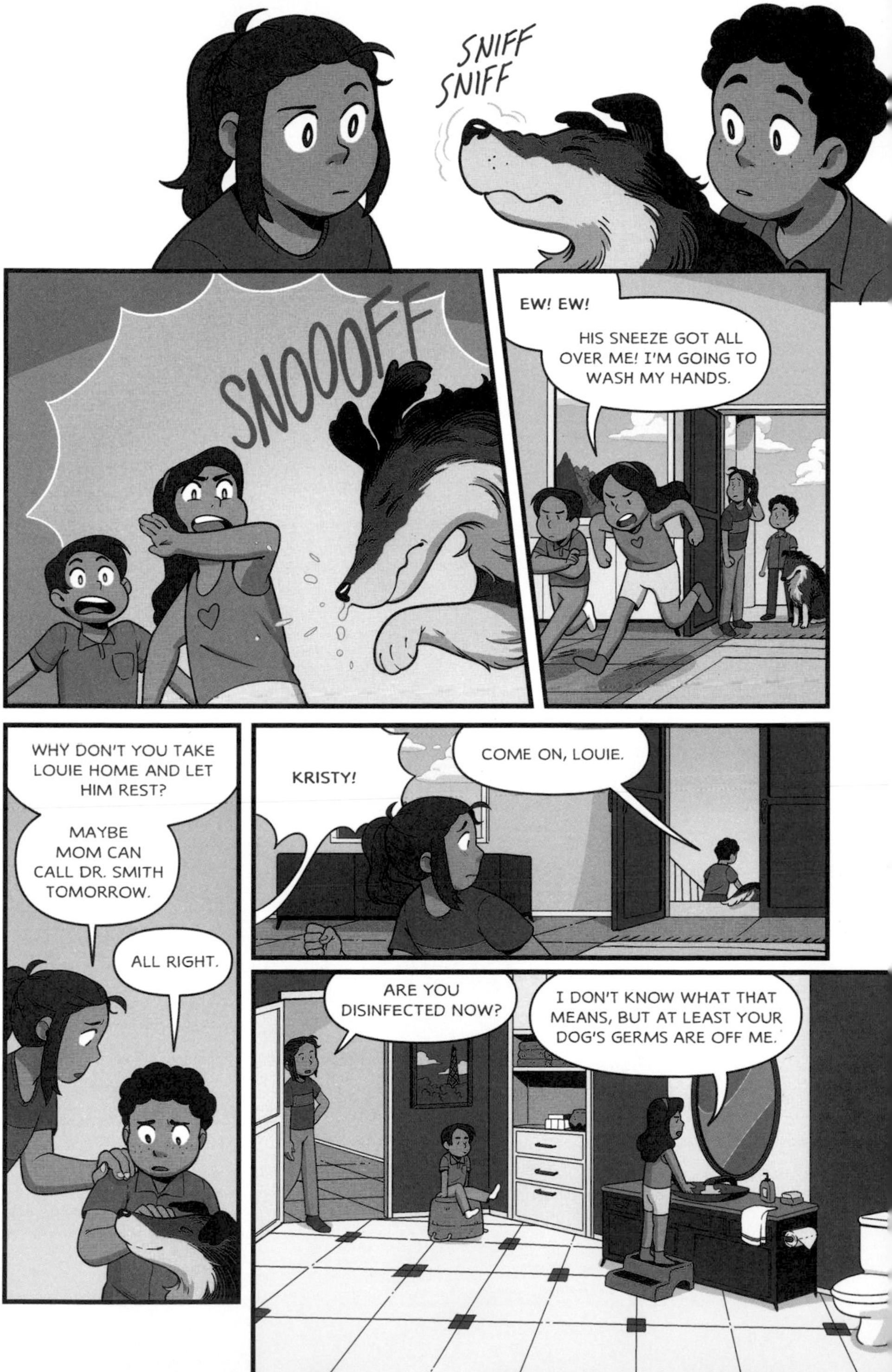
SNIFF
SNIFF
SNOOOFF
EW! EW!
HIS SNEEZE GOT ALL OVER ME! I'M GOING TO WASH MY HANDS.
WHY DON'T YOU TAKE LOUIE HOME AND LET HIM REST?
MAYBE MOM CAN CALL DR. SMITH TOMORROW.
ALL RIGHT.
KRISTY!
COME ON, LOUIE.
ARE YOU DISINFECTED NOW?
I DON'T KNOW WHAT THAT MEANS, BUT AT LEAST YOUR DOG'S GERMS ARE OFF ME.

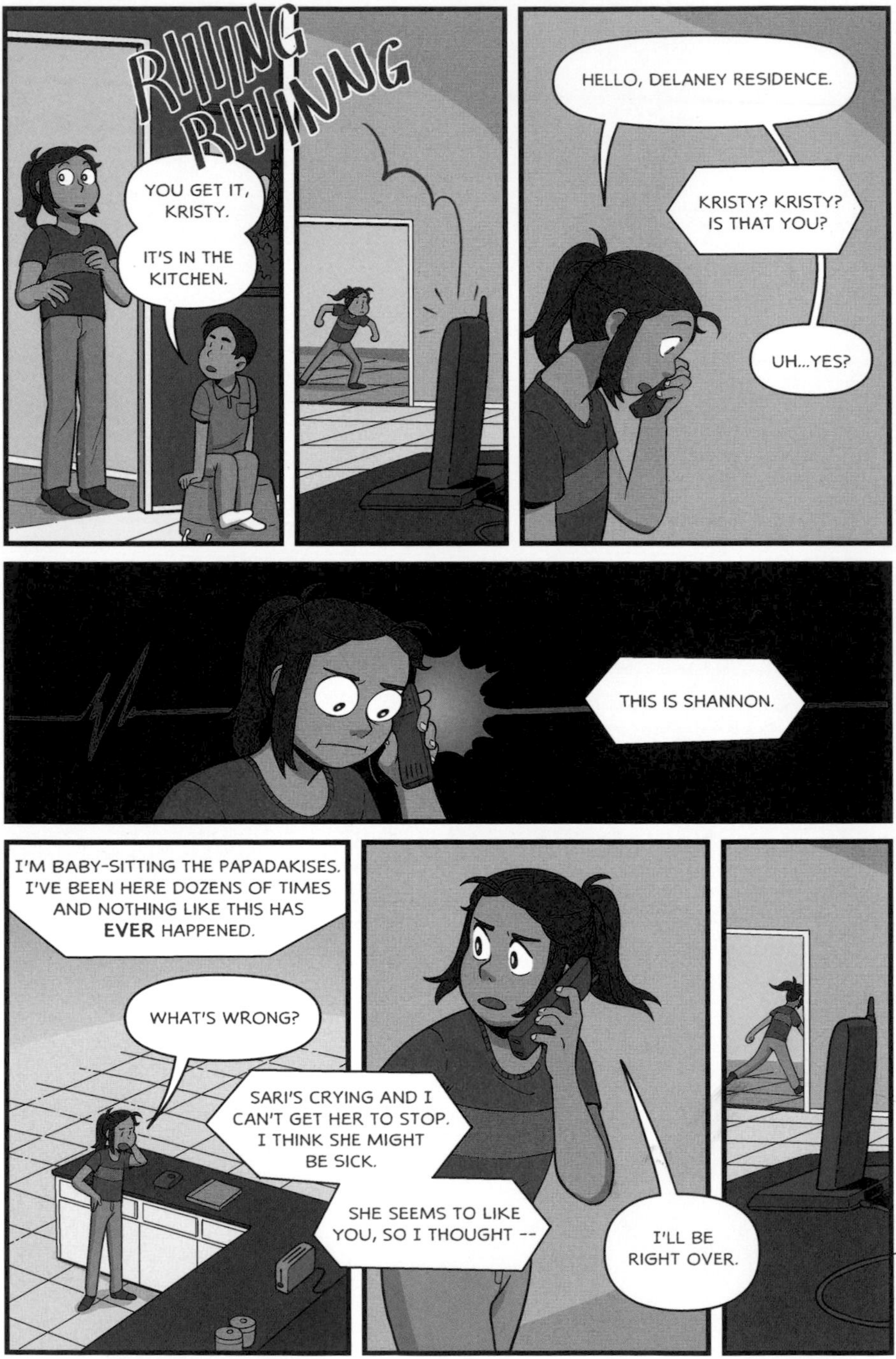
RIIIING
RIIIINNG
YOU GET IT, KRISTY.
IT'S IN THE KITCHEN.
HELLO, DELANEY RESIDENCE.
KRISTY? KRISTY? IS THAT YOU?
UH...YES?
THIS IS SHANNON.
I'M BABY-SITTING THE PAPADAKISES. I'VE BEEN HERE DOZENS OF TIMES AND NOTHING LIKE THIS HAS EVER HAPPENED.
WHAT'S WRONG?
SARI'S CRYING AND I CAN'T GET HER TO STOP. I THINK SHE MIGHT BE SICK.
SHE SEEMS TO LIKE YOU, SO I THOUGHT --
I'LL BE RIGHT OVER.

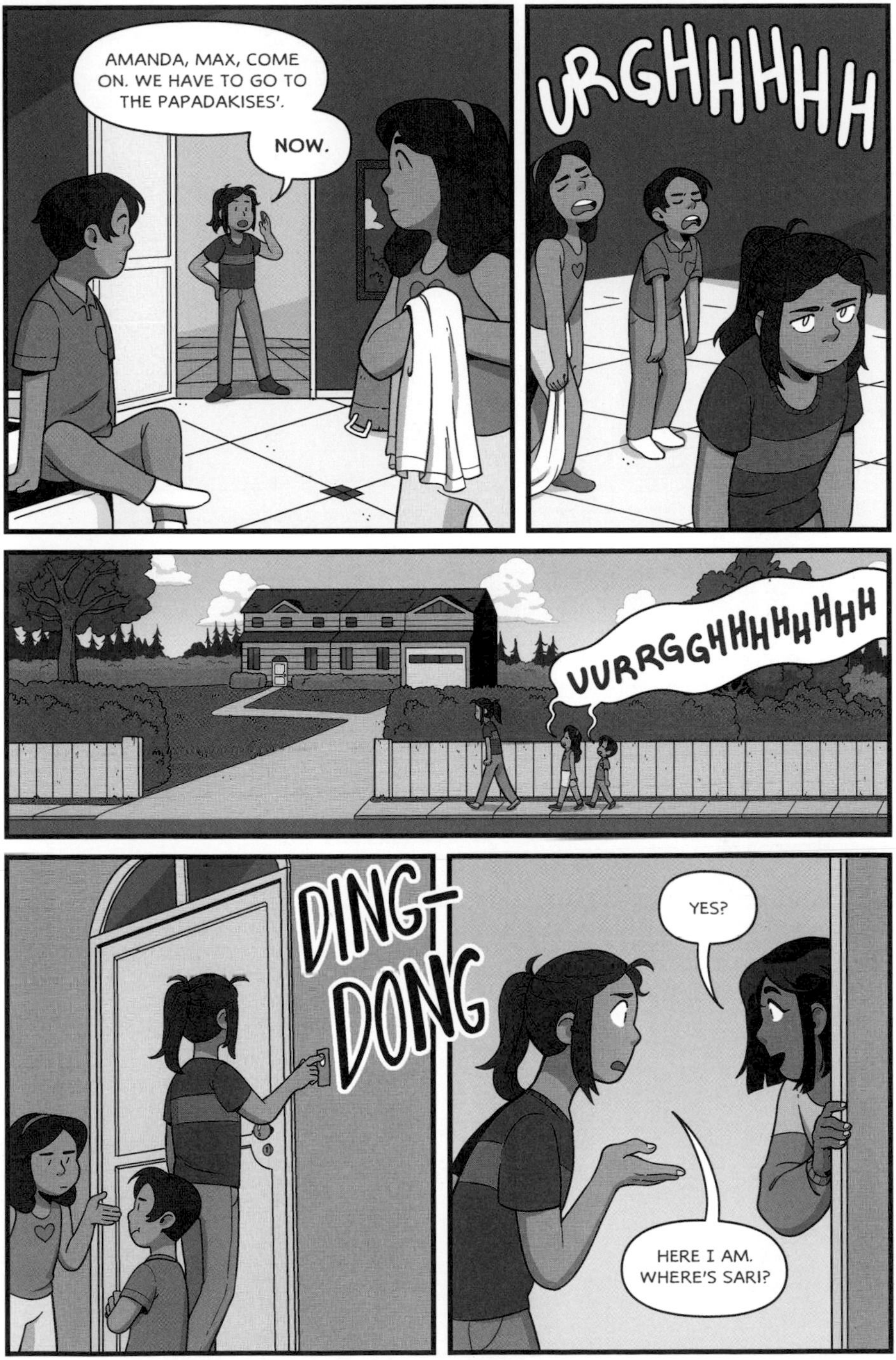
AMANDA, MAX, COME ON. WE HAVE TO GO TO THE PAPADAKISES'.
NOW.
URGHHHHH
VURRGGHHHHHHHH
DING-DONG
YES?
HERE I AM. WHERE'S SARI?

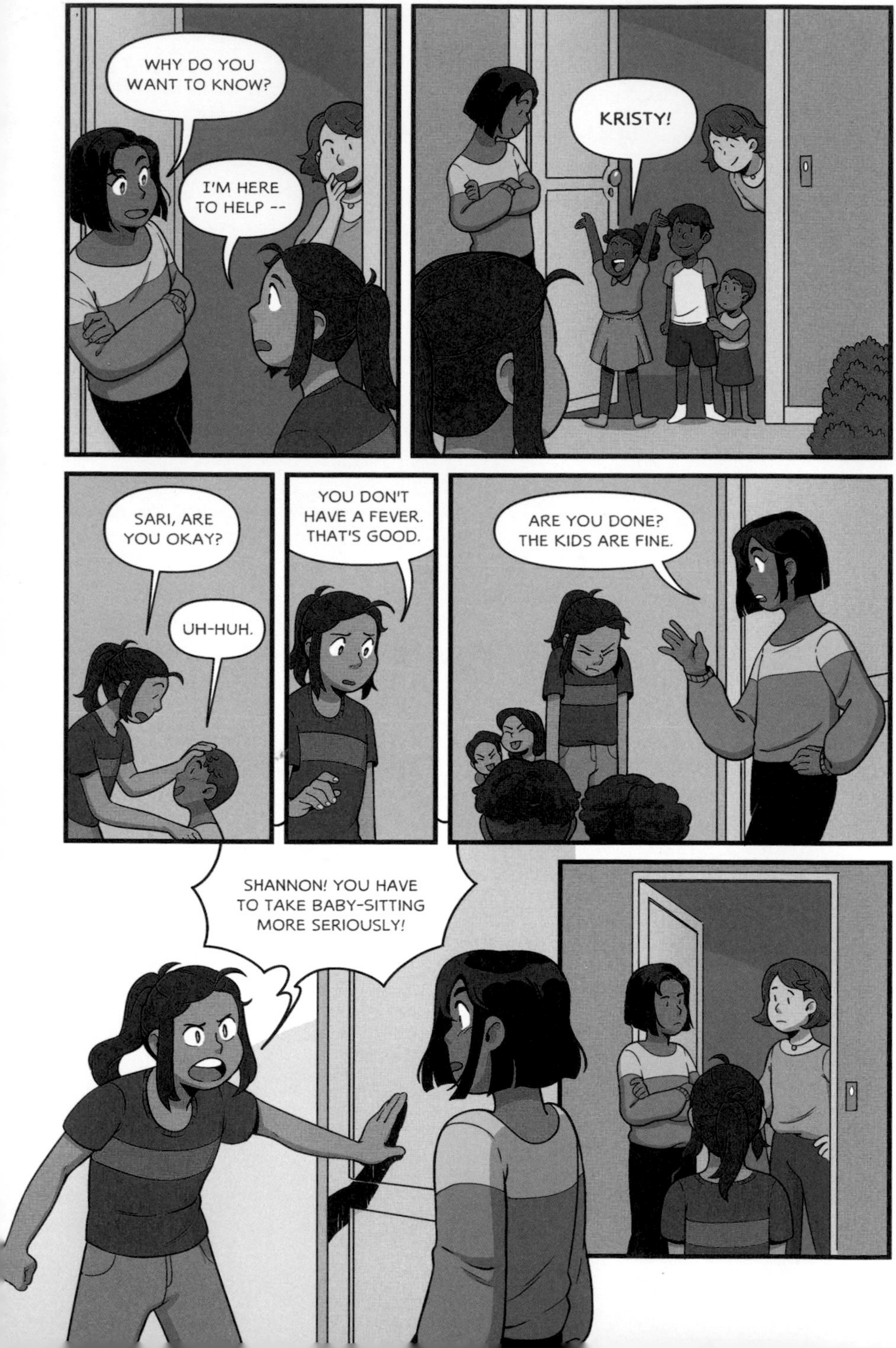
WHY DO YOU WANT TO KNOW?
I'M HERE TO HELP --
KRISTY!
SARI, ARE YOU OKAY?
UH-HUH.
YOU DON'T HAVE A FEVER. THAT'S GOOD.
ARE YOU DONE? THE KIDS ARE FINE.
SHANNON! YOU HAVE TO TAKE BABY-SITTING MORE SERIOUSLY!

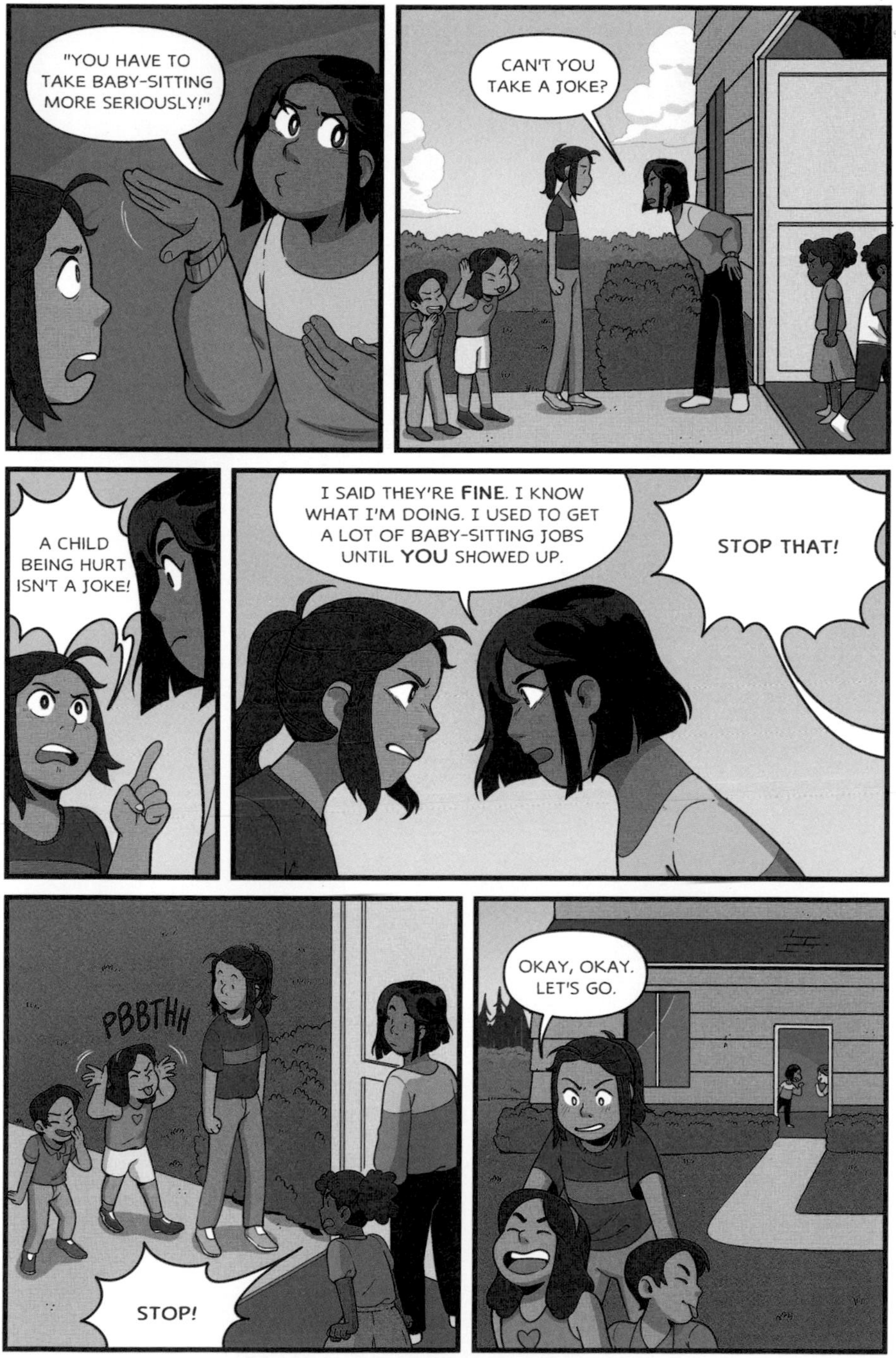
"YOU HAVE TO TAKE BABY-SITTING MORE SERIOUSLY!"
CAN'T YOU TAKE A JOKE?
A CHILD BEING HURT ISN'T A JOKE!
I SAID THEY'RE **FINE**. I KNOW WHAT I'M DOING. I USED TO GET A LOT OF BABY-SITTING JOBS UNTIL **YOU** SHOWED UP.
STOP THAT!
PBBTHH
STOP!
OKAY, OKAY. LET'S GO.

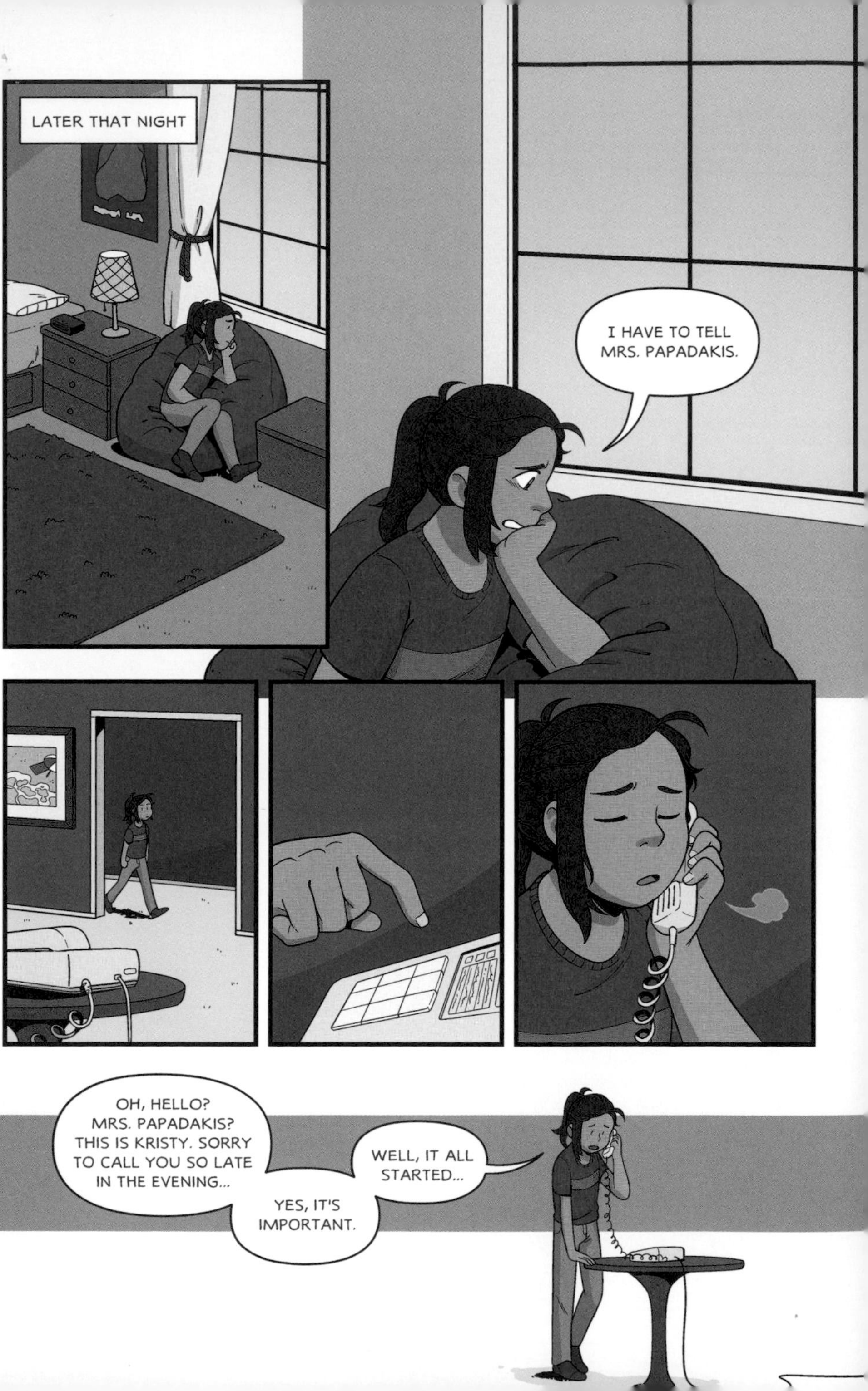
LATER THAT NIGHT
I HAVE TO TELL MRS. PAPADAKIS.
OH, HELLO? MRS. PAPADAKIS? THIS IS KRISTY. SORRY TO CALL YOU SO LATE IN THE EVENING...
YES, IT'S IMPORTANT.
WELL, IT ALL STARTED...

CHAPTER 7

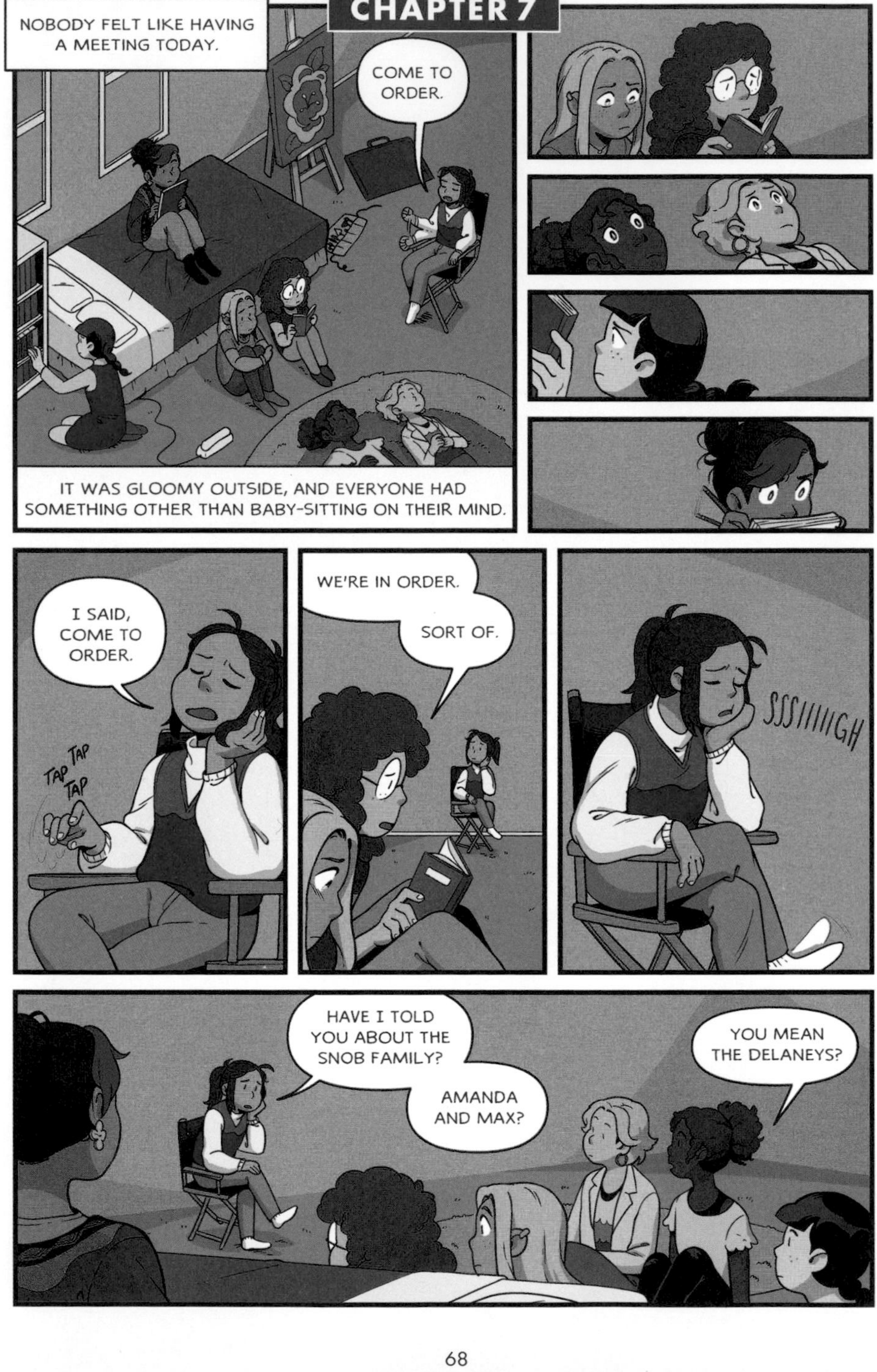

NOBODY FELT LIKE HAVING A MEETING TODAY.
COME TO ORDER.
IT WAS GLOOMY OUTSIDE, AND EVERYONE HAD SOMETHING OTHER THAN BABY-SITTING ON THEIR MIND.
I SAID, COME TO ORDER.
TAP TAP TAP TAP
WE'RE IN ORDER.
SORT OF.
SSSIIIIIGH
HAVE I TOLD YOU ABOUT THE SNOB FAMILY?
AMANDA AND MAX?
YOU MEAN THE DELANEYS?

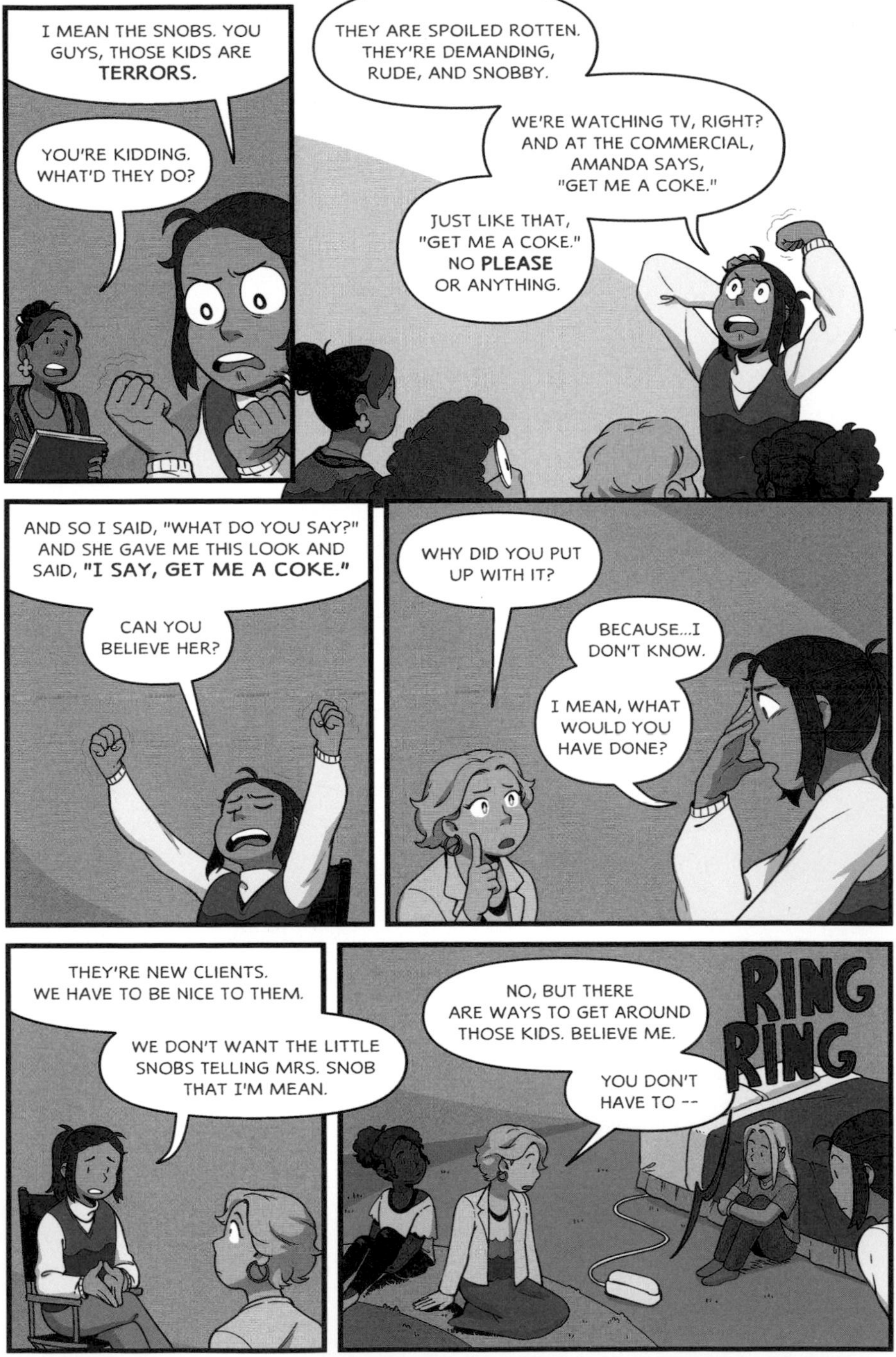

I MEAN THE SNOBS. YOU GUYS, THOSE KIDS ARE **TERRORS.**
YOU'RE KIDDING. WHAT'D THEY DO?
THEY ARE SPOILED ROTTEN. THEY'RE DEMANDING, RUDE, AND SNOBBY.
WE'RE WATCHING TV, RIGHT? AND AT THE COMMERCIAL, AMANDA SAYS, "GET ME A COKE."
JUST LIKE THAT, "GET ME A COKE." NO **PLEASE** OR ANYTHING.
AND SO I SAID, "WHAT DO YOU SAY?" AND SHE GAVE ME THIS LOOK AND SAID, **"I SAY, GET ME A COKE."**
CAN YOU BELIEVE HER?
WHY DID YOU PUT UP WITH IT?
BECAUSE...I DON'T KNOW.
I MEAN, WHAT WOULD YOU HAVE DONE?
THEY'RE NEW CLIENTS. WE HAVE TO BE NICE TO THEM.
WE DON'T WANT THE LITTLE SNOBS TELLING MRS. SNOB THAT I'M MEAN.
NO, BUT THERE ARE WAYS TO GET AROUND THOSE KIDS. BELIEVE ME.
YOU DON'T HAVE TO --
RING RING

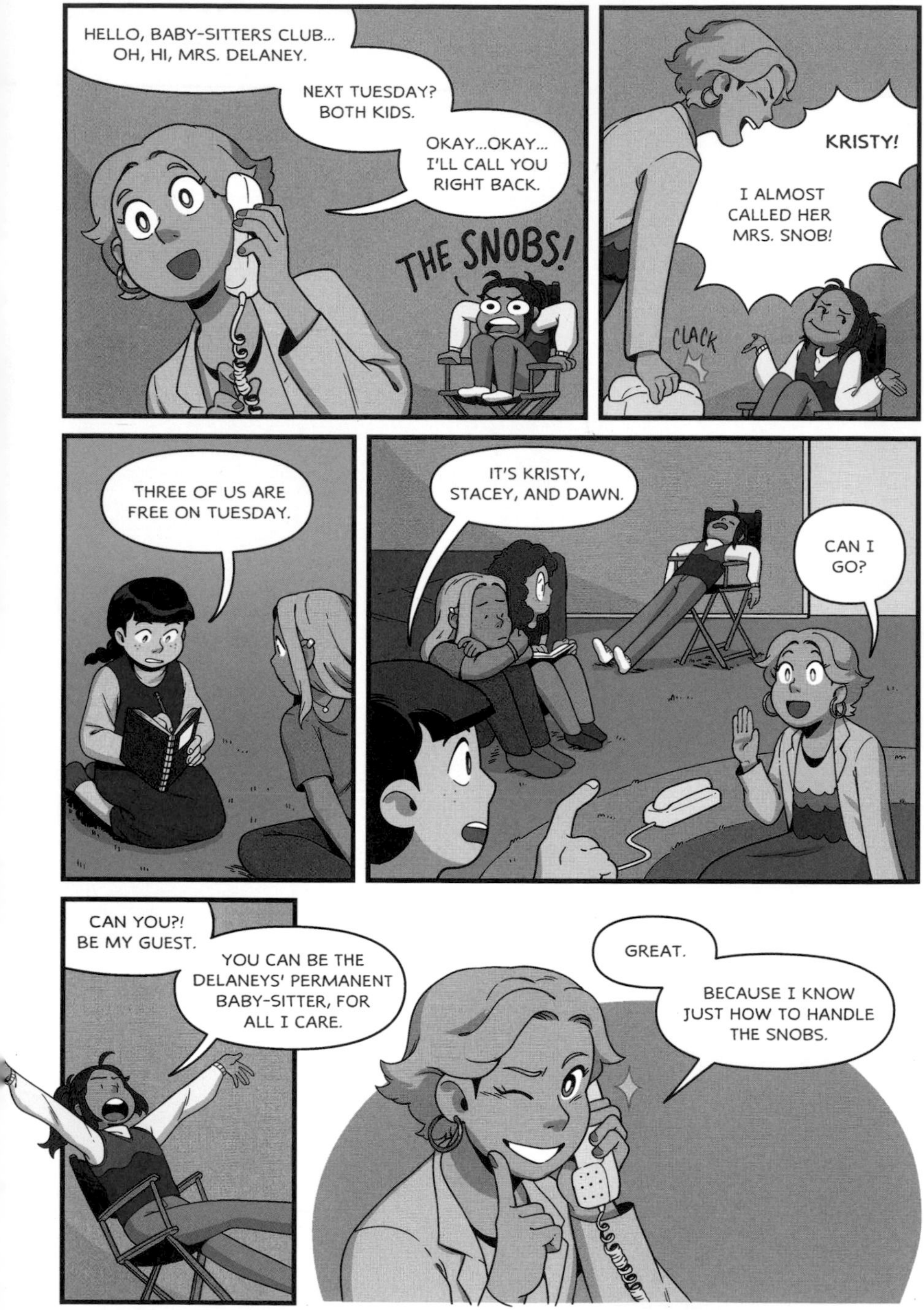
HELLO, BABY-SITTERS CLUB... OH, HI, MRS. DELANEY.
NEXT TUESDAY? BOTH KIDS.
OKAY...OKAY... I'LL CALL YOU RIGHT BACK.
THE SNOBS!
KRISTY!
I ALMOST CALLED HER MRS. SNOB!
CLACK
THREE OF US ARE FREE ON TUESDAY.
IT'S KRISTY, STACEY, AND DAWN.
CAN I GO?
CAN YOU?! BE MY GUEST.
YOU CAN BE THE DELANEYS' PERMANENT BABY-SITTER, FOR ALL I CARE.
GREAT.
BECAUSE I KNOW JUST HOW TO HANDLE THE SNOBS.

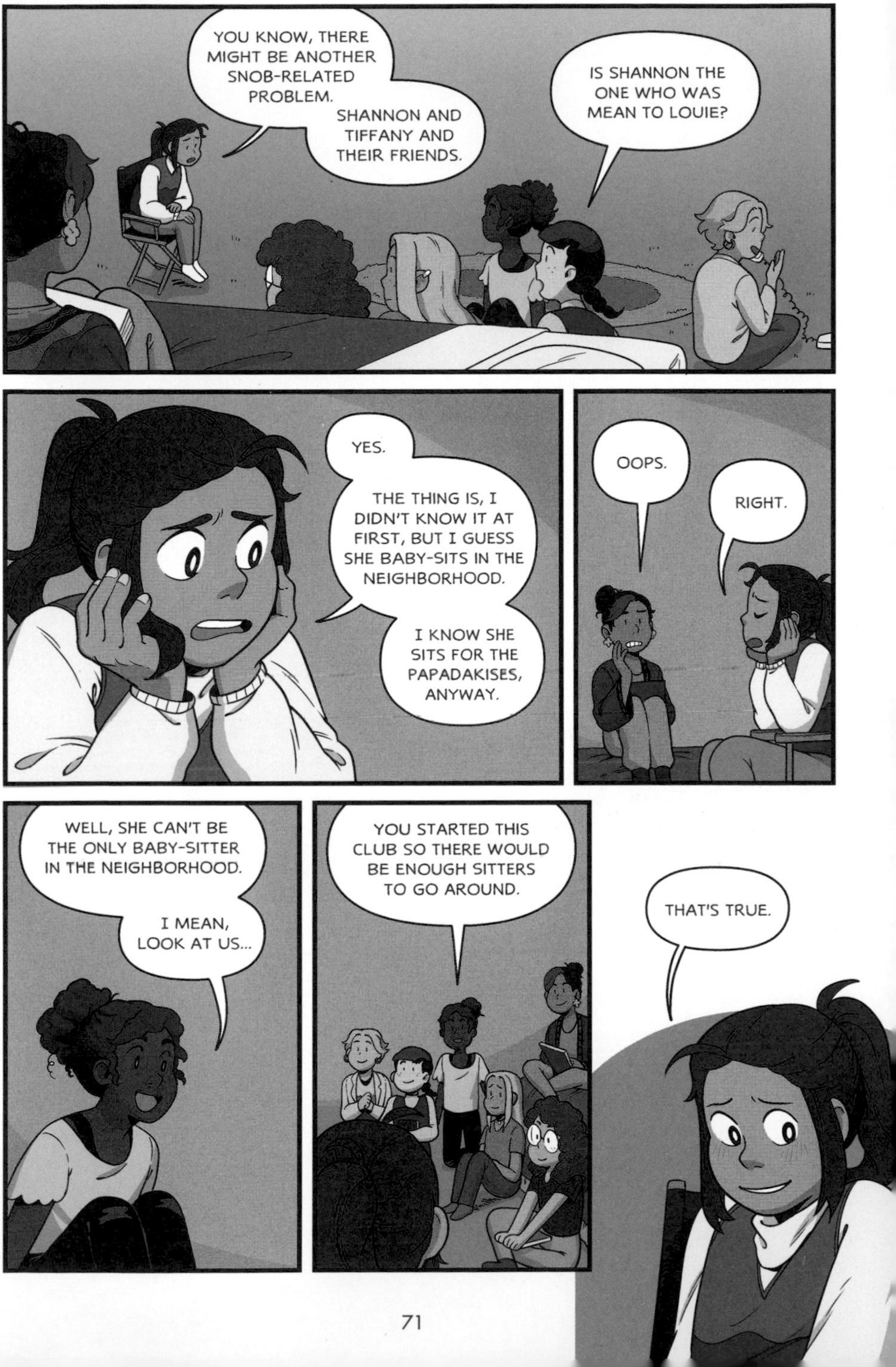
YOU KNOW, THERE MIGHT BE ANOTHER SNOB-RELATED PROBLEM.
SHANNON AND TIFFANY AND THEIR FRIENDS.
IS SHANNON THE ONE WHO WAS MEAN TO LOUIE?
YES.
THE THING IS, I DIDN'T KNOW IT AT FIRST, BUT I GUESS SHE BABY-SITS IN THE NEIGHBORHOOD.
I KNOW SHE SITS FOR THE PAPADAKISES, ANYWAY.
OOPS.
RIGHT.
WELL, SHE CAN'T BE THE ONLY BABY-SITTER IN THE NEIGHBORHOOD.
I MEAN, LOOK AT US...
YOU STARTED THIS CLUB SO THERE WOULD BE ENOUGH SITTERS TO GO AROUND.
THAT'S TRUE.

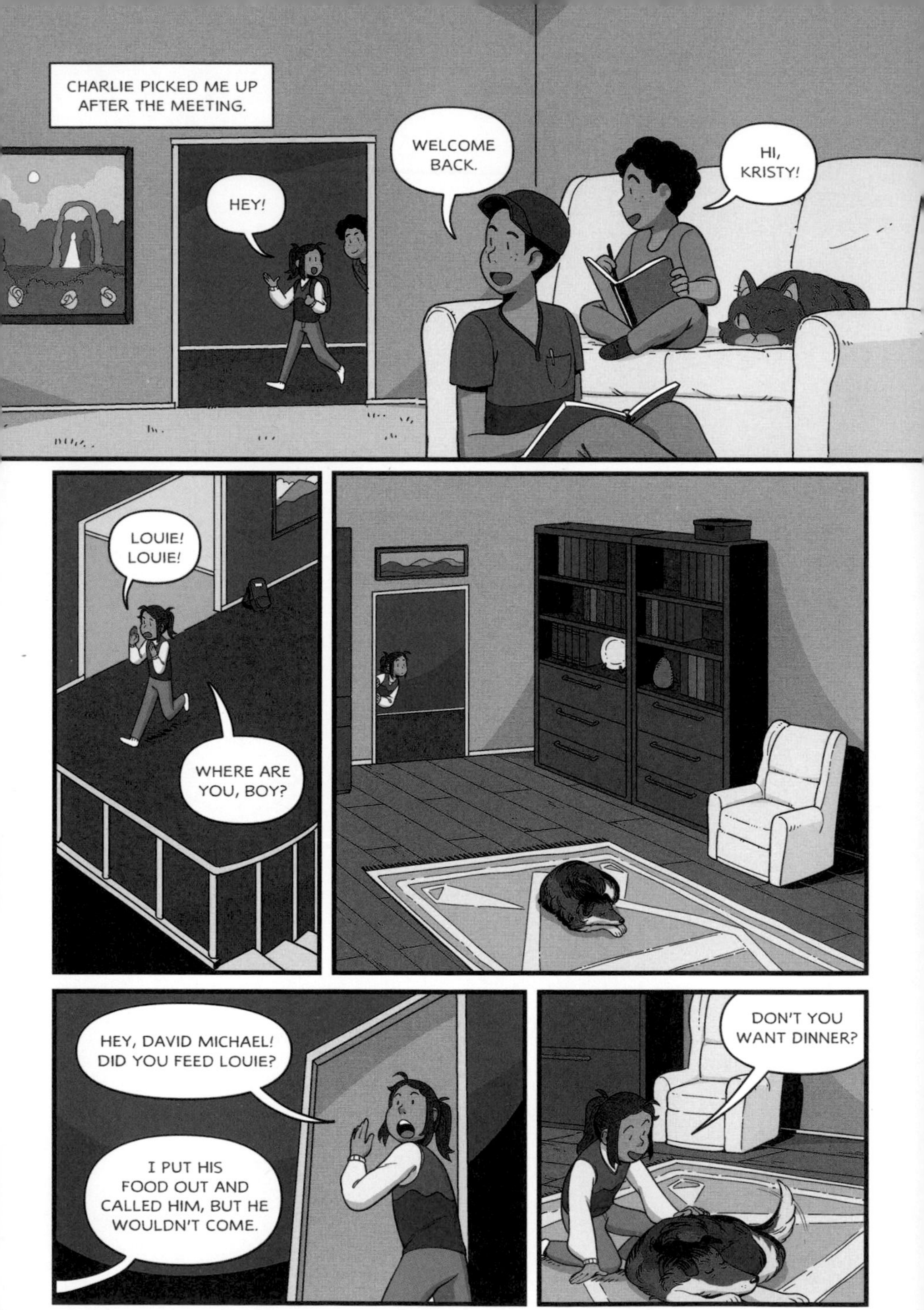
CHARLIE PICKED ME UP AFTER THE MEETING.
HEY!
WELCOME BACK.
HI, KRISTY!
LOUIE! LOUIE!
WHERE ARE YOU, BOY?
HEY, DAVID MICHAEL! DID YOU FEED LOUIE?
I PUT HIS FOOD OUT AND CALLED HIM, BUT HE WOULDN'T COME.
DON'T YOU WANT DINNER?

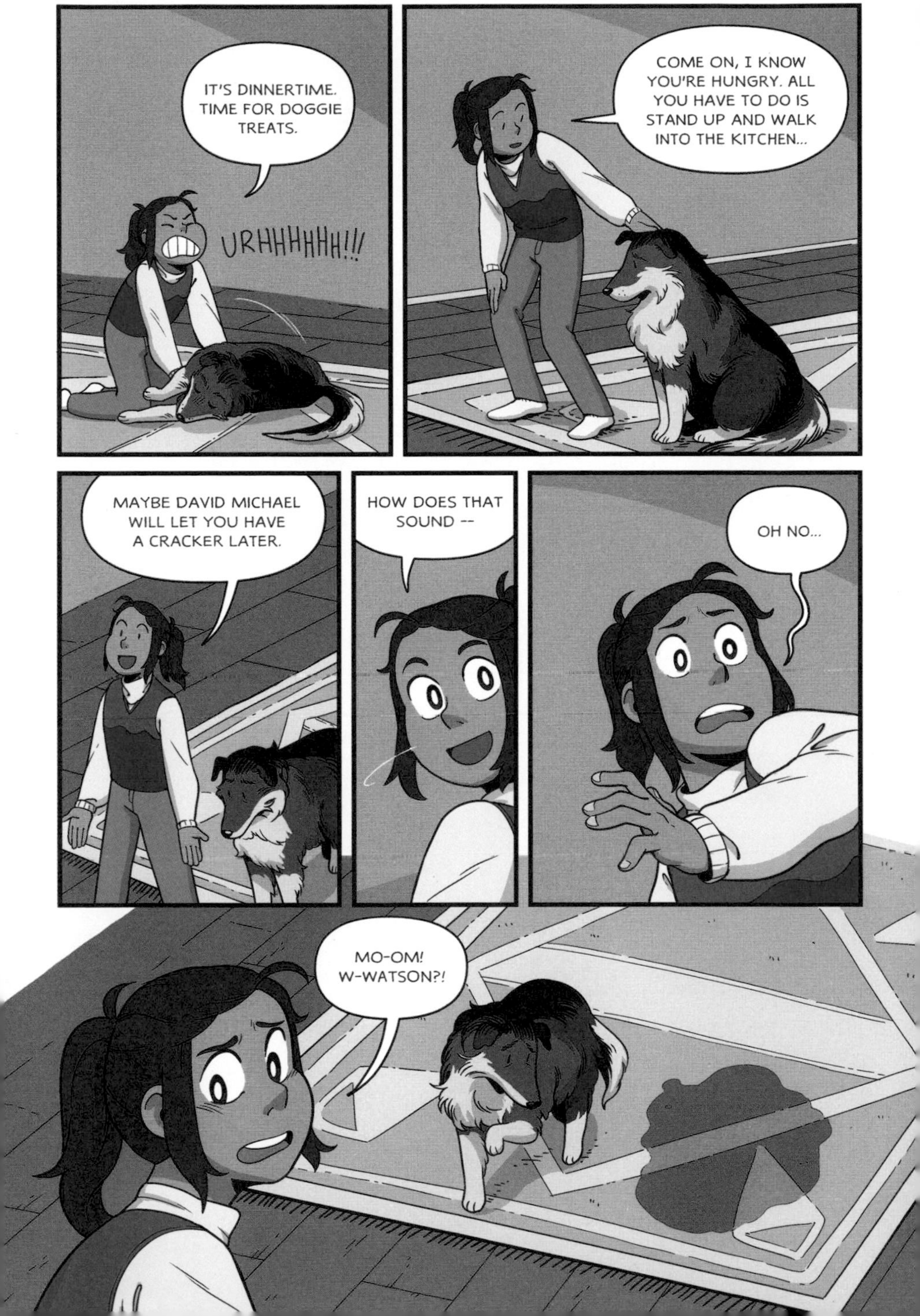
IT'S DINNERTIME. TIME FOR DOGGIE TREATS.
URHHHHHH!!!
COME ON, I KNOW YOU'RE HUNGRY. ALL YOU HAVE TO DO IS STAND UP AND WALK INTO THE KITCHEN...
MAYBE DAVID MICHAEL WILL LET YOU HAVE A CRACKER LATER.
HOW DOES THAT SOUND --
OH NO...
MO-OM! W-WATSON?!

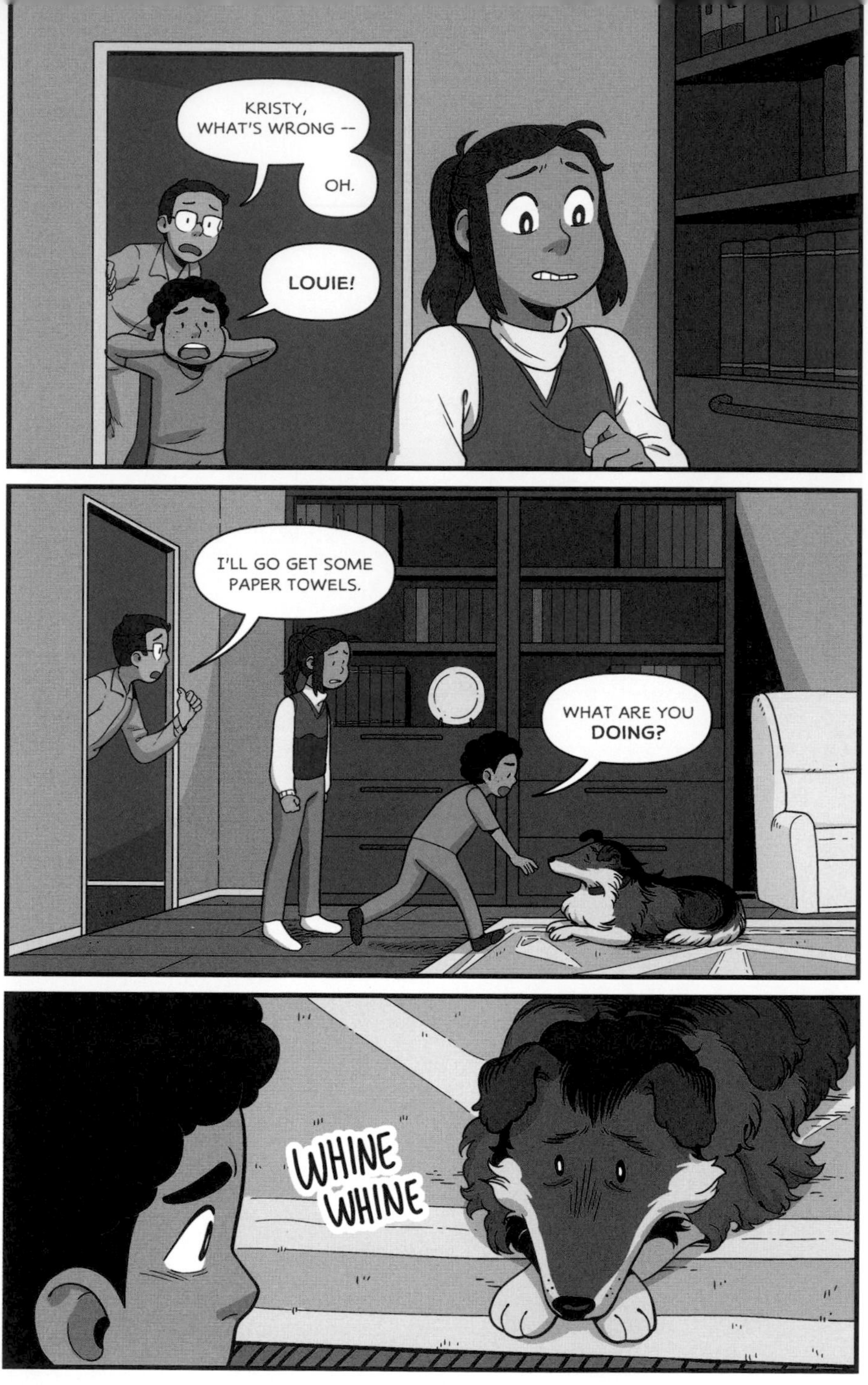
KRISTY, WHAT'S WRONG --
OH.
LOUIE!
I'LL GO GET SOME PAPER TOWELS.
WHAT ARE YOU DOING?
WHINE WHINE

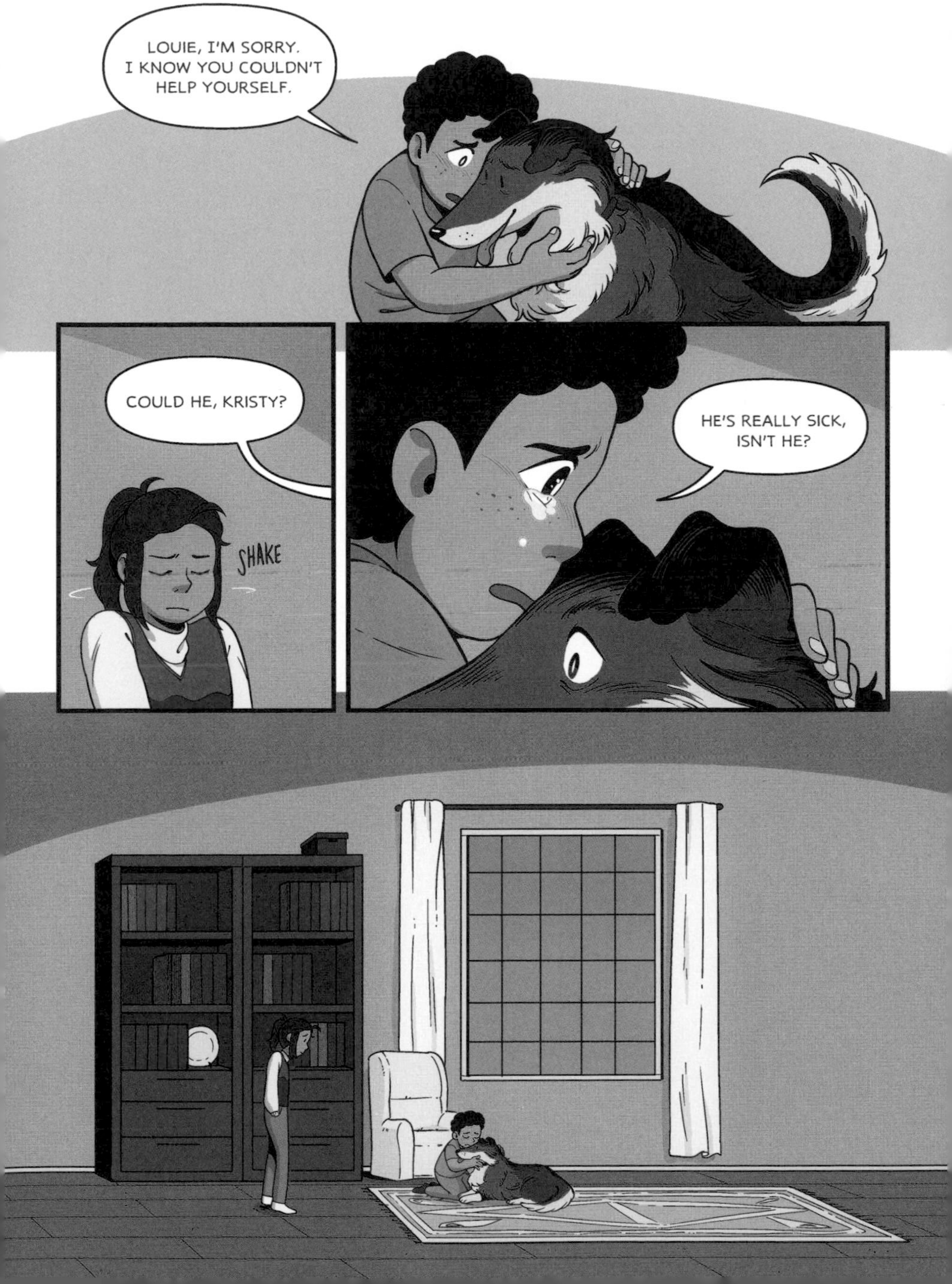
LOUIE, I'M SORRY. I KNOW YOU COULDN'T HELP YOURSELF.
COULD HE, KRISTY?
SHAKE
HE'S REALLY SICK, ISN'T HE?

Tuesday

Okay, so I sat for the Snobs today, and it was no big deal. You just have to know how to handle them. You have to know a little psychology. I read this magazine article called "Getting What You Want: Dealing with Difficult People the Easy Way." It's kind of hard to explain what you're supposed to do, so I'll just give you some examples of how I dealt with the Snobs. I found that once you have tamed them, they're pretty nice little kids.

By the way, my parents have a book called The Taming of the Shrew. I think it might be a play. Now I could write a play called The Taming of the Snobs!

Stacey

CHAPTER 8

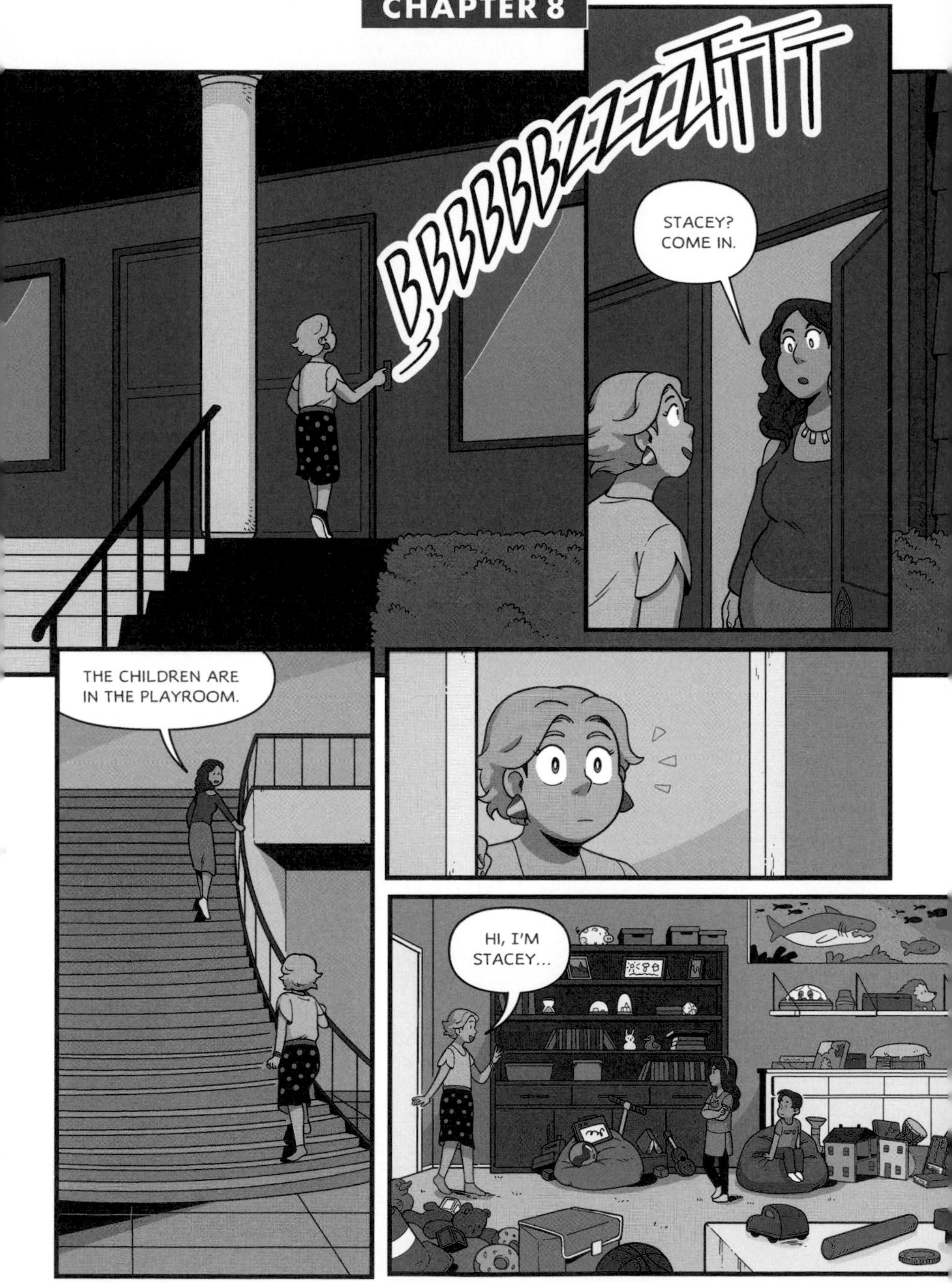
BBBBBZZZZZAAATTT
STACEY? COME IN.
THE CHILDREN ARE IN THE PLAYROOM.
HI, I'M STACEY...

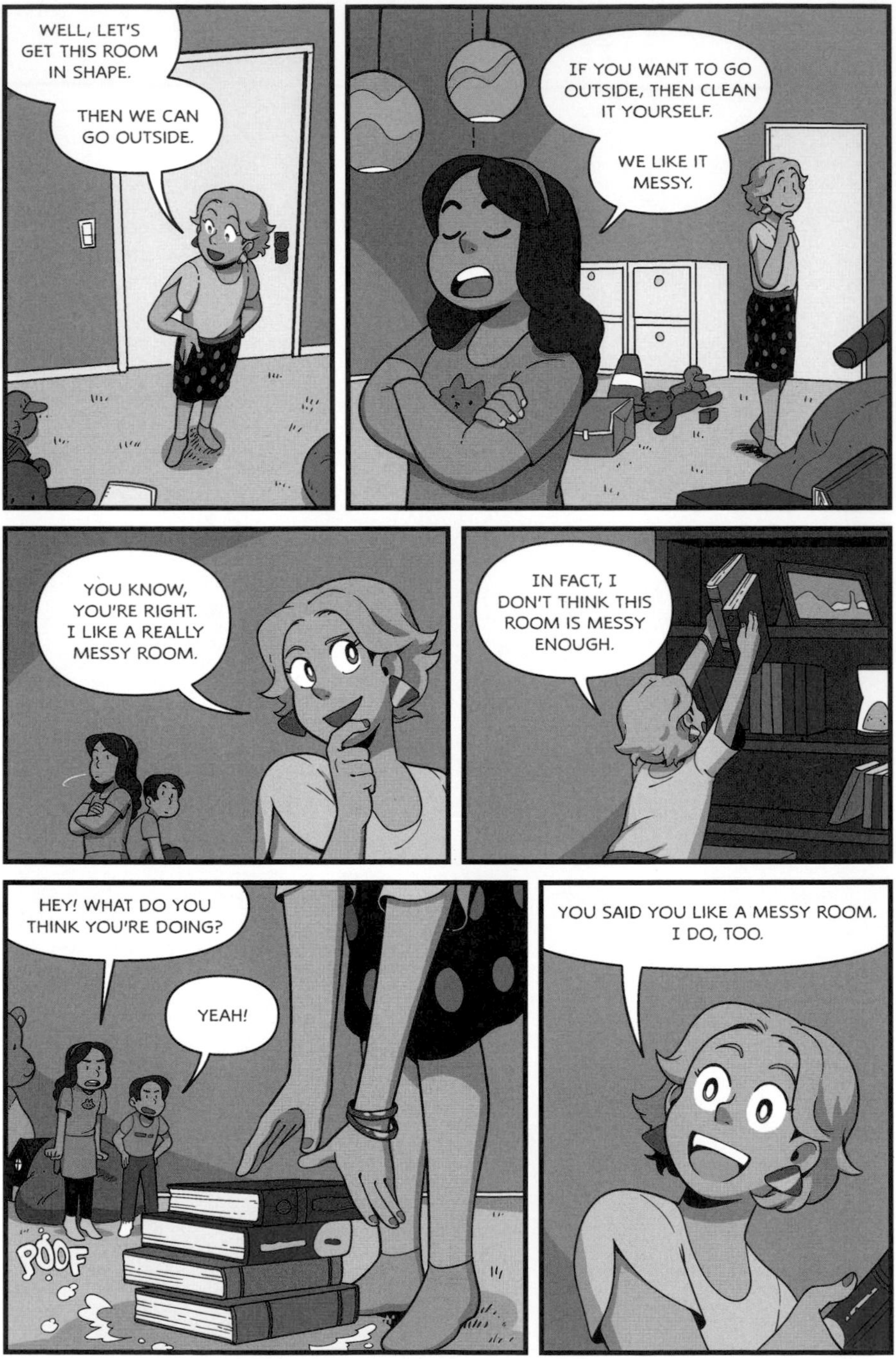
WELL, LET'S GET THIS ROOM IN SHAPE.
THEN WE CAN GO OUTSIDE.
IF YOU WANT TO GO OUTSIDE, THEN CLEAN IT YOURSELF.
WE LIKE IT MESSY.
YOU KNOW, YOU'RE RIGHT. I LIKE A REALLY MESSY ROOM.
IN FACT, I DON'T THINK THIS ROOM IS MESSY ENOUGH.
HEY! WHAT DO YOU THINK YOU'RE DOING?
YEAH!
POOF
YOU SAID YOU LIKE A MESSY ROOM. I DO, TOO.

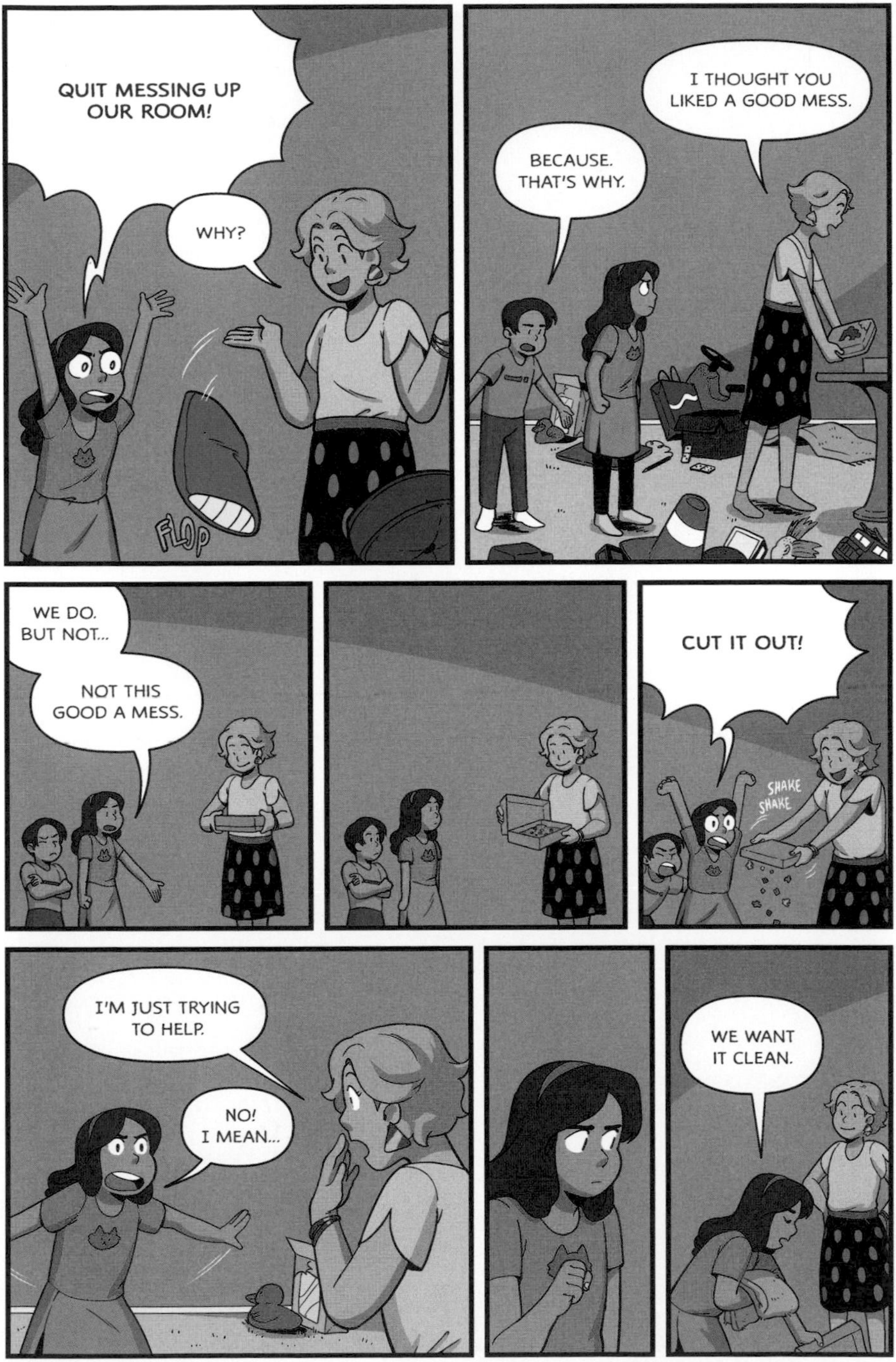
QUIT MESSING UP OUR ROOM!
WHY?
FLOP
BECAUSE. THAT'S WHY.
I THOUGHT YOU LIKED A GOOD MESS.
WE DO. BUT NOT...
NOT THIS GOOD A MESS.
CUT IT OUT!
SHAKE SHAKE
I'M JUST TRYING TO HELP.
NO! I MEAN...
WE WANT IT CLEAN.

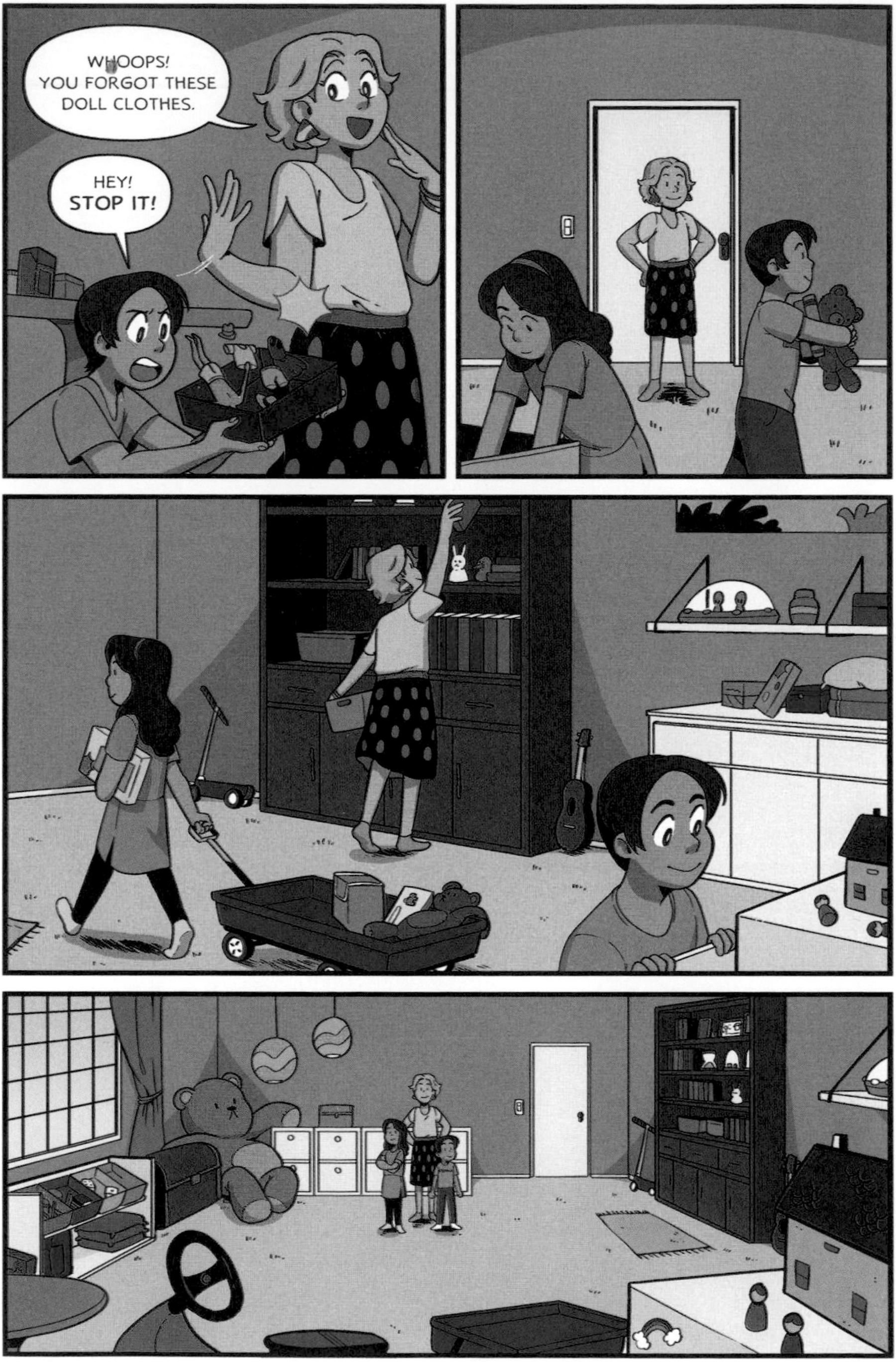
WHOOPS!
YOU FORGOT THESE
DOLL CLOTHES.
HEY!
STOP IT!

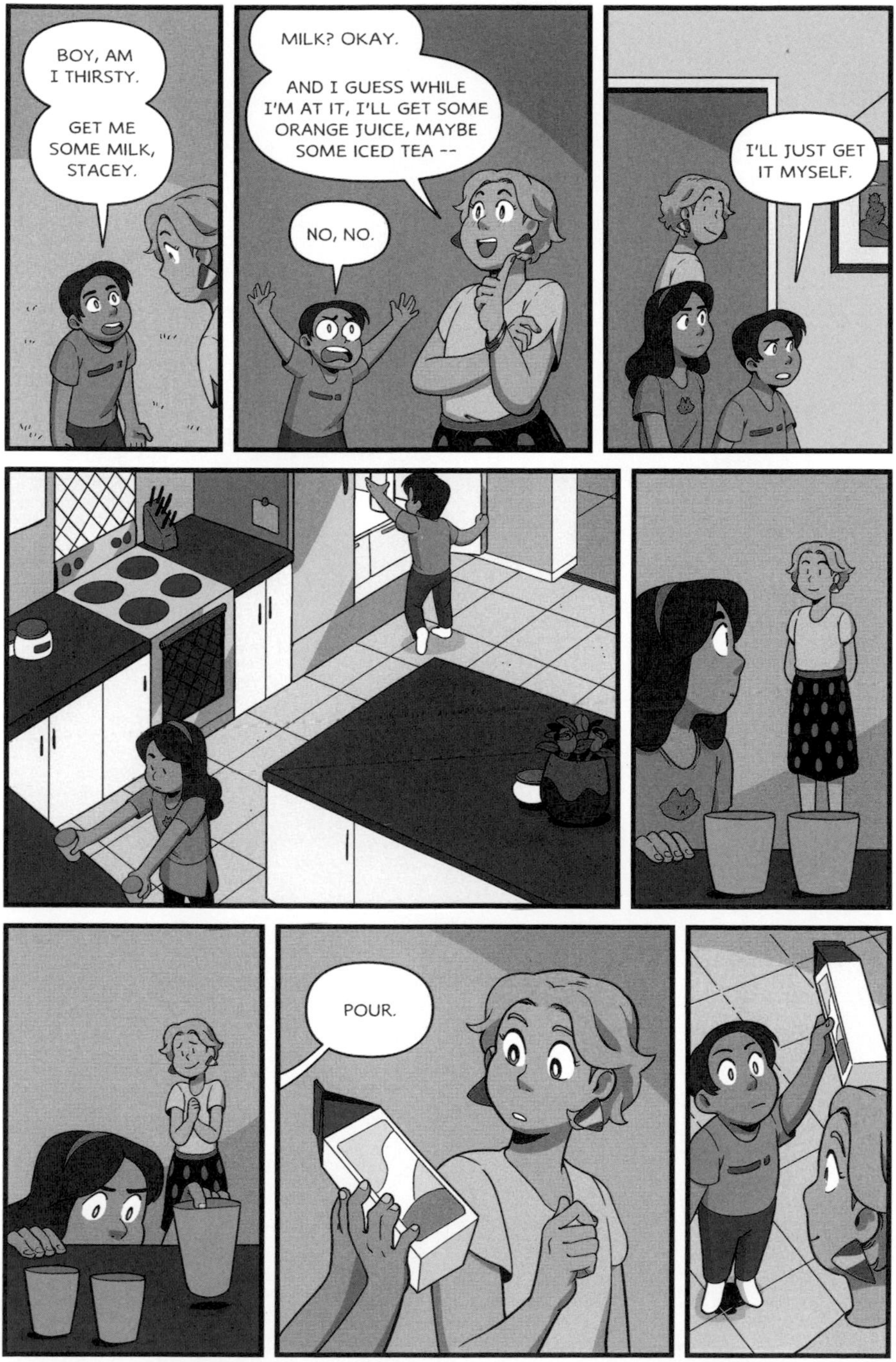
BOY, AM I THIRSTY.
GET ME SOME MILK, STACEY.
MILK? OKAY.
AND I GUESS WHILE I'M AT IT, I'LL GET SOME ORANGE JUICE, MAYBE SOME ICED TEA --
NO, NO.
I'LL JUST GET IT MYSELF.
POUR.

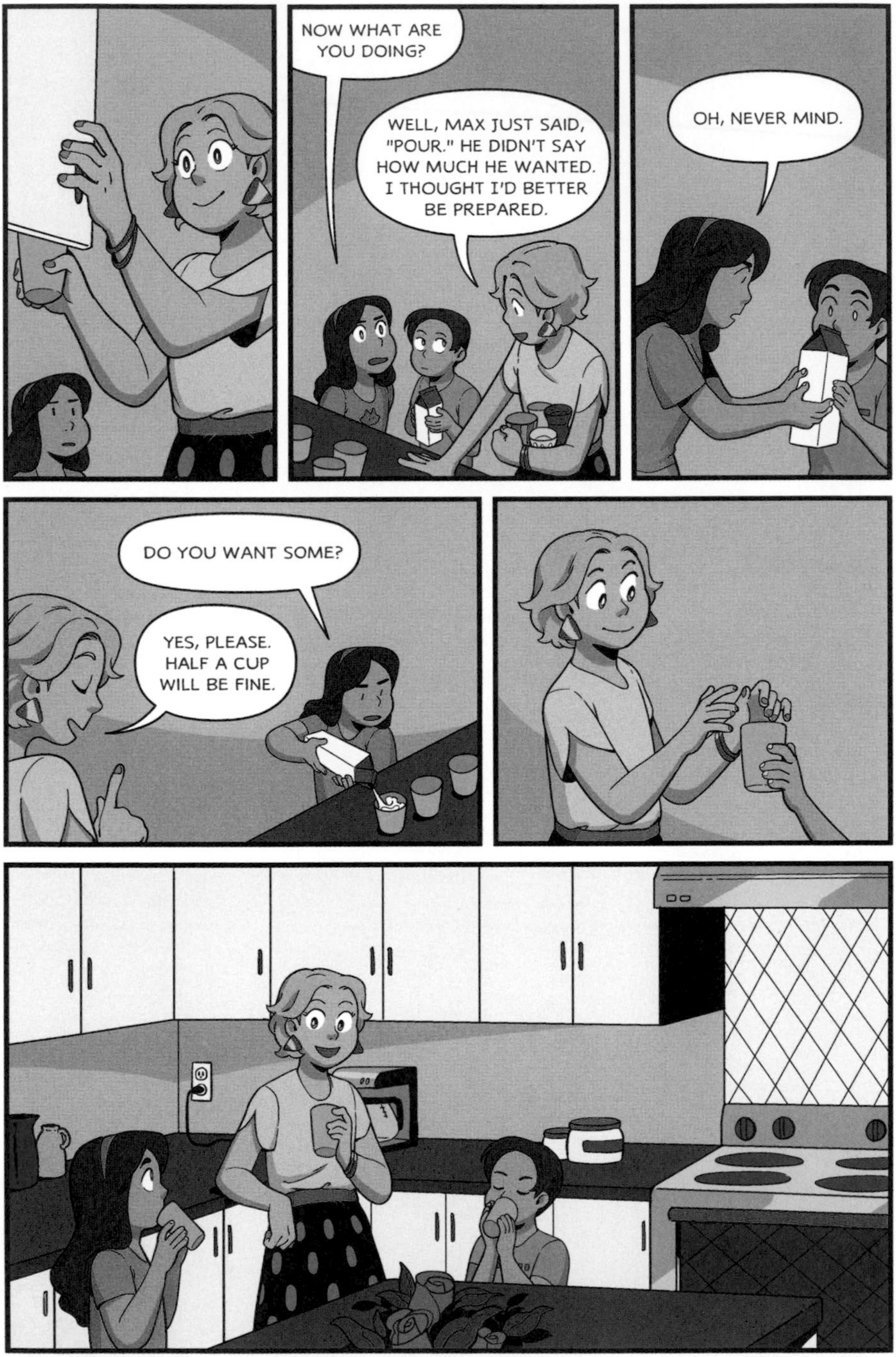
NOW WHAT ARE YOU DOING?
WELL, MAX JUST SAID, "POUR." HE DIDN'T SAY HOW MUCH HE WANTED. I THOUGHT I'D BETTER BE PREPARED.
OH, NEVER MIND.
DO YOU WANT SOME?
YES, PLEASE. HALF A CUP WILL BE FINE.

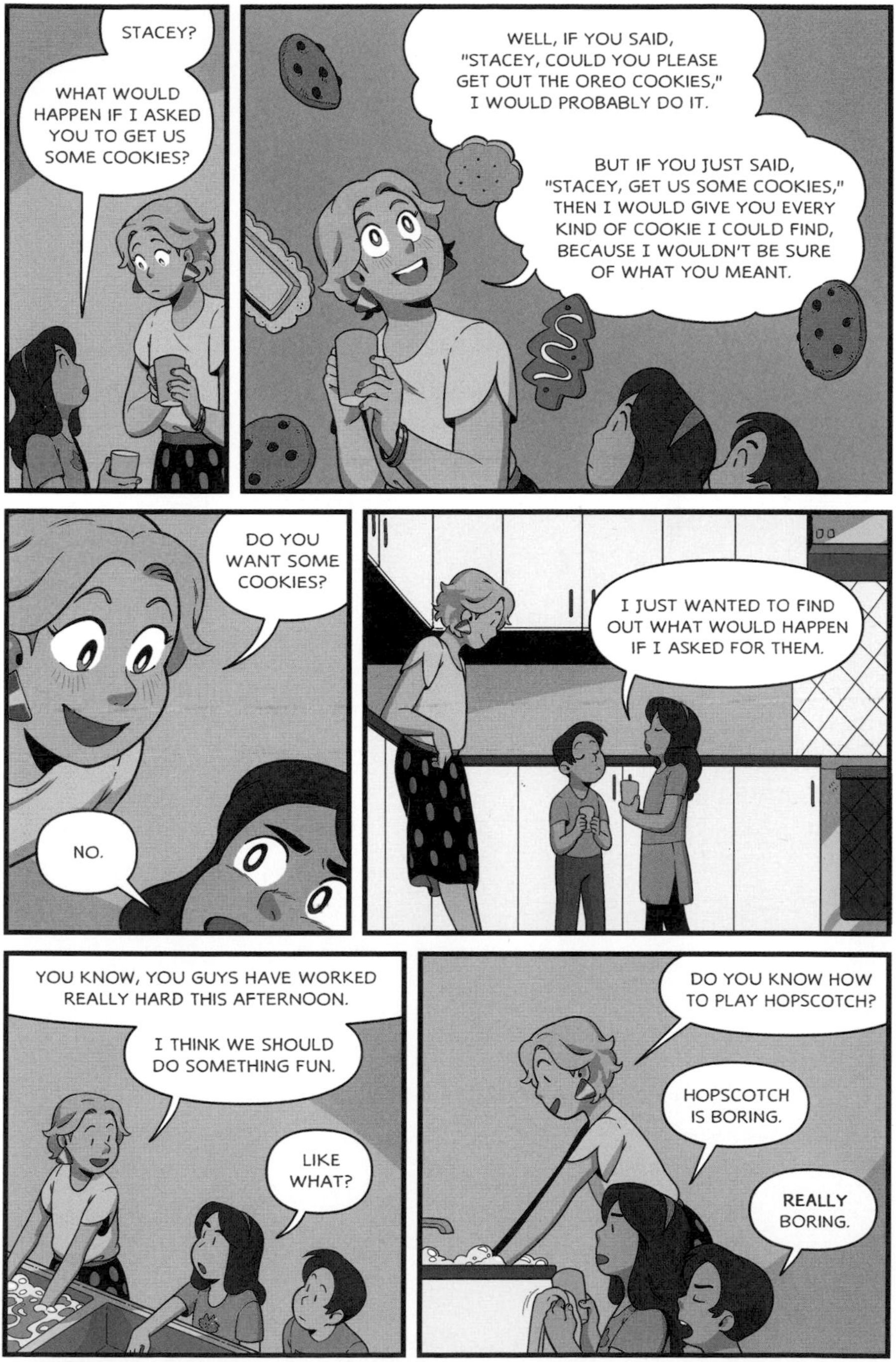
STACEY?
WHAT WOULD HAPPEN IF I ASKED YOU TO GET US SOME COOKIES?
WELL, IF YOU SAID, "STACEY, COULD YOU PLEASE GET OUT THE OREO COOKIES," I WOULD PROBABLY DO IT.
BUT IF YOU JUST SAID, "STACEY, GET US SOME COOKIES," THEN I WOULD GIVE YOU EVERY KIND OF COOKIE I COULD FIND, BECAUSE I WOULDN'T BE SURE OF WHAT YOU MEANT.
DO YOU WANT SOME COOKIES?
NO.
I JUST WANTED TO FIND OUT WHAT WOULD HAPPEN IF I ASKED FOR THEM.
YOU KNOW, YOU GUYS HAVE WORKED REALLY HARD THIS AFTERNOON.
I THINK WE SHOULD DO SOMETHING FUN.
LIKE WHAT?
DO YOU KNOW HOW TO PLAY HOPSCOTCH?
HOPSCOTCH IS BORING.
REALLY BORING.

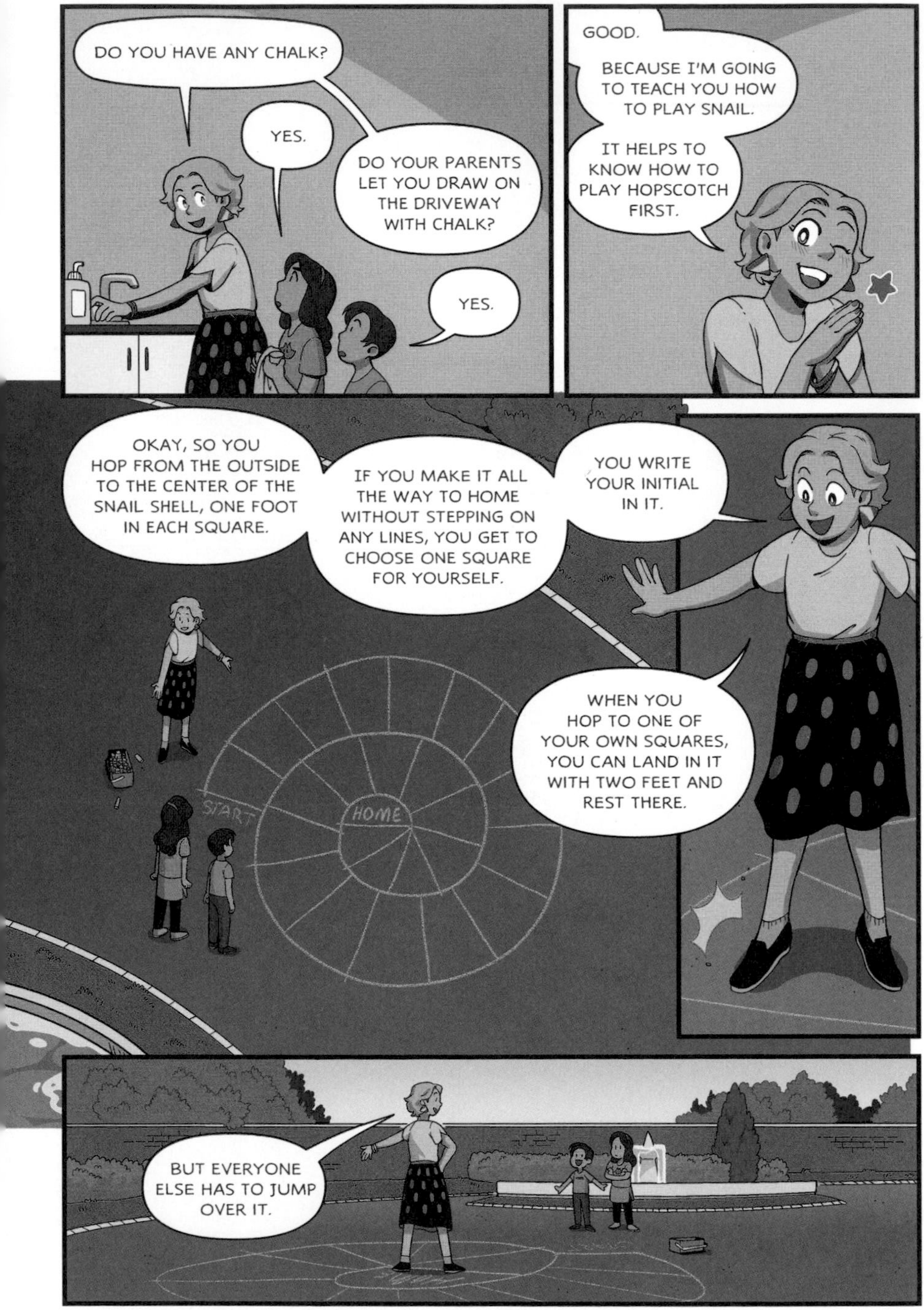
DO YOU HAVE ANY CHALK?
YES.
DO YOUR PARENTS LET YOU DRAW ON THE DRIVEWAY WITH CHALK?
YES.
GOOD.
BECAUSE I'M GOING TO TEACH YOU HOW TO PLAY SNAIL.
IT HELPS TO KNOW HOW TO PLAY HOPSCOTCH FIRST.
OKAY, SO YOU HOP FROM THE OUTSIDE TO THE CENTER OF THE SNAIL SHELL, ONE FOOT IN EACH SQUARE.
IF YOU MAKE IT ALL THE WAY TO HOME WITHOUT STEPPING ON ANY LINES, YOU GET TO CHOOSE ONE SQUARE FOR YOURSELF.
YOU WRITE YOUR INITIAL IN IT.
START
HOME
WHEN YOU HOP TO ONE OF YOUR OWN SQUARES, YOU CAN LAND IN IT WITH TWO FEET AND REST THERE.
BUT EVERYONE ELSE HAS TO JUMP OVER IT.

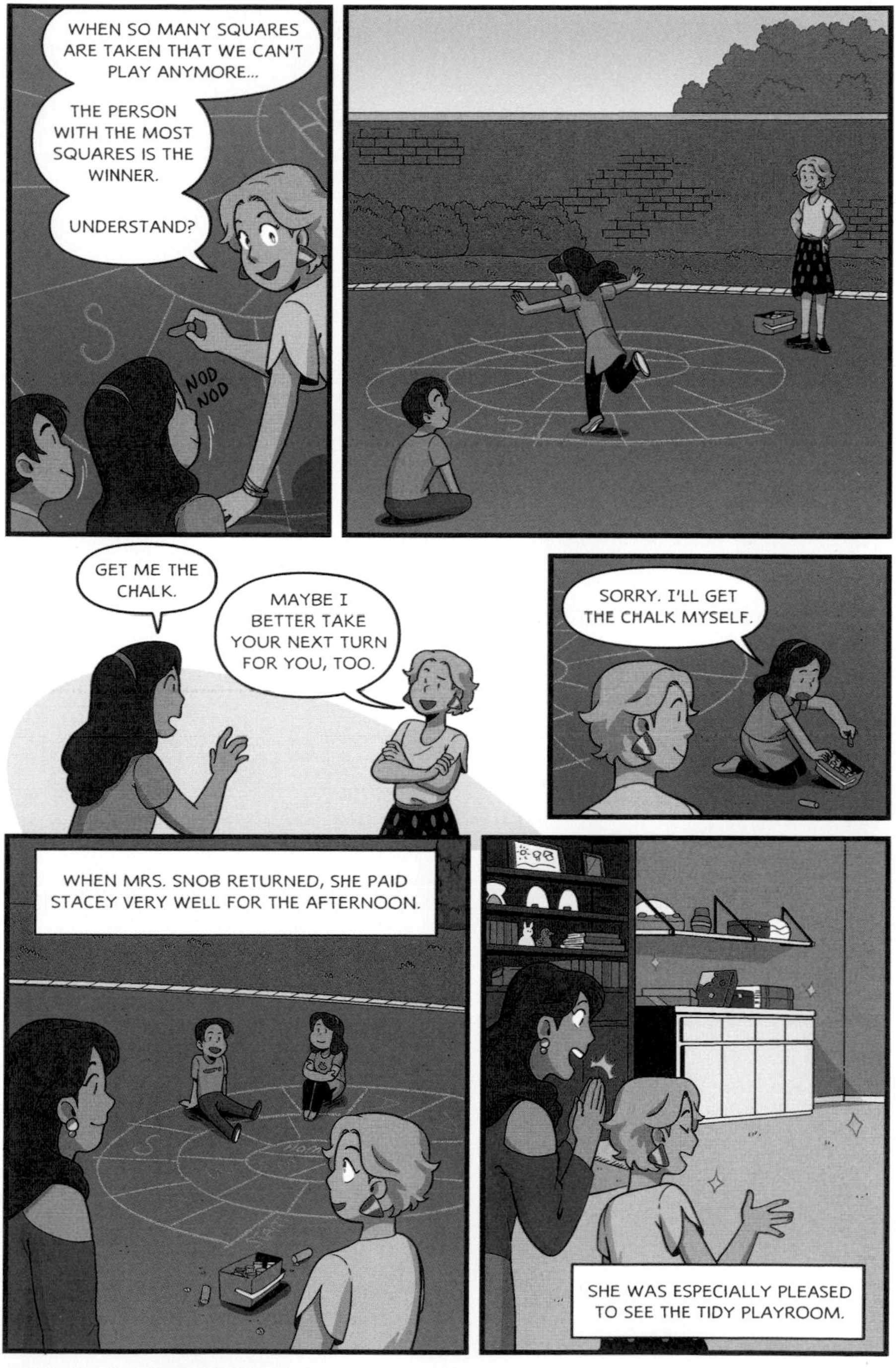
WHEN SO MANY SQUARES ARE TAKEN THAT WE CAN'T PLAY ANYMORE...
THE PERSON WITH THE MOST SQUARES IS THE WINNER.
UNDERSTAND?
NOD NOD
GET ME THE CHALK.
MAYBE I BETTER TAKE YOUR NEXT TURN FOR YOU, TOO.
SORRY. I'LL GET THE CHALK MYSELF.
WHEN MRS. SNOB RETURNED, SHE PAID STACEY VERY WELL FOR THE AFTERNOON.
SHE WAS ESPECIALLY PLEASED TO SEE THE TIDY PLAYROOM.

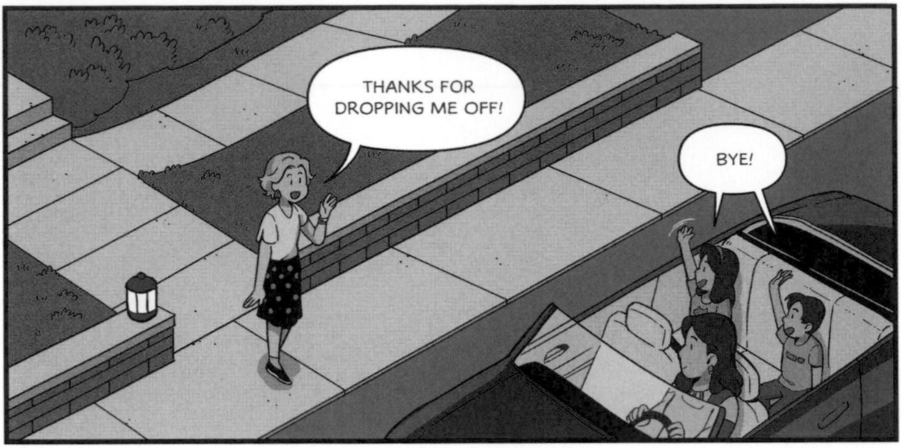
THANKS FOR DROPPING ME OFF!
BYE!

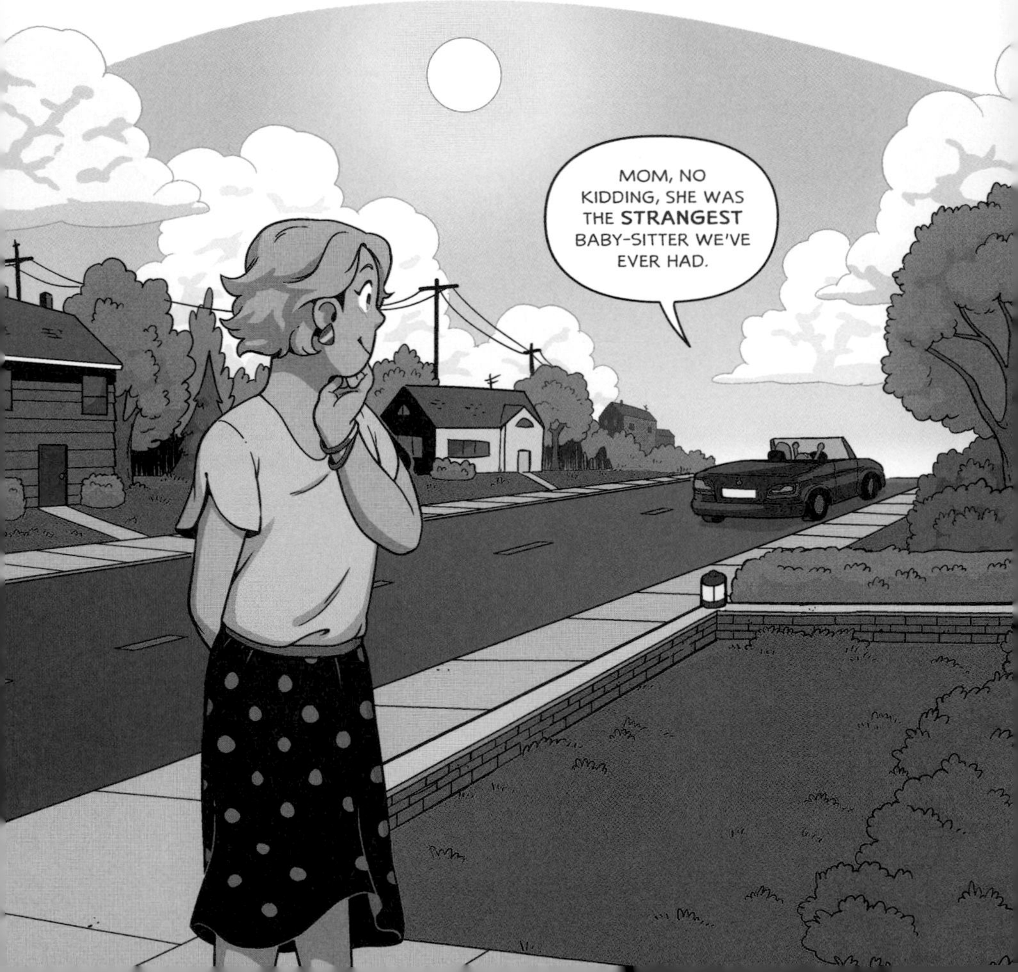
MOM, NO KIDDING, SHE WAS THE **STRANGEST** BABY-SITTER WE'VE EVER HAD.

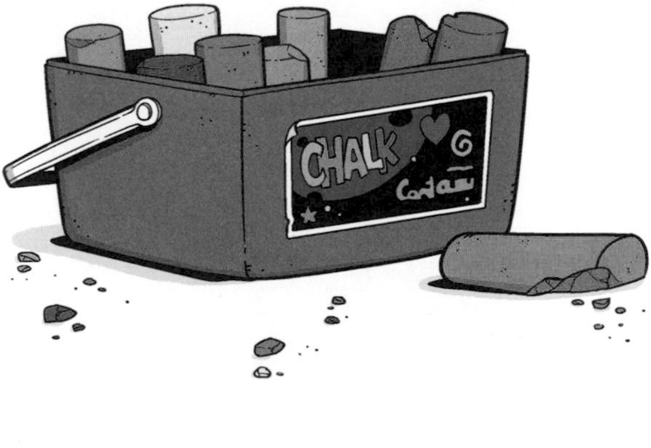
CHALK

CHAPTER 9

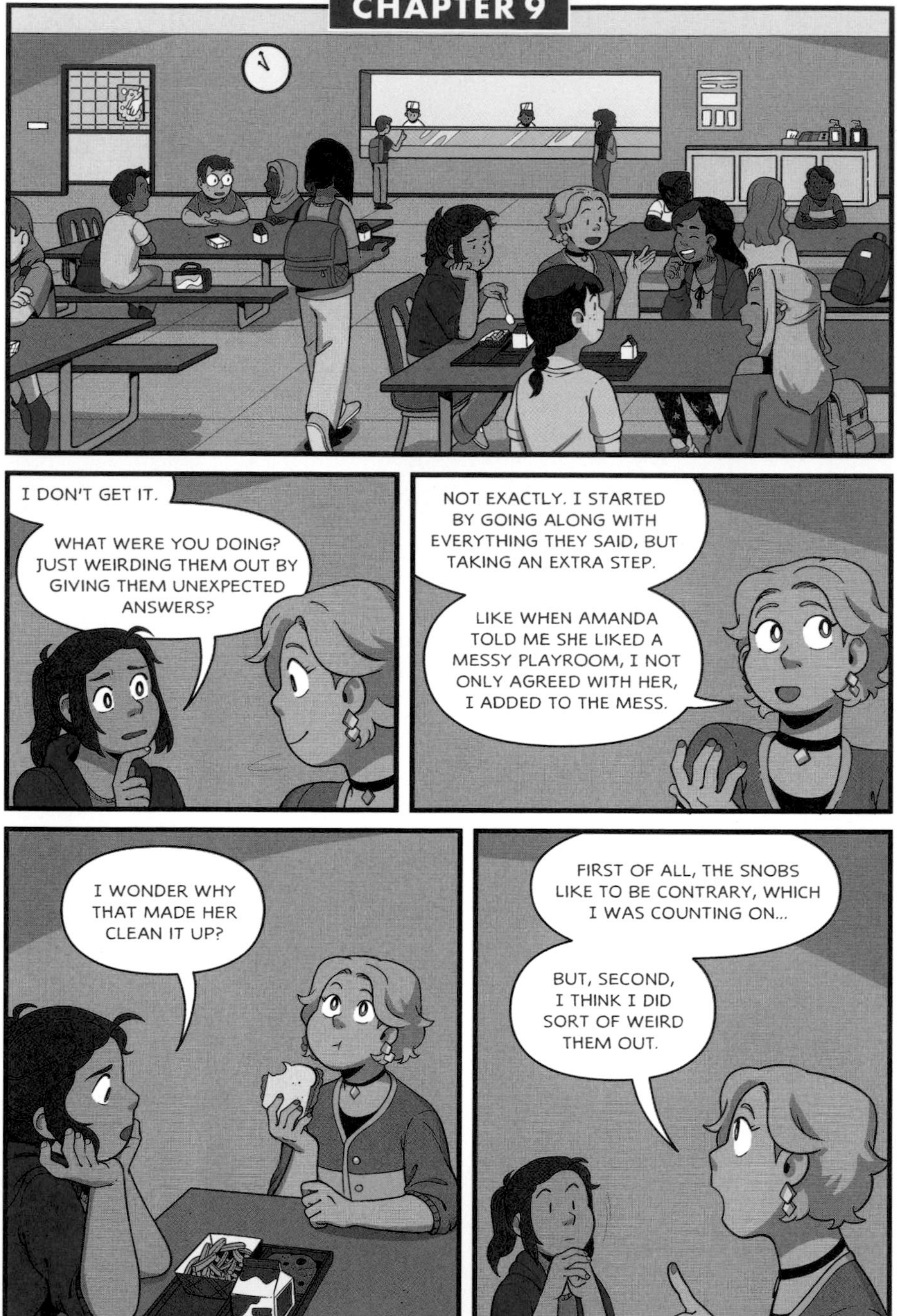
I DON'T GET IT.
WHAT WERE YOU DOING? JUST WEIRDING THEM OUT BY GIVING THEM UNEXPECTED ANSWERS?
NOT EXACTLY. I STARTED BY GOING ALONG WITH EVERYTHING THEY SAID, BUT TAKING AN EXTRA STEP.
LIKE WHEN AMANDA TOLD ME SHE LIKED A MESSY PLAYROOM, I NOT ONLY AGREED WITH HER, I ADDED TO THE MESS.
I WONDER WHY THAT MADE HER CLEAN IT UP?
FIRST OF ALL, THE SNOBS LIKE TO BE CONTRARY, WHICH I WAS COUNTING ON...
BUT, SECOND, I THINK I DID SORT OF WEIRD THEM OUT.

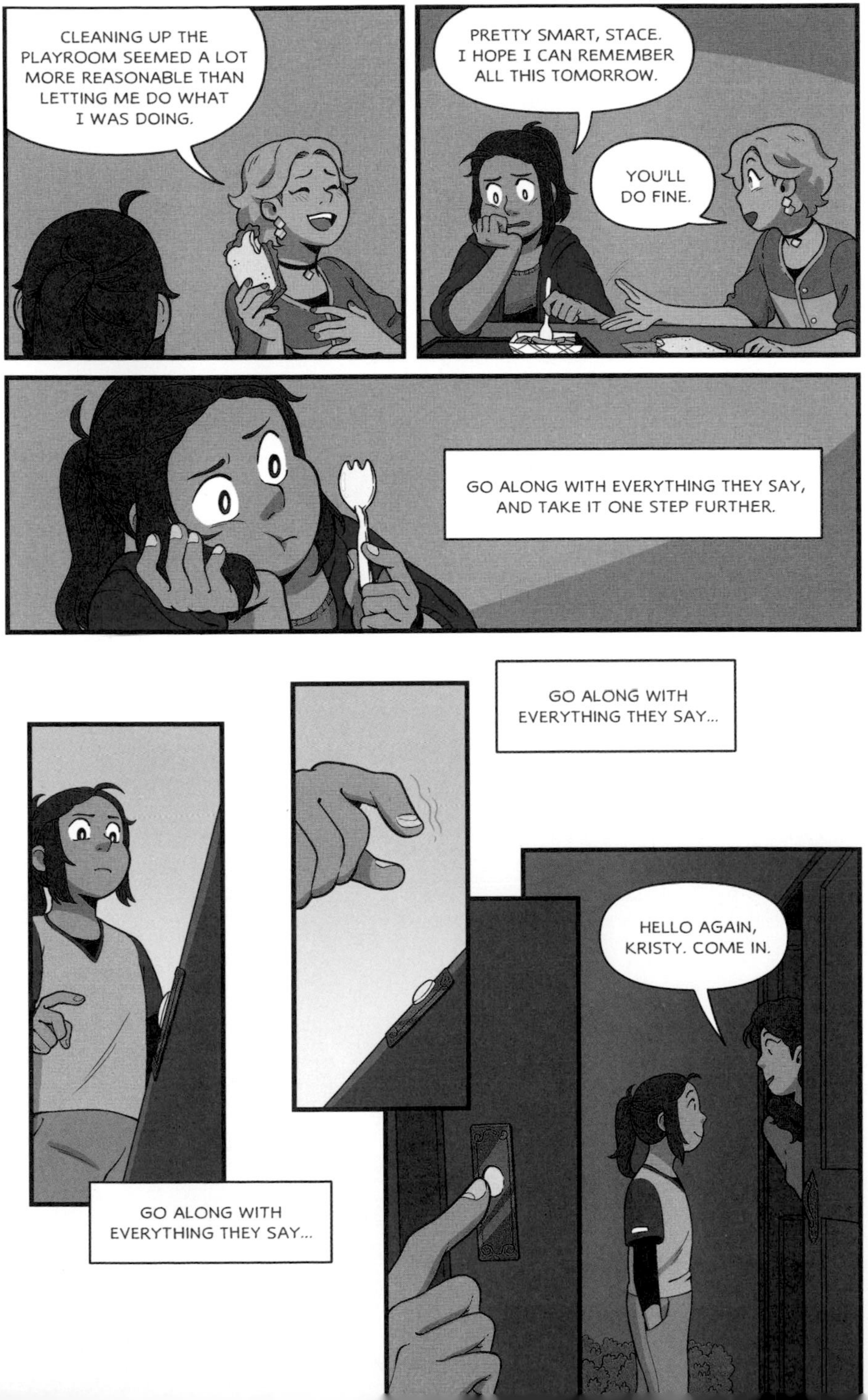
CLEANING UP THE PLAYROOM SEEMED A LOT MORE REASONABLE THAN LETTING ME DO WHAT I WAS DOING.
PRETTY SMART, STACE. I HOPE I CAN REMEMBER ALL THIS TOMORROW.
YOU'LL DO FINE.
GO ALONG WITH EVERYTHING THEY SAY, AND TAKE IT ONE STEP FURTHER.
GO ALONG WITH EVERYTHING THEY SAY...
GO ALONG WITH EVERYTHING THEY SAY...
HELLO AGAIN, KRISTY. COME IN.

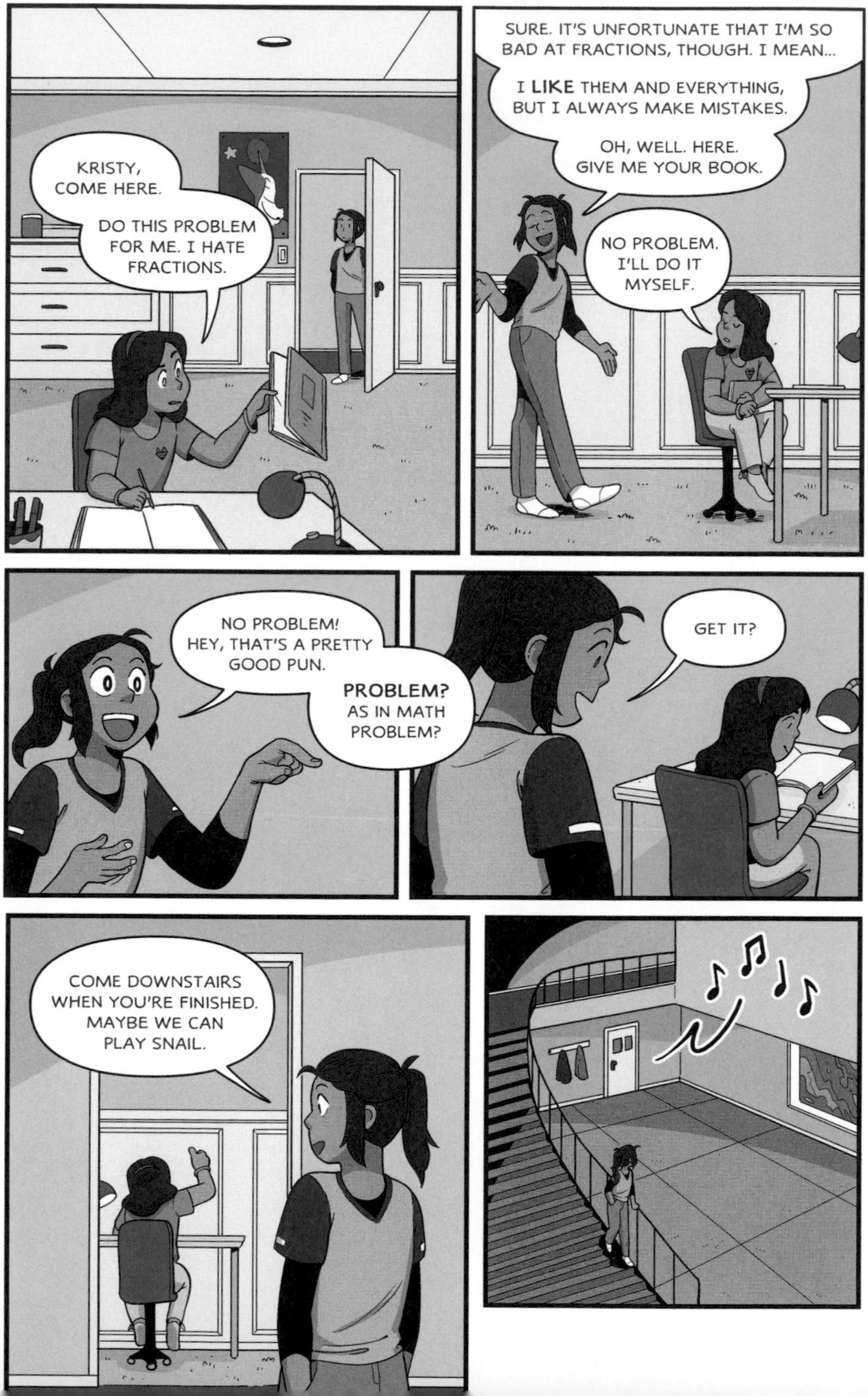
KRISTY, COME HERE.
DO THIS PROBLEM FOR ME. I HATE FRACTIONS.
SURE. IT'S UNFORTUNATE THAT I'M SO BAD AT FRACTIONS, THOUGH. I MEAN...
I **LIKE** THEM AND EVERYTHING, BUT I ALWAYS MAKE MISTAKES.
OH, WELL. HERE. GIVE ME YOUR BOOK.
NO PROBLEM. I'LL DO IT MYSELF.
NO PROBLEM! HEY, THAT'S A PRETTY GOOD PUN.
PROBLEM? AS IN MATH PROBLEM?
GET IT?
COME DOWNSTAIRS WHEN YOU'RE FINISHED. MAYBE WE CAN PLAY SNAIL.

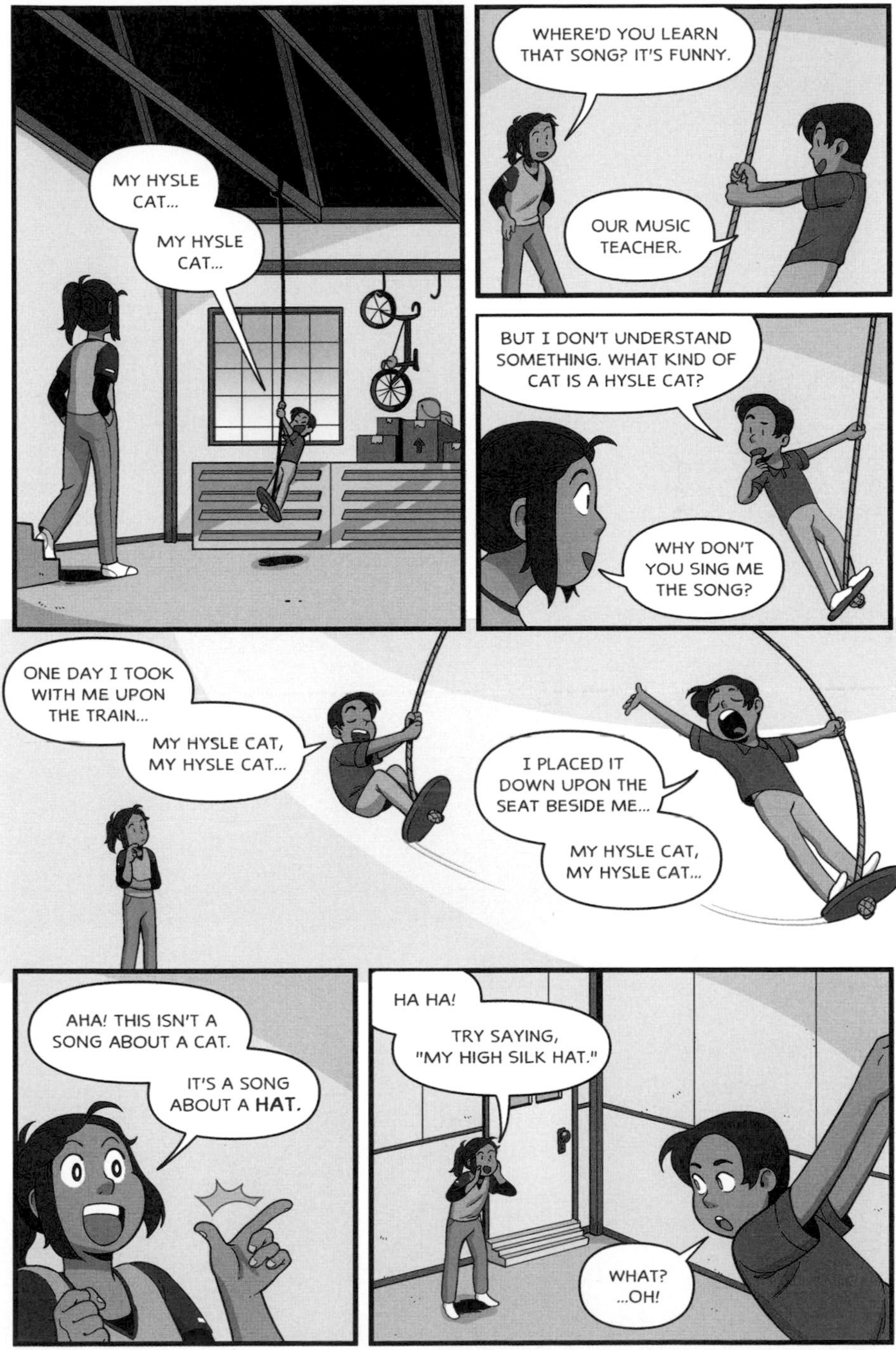
MY HYSLE CAT...
MY HYSLE CAT...
WHERE'D YOU LEARN THAT SONG? IT'S FUNNY.
OUR MUSIC TEACHER.
BUT I DON'T UNDERSTAND SOMETHING. WHAT KIND OF CAT IS A HYSLE CAT?
WHY DON'T YOU SING ME THE SONG?
ONE DAY I TOOK WITH ME UPON THE TRAIN...
MY HYSLE CAT, MY HYSLE CAT...
I PLACED IT DOWN UPON THE SEAT BESIDE ME...
MY HYSLE CAT, MY HYSLE CAT...
AHA! THIS ISN'T A SONG ABOUT A CAT.
IT'S A SONG ABOUT A HAT.
HA HA!
TRY SAYING, "MY HIGH SILK HAT."
WHAT? ...OH!

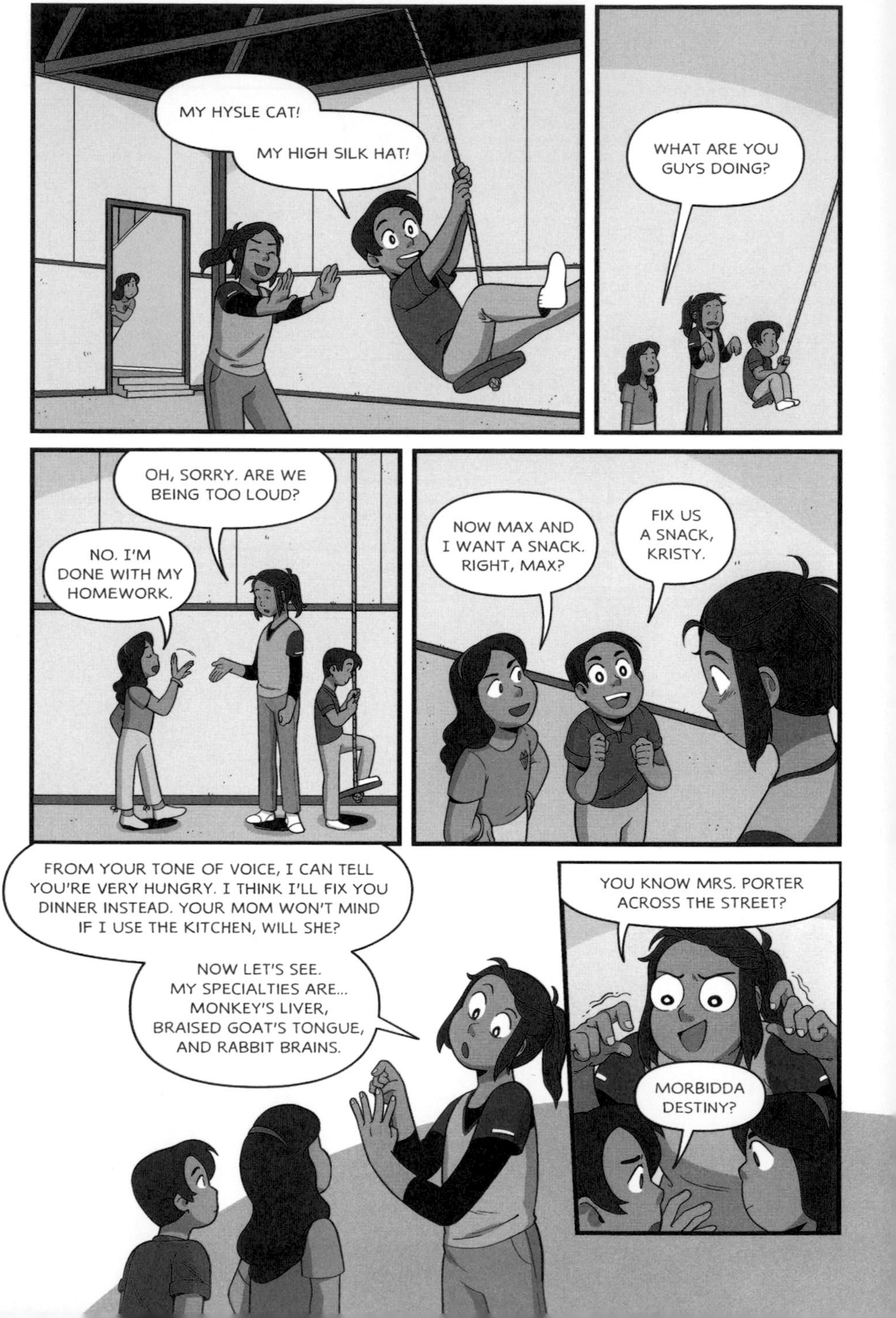
MY HYSLE CAT!
MY HIGH SILK HAT!
WHAT ARE YOU GUYS DOING?
OH, SORRY. ARE WE BEING TOO LOUD?
NO. I'M DONE WITH MY HOMEWORK.
NOW MAX AND I WANT A SNACK. RIGHT, MAX?
FIX US A SNACK, KRISTY.
FROM YOUR TONE OF VOICE, I CAN TELL YOU'RE VERY HUNGRY. I THINK I'LL FIX YOU DINNER INSTEAD. YOUR MOM WON'T MIND IF I USE THE KITCHEN, WILL SHE?
NOW LET'S SEE. MY SPECIALTIES ARE... MONKEY'S LIVER, BRAISED GOAT'S TONGUE, AND RABBIT BRAINS.
YOU KNOW MRS. PORTER ACROSS THE STREET?
MORBIDDA DESTINY?

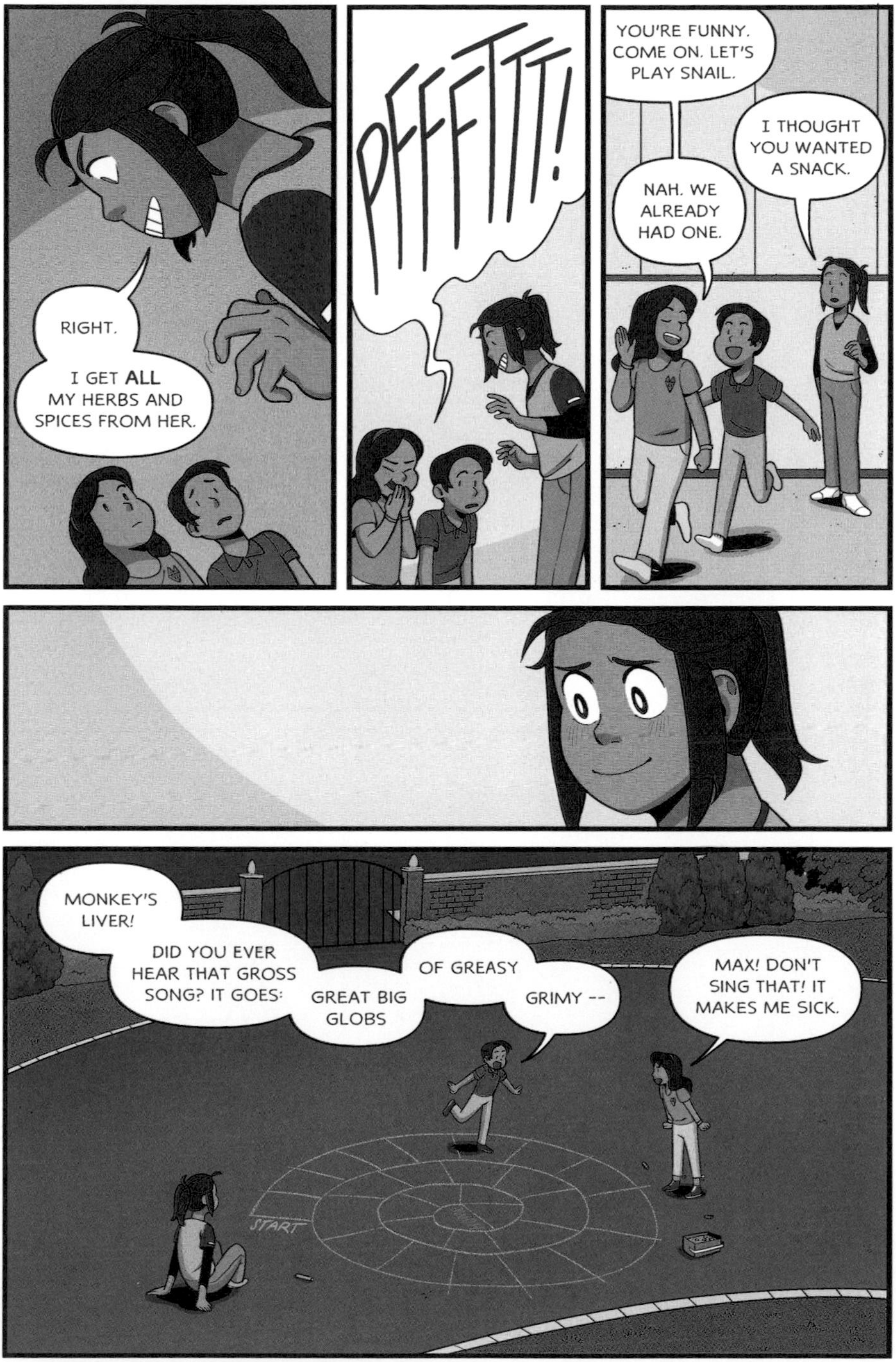
RIGHT.
I GET **ALL** MY HERBS AND SPICES FROM HER.
PFFFTTT!
YOU'RE FUNNY. COME ON. LET'S PLAY SNAIL.
NAH. WE ALREADY HAD ONE.
I THOUGHT YOU WANTED A SNACK.
MONKEY'S LIVER!
DID YOU EVER HEAR THAT GROSS SONG? IT GOES:
GREAT BIG GLOBS
OF GREASY
GRIMY --
MAX! DON'T SING THAT! IT MAKES ME SICK.
START

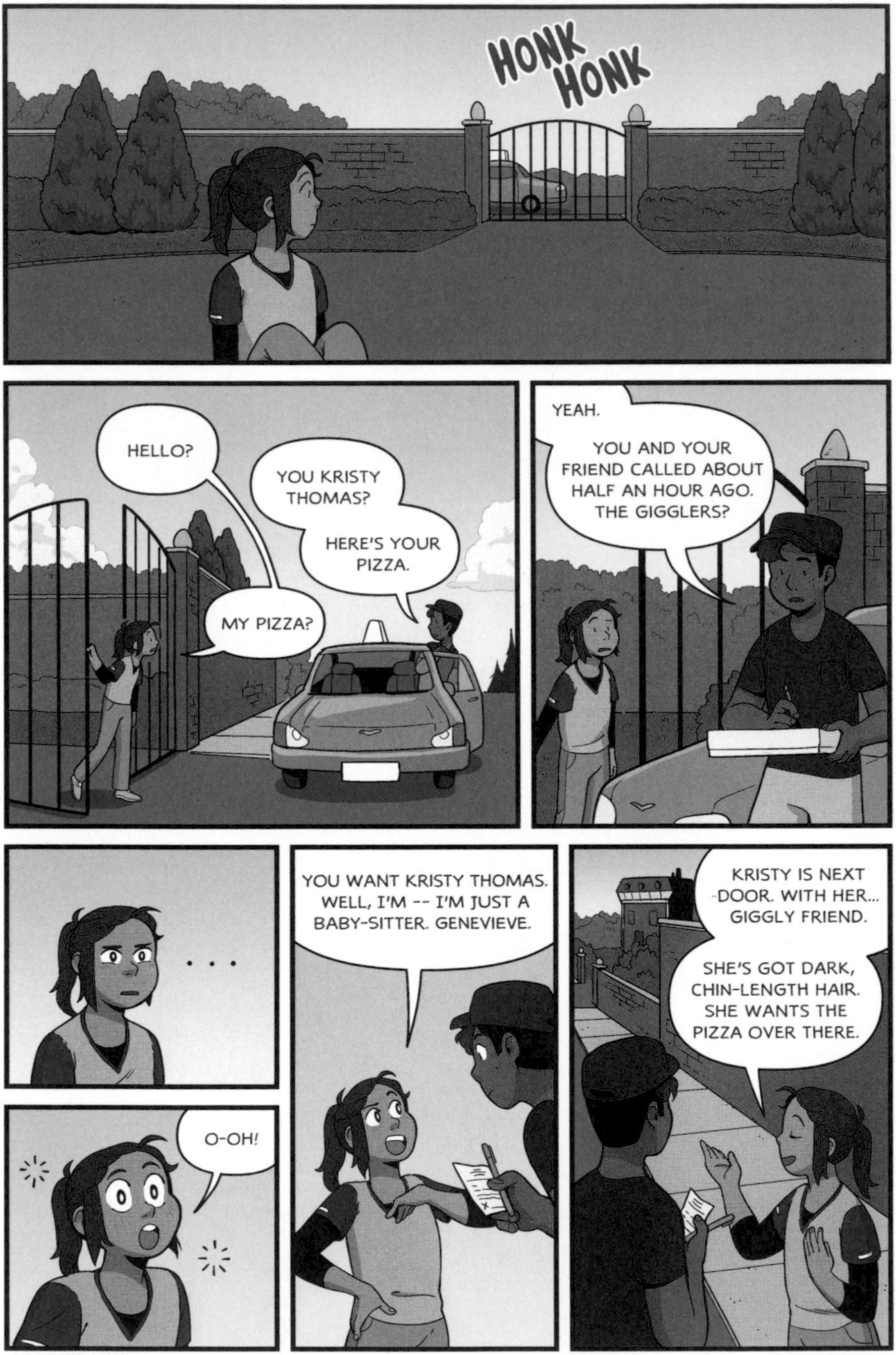
HONK
HONK
HELLO?
YOU KRISTY THOMAS?
HERE'S YOUR PIZZA.
MY PIZZA?
YEAH.
YOU AND YOUR FRIEND CALLED ABOUT HALF AN HOUR AGO. THE GIGGLERS?
. . .
O-OH!
YOU WANT KRISTY THOMAS. WELL, I'M -- I'M JUST A BABY-SITTER. GENEVIEVE.
KRISTY IS NEXT -DOOR. WITH HER... GIGGLY FRIEND.
SHE'S GOT DARK, CHIN-LENGTH HAIR. SHE WANTS THE PIZZA OVER THERE.

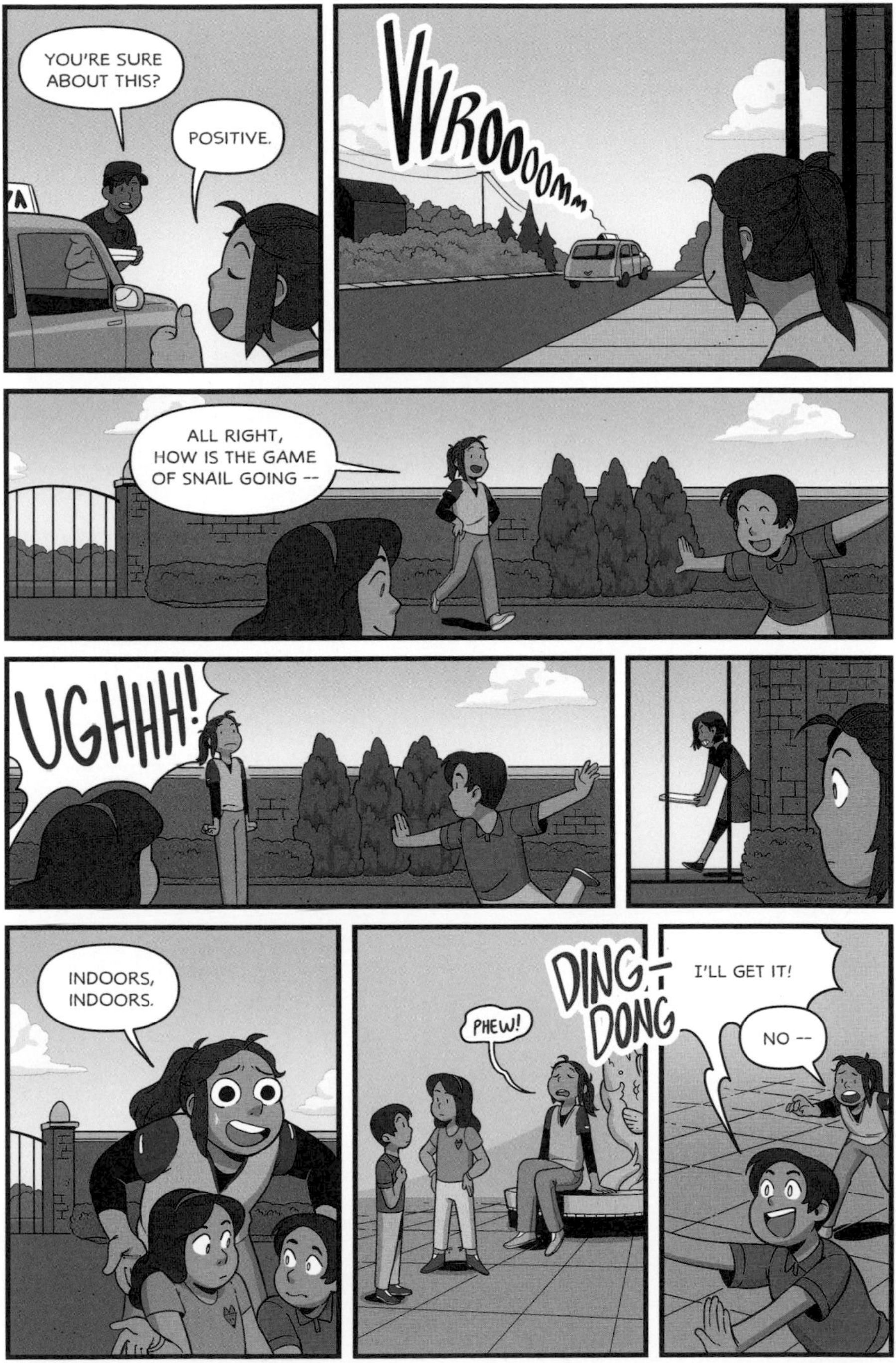
YOU'RE SURE ABOUT THIS?
POSITIVE.
VVROOOOMM
ALL RIGHT, HOW IS THE GAME OF SNAIL GOING --
UGHHH!
INDOORS, INDOORS.
PHEW!
DING-DONG
I'LL GET IT!
NO --

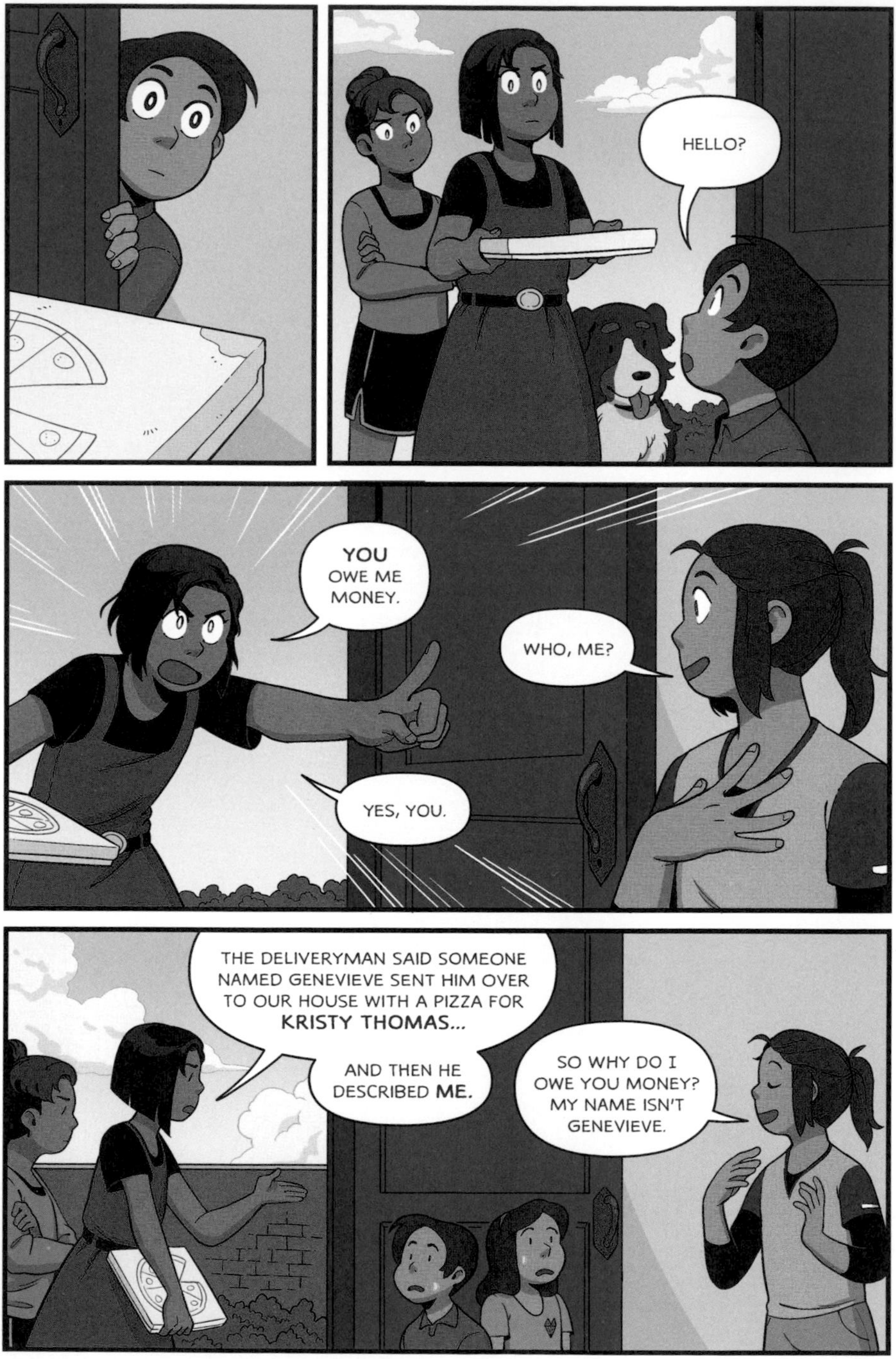
HELLO?
YOU OWE ME MONEY.
WHO, ME?
YES, YOU.
THE DELIVERYMAN SAID SOMEONE NAMED GENEVIEVE SENT HIM OVER TO OUR HOUSE WITH A PIZZA FOR KRISTY THOMAS...
AND THEN HE DESCRIBED ME.
SO WHY DO I OWE YOU MONEY? MY NAME ISN'T GENEVIEVE.

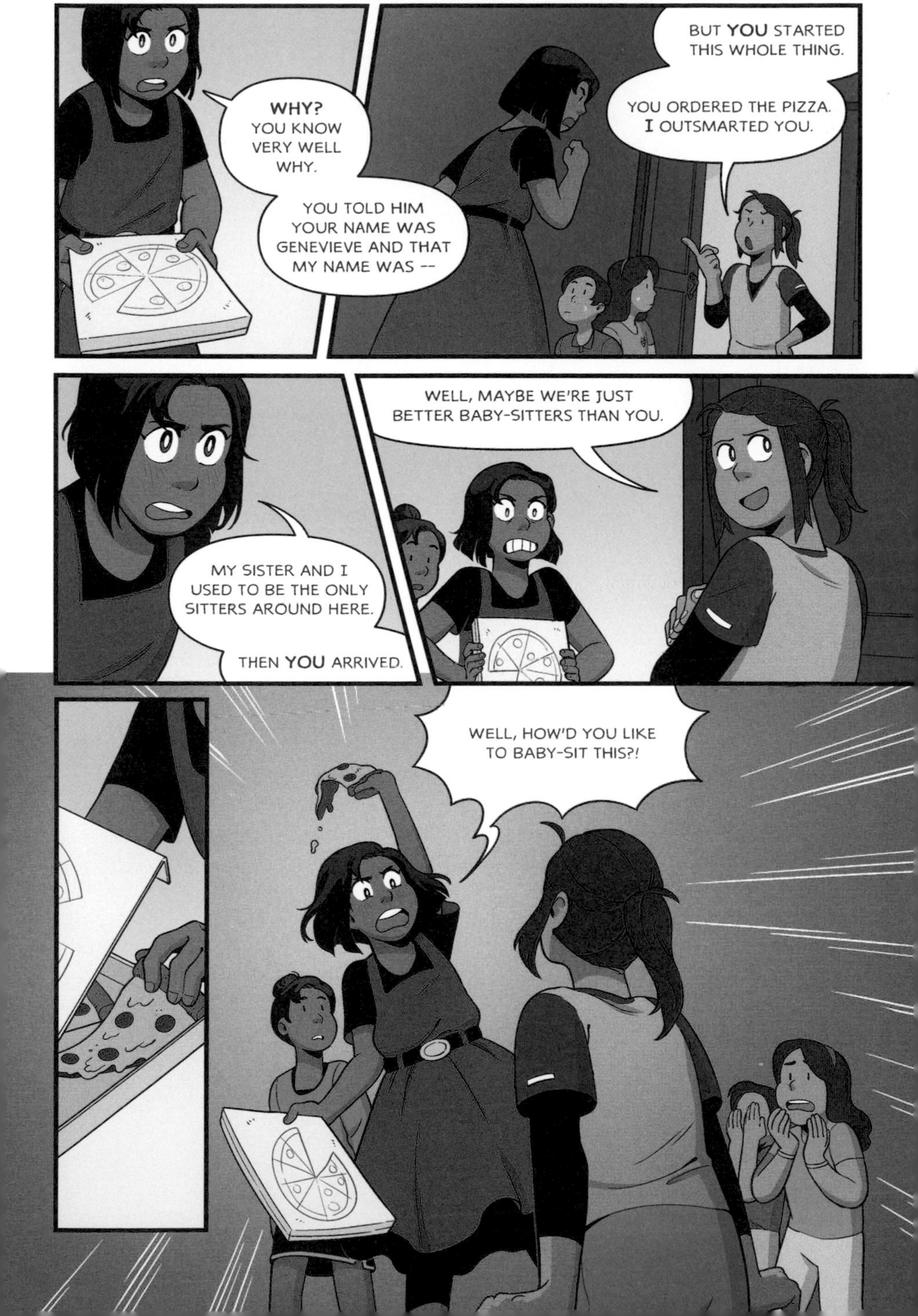
WHY? YOU KNOW VERY WELL WHY.
YOU TOLD HIM YOUR NAME WAS GENEVIEVE AND THAT MY NAME WAS --
BUT YOU STARTED THIS WHOLE THING.
YOU ORDERED THE PIZZA. I OUTSMARTED YOU.
MY SISTER AND I USED TO BE THE ONLY SITTERS AROUND HERE.
THEN YOU ARRIVED.
WELL, MAYBE WE'RE JUST BETTER BABY-SITTERS THAN YOU.
WELL, HOW'D YOU LIKE TO BABY-SIT THIS?!

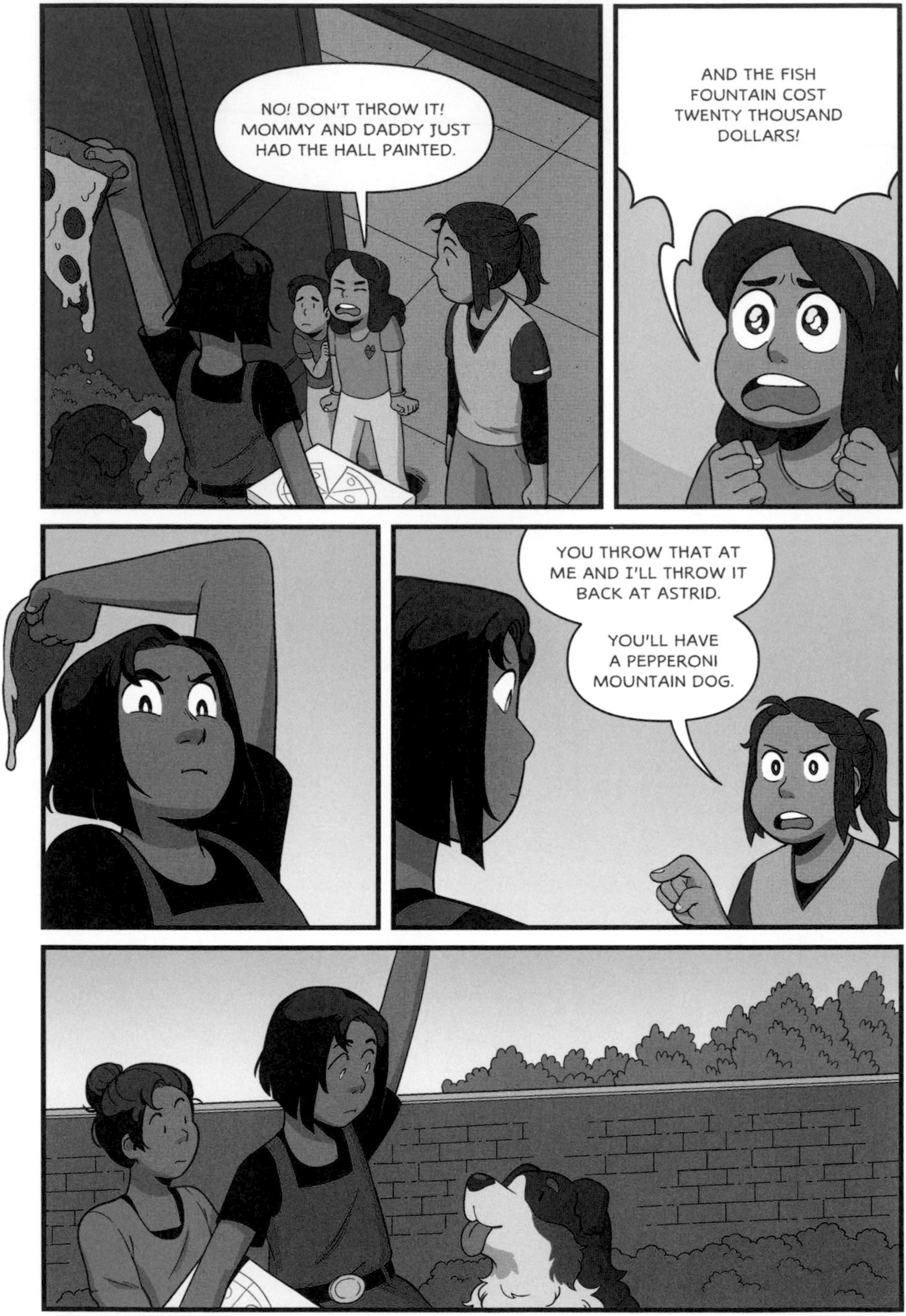
NO! DON'T THROW IT! MOMMY AND DADDY JUST HAD THE HALL PAINTED.
AND THE FISH FOUNTAIN COST TWENTY THOUSAND DOLLARS!
YOU THROW THAT AT ME AND I'LL THROW IT BACK AT ASTRID.
YOU'LL HAVE A PEPPERONI MOUNTAIN DOG.

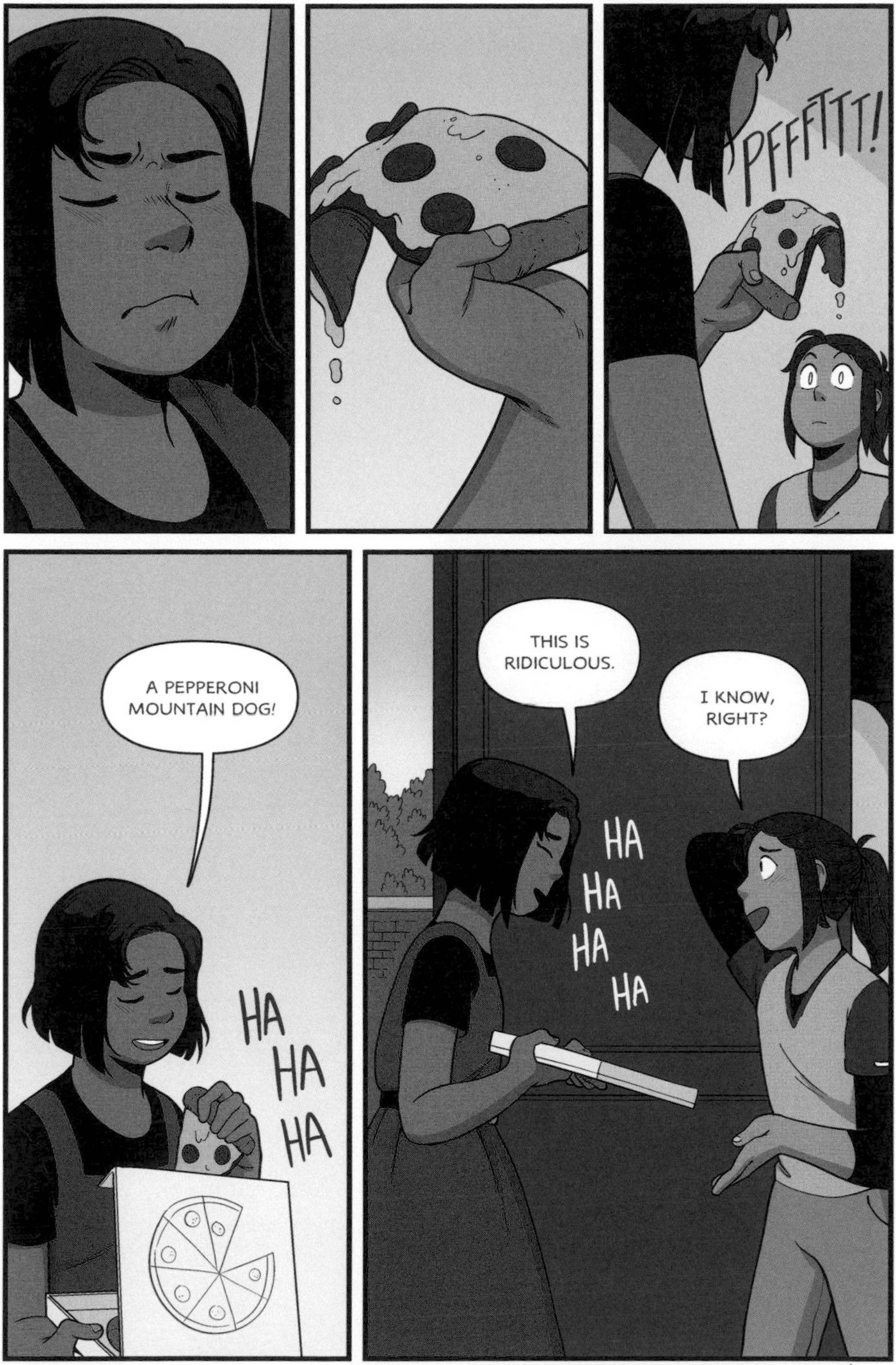
PFFFTTT!
A PEPPERONI MOUNTAIN DOG!
HA
HA
HA
THIS IS RIDICULOUS.
HA
HA
HA
HA
I KNOW, RIGHT?

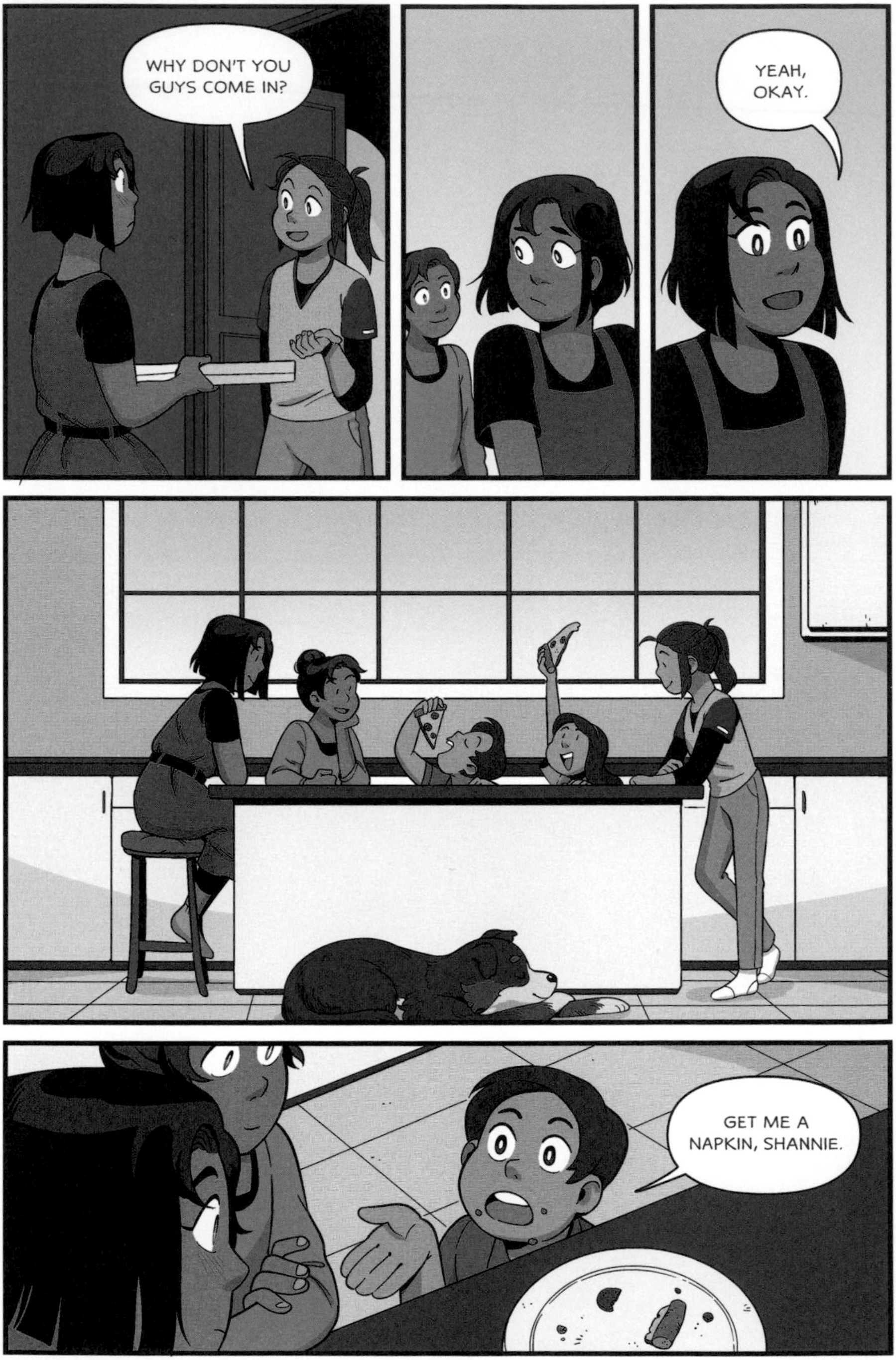
WHY DON'T YOU GUYS COME IN?
YEAH, OKAY.
GET ME A NAPKIN, SHANNIE.

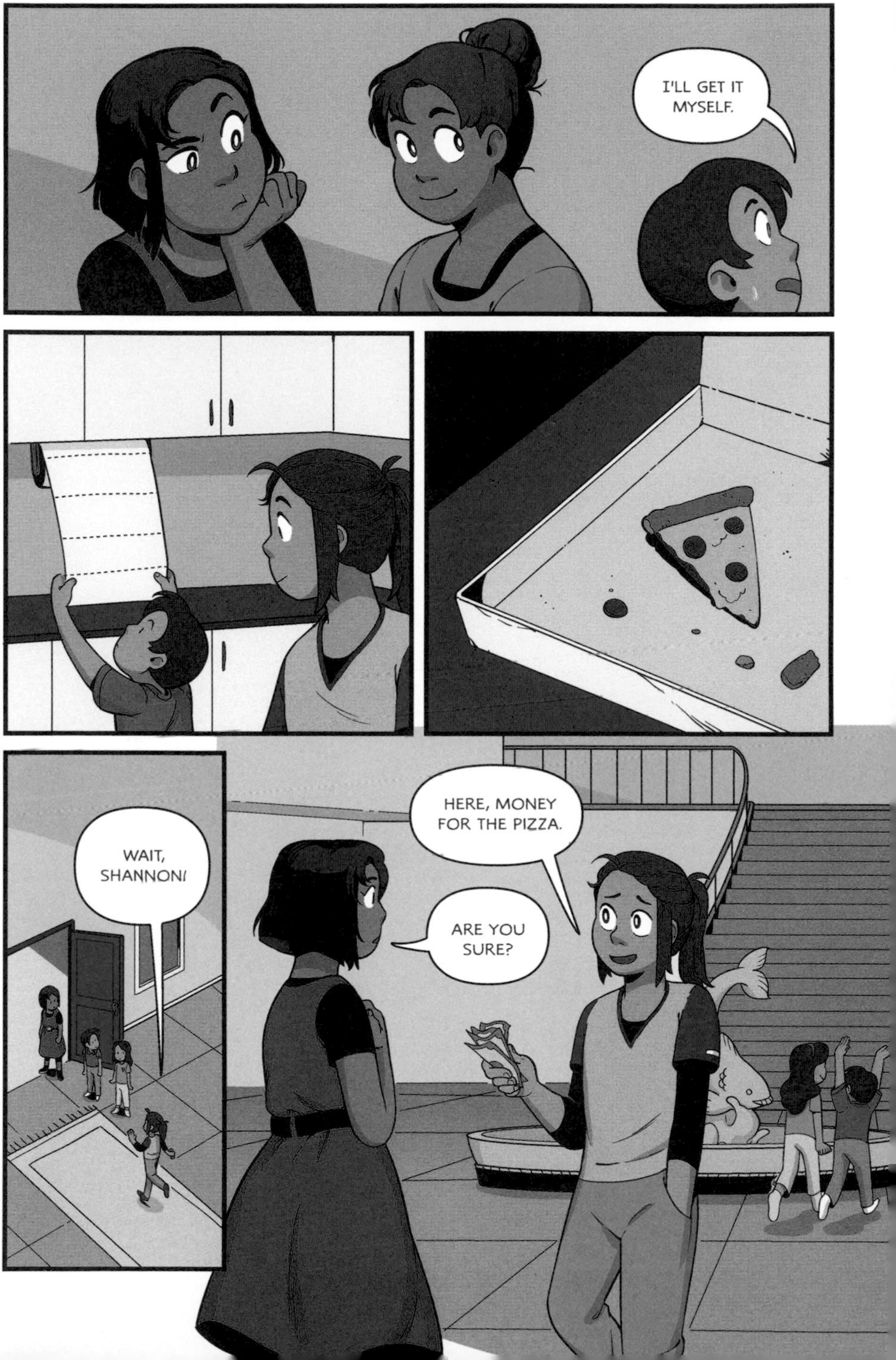
I'LL GET IT MYSELF.
WAIT, SHANNON!
HERE, MONEY FOR THE PIZZA.
ARE YOU SURE?

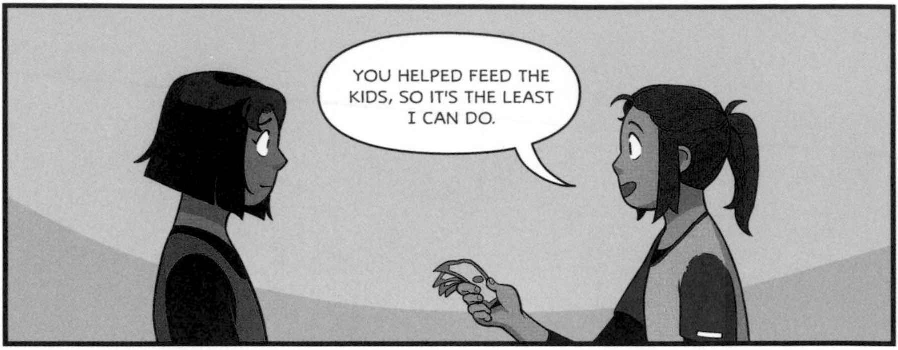
YOU HELPED FEED THE KIDS, SO IT'S THE LEAST I CAN DO.

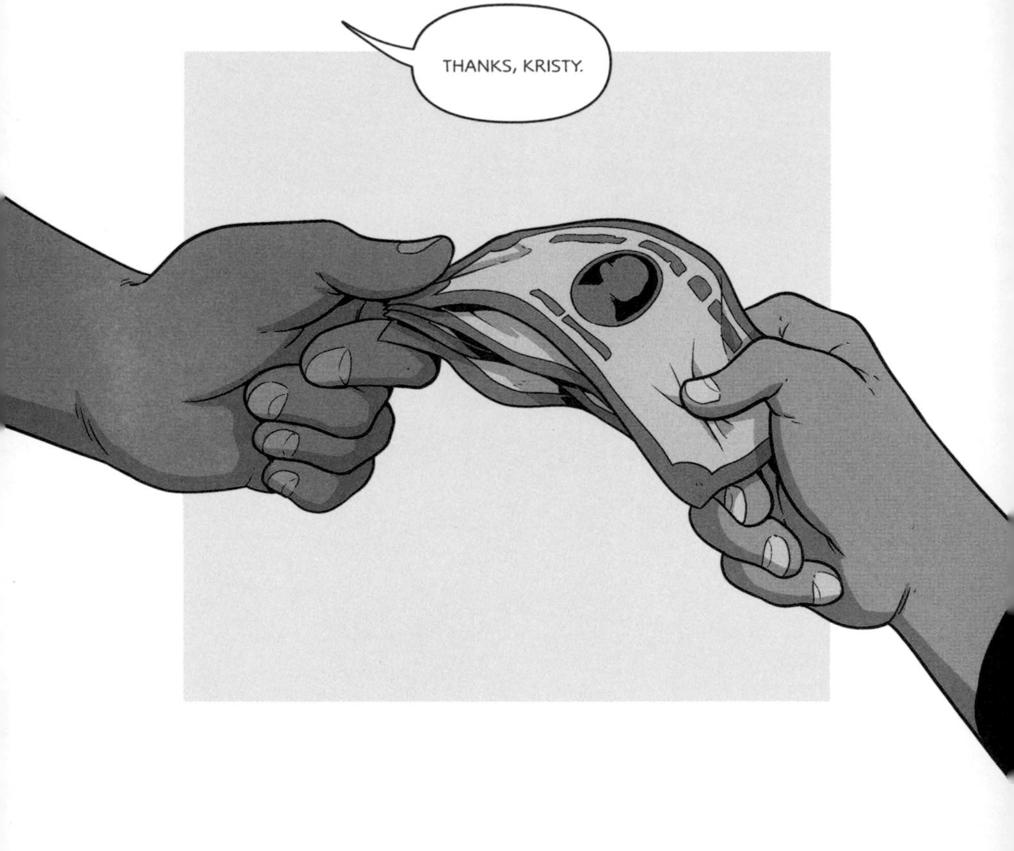
THANKS, KRISTY.

Saturday

   Chicken pocks! The only way your going
to apreciat what I wright here is if you
rember how it felt to have the chicken
pocks. I do sort of. I was seven when I
had them and it was not plesent. I itched
and had a feever and my mom said Don't
scratch but it was the only thing I
wanted to do. So keep that in mind.
   OK so Malory, Jessi, and I sat for
Malory's brothers and sisters. The triplets
and Margo and Claire were all ~~rek recov~~
getting over the chicken pox. They were
not felling very good. What a night we had.
Orders, orders, orders...

                              * Claudia *

CHAPTER 10

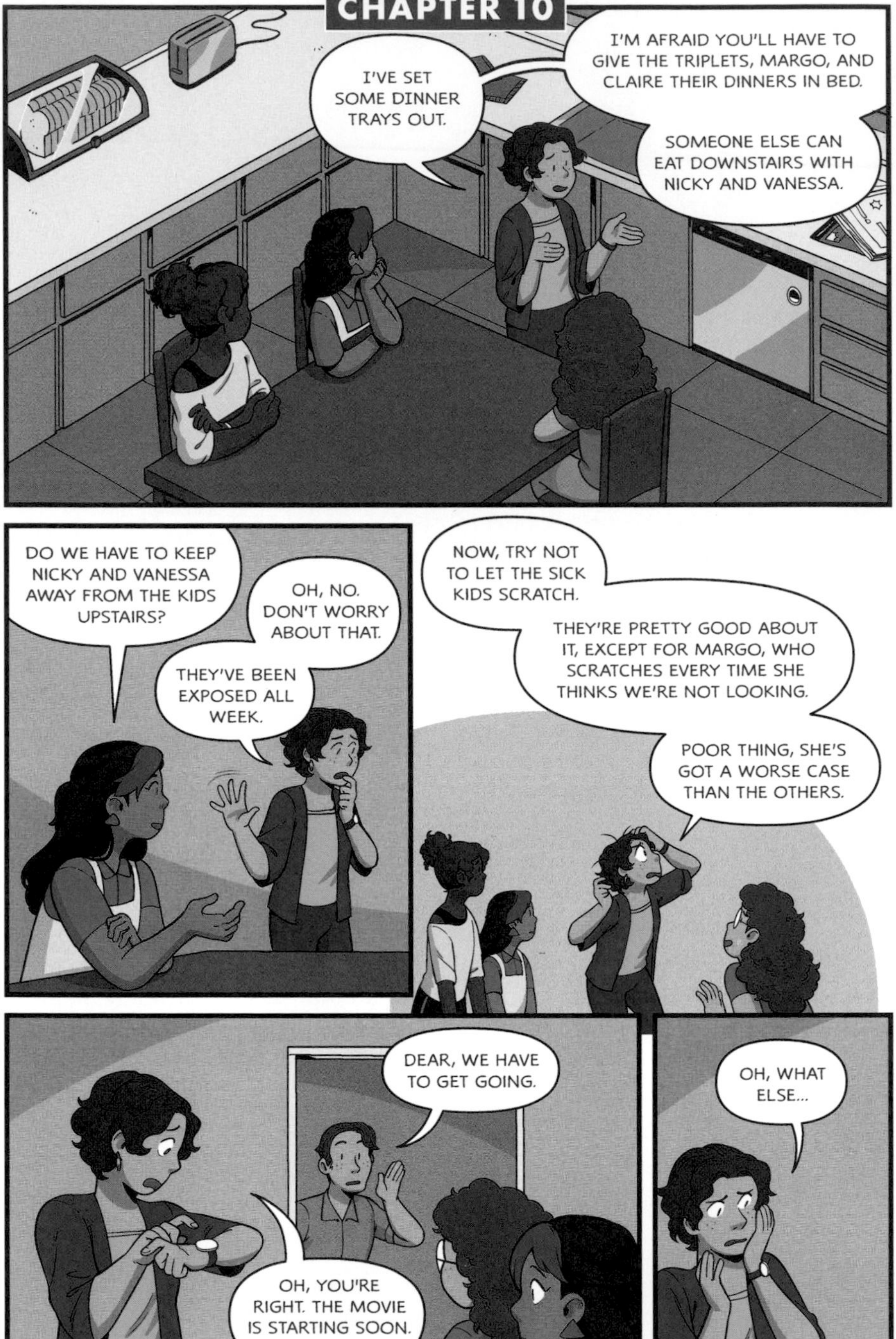
I'VE SET SOME DINNER TRAYS OUT.
I'M AFRAID YOU'LL HAVE TO GIVE THE TRIPLETS, MARGO, AND CLAIRE THEIR DINNERS IN BED.
SOMEONE ELSE CAN EAT DOWNSTAIRS WITH NICKY AND VANESSA.
DO WE HAVE TO KEEP NICKY AND VANESSA AWAY FROM THE KIDS UPSTAIRS?
OH, NO. DON'T WORRY ABOUT THAT.
THEY'VE BEEN EXPOSED ALL WEEK.
NOW, TRY NOT TO LET THE SICK KIDS SCRATCH.
THEY'RE PRETTY GOOD ABOUT IT, EXCEPT FOR MARGO, WHO SCRATCHES EVERY TIME SHE THINKS WE'RE NOT LOOKING.
POOR THING, SHE'S GOT A WORSE CASE THAN THE OTHERS.
DEAR, WE HAVE TO GET GOING.
OH, YOU'RE RIGHT. THE MOVIE IS STARTING SOON.
OH, WHAT ELSE...

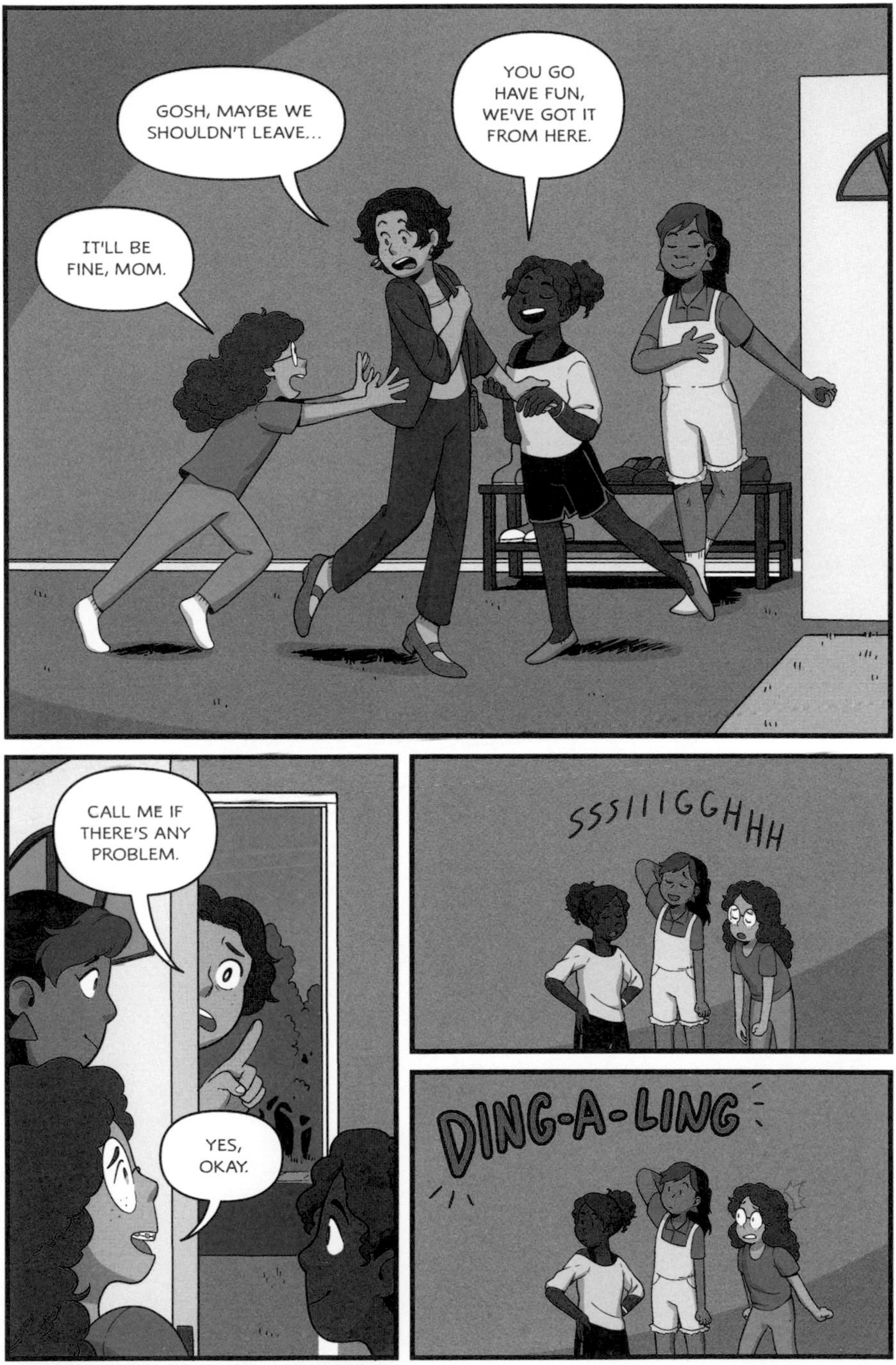
GOSH, MAYBE WE SHOULDN'T LEAVE...
YOU GO HAVE FUN, WE'VE GOT IT FROM HERE.
IT'LL BE FINE, MOM.
CALL ME IF THERE'S ANY PROBLEM.
YES, OKAY.
SSSIIIGGHHHH
DING-A-LING

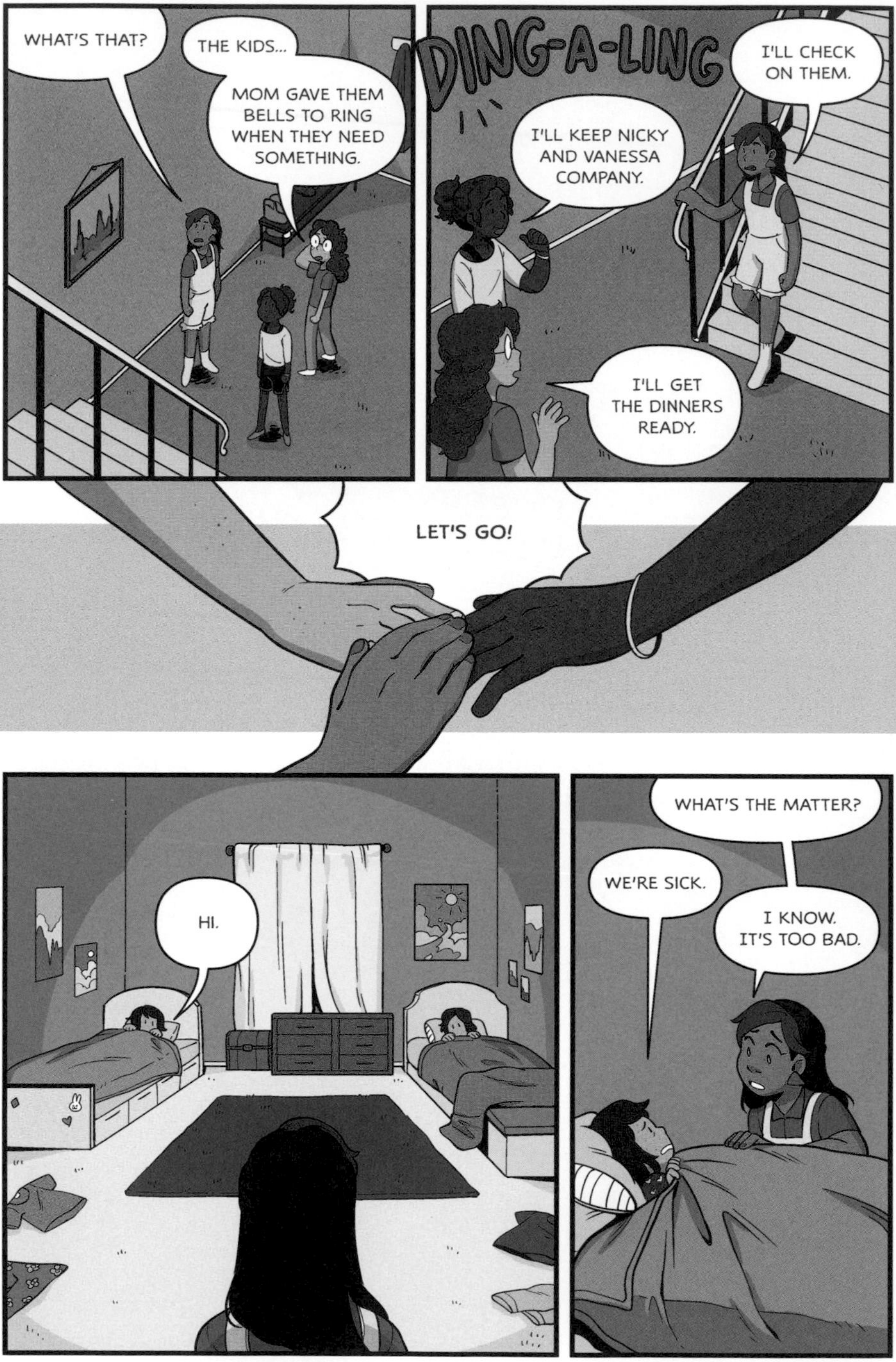
WHAT'S THAT?
THE KIDS...
MOM GAVE THEM BELLS TO RING WHEN THEY NEED SOMETHING.
DING-A-LING
I'LL CHECK ON THEM.
I'LL KEEP NICKY AND VANESSA COMPANY.
I'LL GET THE DINNERS READY.
LET'S GO!
HI.
WHAT'S THE MATTER?
WE'RE SICK.
I KNOW. IT'S TOO BAD.

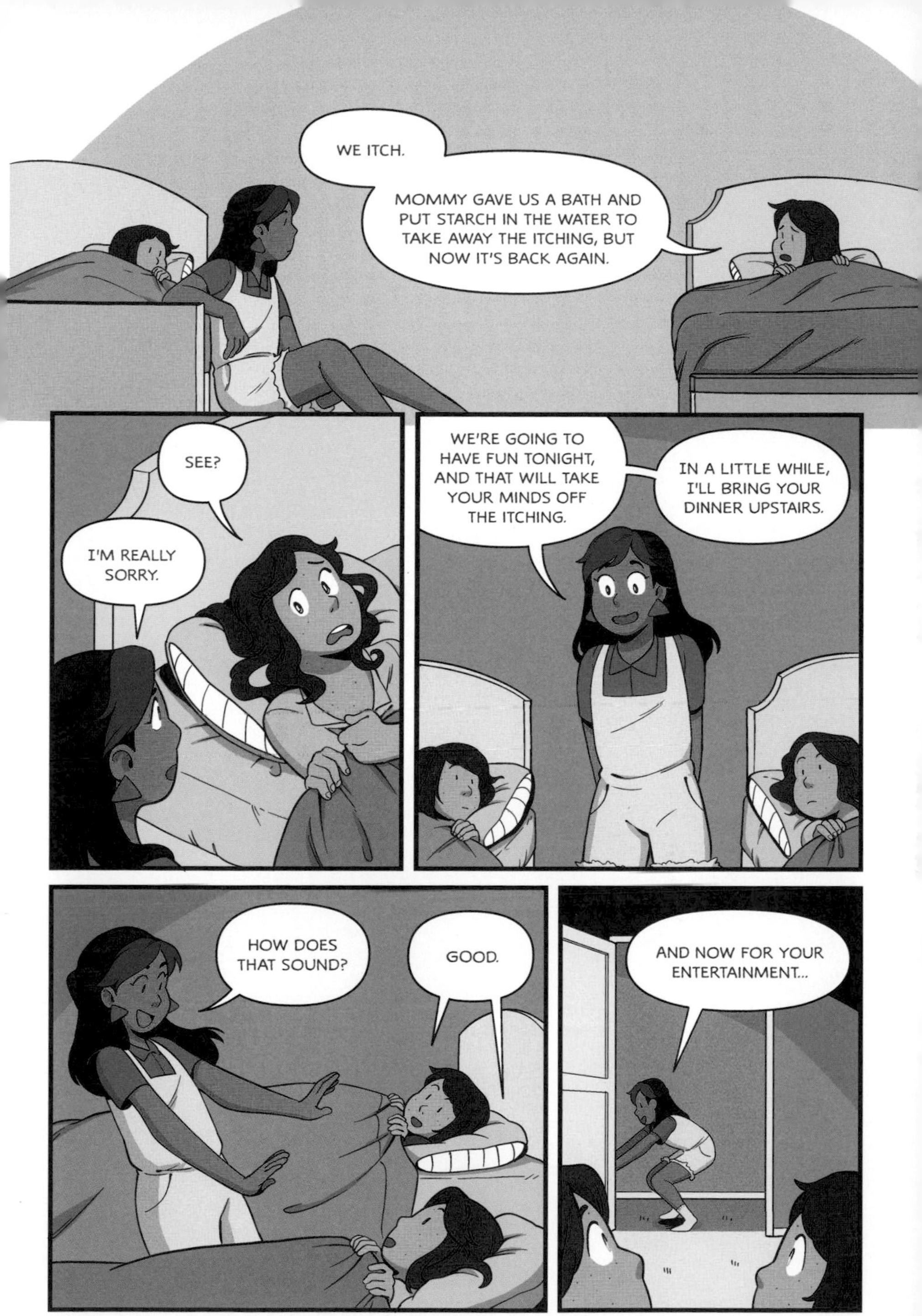
WE ITCH.
MOMMY GAVE US A BATH AND PUT STARCH IN THE WATER TO TAKE AWAY THE ITCHING, BUT NOW IT'S BACK AGAIN.
SEE?
I'M REALLY SORRY.
WE'RE GOING TO HAVE FUN TONIGHT, AND THAT WILL TAKE YOUR MINDS OFF THE ITCHING.
IN A LITTLE WHILE, I'LL BRING YOUR DINNER UPSTAIRS.
HOW DOES THAT SOUND?
GOOD.
AND NOW FOR YOUR ENTERTAINMENT...

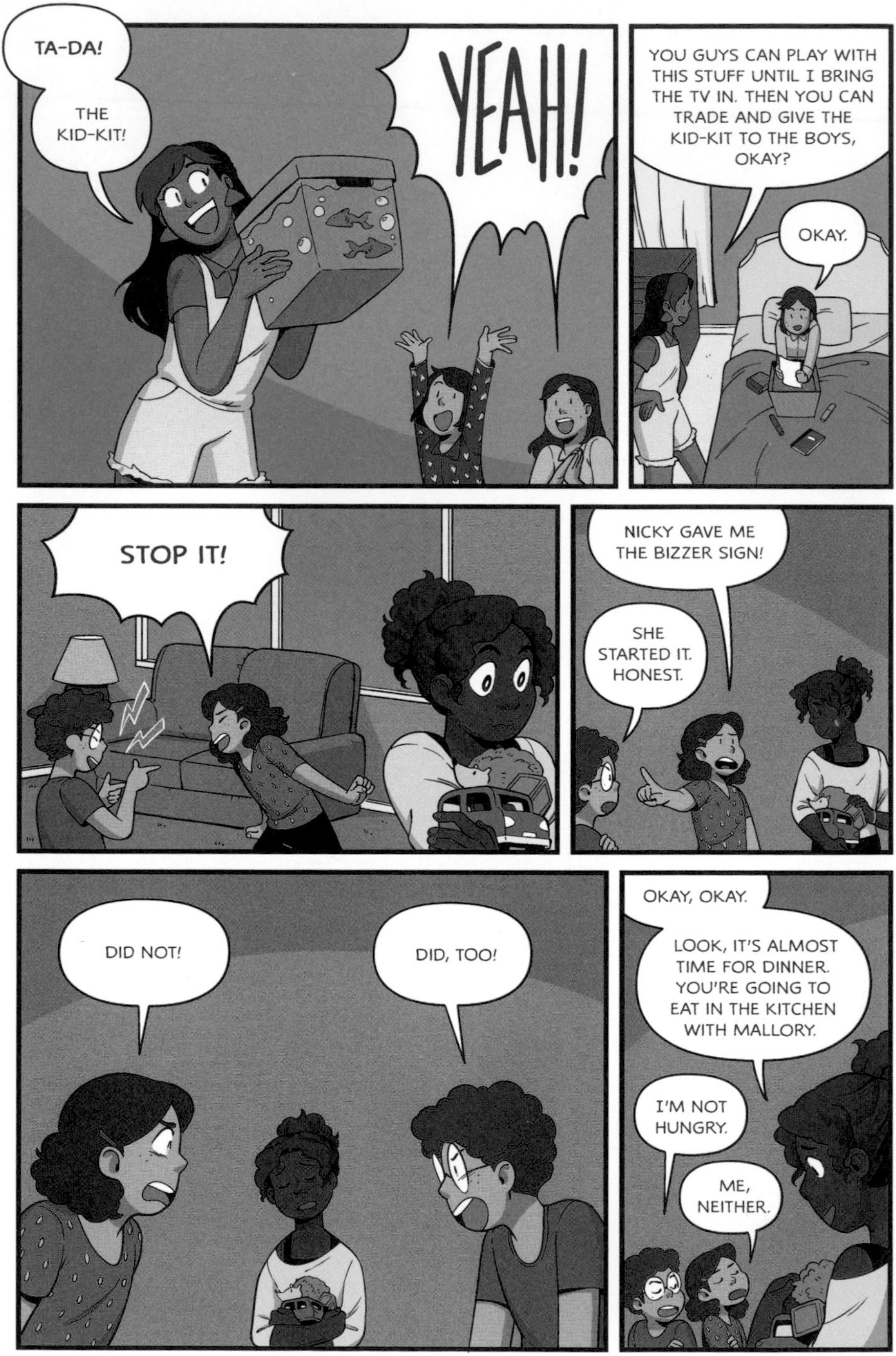
TA-DA!
THE KID-KIT!
YEAH!
YOU GUYS CAN PLAY WITH THIS STUFF UNTIL I BRING THE TV IN. THEN YOU CAN TRADE AND GIVE THE KID-KIT TO THE BOYS, OKAY?
OKAY.
STOP IT!
NICKY GAVE ME THE BIZZER SIGN!
SHE STARTED IT. HONEST.
DID NOT!
DID, TOO!
OKAY, OKAY.
LOOK, IT'S ALMOST TIME FOR DINNER. YOU'RE GOING TO EAT IN THE KITCHEN WITH MALLORY.
I'M NOT HUNGRY.
ME, NEITHER.

NOT EVEN FOR...

CREAM CHEESE AND JELLY SANDWICHES?

WELL, MAYBE...

TINKLE TINKLE

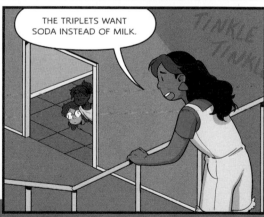

THE TRIPLETS WANT SODA INSTEAD OF MILK.

TINKLE TINKLE

DING-A-LING

I THINK THAT'S THE GIRLS. CAN YOU CHECK ON THEM?

SURE.

DING-A-LING

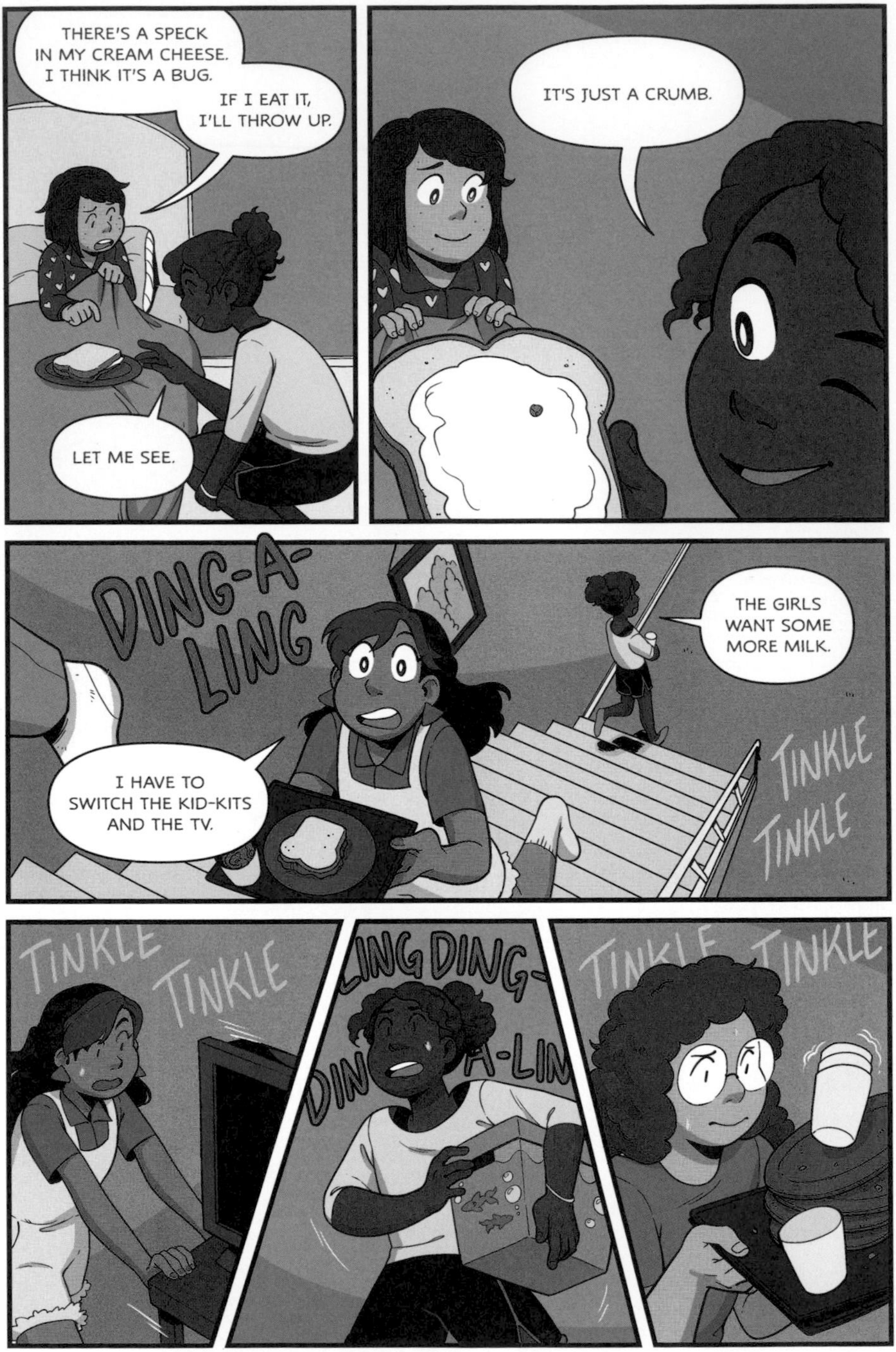
THERE'S A SPECK IN MY CREAM CHEESE. I THINK IT'S A BUG.
IF I EAT IT, I'LL THROW UP.
LET ME SEE.
IT'S JUST A CRUMB.
DING-A-LING
THE GIRLS WANT SOME MORE MILK.
I HAVE TO SWITCH THE KID-KITS AND THE TV.
TINKLE TINKLE
TINKLE TINKLE
DING-A-LING
TINKLE TINKLE

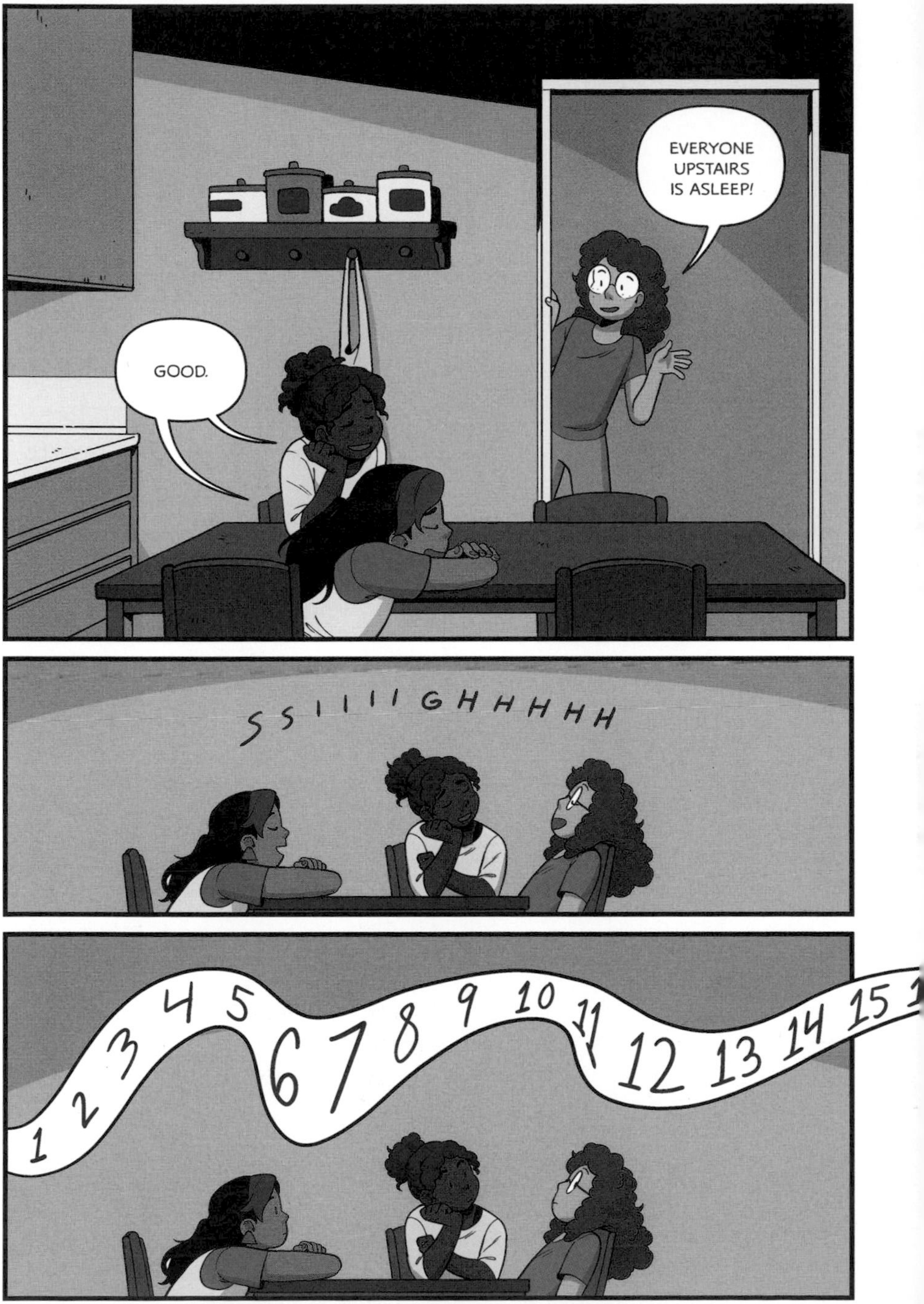
EVERYONE UPSTAIRS IS ASLEEP!
GOOD.
SSIIIIGHHHHH
1 2 3 4 5 6 7 8 9 10 11 12 13 14 15

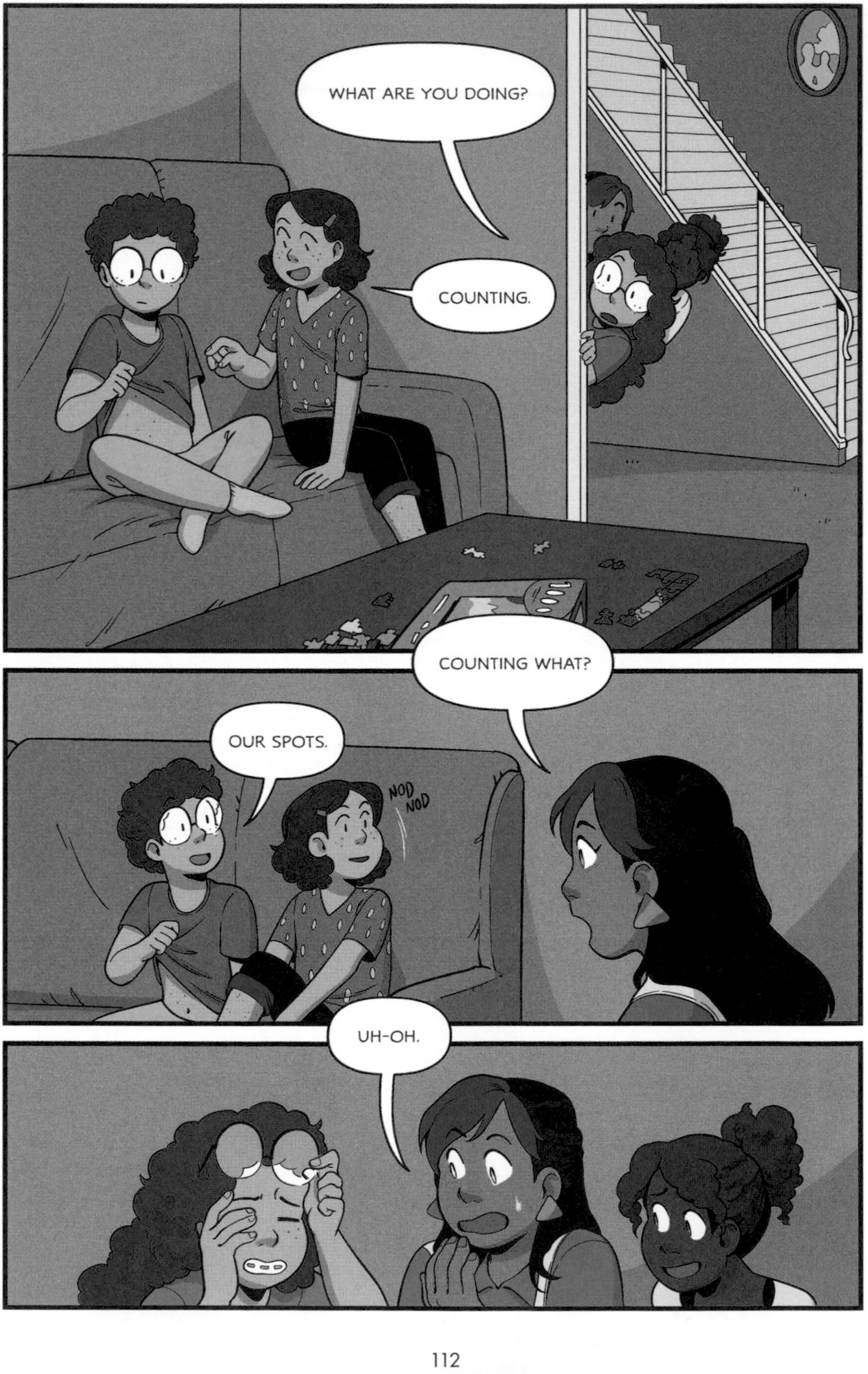
WHAT ARE YOU DOING?
COUNTING.
COUNTING WHAT?
OUR SPOTS.
NOD NOD
UH-OH.

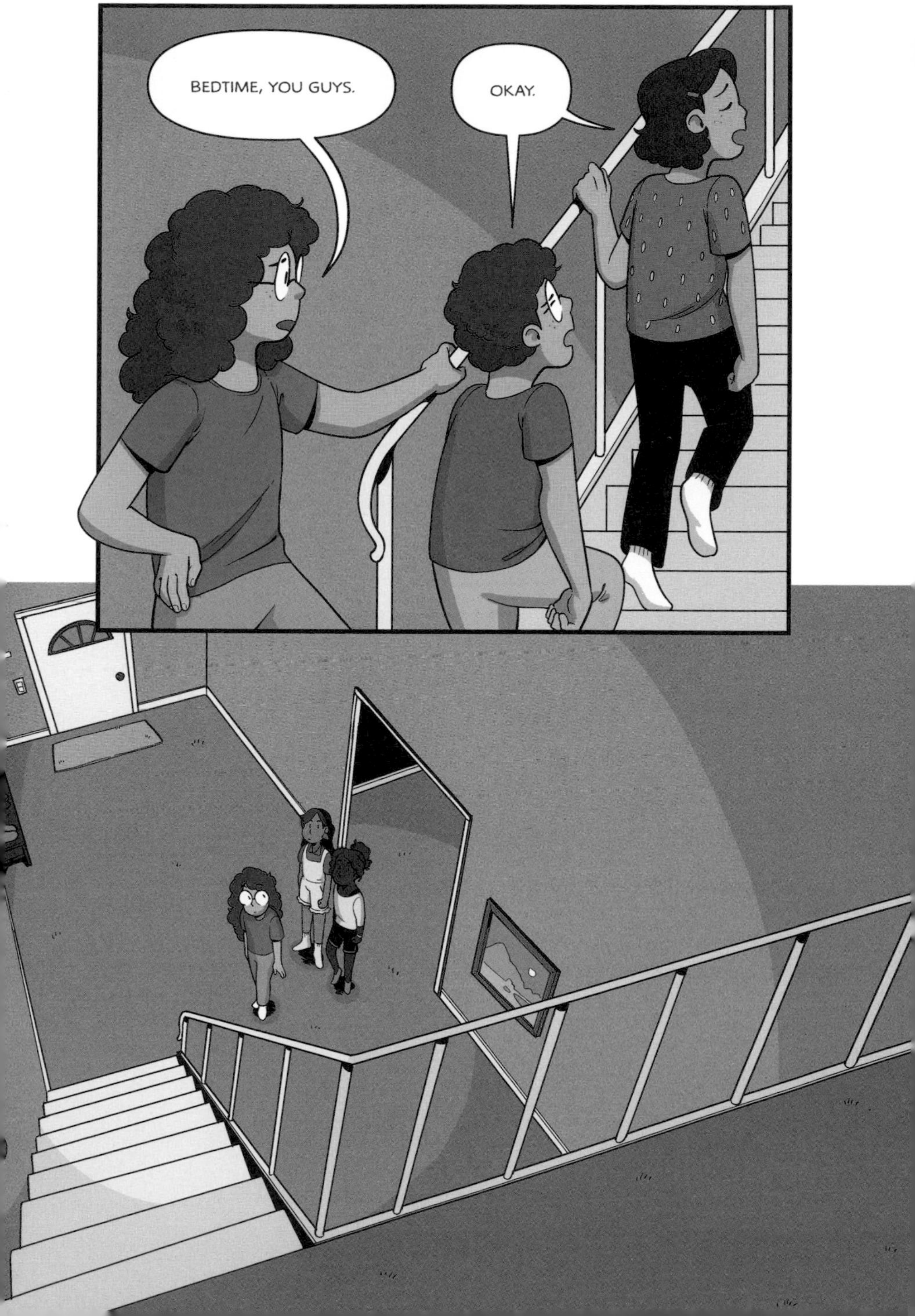
BEDTIME, YOU GUYS.
OKAY.

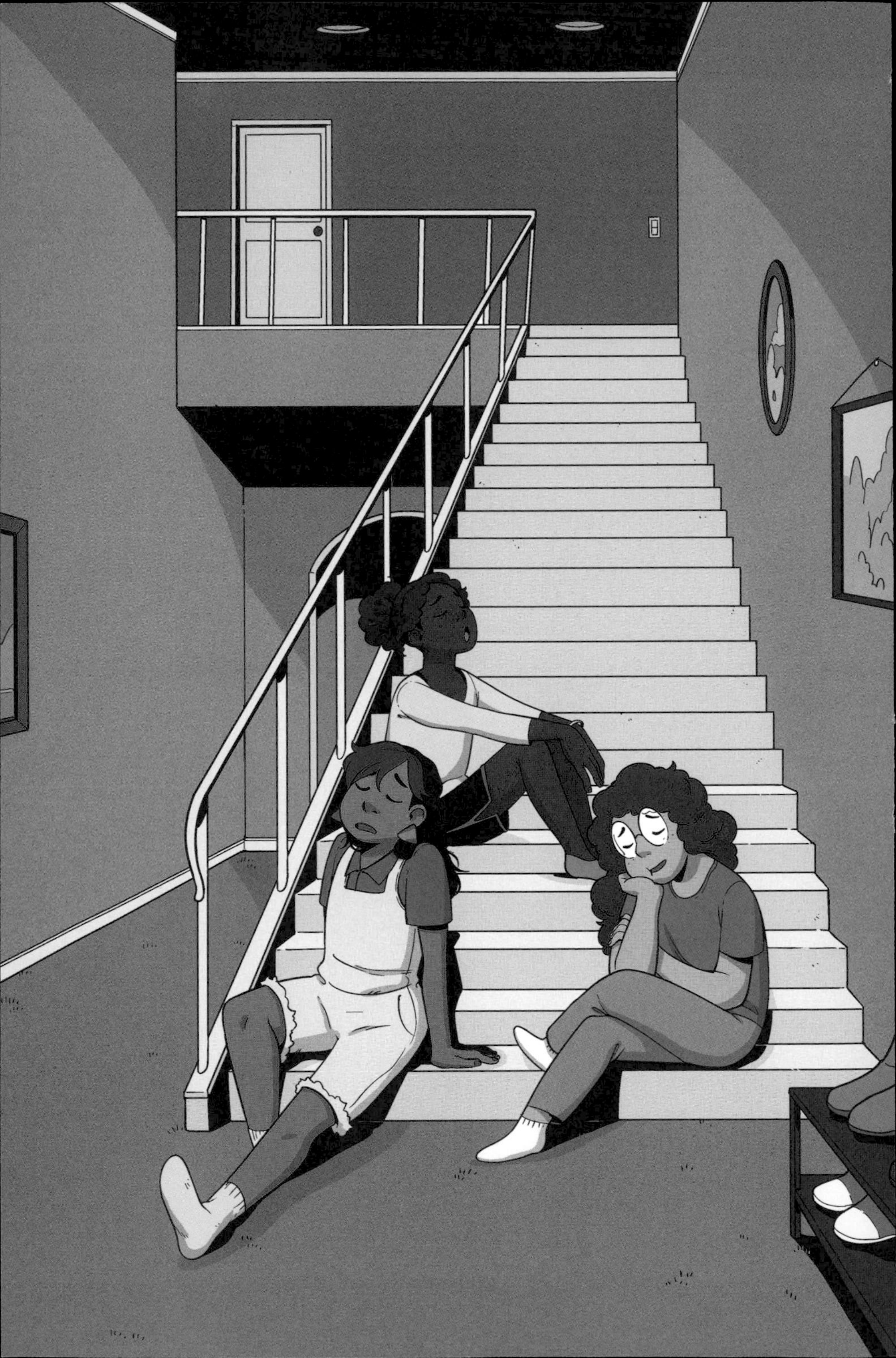

CHAPTER 11

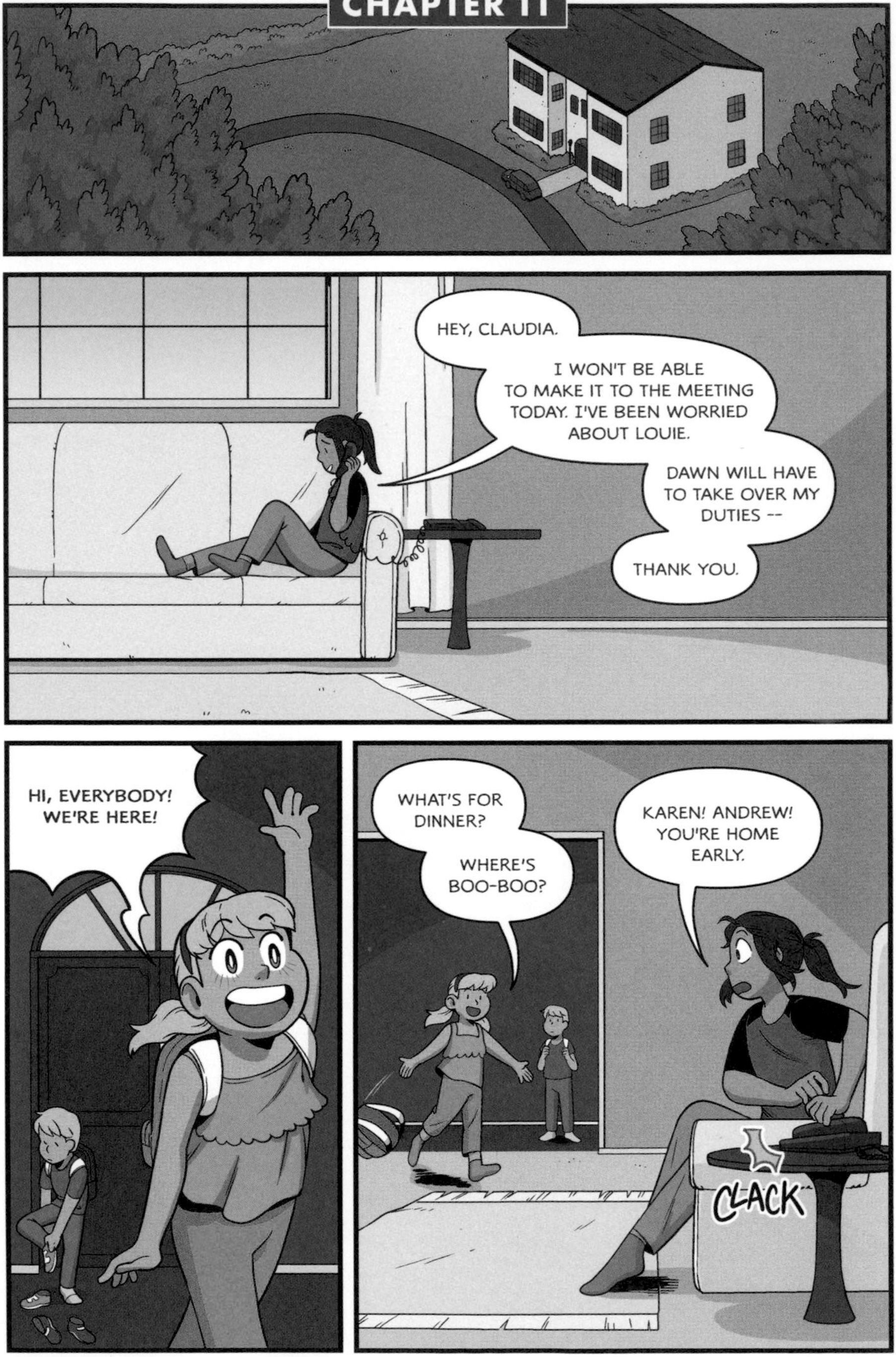
HEY, CLAUDIA.
I WON'T BE ABLE TO MAKE IT TO THE MEETING TODAY. I'VE BEEN WORRIED ABOUT LOUIE.
DAWN WILL HAVE TO TAKE OVER MY DUTIES --
THANK YOU.
HI, EVERYBODY! WE'RE HERE!
WHAT'S FOR DINNER?
WHERE'S BOO-BOO?
KAREN! ANDREW! YOU'RE HOME EARLY.
CLACK

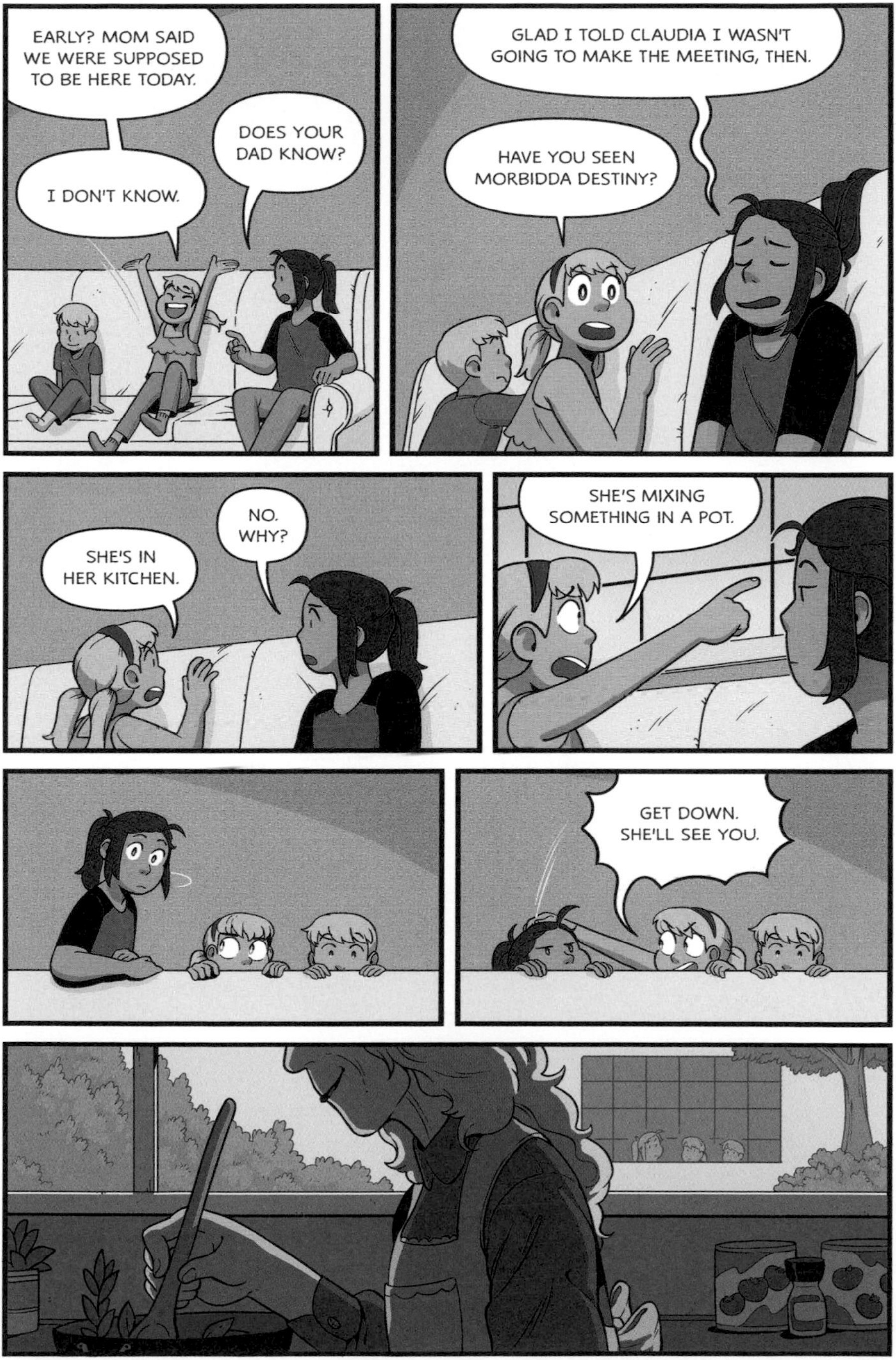
EARLY? MOM SAID WE WERE SUPPOSED TO BE HERE TODAY.
I DON'T KNOW.
DOES YOUR DAD KNOW?
GLAD I TOLD CLAUDIA I WASN'T GOING TO MAKE THE MEETING, THEN.
HAVE YOU SEEN MORBIDDA DESTINY?
SHE'S IN HER KITCHEN.
NO. WHY?
SHE'S MIXING SOMETHING IN A POT.
GET DOWN. SHE'LL SEE YOU.

I THINK SHE'S MIXING A WICKED WITCH'S BREW!

SHE'S STIRRING UP A BREW THAT'S GOING TO GROW FUR ALL OVER ANDREW OR --

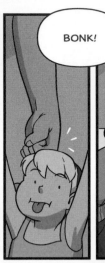

BONK!

YOU KNOW SHE CAN'T DO STUFF LIKE THAT. SHE'S PROBABLY MAKING SOUP.

KRISTY?

OH, ANDREW...

WHERE'S BOO-BOO?

YOU'RE NOT GOING TO GROW FUR. DON'T GIVE IT A SECOND THOUGHT.

EEEE! HE'S GROWING FANGS!

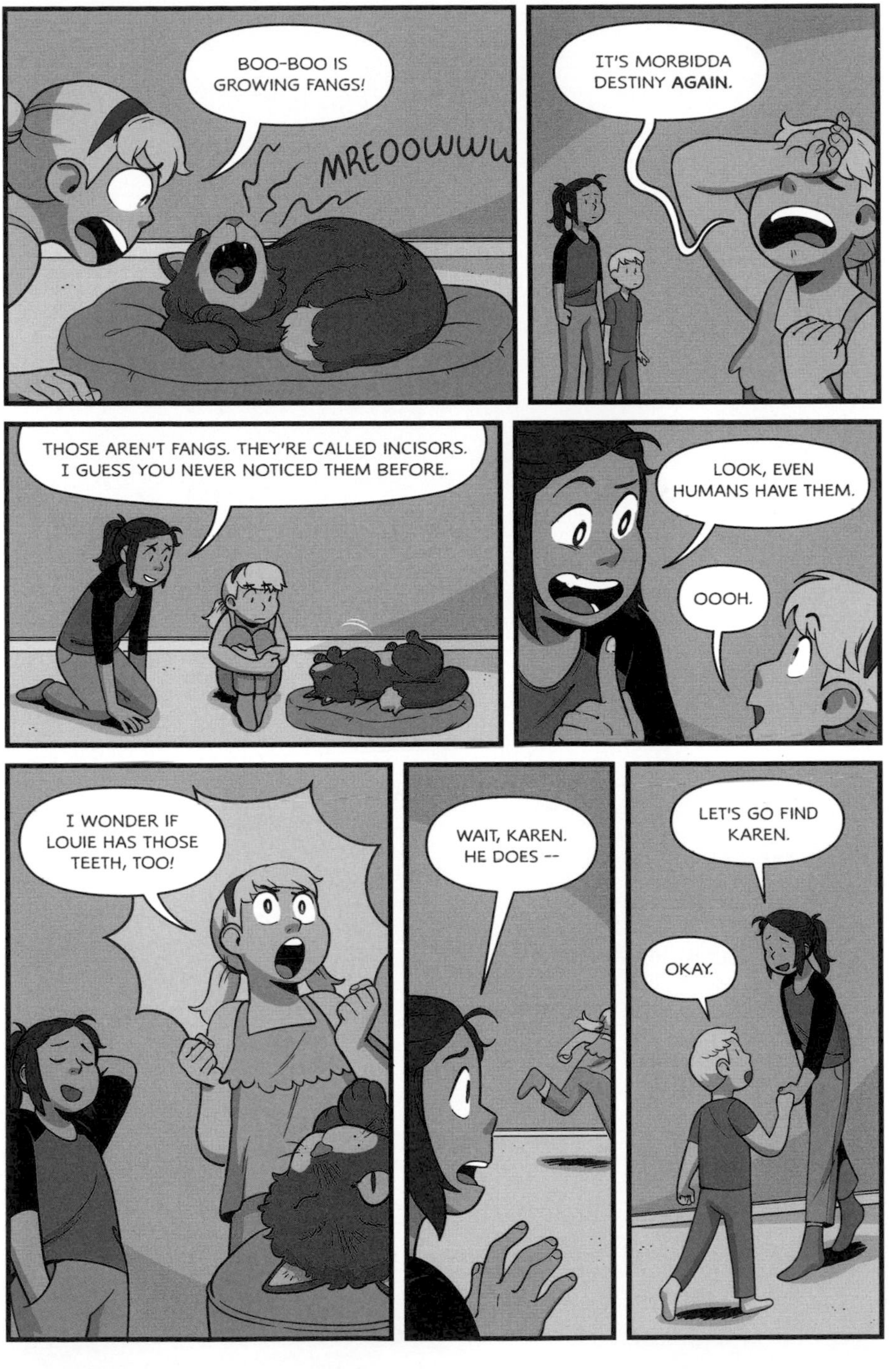

BOO-BOO IS GROWING FANGS!
MREOOWWW
IT'S MORBIDDA DESTINY **AGAIN.**
THOSE AREN'T FANGS. THEY'RE CALLED INCISORS. I GUESS YOU NEVER NOTICED THEM BEFORE.
LOOK, EVEN HUMANS HAVE THEM.
OOOH.
I WONDER IF LOUIE HAS THOSE TEETH, TOO!
WAIT, KAREN. HE DOES --
LET'S GO FIND KAREN.
OKAY.

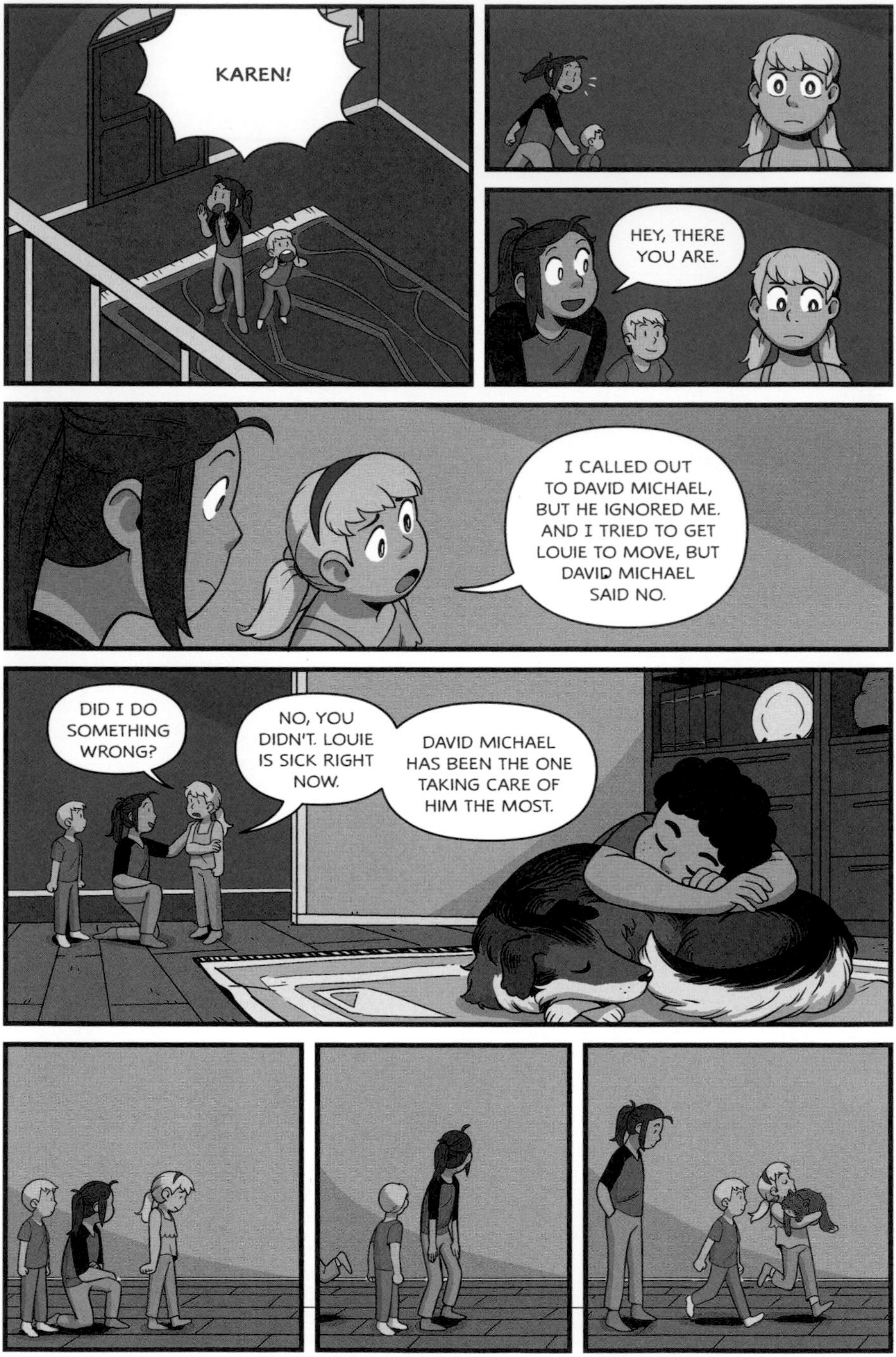
KAREN!
HEY, THERE YOU ARE.
I CALLED OUT TO DAVID MICHAEL, BUT HE IGNORED ME. AND I TRIED TO GET LOUIE TO MOVE, BUT DAVID MICHAEL SAID NO.
DID I DO SOMETHING WRONG?
NO, YOU DIDN'T. LOUIE IS SICK RIGHT NOW.
DAVID MICHAEL HAS BEEN THE ONE TAKING CARE OF HIM THE MOST.

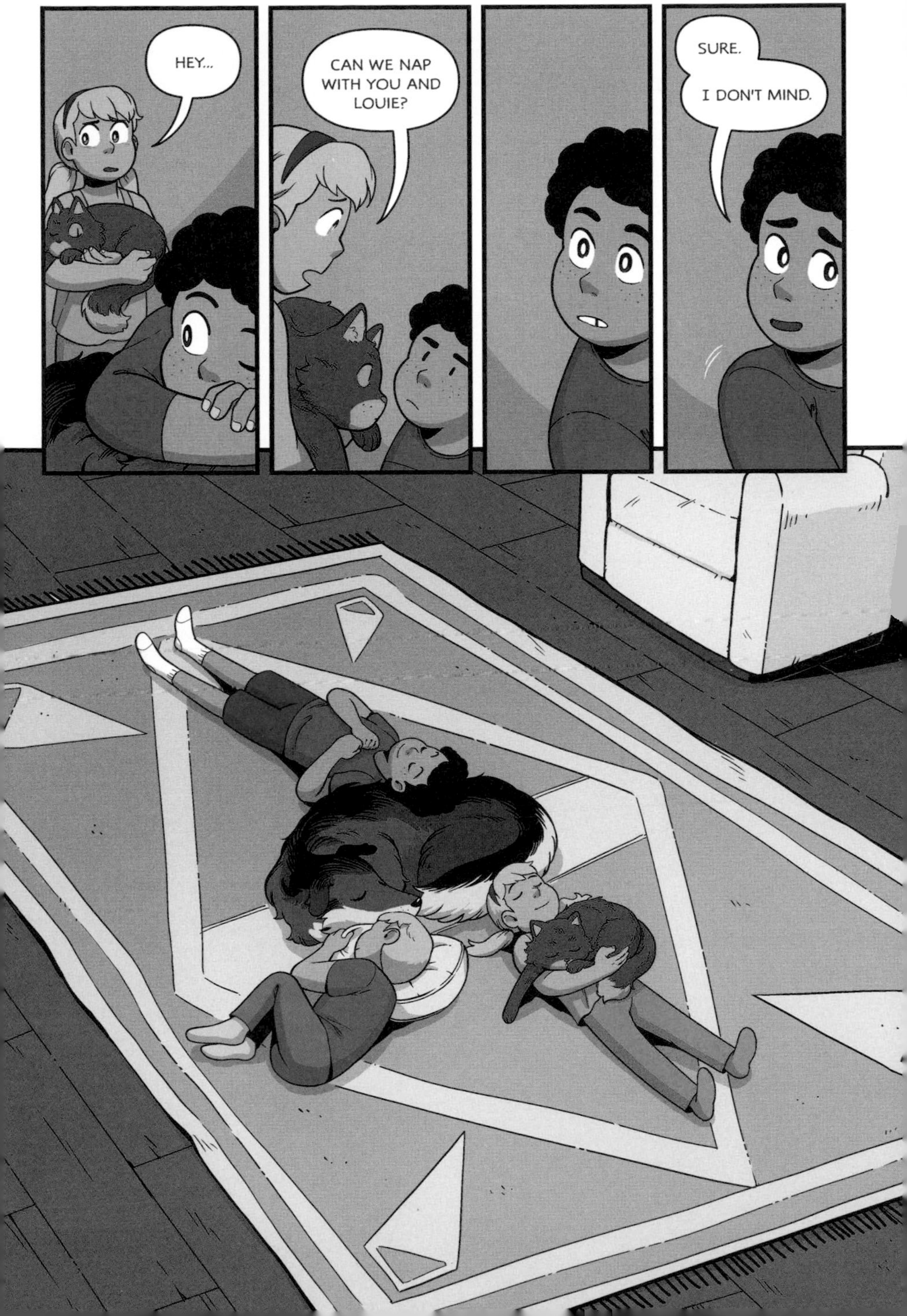
HEY...
CAN WE NAP WITH YOU AND LOUIE?
SURE.
I DON'T MIND.

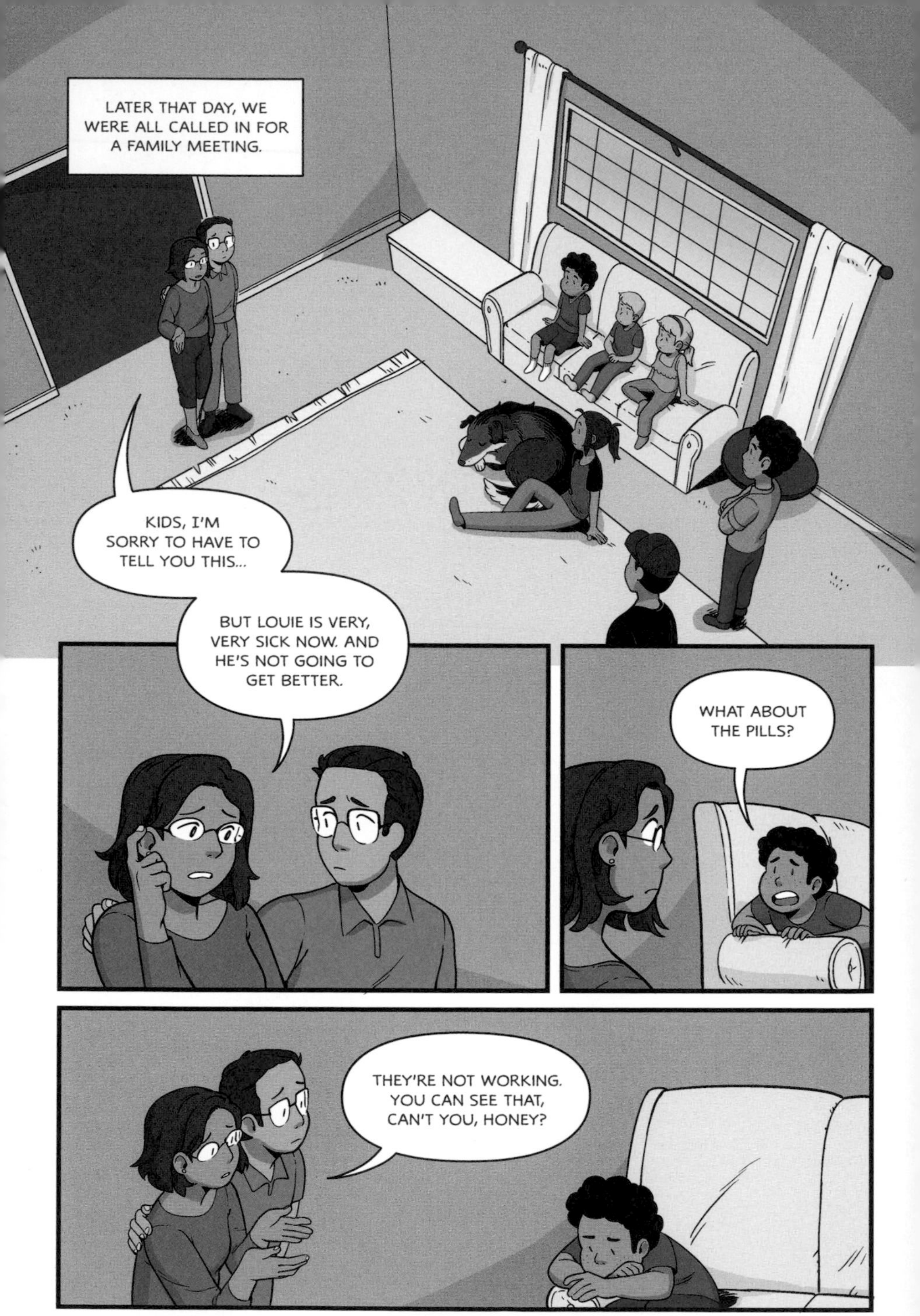

LATER THAT DAY, WE WERE ALL CALLED IN FOR A FAMILY MEETING.
KIDS, I'M SORRY TO HAVE TO TELL YOU THIS...
BUT LOUIE IS VERY, VERY SICK NOW. AND HE'S NOT GOING TO GET BETTER.
WHAT ABOUT THE PILLS?
THEY'RE NOT WORKING. YOU CAN SEE THAT, CAN'T YOU, HONEY?

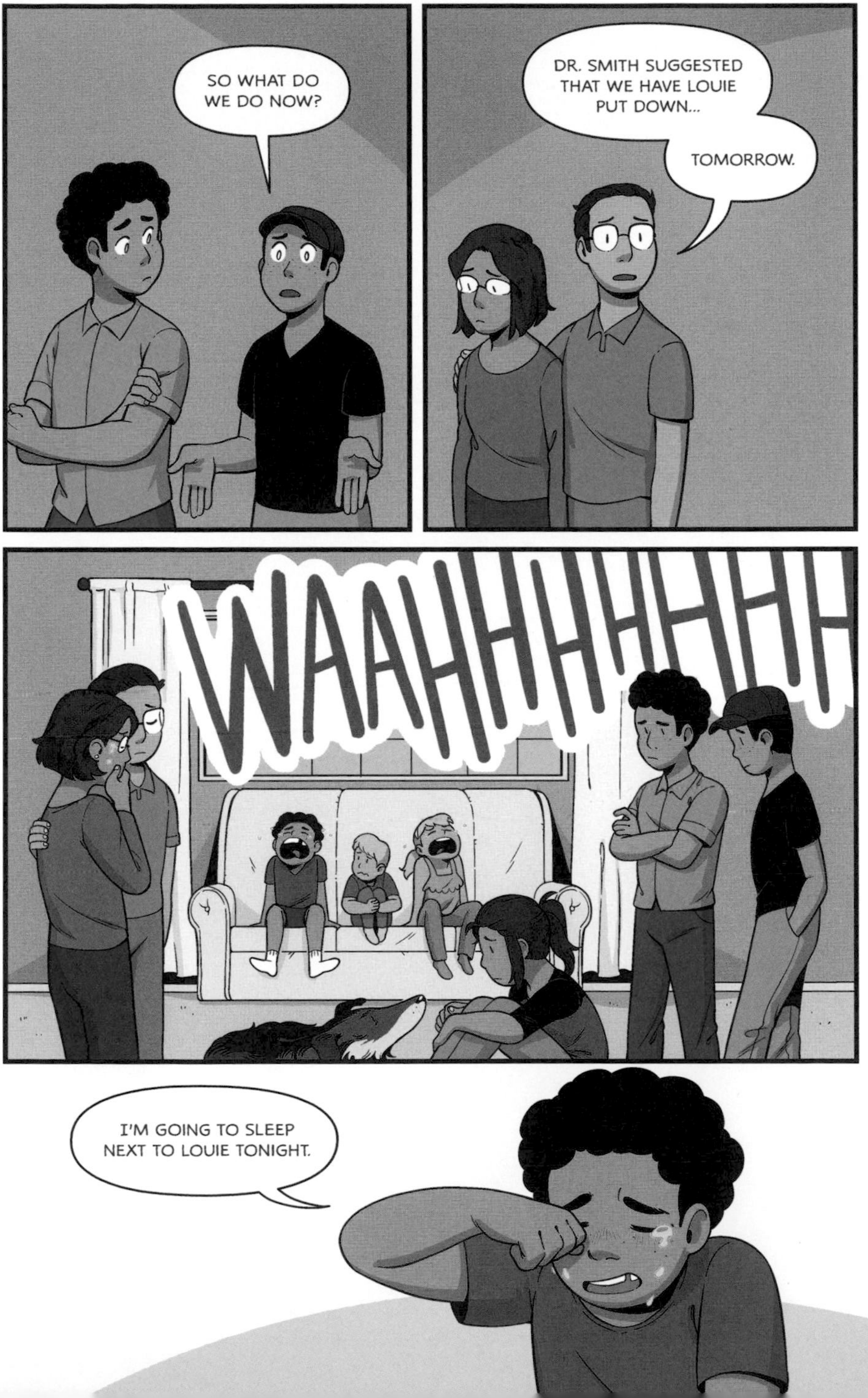
SO WHAT DO WE DO NOW?
DR. SMITH SUGGESTED THAT WE HAVE LOUIE PUT DOWN...
TOMORROW.
WAAHHHHHHHH
I'M GOING TO SLEEP NEXT TO LOUIE TONIGHT.

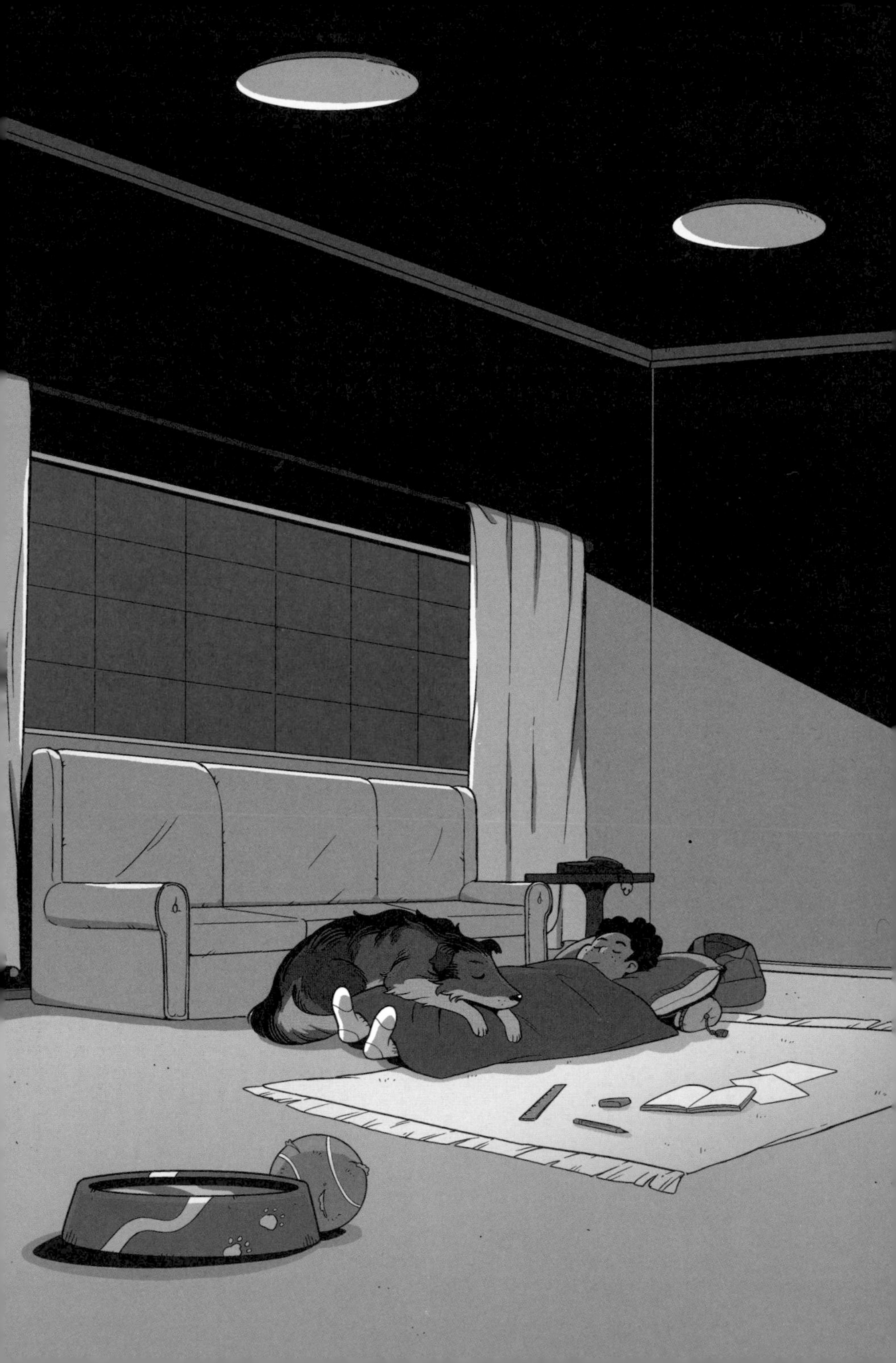

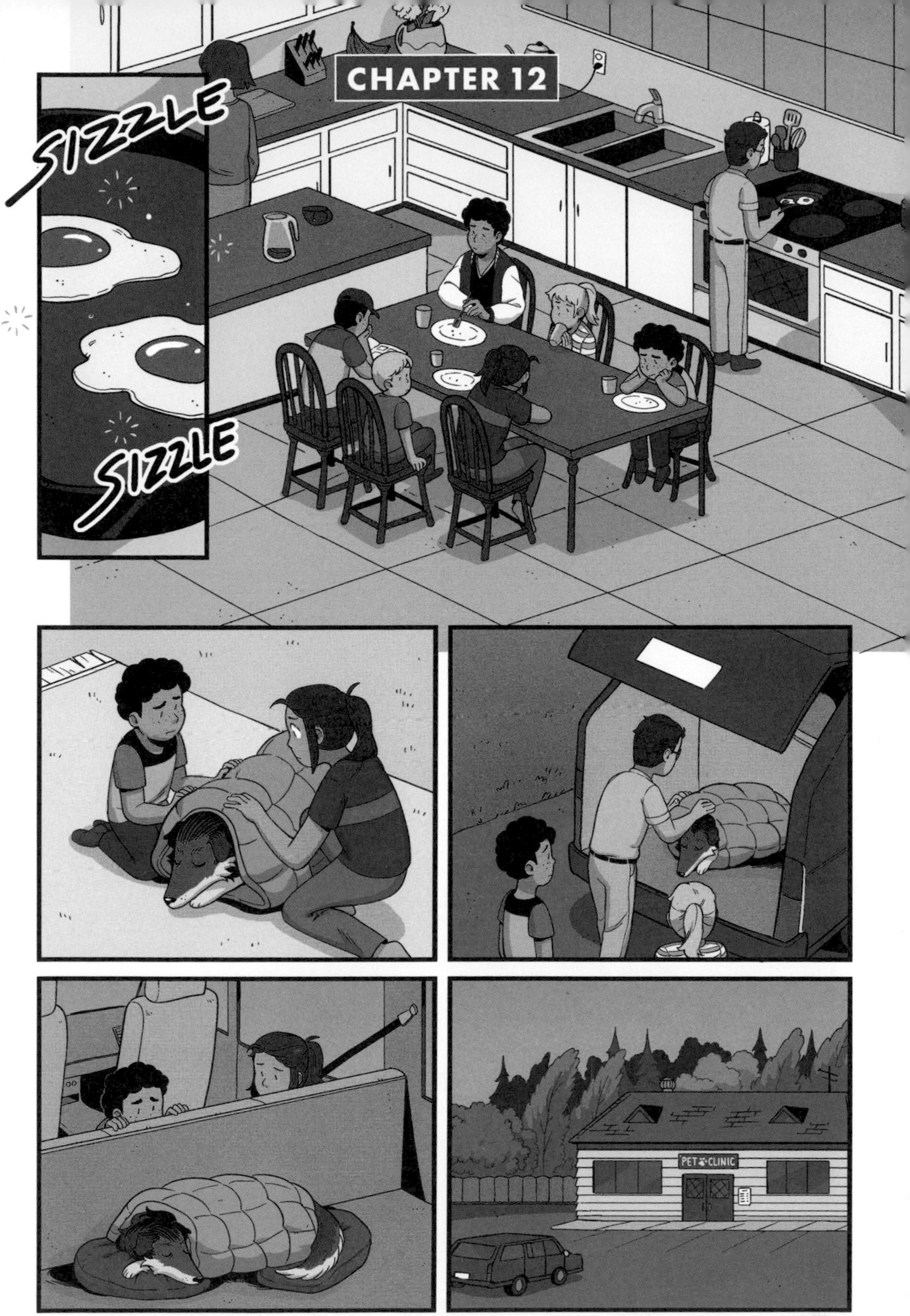
CHAPTER 12
SIZZLE
SIZZLE
PET CLINIC

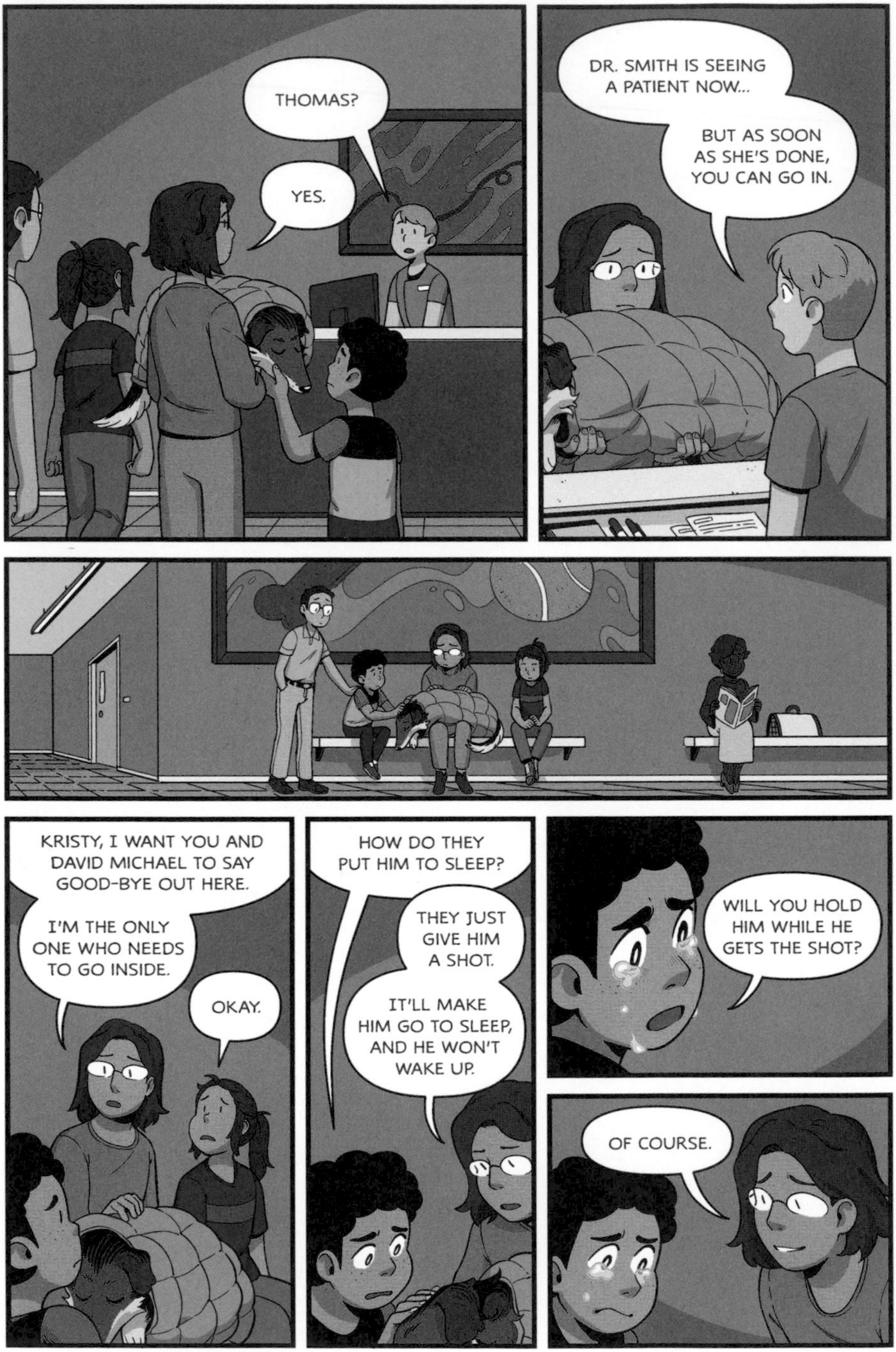
THOMAS?
YES.
DR. SMITH IS SEEING A PATIENT NOW...
BUT AS SOON AS SHE'S DONE, YOU CAN GO IN.
KRISTY, I WANT YOU AND DAVID MICHAEL TO SAY GOOD-BYE OUT HERE.
I'M THE ONLY ONE WHO NEEDS TO GO INSIDE.
OKAY.
HOW DO THEY PUT HIM TO SLEEP?
THEY JUST GIVE HIM A SHOT.
IT'LL MAKE HIM GO TO SLEEP, AND HE WON'T WAKE UP.
WILL YOU HOLD HIM WHILE HE GETS THE SHOT?
OF COURSE.

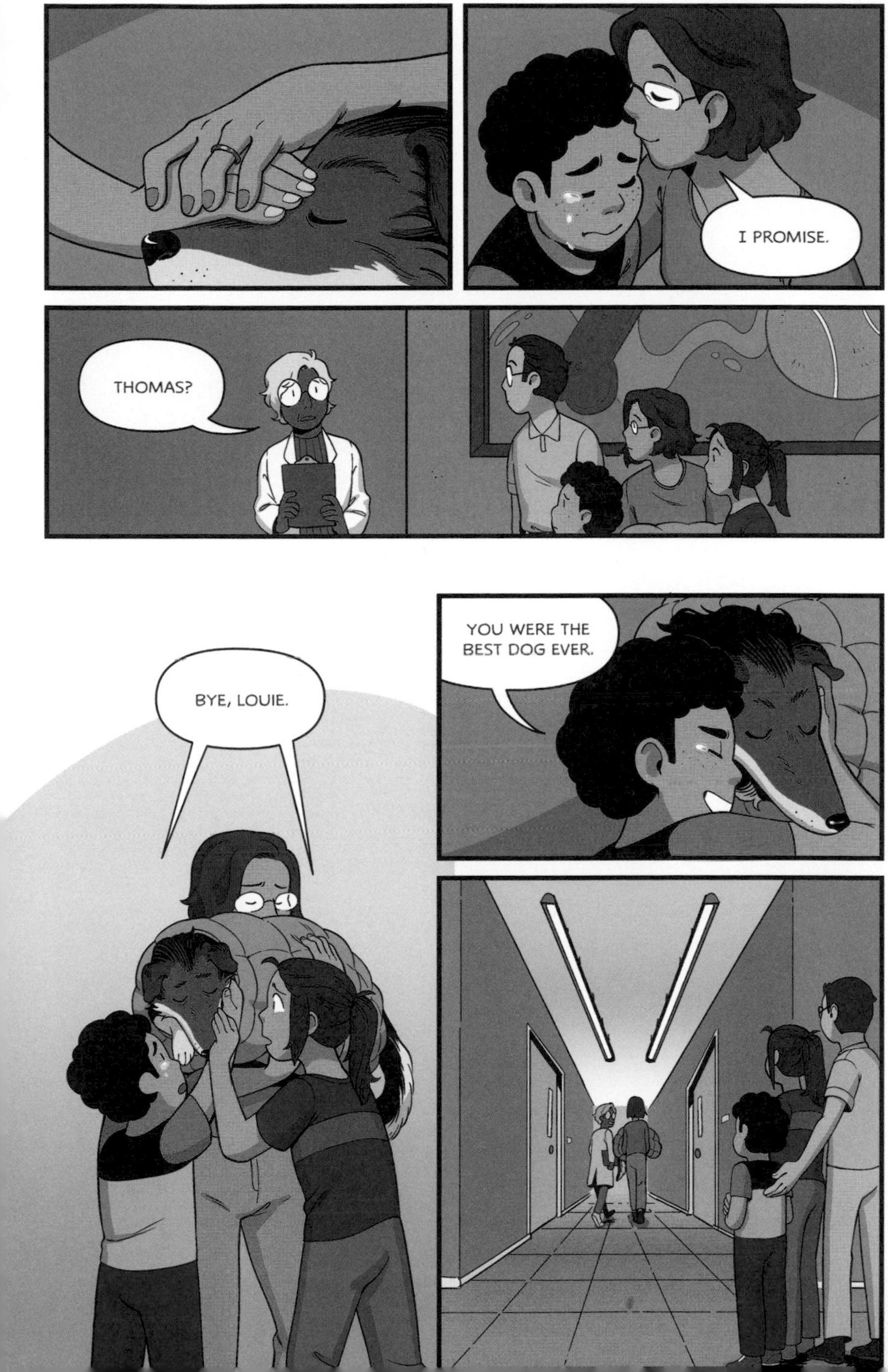
I PROMISE.
THOMAS?
YOU WERE THE BEST DOG EVER.
BYE, LOUIE.

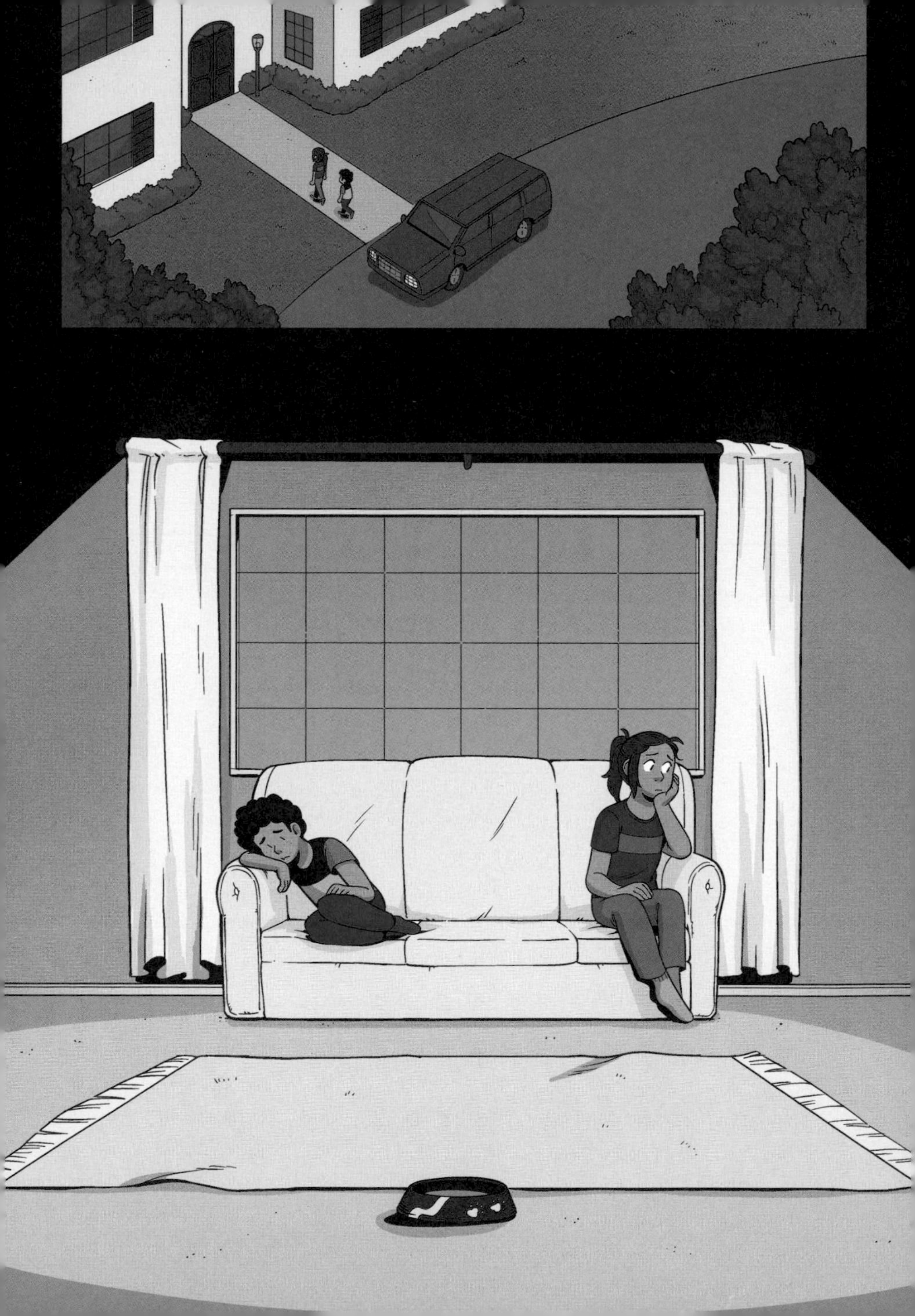

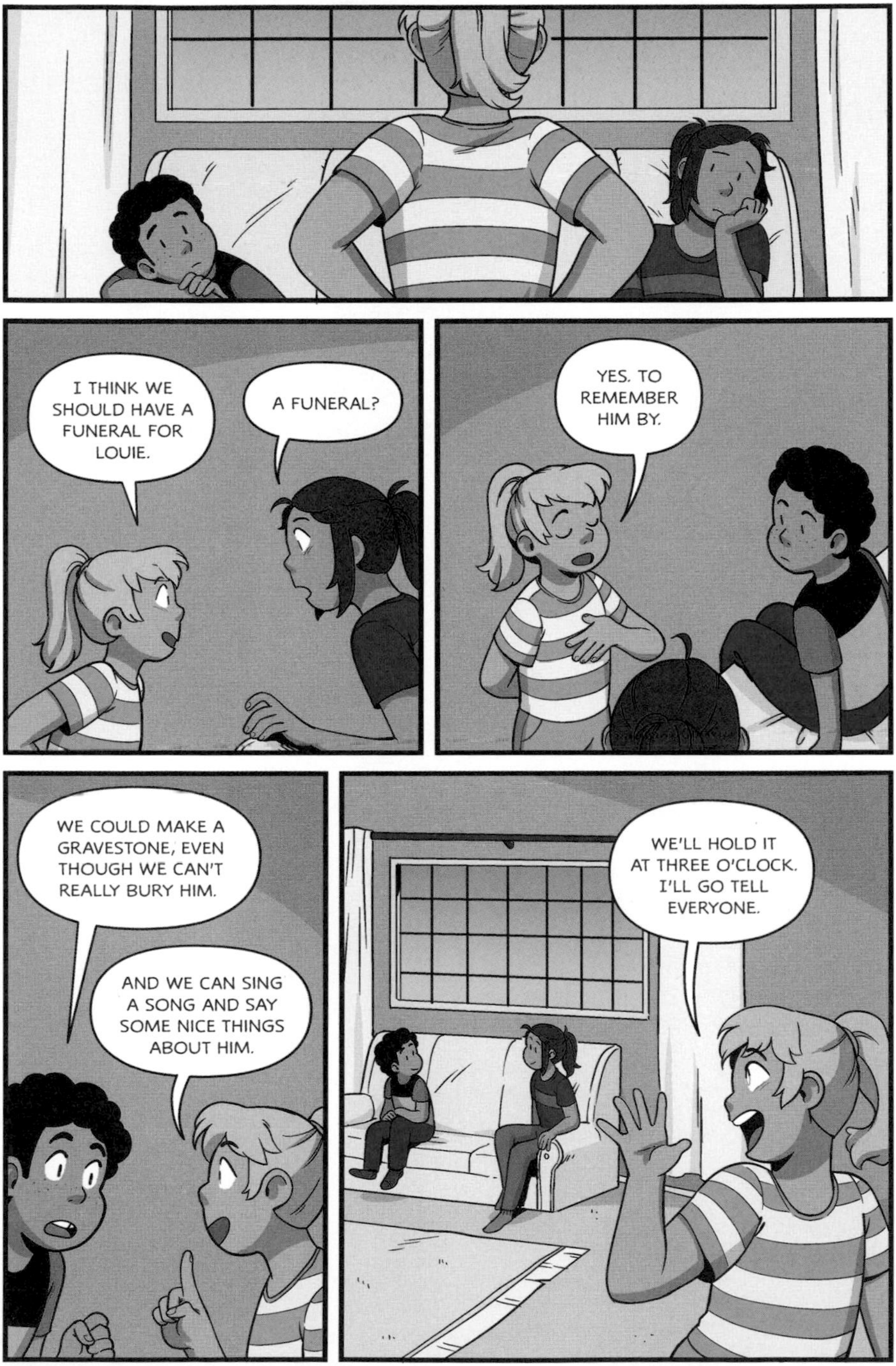
I THINK WE SHOULD HAVE A FUNERAL FOR LOUIE.
A FUNERAL?
YES. TO REMEMBER HIM BY.
WE COULD MAKE A GRAVESTONE, EVEN THOUGH WE CAN'T REALLY BURY HIM.
AND WE CAN SING A SONG AND SAY SOME NICE THINGS ABOUT HIM.
WE'LL HOLD IT AT THREE O'CLOCK. I'LL GO TELL EVERYONE.

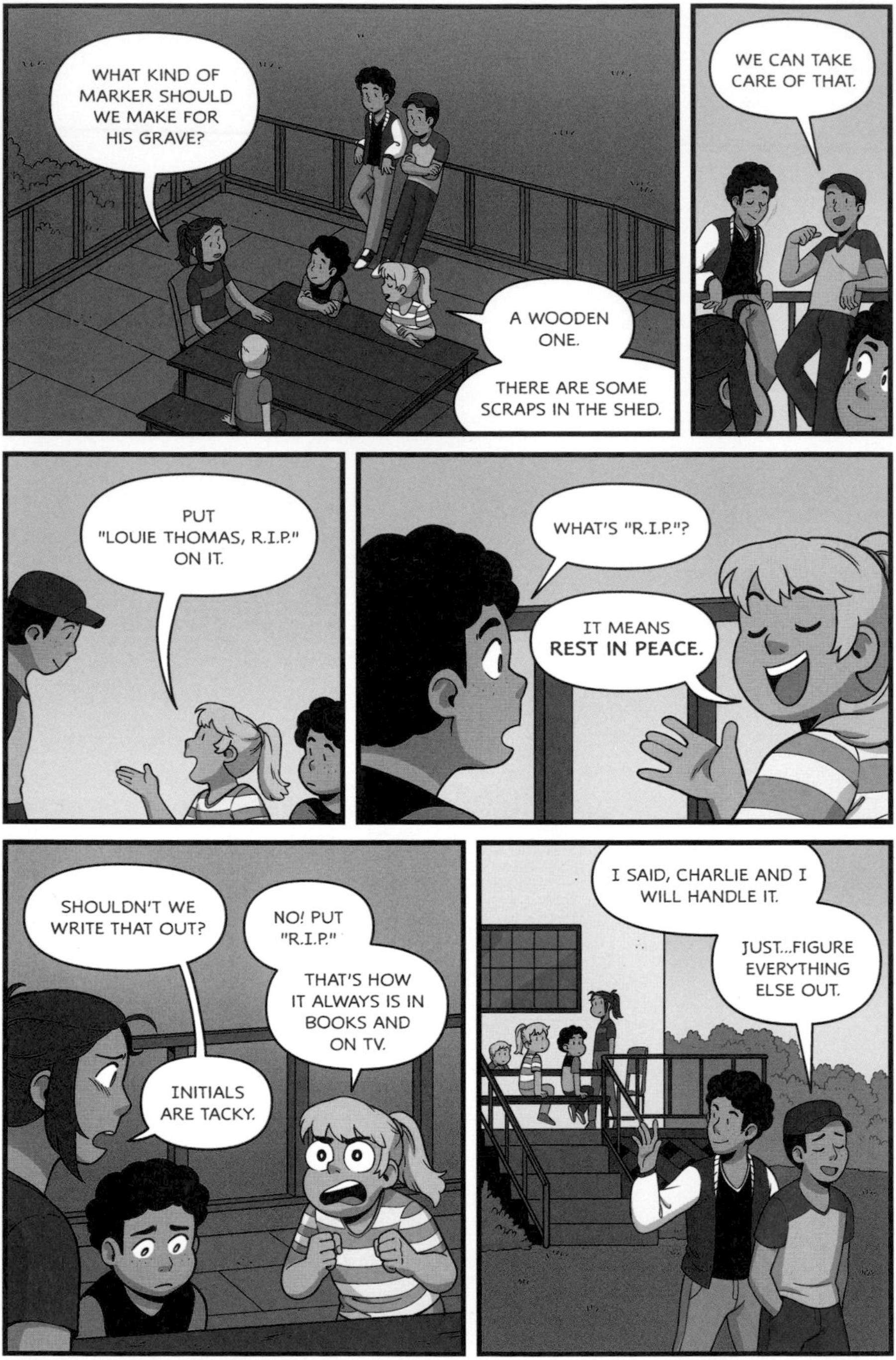
WHAT KIND OF MARKER SHOULD WE MAKE FOR HIS GRAVE?
A WOODEN ONE.
THERE ARE SOME SCRAPS IN THE SHED.
WE CAN TAKE CARE OF THAT.
PUT "LOUIE THOMAS, R.I.P." ON IT.
WHAT'S "R.I.P."?
IT MEANS **REST IN PEACE.**
SHOULDN'T WE WRITE THAT OUT?
INITIALS ARE TACKY.
NO! PUT "R.I.P."
THAT'S HOW IT ALWAYS IS IN BOOKS AND ON TV.
I SAID, CHARLIE AND I WILL HANDLE IT.
JUST...FIGURE EVERYTHING ELSE OUT.

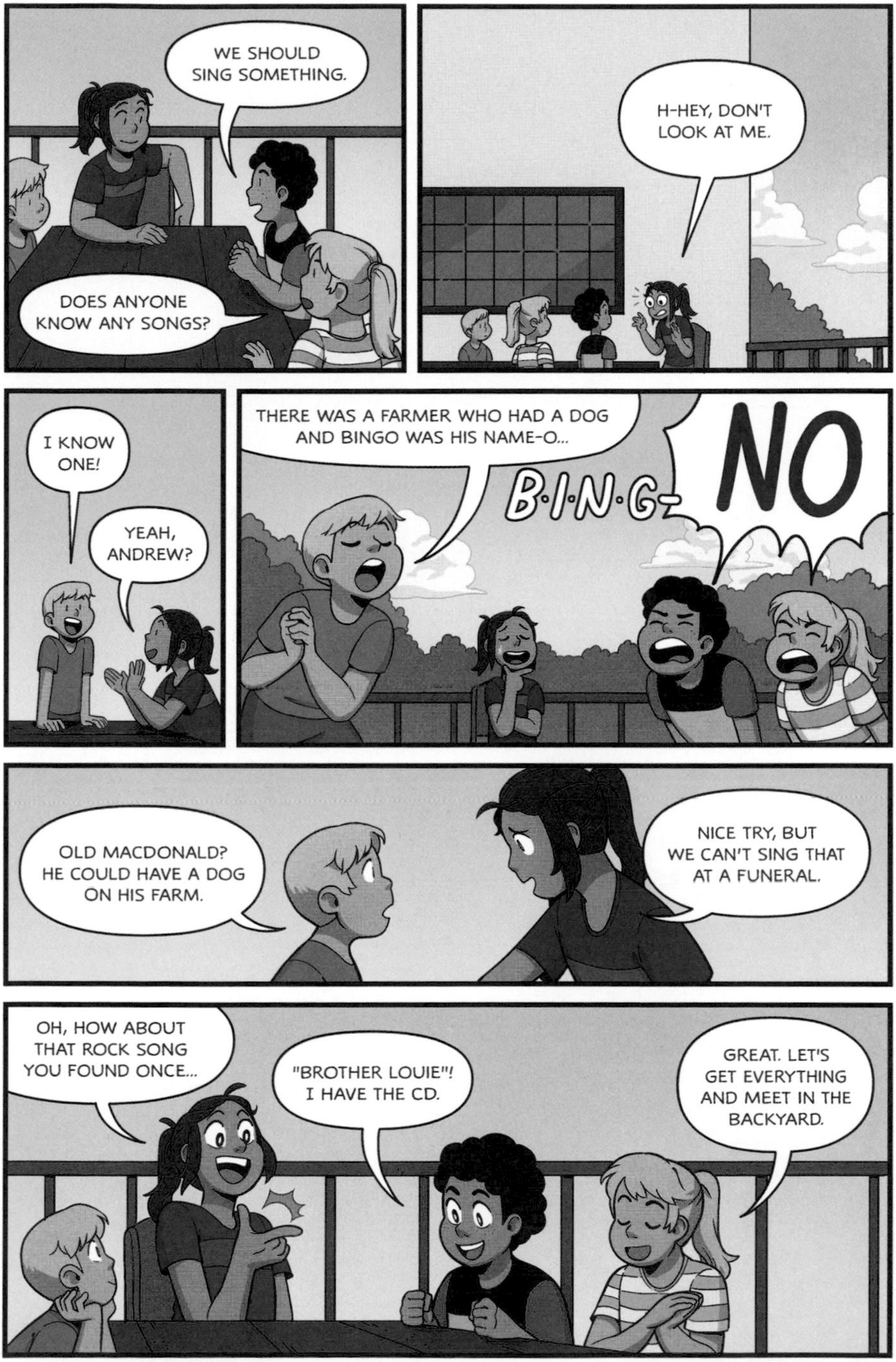
WE SHOULD SING SOMETHING.
DOES ANYONE KNOW ANY SONGS?
H-HEY, DON'T LOOK AT ME.
I KNOW ONE!
YEAH, ANDREW?
THERE WAS A FARMER WHO HAD A DOG AND BINGO WAS HIS NAME-O...
B-I-N-G-
NO
OLD MACDONALD? HE COULD HAVE A DOG ON HIS FARM.
NICE TRY, BUT WE CAN'T SING THAT AT A FUNERAL.
OH, HOW ABOUT THAT ROCK SONG YOU FOUND ONCE...
"BROTHER LOUIE"! I HAVE THE CD.
GREAT. LET'S GET EVERYTHING AND MEET IN THE BACKYARD.

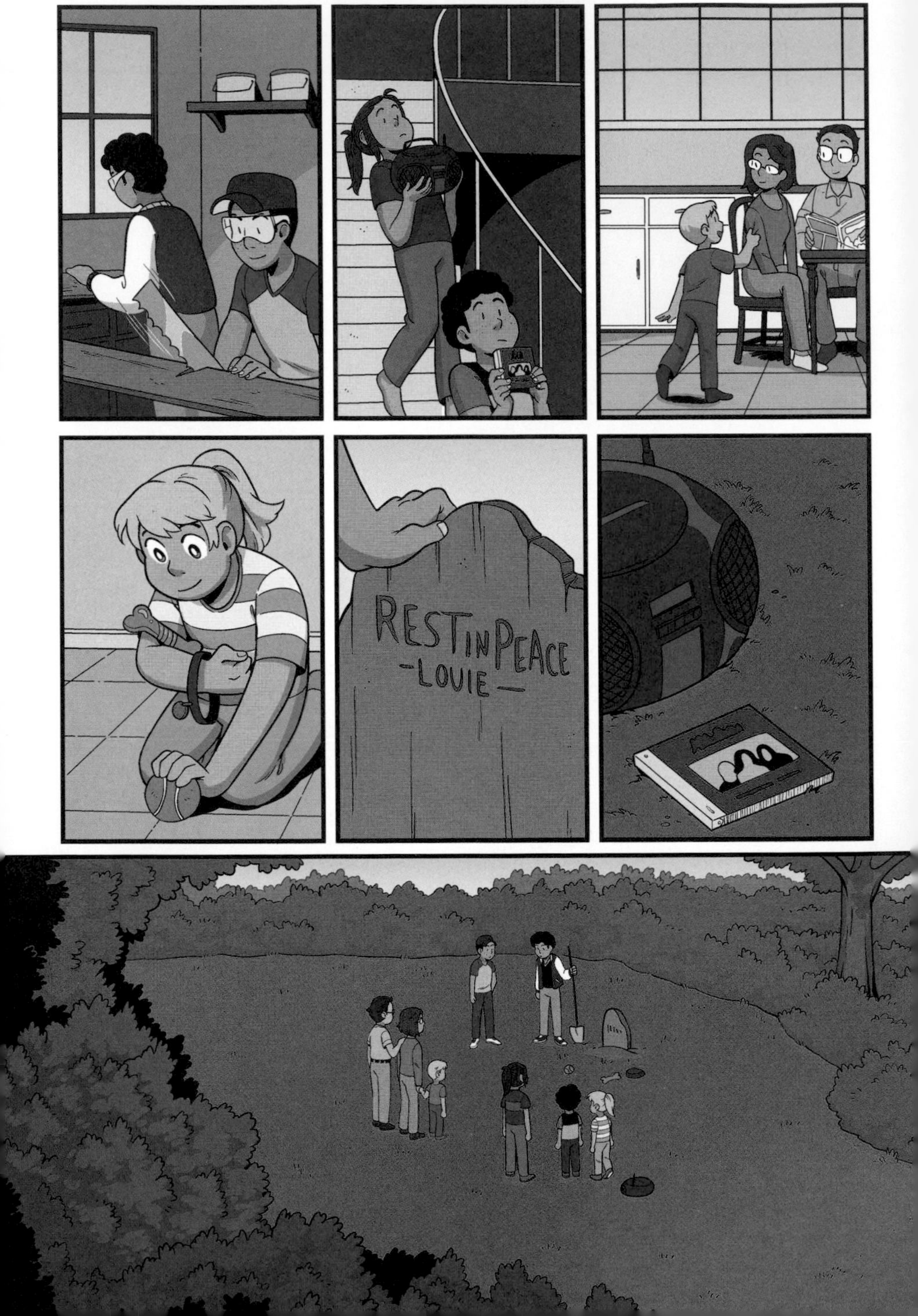
REST IN PEACE
-LOUIE-

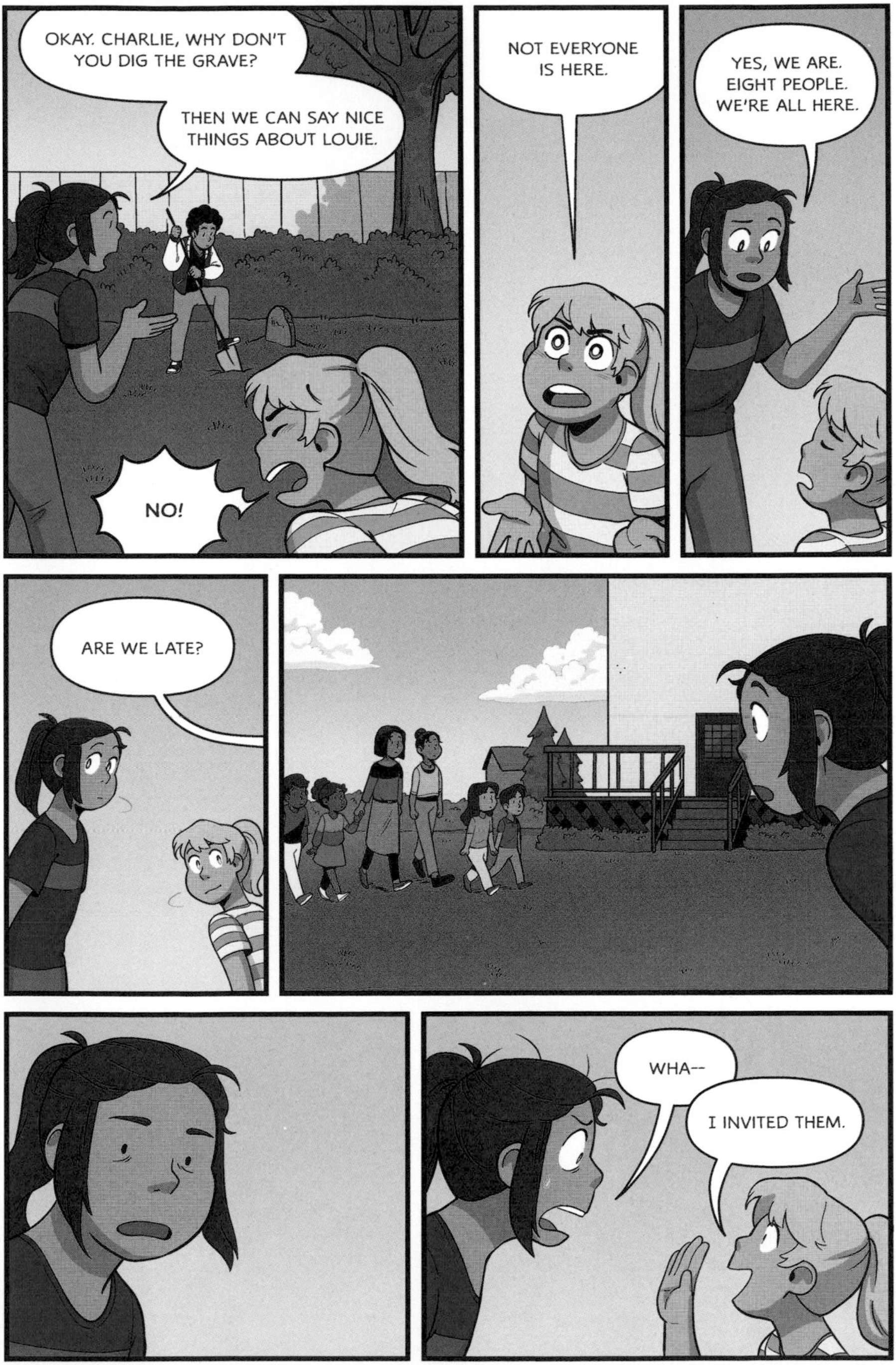

OKAY. CHARLIE, WHY DON'T YOU DIG THE GRAVE?
THEN WE CAN SAY NICE THINGS ABOUT LOUIE.
NO!
NOT EVERYONE IS HERE.
YES, WE ARE. EIGHT PEOPLE. WE'RE ALL HERE.
ARE WE LATE?
WHA--
I INVITED THEM.

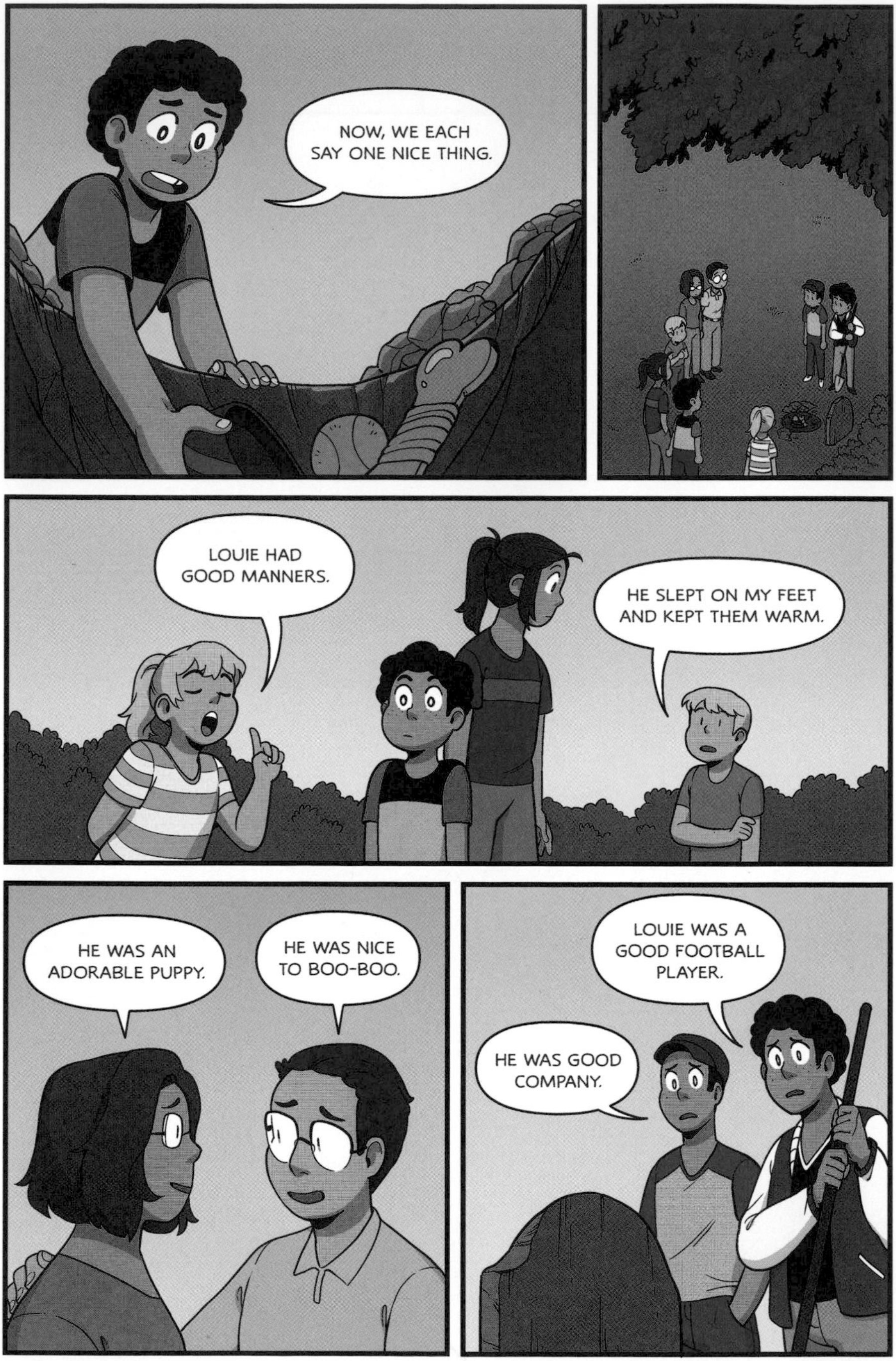
NOW, WE EACH SAY ONE NICE THING.
LOUIE HAD GOOD MANNERS.
HE SLEPT ON MY FEET AND KEPT THEM WARM.
HE WAS AN ADORABLE PUPPY.
HE WAS NICE TO BOO-BOO.
LOUIE WAS A GOOD FOOTBALL PLAYER.
HE WAS GOOD COMPANY.

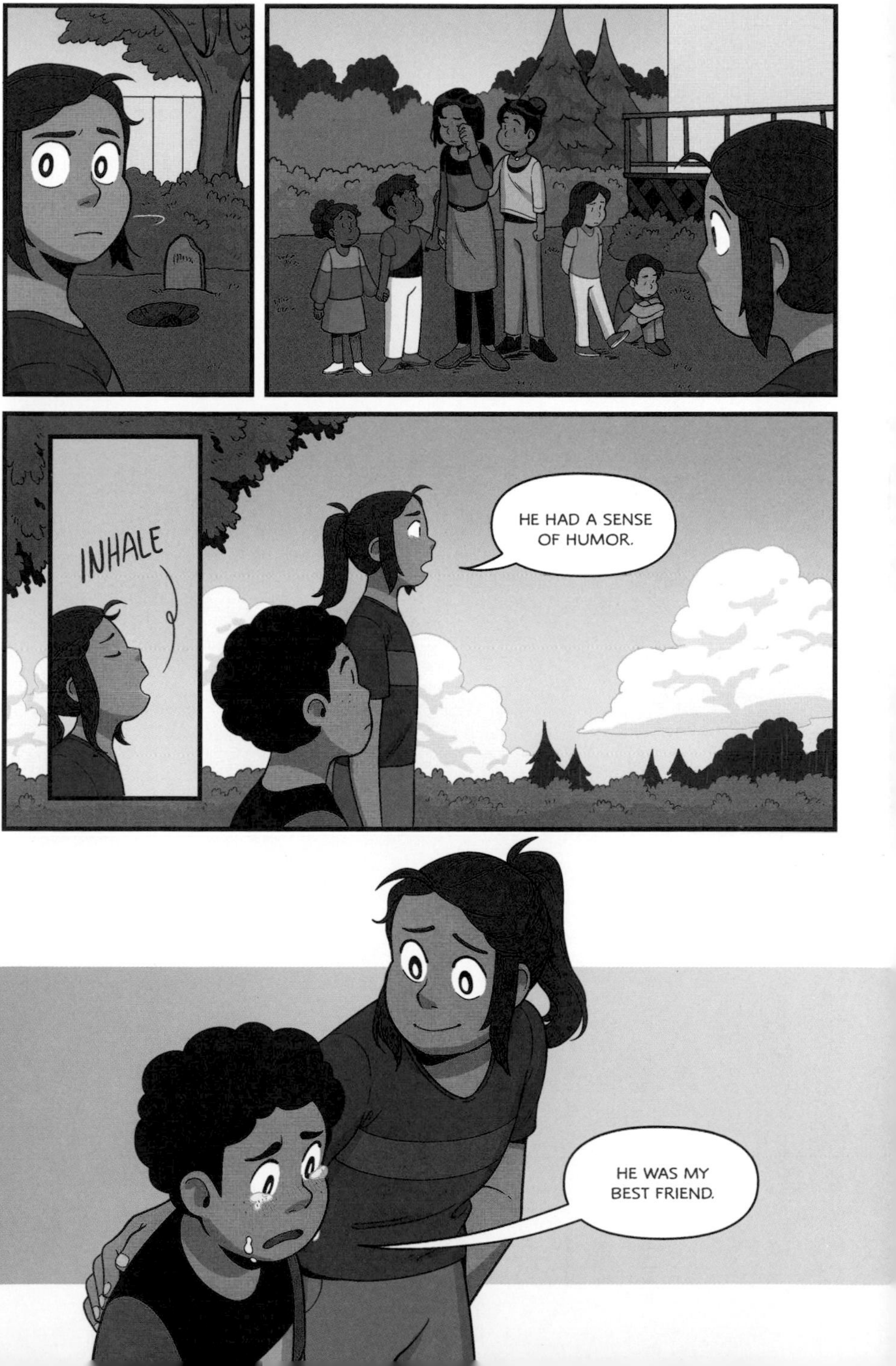
INHALE
HE HAD A SENSE OF HUMOR.
HE WAS MY BEST FRIEND.

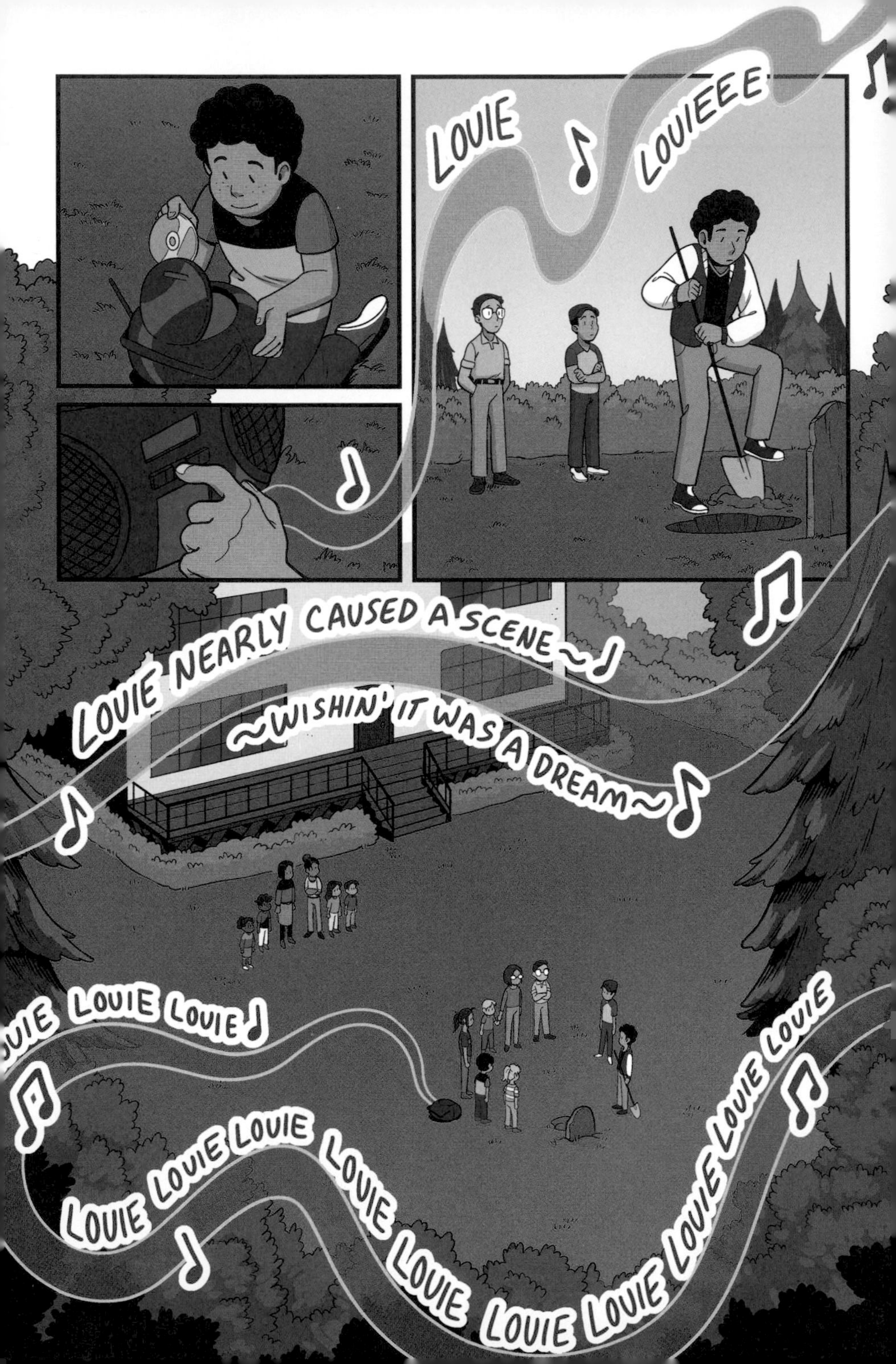
LOUIE
LOUIEEE
LOUIE NEARLY CAUSED A SCENE~
~WISHIN' IT WAS A DREAM~
UIE LOUIE LOUIE
LOUIE LOUIE LOUIE LOUIE
LOUIE LOUIE LOUIE LOUIE LOUIE LOUIE

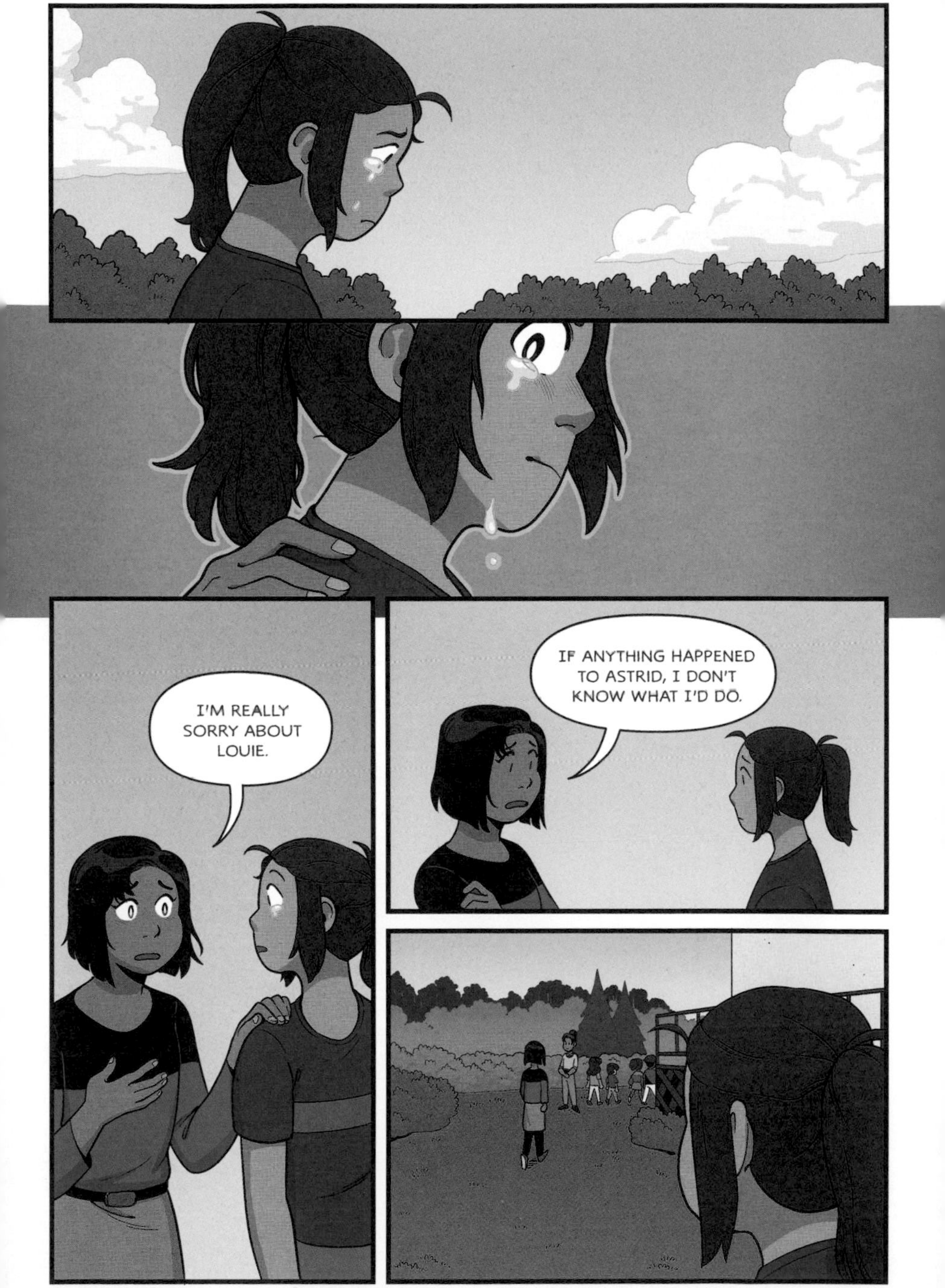
I'M REALLY SORRY ABOUT LOUIE.
IF ANYTHING HAPPENED TO ASTRID, I DON'T KNOW WHAT I'D DO.

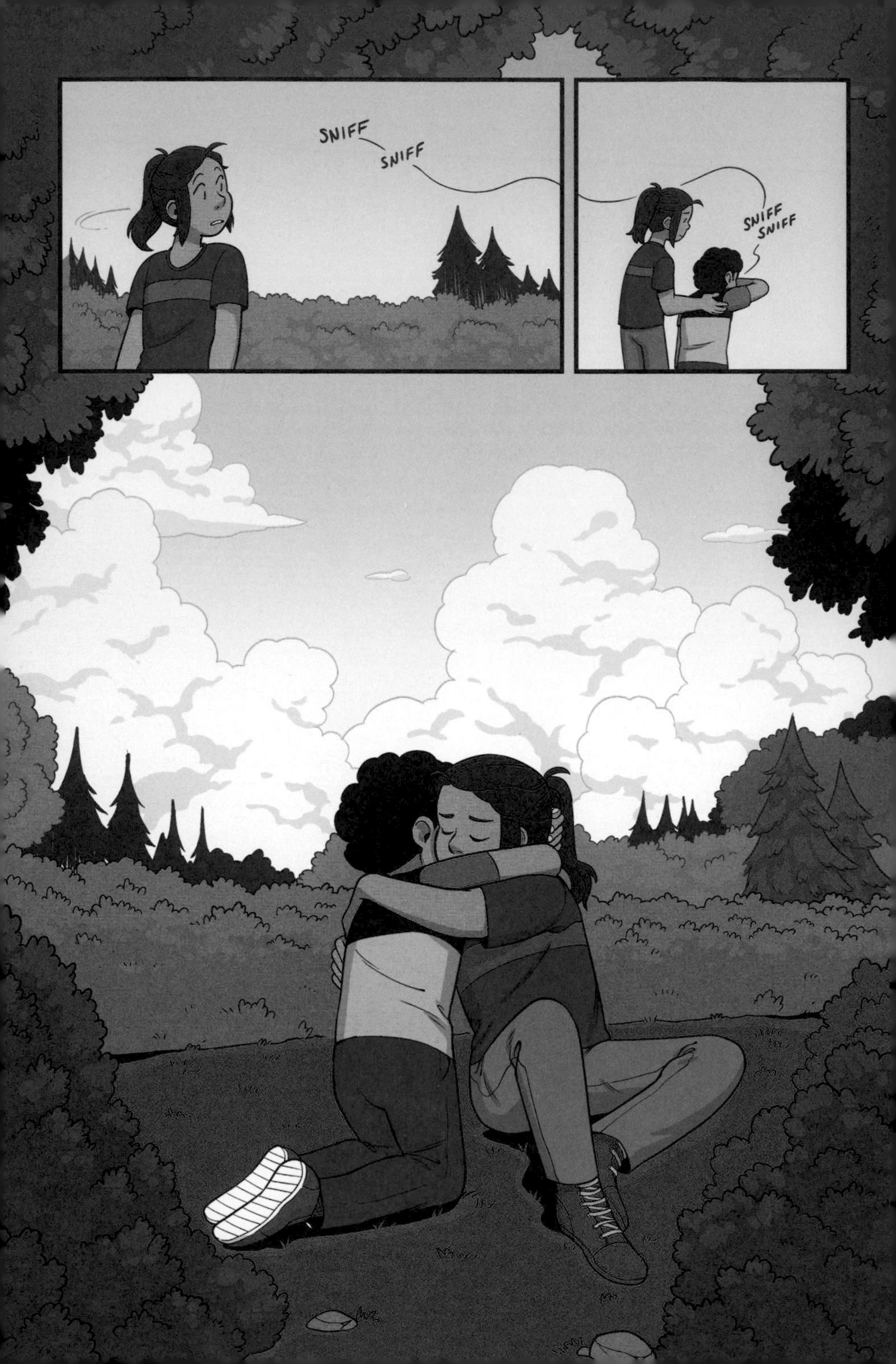
SNIFF
SNIFF
SNIFF
SNIFF

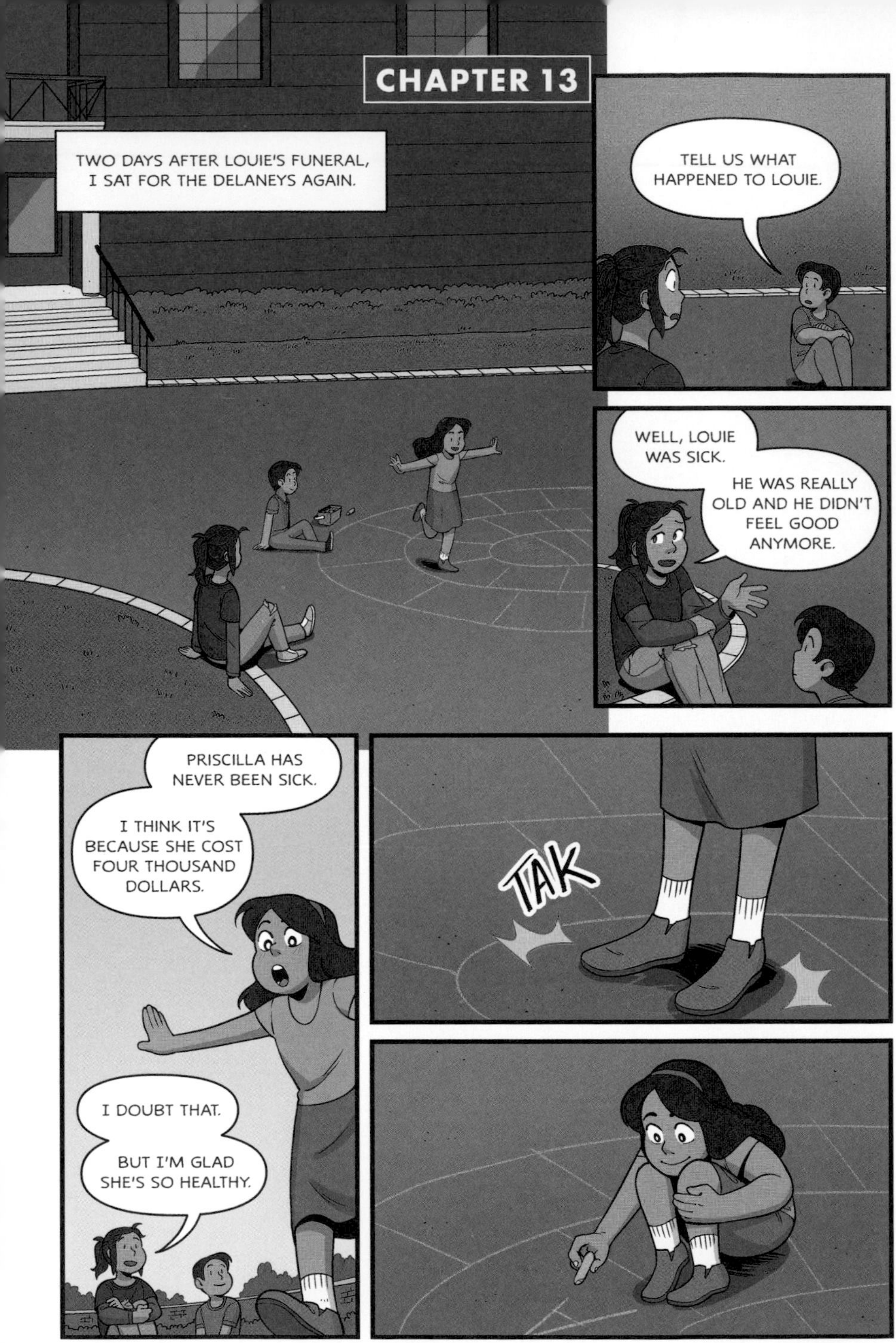
CHAPTER 13
TWO DAYS AFTER LOUIE'S FUNERAL, I SAT FOR THE DELANEYS AGAIN.
TELL US WHAT HAPPENED TO LOUIE.
WELL, LOUIE WAS SICK.
HE WAS REALLY OLD AND HE DIDN'T FEEL GOOD ANYMORE.
PRISCILLA HAS NEVER BEEN SICK.
I THINK IT'S BECAUSE SHE COST FOUR THOUSAND DOLLARS.
I DOUBT THAT.
BUT I'M GLAD SHE'S SO HEALTHY.
TAK

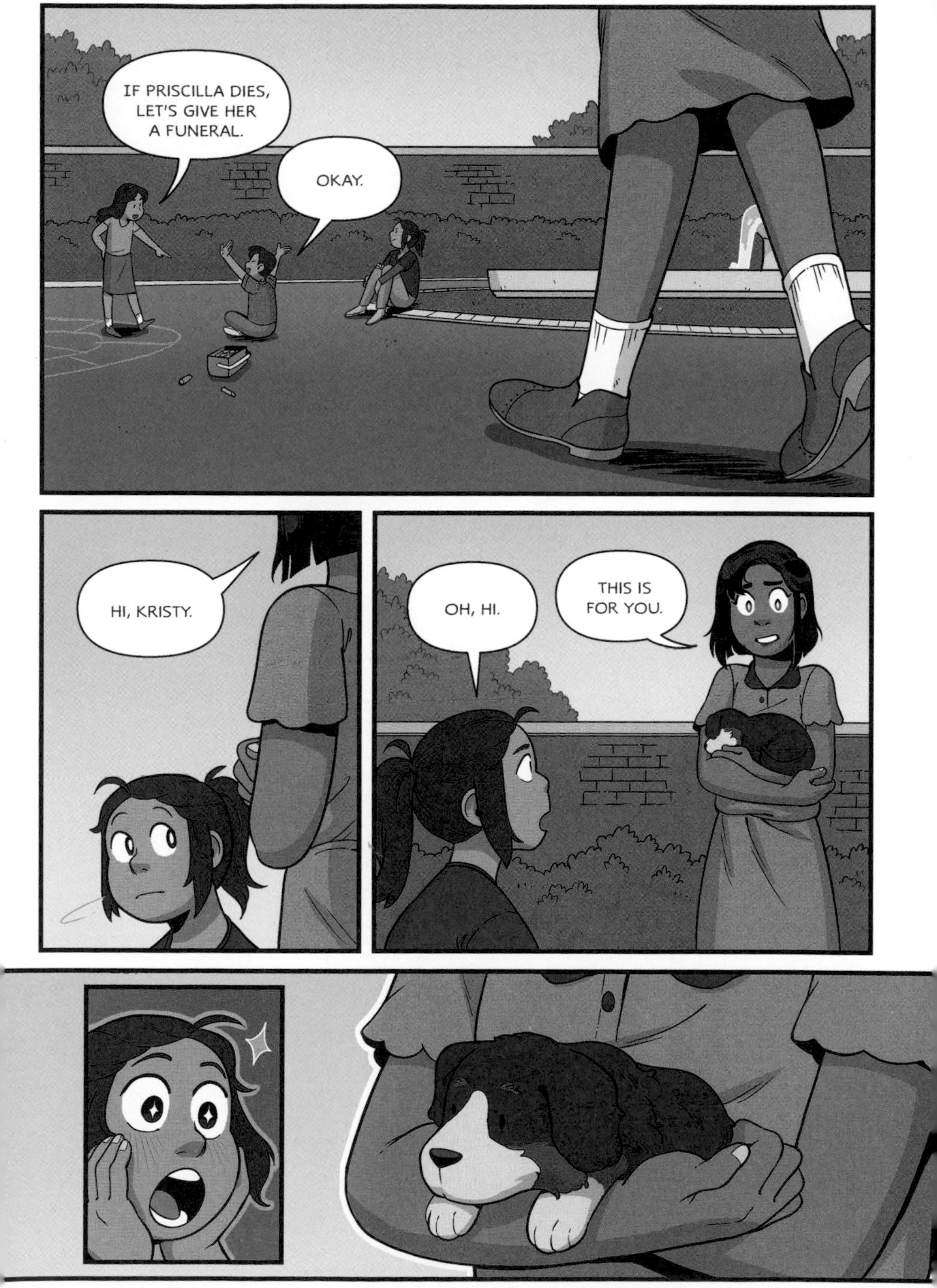
IF PRISCILLA DIES, LET'S GIVE HER A FUNERAL.
OKAY.
HI, KRISTY.
OH, HI.
THIS IS FOR YOU.

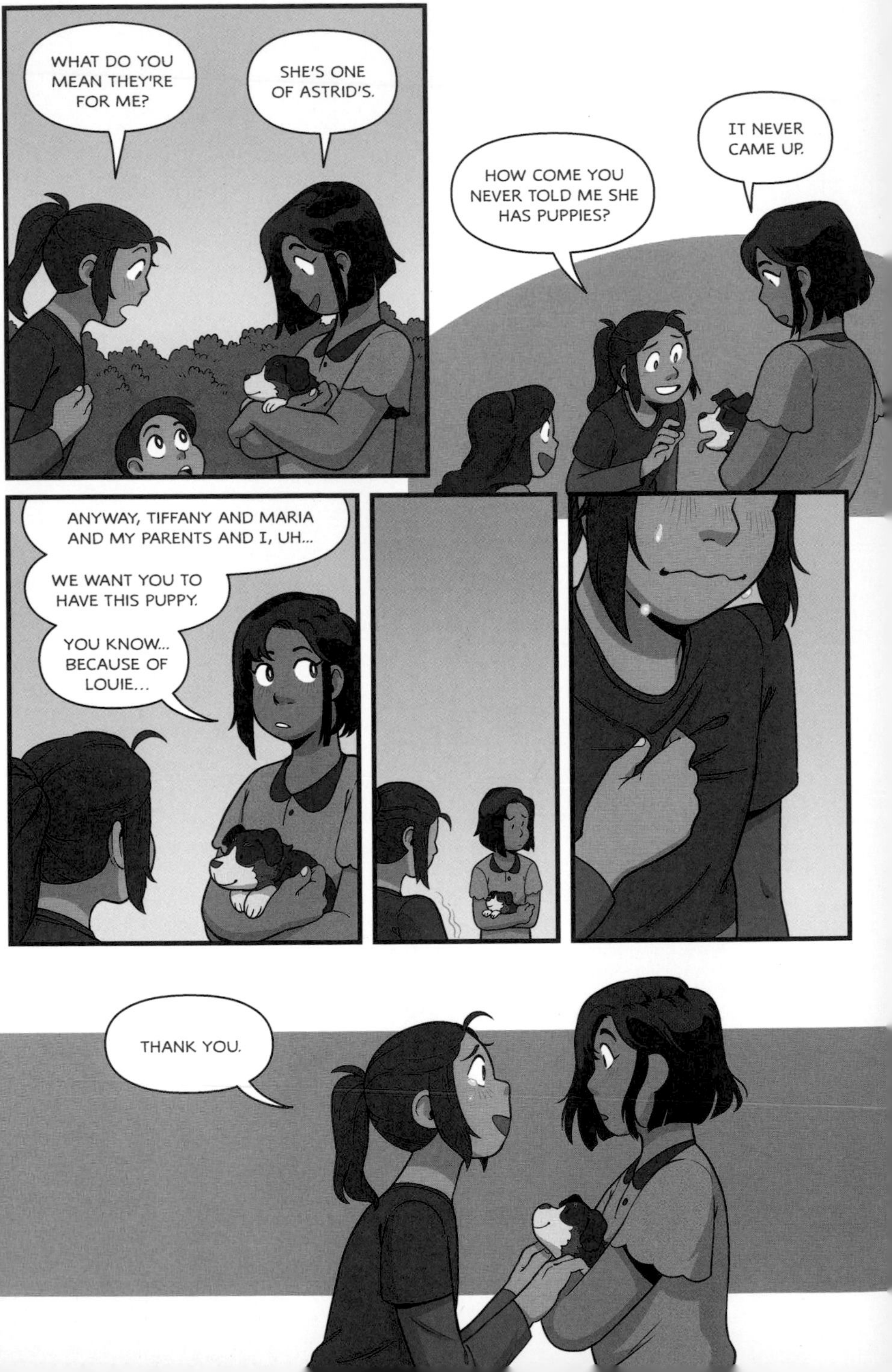
WHAT DO YOU MEAN THEY'RE FOR ME?
SHE'S ONE OF ASTRID'S.
HOW COME YOU NEVER TOLD ME SHE HAS PUPPIES?
IT NEVER CAME UP.
ANYWAY, TIFFANY AND MARIA AND MY PARENTS AND I, UH...
WE WANT YOU TO HAVE THIS PUPPY.
YOU KNOW... BECAUSE OF LOUIE...
THANK YOU.

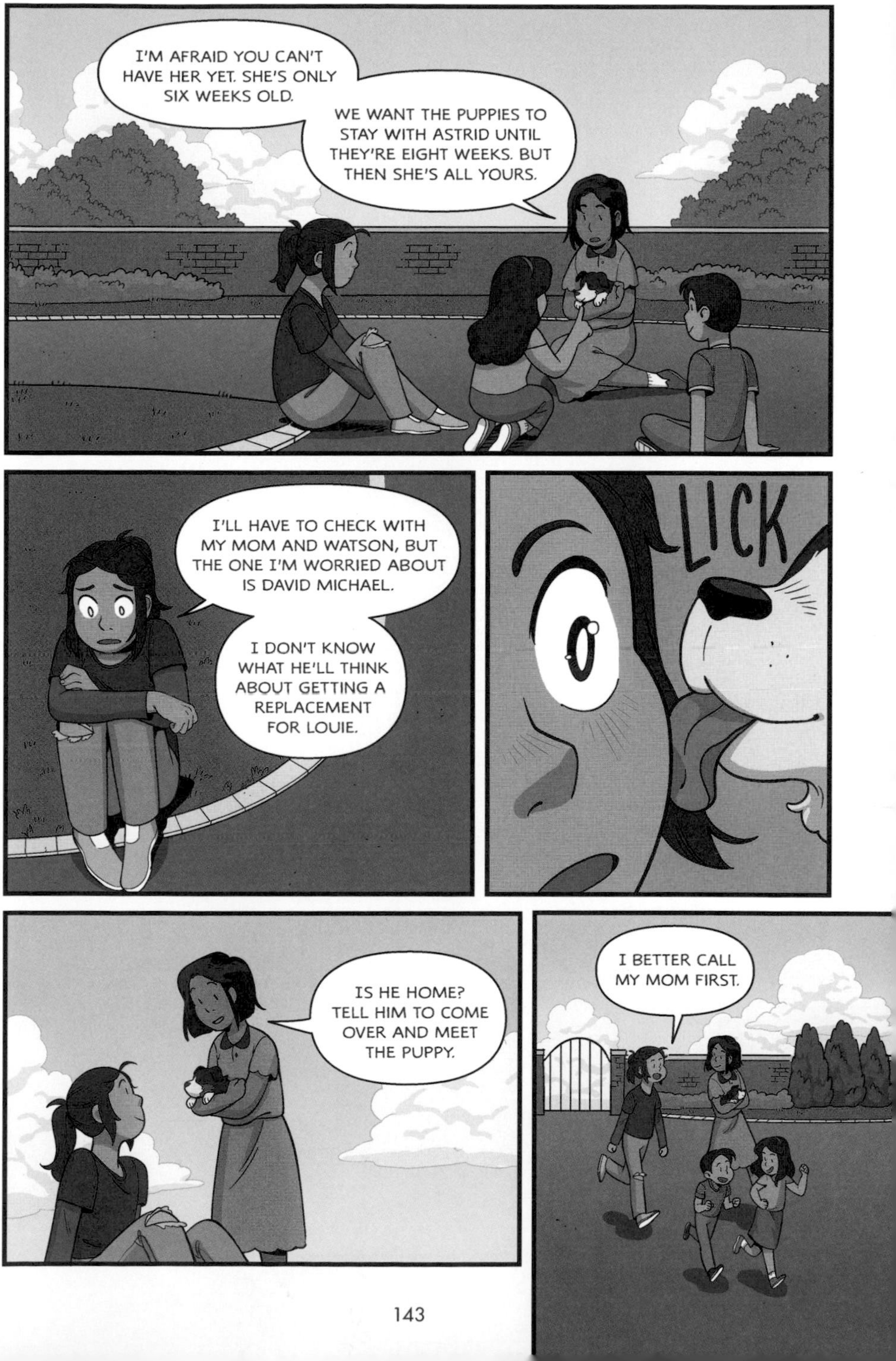
I'M AFRAID YOU CAN'T HAVE HER YET. SHE'S ONLY SIX WEEKS OLD.
WE WANT THE PUPPIES TO STAY WITH ASTRID UNTIL THEY'RE EIGHT WEEKS. BUT THEN SHE'S ALL YOURS.
I'LL HAVE TO CHECK WITH MY MOM AND WATSON, BUT THE ONE I'M WORRIED ABOUT IS DAVID MICHAEL.
I DON'T KNOW WHAT HE'LL THINK ABOUT GETTING A REPLACEMENT FOR LOUIE.
LICK
IS HE HOME? TELL HIM TO COME OVER AND MEET THE PUPPY.
I BETTER CALL MY MOM FIRST.

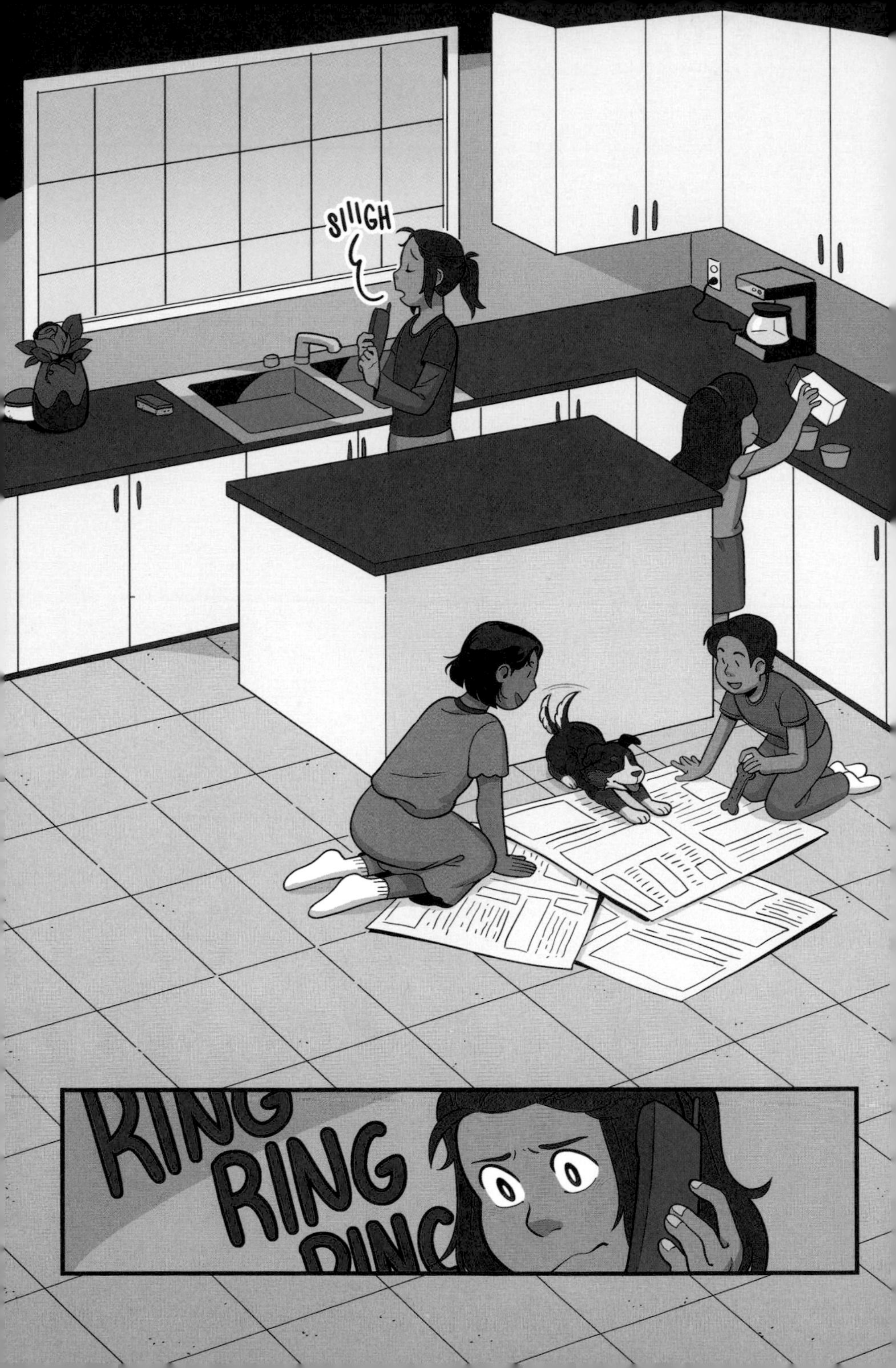
SIIIGH
RING
RING
RING

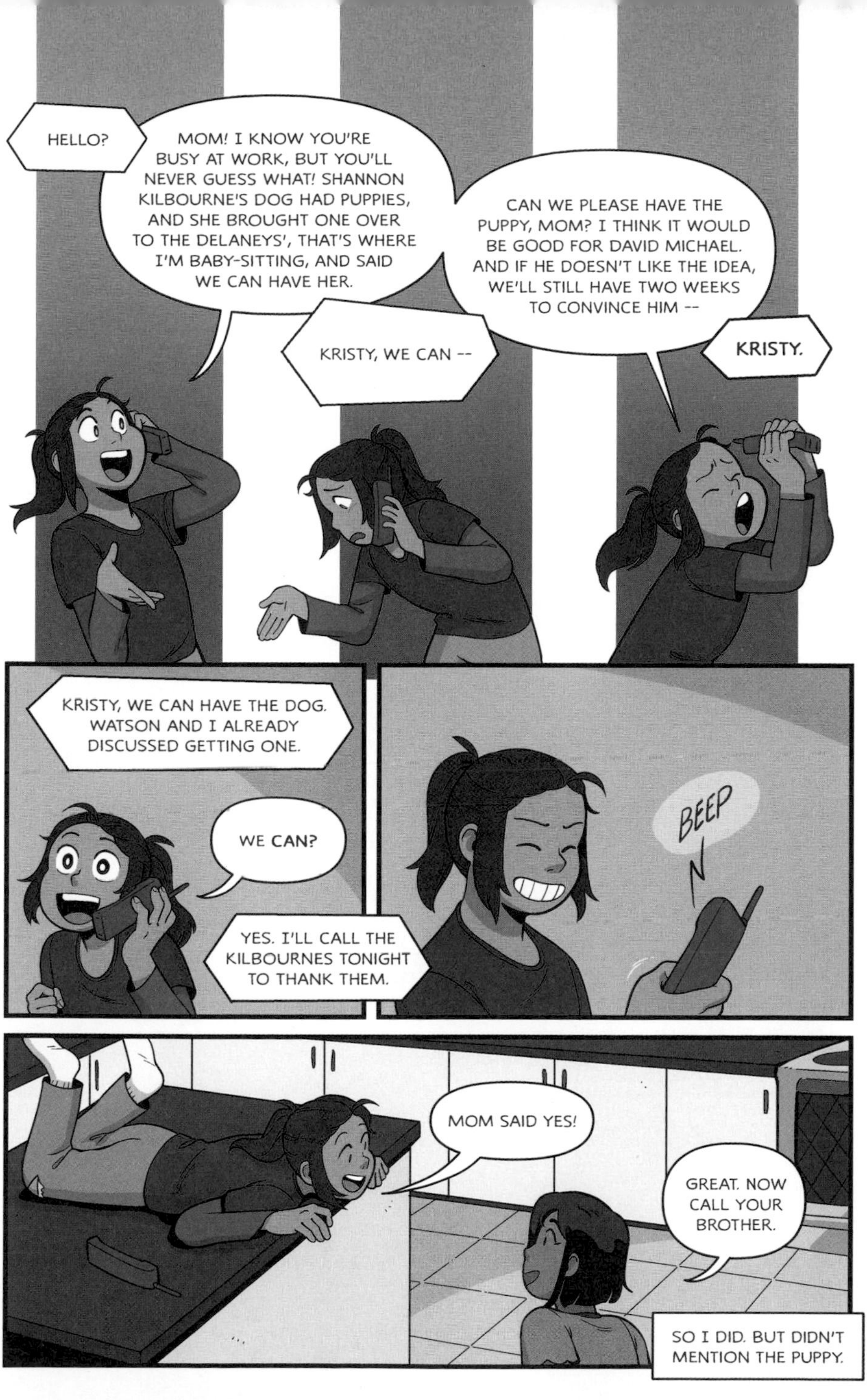
HELLO?
MOM! I KNOW YOU'RE BUSY AT WORK, BUT YOU'LL NEVER GUESS WHAT! SHANNON KILBOURNE'S DOG HAD PUPPIES, AND SHE BROUGHT ONE OVER TO THE DELANEYS', THAT'S WHERE I'M BABY-SITTING, AND SAID WE CAN HAVE HER.
KRISTY, WE CAN --
CAN WE PLEASE HAVE THE PUPPY, MOM? I THINK IT WOULD BE GOOD FOR DAVID MICHAEL. AND IF HE DOESN'T LIKE THE IDEA, WE'LL STILL HAVE TWO WEEKS TO CONVINCE HIM --
KRISTY.
KRISTY, WE CAN HAVE THE DOG. WATSON AND I ALREADY DISCUSSED GETTING ONE.
WE CAN?
YES. I'LL CALL THE KILBOURNES TONIGHT TO THANK THEM.
BEEP
MOM SAID YES!
GREAT. NOW CALL YOUR BROTHER.
SO I DID. BUT DIDN'T MENTION THE PUPPY.

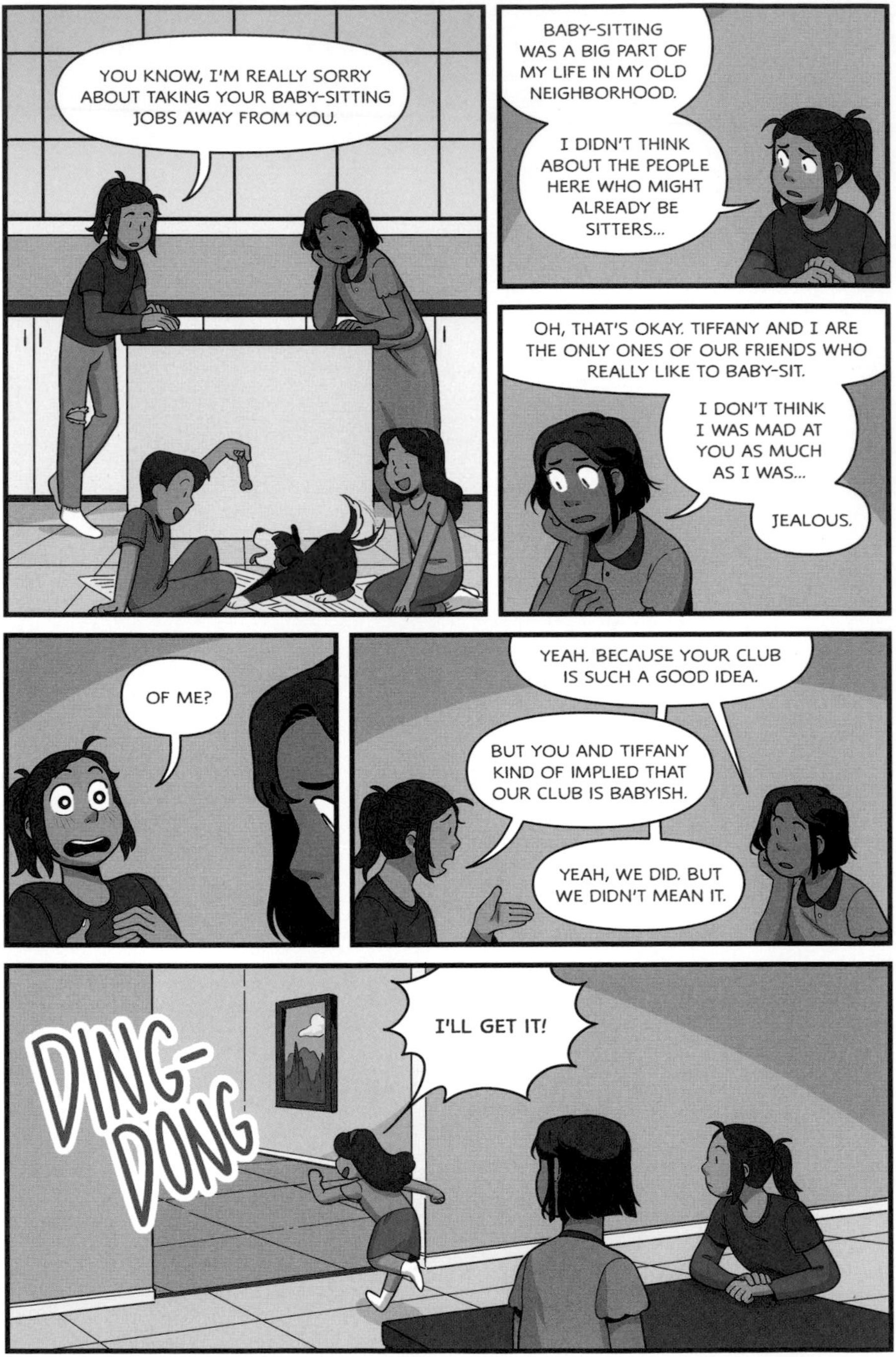
YOU KNOW, I'M REALLY SORRY ABOUT TAKING YOUR BABY-SITTING JOBS AWAY FROM YOU.
BABY-SITTING WAS A BIG PART OF MY LIFE IN MY OLD NEIGHBORHOOD.
I DIDN'T THINK ABOUT THE PEOPLE HERE WHO MIGHT ALREADY BE SITTERS...
OH, THAT'S OKAY. TIFFANY AND I ARE THE ONLY ONES OF OUR FRIENDS WHO REALLY LIKE TO BABY-SIT.
I DON'T THINK I WAS MAD AT YOU AS MUCH AS I WAS...
JEALOUS.
OF ME?
YEAH. BECAUSE YOUR CLUB IS SUCH A GOOD IDEA.
BUT YOU AND TIFFANY KIND OF IMPLIED THAT OUR CLUB IS BABYISH.
YEAH, WE DID. BUT WE DIDN'T MEAN IT.
DING-DONG
I'LL GET IT!

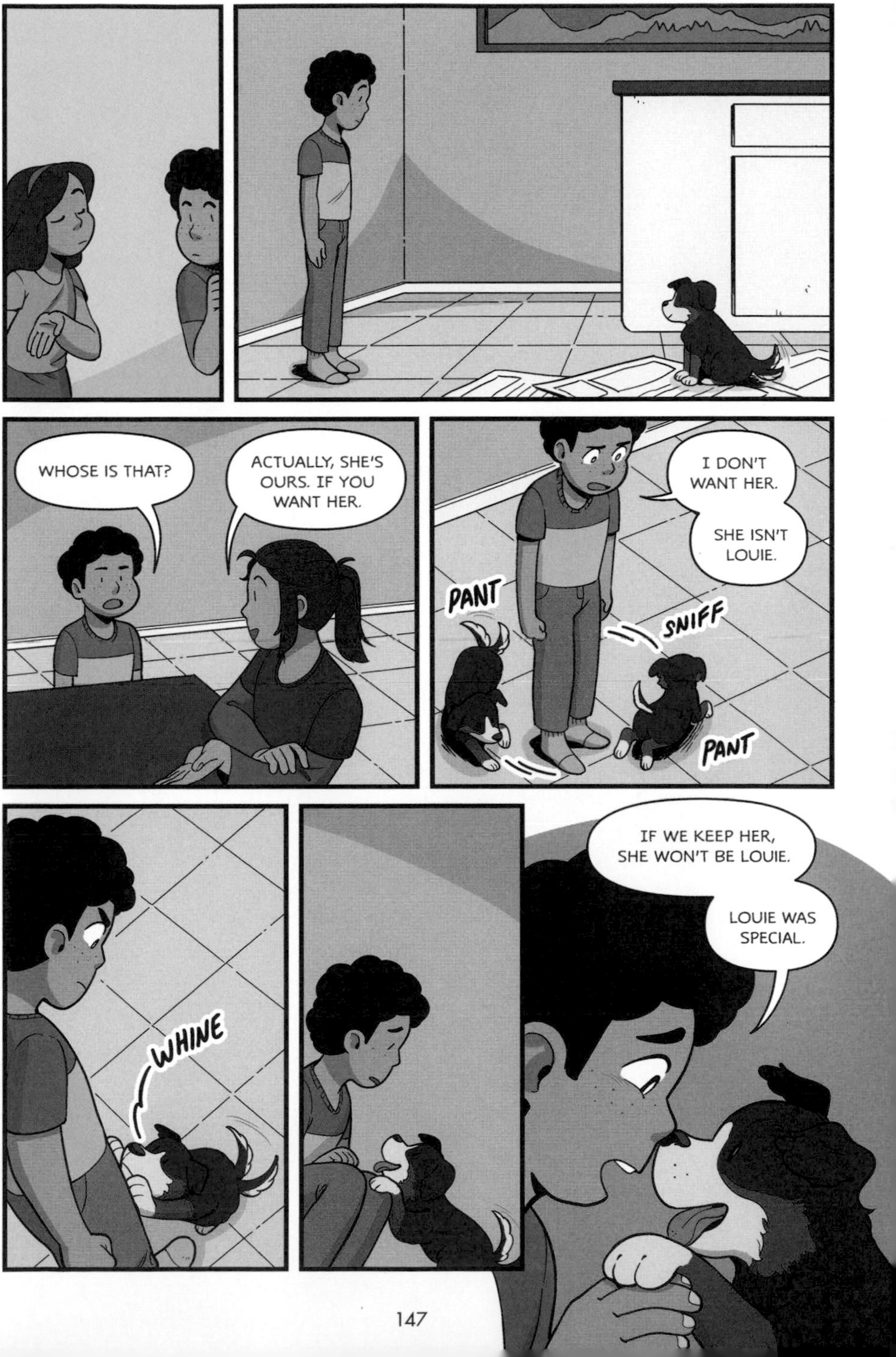
WHOSE IS THAT?
ACTUALLY, SHE'S OURS. IF YOU WANT HER.
I DON'T WANT HER.
SHE ISN'T LOUIE.
PANT
SNIFF
PANT
WHINE
IF WE KEEP HER, SHE WON'T BE LOUIE.
LOUIE WAS SPECIAL.

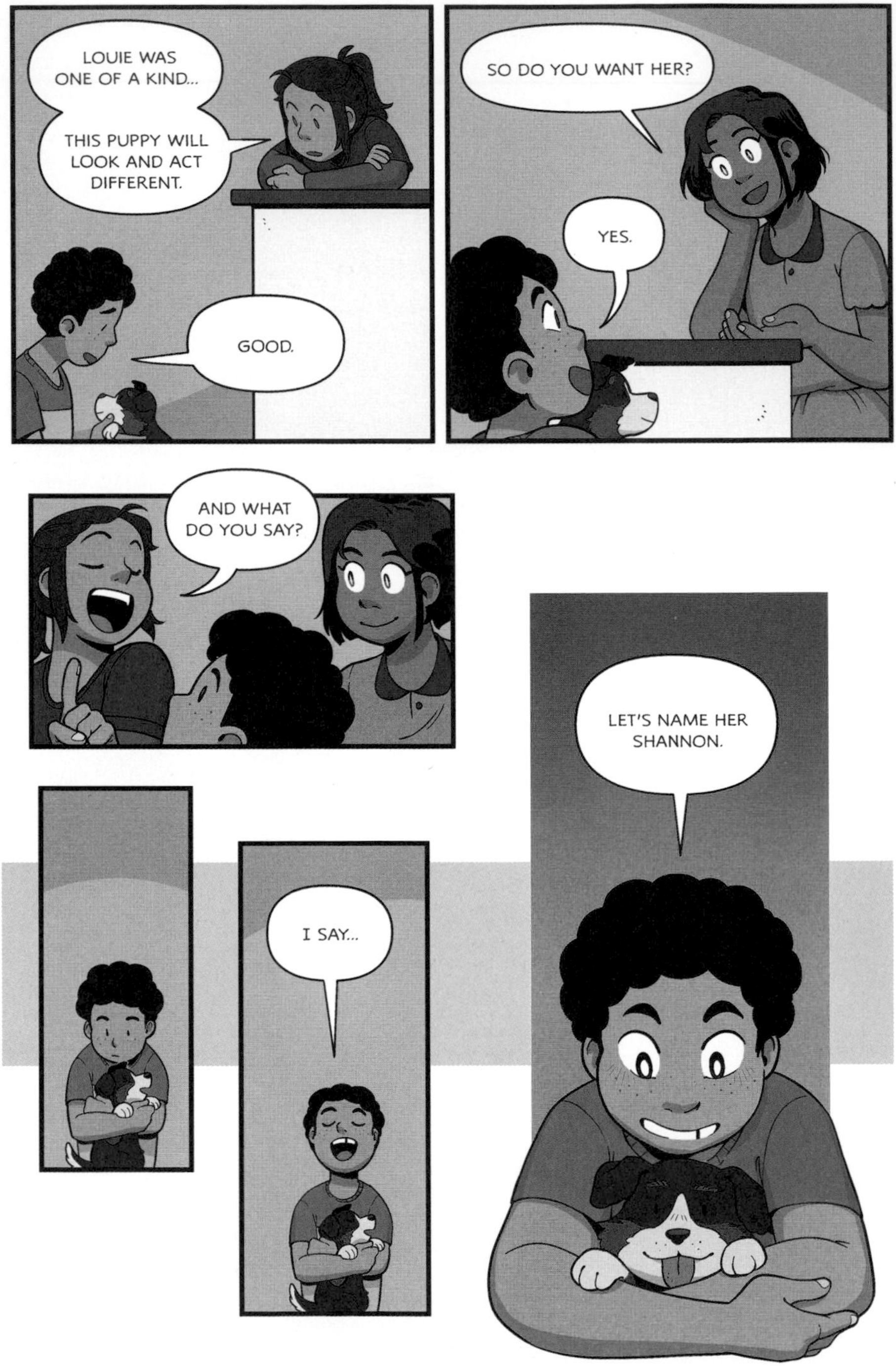
LOUIE WAS ONE OF A KIND...
THIS PUPPY WILL LOOK AND ACT DIFFERENT.
GOOD.
SO DO YOU WANT HER?
YES.
AND WHAT DO YOU SAY?
I SAY...
LET'S NAME HER SHANNON.

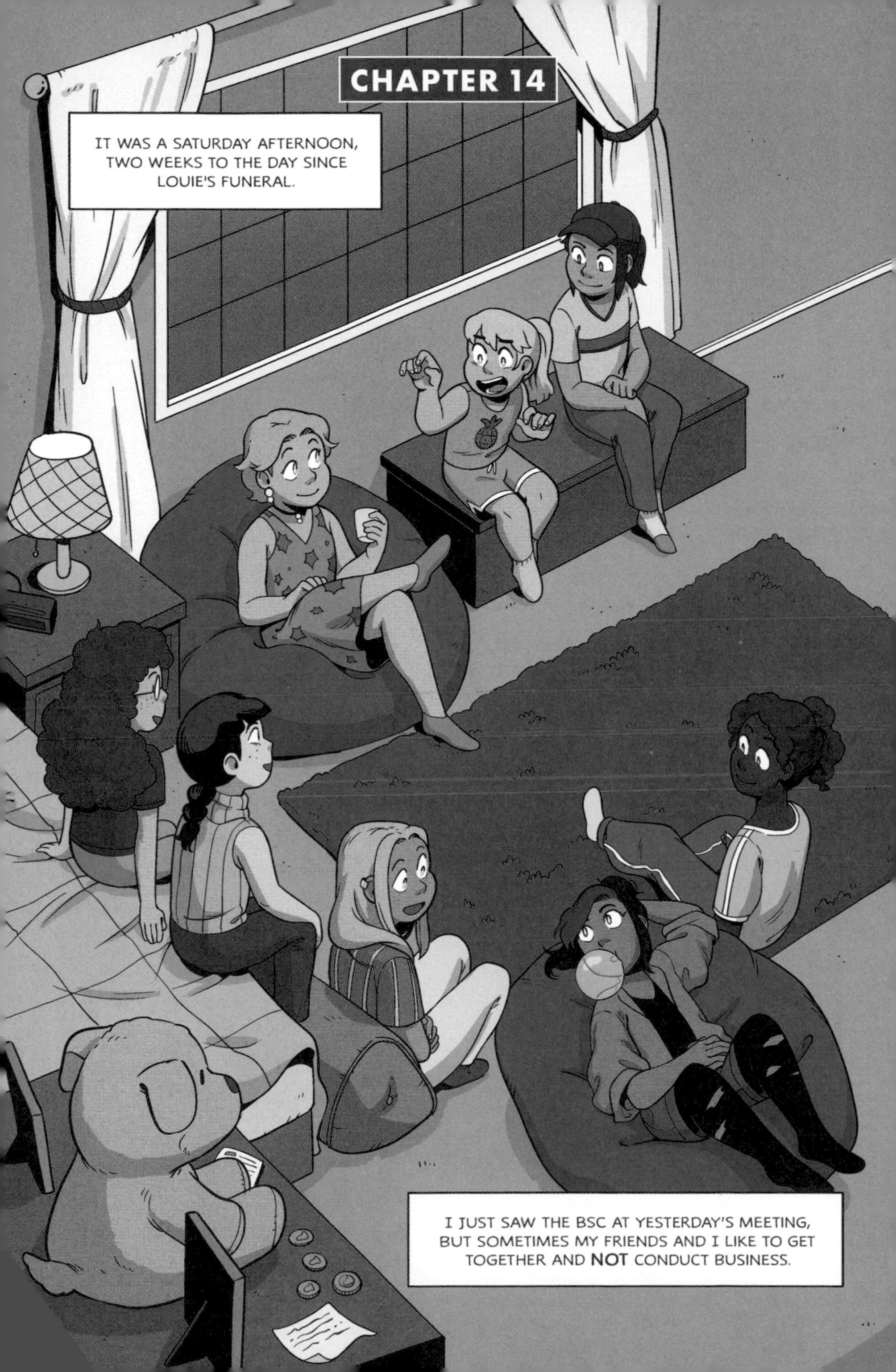
CHAPTER 14
IT WAS A SATURDAY AFTERNOON, TWO WEEKS TO THE DAY SINCE LOUIE'S FUNERAL.
I JUST SAW THE BSC AT YESTERDAY'S MEETING, BUT SOMETIMES MY FRIENDS AND I LIKE TO GET TOGETHER AND **NOT** CONDUCT BUSINESS.

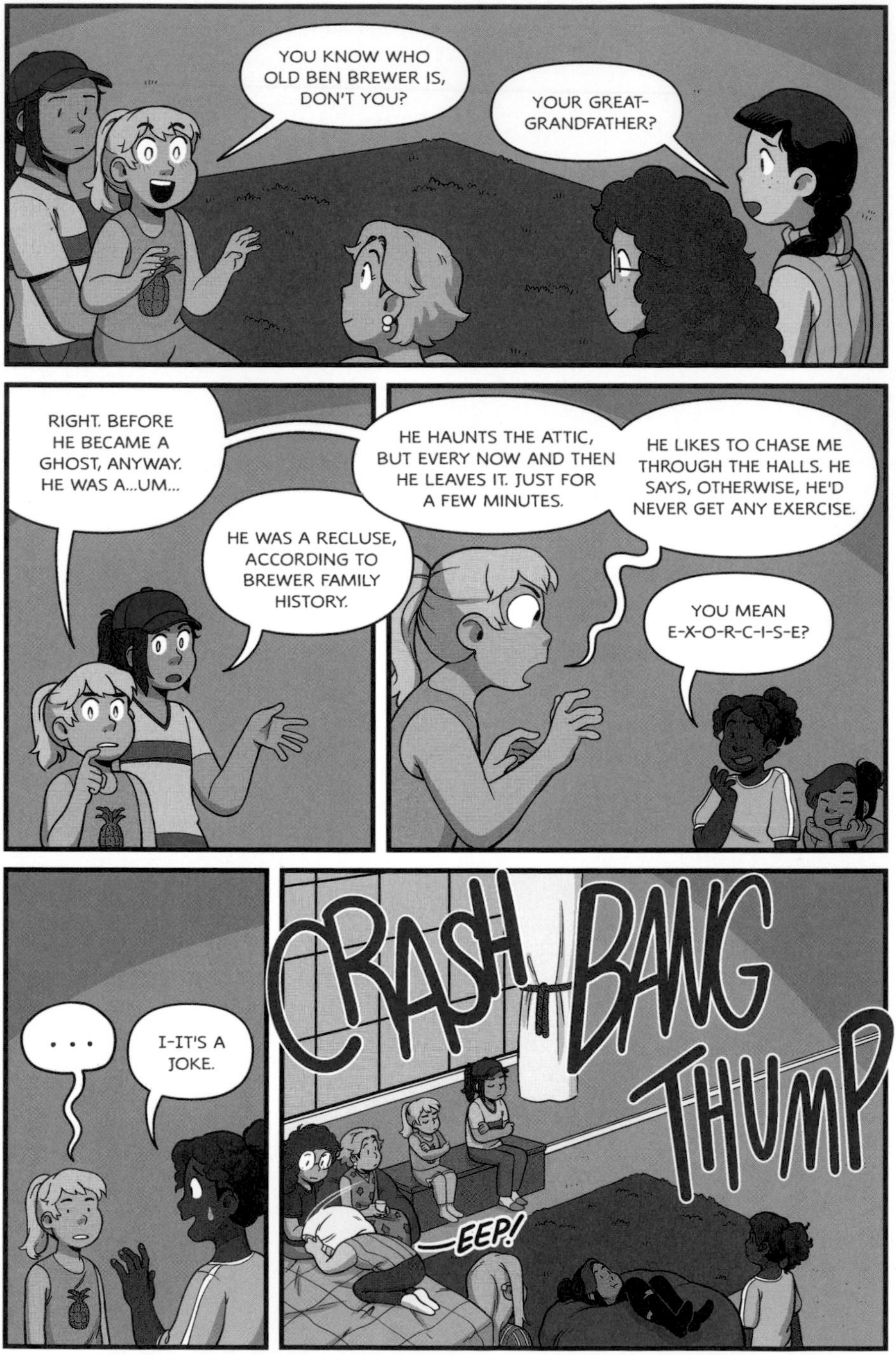

YOU KNOW WHO OLD BEN BREWER IS, DON'T YOU?
YOUR GREAT-GRANDFATHER?
RIGHT. BEFORE HE BECAME A GHOST, ANYWAY. HE WAS A...UM...
HE WAS A RECLUSE, ACCORDING TO BREWER FAMILY HISTORY.
HE HAUNTS THE ATTIC, BUT EVERY NOW AND THEN HE LEAVES IT. JUST FOR A FEW MINUTES.
HE LIKES TO CHASE ME THROUGH THE HALLS. HE SAYS, OTHERWISE, HE'D NEVER GET ANY EXERCISE.
YOU MEAN E-X-O-R-C-I-S-E?
. . .
I-IT'S A JOKE.
CRASH
BANG
THUMP
—EEP!

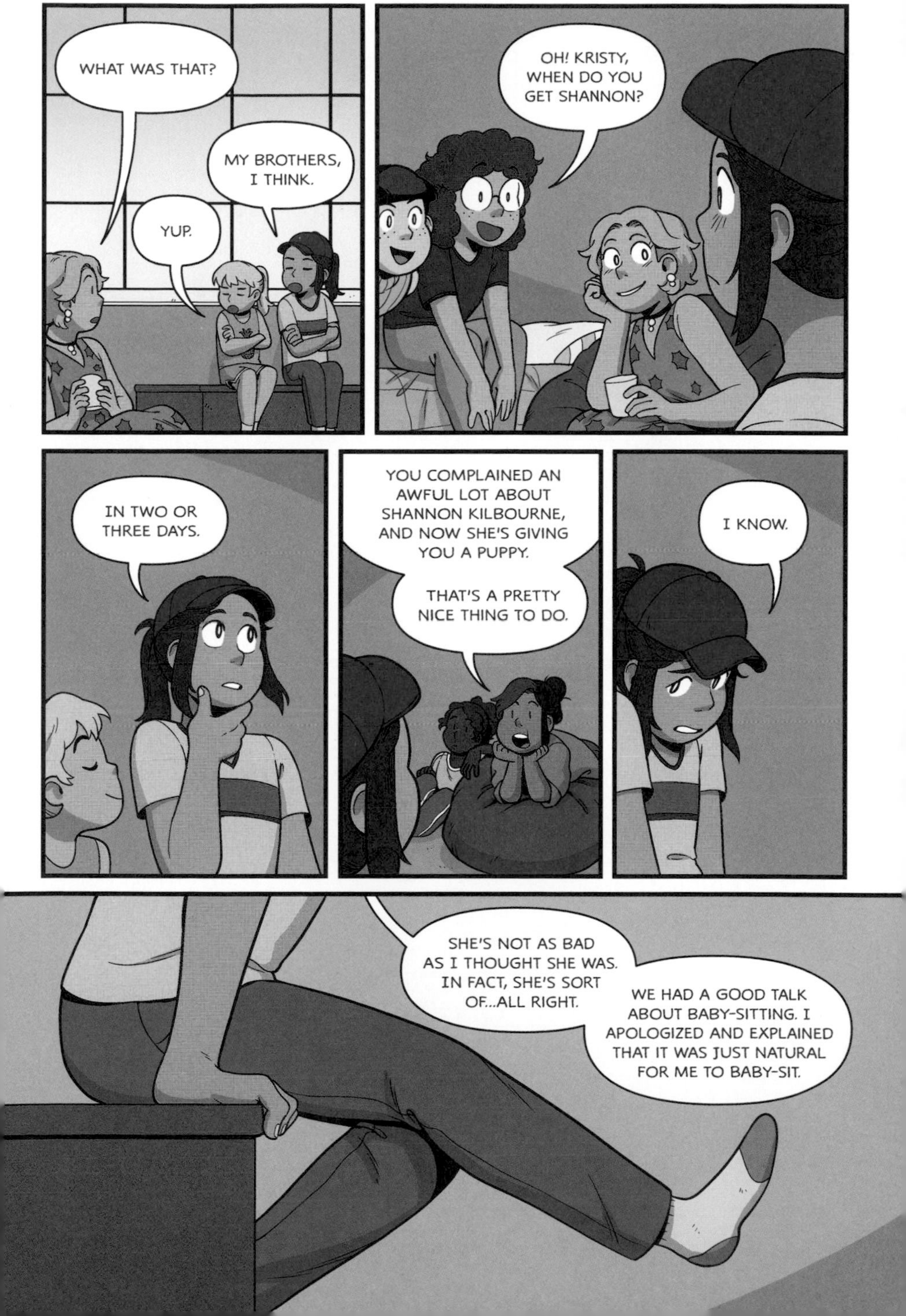
WHAT WAS THAT?
MY BROTHERS, I THINK.
YUP.
OH! KRISTY, WHEN DO YOU GET SHANNON?
IN TWO OR THREE DAYS.
YOU COMPLAINED AN AWFUL LOT ABOUT SHANNON KILBOURNE, AND NOW SHE'S GIVING YOU A PUPPY.
THAT'S A PRETTY NICE THING TO DO.
I KNOW.
SHE'S NOT AS BAD AS I THOUGHT SHE WAS. IN FACT, SHE'S SORT OF...ALL RIGHT.
WE HAD A GOOD TALK ABOUT BABY-SITTING. I APOLOGIZED AND EXPLAINED THAT IT WAS JUST NATURAL FOR ME TO BABY-SIT.

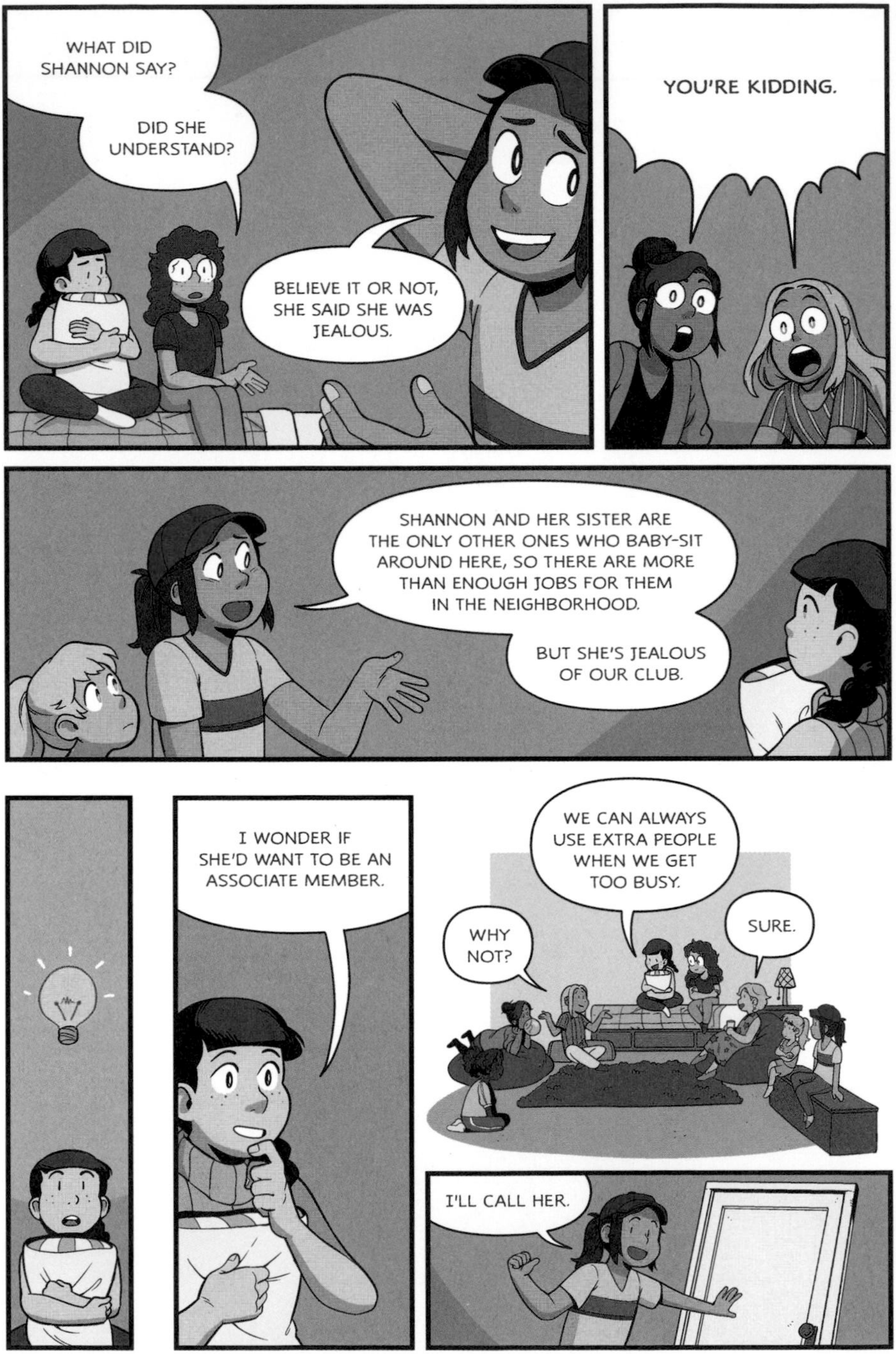
WHAT DID SHANNON SAY?
DID SHE UNDERSTAND?
BELIEVE IT OR NOT, SHE SAID SHE WAS JEALOUS.
YOU'RE KIDDING.
SHANNON AND HER SISTER ARE THE ONLY OTHER ONES WHO BABY-SIT AROUND HERE, SO THERE ARE MORE THAN ENOUGH JOBS FOR THEM IN THE NEIGHBORHOOD.
BUT SHE'S JEALOUS OF OUR CLUB.
I WONDER IF SHE'D WANT TO BE AN ASSOCIATE MEMBER.
WE CAN ALWAYS USE EXTRA PEOPLE WHEN WE GET TOO BUSY.
WHY NOT?
SURE.
I'LL CALL HER.

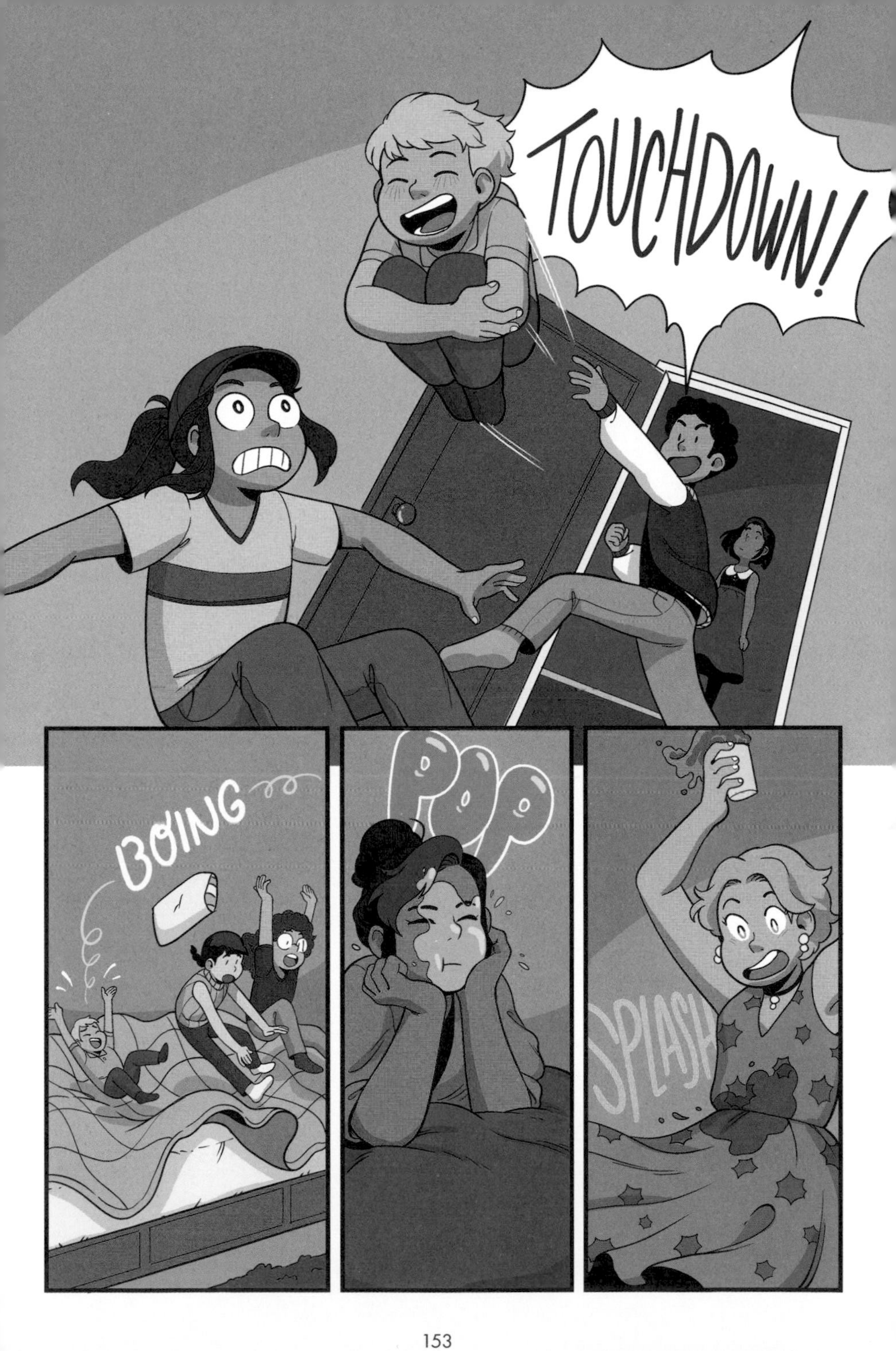
TOUCHDOWN!
BOING
POP
SPLASH

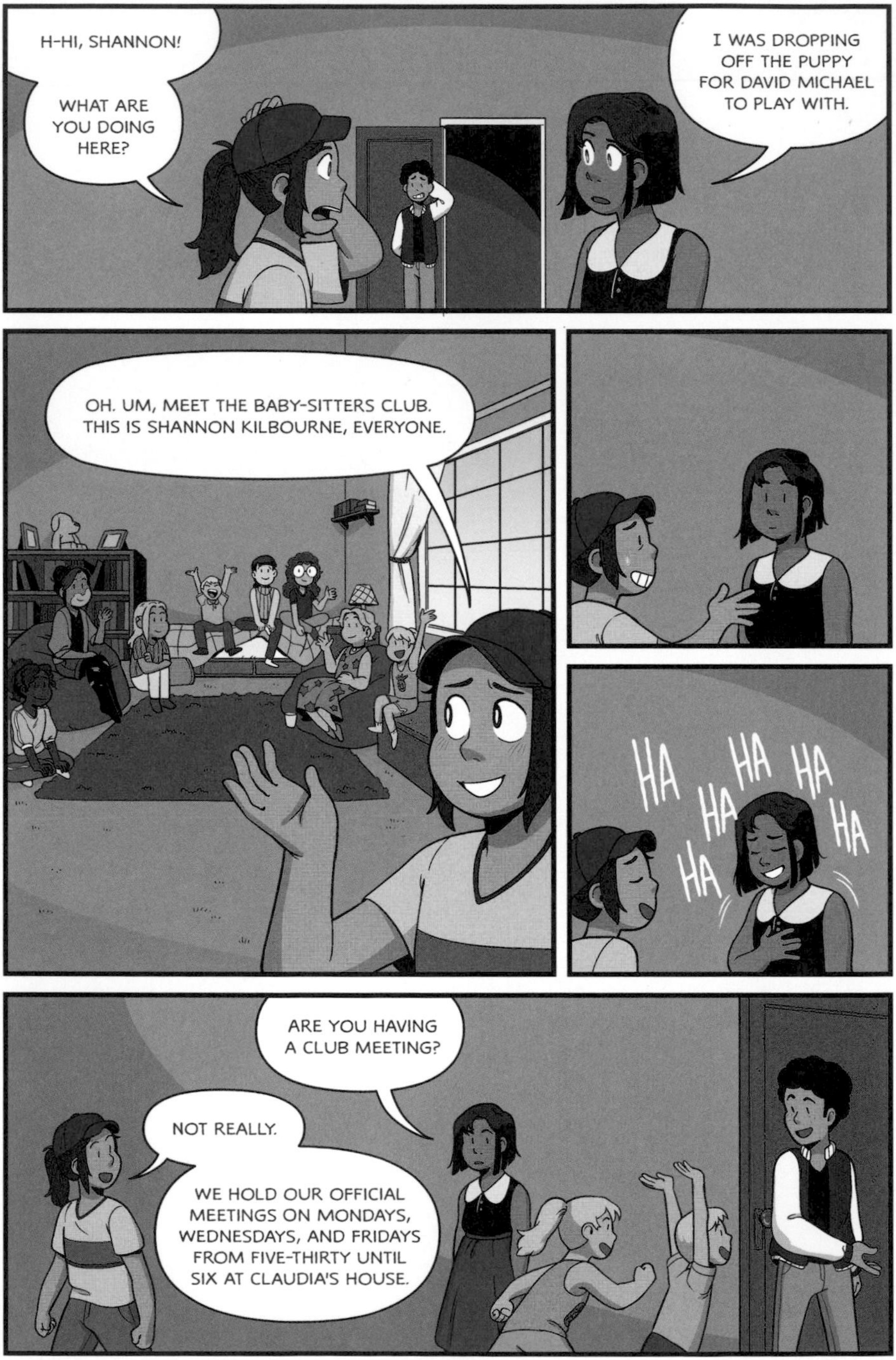

H-HI, SHANNON!
WHAT ARE YOU DOING HERE?
I WAS DROPPING OFF THE PUPPY FOR DAVID MICHAEL TO PLAY WITH.
OH. UM, MEET THE BABY-SITTERS CLUB. THIS IS SHANNON KILBOURNE, EVERYONE.
HA HA HA HA HA HA HA
ARE YOU HAVING A CLUB MEETING?
NOT REALLY.
WE HOLD OUR OFFICIAL MEETINGS ON MONDAYS, WEDNESDAYS, AND FRIDAYS FROM FIVE-THIRTY UNTIL SIX AT CLAUDIA'S HOUSE.

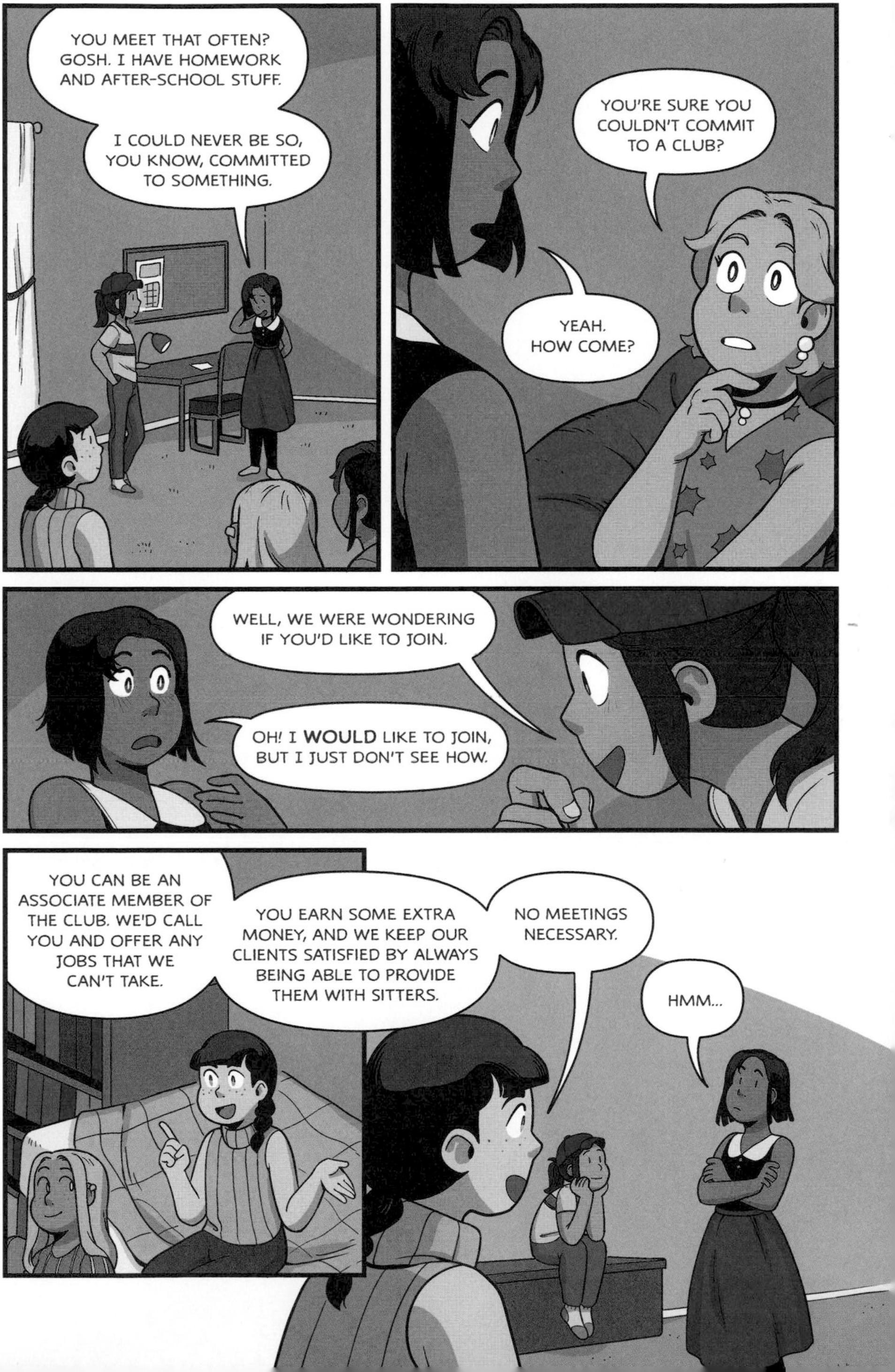
YOU MEET THAT OFTEN? GOSH. I HAVE HOMEWORK AND AFTER-SCHOOL STUFF.
I COULD NEVER BE SO, YOU KNOW, COMMITTED TO SOMETHING.
YOU'RE SURE YOU COULDN'T COMMIT TO A CLUB?
YEAH. HOW COME?
WELL, WE WERE WONDERING IF YOU'D LIKE TO JOIN.
OH! I **WOULD** LIKE TO JOIN, BUT I JUST DON'T SEE HOW.
YOU CAN BE AN ASSOCIATE MEMBER OF THE CLUB. WE'D CALL YOU AND OFFER ANY JOBS THAT WE CAN'T TAKE.
YOU EARN SOME EXTRA MONEY, AND WE KEEP OUR CLIENTS SATISFIED BY ALWAYS BEING ABLE TO PROVIDE THEM WITH SITTERS.
NO MEETINGS NECESSARY.
HMM...

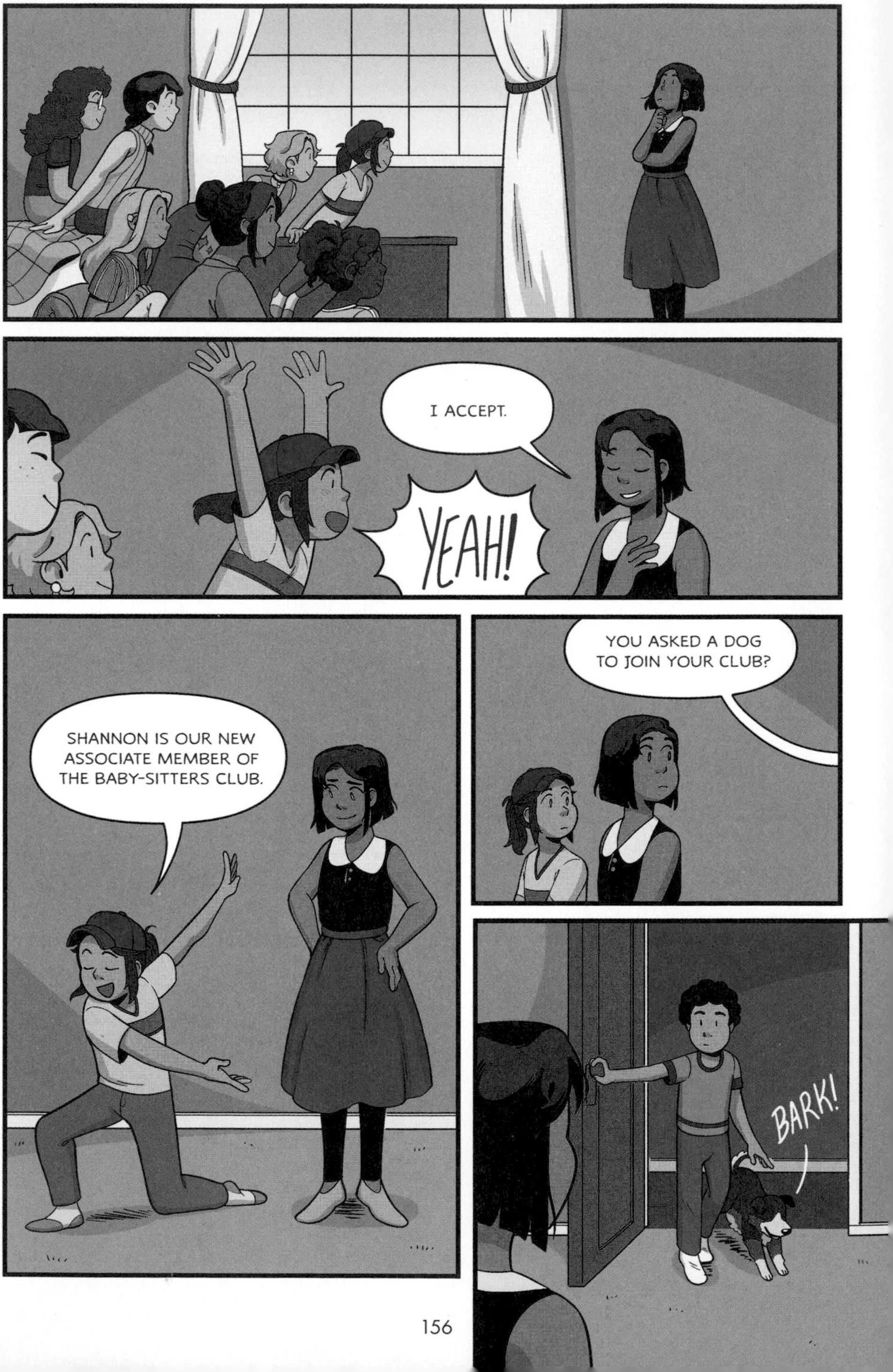
I ACCEPT.
YEAH!
SHANNON IS OUR NEW ASSOCIATE MEMBER OF THE BABY-SITTERS CLUB.
YOU ASKED A DOG TO JOIN YOUR CLUB?
BARK!

NO, SILLY. THE **HUMAN** SHANNON.

I KNOW.

LOUIE HAD LEFT A SORT OF LEGACY.

HE'D BROUGHT SHANNON AND ME TOGETHER SO WE COULD BE FRIENDS INSTEAD OF ENEMIES.

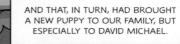

AND THAT, IN TURN, HAD BROUGHT A NEW PUPPY TO OUR FAMILY, BUT ESPECIALLY TO DAVID MICHAEL.

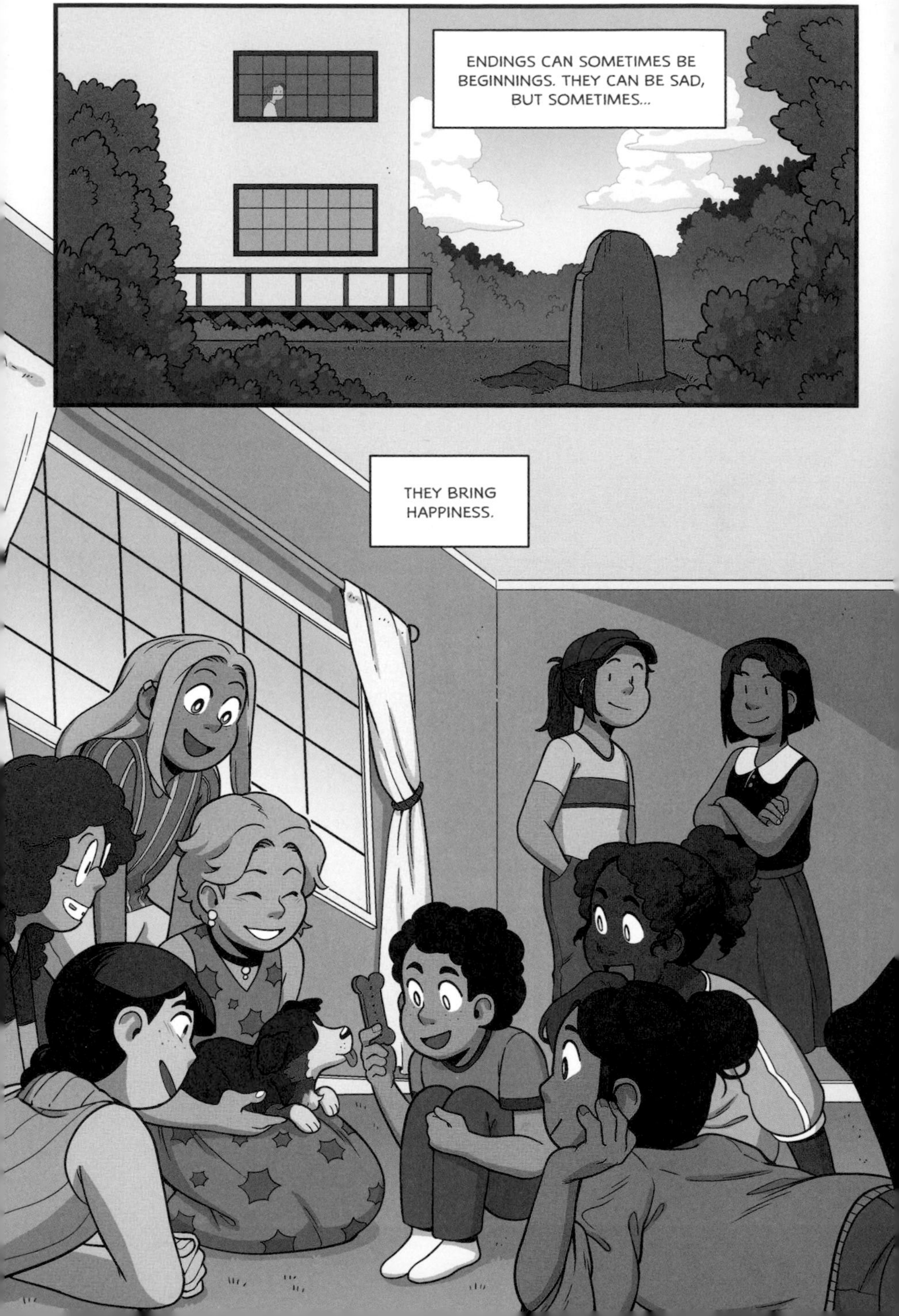
ENDINGS CAN SOMETIMES BE BEGINNINGS. THEY CAN BE SAD, BUT SOMETIMES...
THEY BRING HAPPINESS.